OBSIDIAN ORACLE

IRONMOON

BOOK FOUR

MERRY RAVENELL

9 SWORDS

DEDICATION

Earning a crown takes a while.
For everyone who waited seven years for this.
Absolute legends.

GABEL - THEN I WILL BE ENDLESS

She could not see him like this.

Gabel moved off to the side so his panting wouldn't worry her. She was not comatose, just drifting on tides of unrelenting pain as Aaron warred for her soul from the other side.

You are mine, buttercup, and I am yours. You are not his. You have never *been his, no matter how much he wanted to think he could have you.*

I do *know how to keep what is mine. I swore you would never be his, and if I have to fight his designs on you for eternity, then I will fight him for eternity. If it will never end, then I will be endless.*

He barred his teeth, then twisted around to examine the injury on his leg. Aaron had torn him open again.

No matter. He could endure the pain as long as the leg remained functional. The *functional* part did seem to be of some concern.

She was not a little wolf, but she seemed so very small. She panted shallow, pained breaths. Every few heartbeats, a rictus shook her body.

He sniffed her ruff. The grief and agony rising off it made him quiver for a second before it stoked cold, cruel fury.

Then I will be endless.

He licked her snout.

She opened her eyes. They were glassy, staring, tormented. The one facing him, her left eye, had the Moon suspended in the iris, sinking low on a dark horizon.

She saw him across the Moon's curve, across tides of pain, like a ship captain might see a lighthouse in the far distance—or *hope* he saw that, and it wasn't some cruel trick of the night.

What did the Silvery Sky Bitch torment her with now? Why had the Silvery Sky Bitch allowed Aaron's Mark to mean anything?

Three days and it had not festered. It remained a raw, cruel wound raked into her silvery shoulder.

It would heal, then it would fade, but the damage was done.

She could have simply spared his life and held him prisoner. Why had she commanded him to kill Aaron?

How do I free you from him? Must I chase him into the next world and devour his soul?

Gabel settled down next to her and rested his chin on her shoulder, ears perked and senses alert. The IceMaw might come looking for them. Well, for *her*. He had defeated Aaron in combat. He had killed Aaron because Gianna had begged him to. Whatever the IceMaw made of that was their concern.

A rictus shook her, and she whimpered in her throat, a sound of pure pain and anguish.

He slicked his ears and pressed closer to her, rubbing his jowl along her side.

I should never have given you up. I should have defied the Moon, defied you, endured your fury and anger.

I should have stolen you from Magnes. I should have stolen you from SableFur. I should have howled to that cursed pack you are mine.

*You **ARE** mine. Your place is at **MY** side. No longer will I let you wander from my gaze. No longer will I even share you with the world or the Goddess who thinks you belong to HER, or the monster who thinks you are HIS.*

*You. Are. **MINE.***

I am the Destroyer, and I have chosen destruction. Let it all burn. Let it all wither. Let it all fall apart and rot into the ground. I will be king of what remains, just as you have always told me, and I will dance on ashes... with you safe at my side.

Some of her torment eased. It echoed through their bond like hoofbeats, but she was too far away, and the source beyond his reach.

How strange: it was as if he could see her running towards him, harried by something he *knew* was there, that he perceived, but he was powerless to go to her, or to deal with the monster.

She would have to fight the monster on her own a while longer. He needed to get her physical body somewhere safe.

But where?

The RedWater and other smaller packs he had not gotten around to conquering stood between him and IronMoon. The bulk of his army was in SableFur, far to the north. He had none of his human implements of life. He was wounded, and Gianna was broken.

He sniffed the Mark on her shoulder again, fascinated with the wanton, horrifying cruelty that was quite unlike anything he had ever considered. Even looking at it made his soul clench in fury and pain.

She could not possibly have consented to being Marked by Aaron.

He drank deep of her torment and agony. Under that was *her*, his Queen, the rare night-blooming cereus that only came one night of the year. *"Or did you trick* him, *my ambitious queen? Did you do it to trap him and bind him?"*

She did not answer. She might not have even heard his words across the waves of suffering.

He had been in agony for days after surrendering her to the Oracles. The pain had been immeasurable, and the madness cloaked his mind. All he remembered was a soul-deep agony beyond description and her screams as he had left her with the Oracles of SableFur.

She would not be well for days yet, if history followed this course that had been set.

"I swore to you if you were lost on the Tides, I would come find you." But he did not have the tourmaline. His spear was back in IronMoon's heart—and it had never taken him to the Tides. It had taken him to the place where their souls had joined. *"And I swore I would build a tower to the Moon and gouge out Her Eye if you were not returned to me."*

Faithless Moon. Too early to plan an invasion on Her domain. But the time would come.

Then I will be endless.

He rubbed his jowl in her fur again, inhaling deeply, questing for the scent of the rare flower under the layers of ash and agony. *"Where shall I take you now? I cannot risk the world finding you before you are ready to be found once more."*

An idea formed, slowly, as the map of his ruined domain unfurled in his mind.

He grinned.

Perfect.

THIS IS THE END

The salt of the Tides didn't usually smell of sunlight, and there was no sun here: just the furious storm-lanced sky.

Aaron's howls tore at my mind, and I tumbled across the Tides, water-logged and helpless, without even the shattered remains of the Oracle of Mirrors' shards to protect me. Gabel's voice pulled from some other direction, his teeth digging into my soul and *pulling*.

I swore I would come onto the Tides to find you, buttercup.

My soul tried to tear out of my body and sink into the Tides, where the howls could not reach me.

I swam, bobbing and sinking in my nightmares, paddling desperately for shore as the storm blew in, and the Scythe-Moon's edge pressed into the horizon.

No! I screamed, gulping down Tides, feeling full and heavy and my pelt dragging me down as two wolves tore at me, but I could not move either. Something kept me weighed down and buoyed at the same time.

I was the fulcrum: the point on which light and dark tipped.

The scent of salt and ocean got worse. I paddled in the direction of Gabel's maw pulling my soul, but the Tides kept tossing me, and Aaron's howls *pulled* the currents like wind.

I gulped down a mouthful of water. I choked. How long had I been swimming?

I will never let him have you. You are mine.

Two voices told me that: a voice of howls and wind, and a voice of ash and burning.

You/You are/are mine/mine.

Anguish ripped through me, rending my soul into pieces. I choked and prayed for something beyond death.

Prayed for it to just end.

But you ended it, little wolf. This IS the end.

But how could it be the end when it felt endless?

The Moon's burning, lashing voice seared through me, driving into me like rain, and I tumbled through the Tides, then through the storm that lashed the jungle temple, where the scales whipped and dangled and clanged.

My paw caught something in the water. Fleshy, perhaps. Sandy, maybe. I choked. My other paw scratched the surface.

This is the end?

I heaved with the last of my strength and pulled myself onto whatever island I had found—

IT WAS TOO BRIGHT.

My skin was too tight, but it also felt too loose.

There was a strange taste in my mouth. Salty and bloody.

Aaron's howls echoed across a vast, vast distance, and my tattered soul strained to hear his song.

"Buttercup."

My name in the lupine language. A scent of ash and burning.

Two leathery forelegs with tufts of matted fur around the

ankles, huge claws. A large, leathery body, oily and fetid. Then movement, and a leather death's-head face with massive orange fangs and breath that smelled of carrion and ash, glowing yellow-green-eyes, and tiny little triangles of battered leather ears.

"Buttercup," he growled softly. *"Come to me."*

My soul felt too small and weak to animate my body. *"Gabel?"*

"I am here."

"Where is here?"

...This IS the end...

"SaltPaw."

It took a few more minutes for my eyes to focus on the world and process my aching corporeal form.

Gabel stood over me now. His rat-tail wagged so hard it slapped his haunches with a sound like a whip hitting a side of meat.

"Gabel." I whispered. I was on my side, staring up at him with one eyeball.

"Buttercup." He lowered his snout to me.

"You smell like fish." He also smelled like Gabel: ash, burning, his breath with the undercurrent of carrion. But his breath definitely smelled like fish. In fact, *everything* smelled of salt and sunlight and something fishy and seaweed-y.

He chuckled.

"Are we on the Tides?"

He slicked his leathery little ear-triangles down. *"No. We are at SaltPaw."*

Oh, yes, he had said that.

He cocked his head to the side. *"Were you on the Tides again? Is that where you have been?"*

I struggled to roll to my chest. *"In them."*

It was too much effort. I flopped back and panted.

Gabel grabbed something on my other side and pulled.

He had me on a very large dog bed it looked like. And I was

on a wooden deck amid white-yellow dunes dotted with ocean grasses, and not far in the distance, was a rocky beach with a dark ocean chewing away at it. On my other side was the patio door to a house. Just a house.

An unremarkable beachy-looking house. Human house, clearly. On stilts, overlooking the beach and ocean.

I stared, dazed, at the sunny ocean.

...*Gianna*...

I snapped my jaw shut against a howl. A shudder wracked my aching body.

On the deck next to my bed was a fish, half a fish, and some fish guts. The only sound was the ocean. The breeze smelled of ocean and sun and salt and summer and sand and dunes. There were no clouds on the horizon, and only white, happy, puffy clouds overhead in the brilliant, piercing blue sky.

It reminded me of one of the first visions I'd had for Gabel: the one where I'd been in a sandy forest by a beach just like this one. I turned my head to look up the line of the beach, and could just make out some trees that shadowed the coastline.

What had that vision been? I'd seen the three runes in that one, hadn't I?

The Meat-Man vision. It had been the petitioner wolf's vision, the first time I'd seen Aaron. It'd been a pretty standard-issue dream about crossing a political boundary, but in it there'd been the three runes—clues for *me*.

My mind rocked in my skull, swinging back and forth like the jangling of the scales from my visions. Was I trapped in the tourmaline? Because last I knew, Gabel did not own a beach house in the middle of nowhere. Gabel had never even *been* to the beach. Hell, *I* had never been to the beach except in my visions, and this was not a pristine tropical beach with blue waters and white sand, but it also wasn't the dark, rocky, frigid ocean-edge of my dreams. *"Where are we?"*

He sat back down, his tail still wagging across the wood. *"For the third time: SaltPaw."*

"The pack that ran and hid from you to avoid getting conquered? That SaltPaw?" Aaron's howl tugged from a far distance.

"It seems they kept running." He looked around the little beachy cove.

He was sitting a bit oddly—and after another murky moment, I realized why. One of his hind legs was injured.

His tongue dangled between his massive fangs. *"I am fine. It is healing."*

It looked terrible: pink blooms slashed into his dark hide.

He glanced at it, then turned his attention back to me, unconcerned. *"You need not worry for me. Now. Would you like to eat this yourself, or shall I keep feeding you?"*

He placed one paw over the half-fish.

"You fed *me? Like a puppy?"* Lupine-form pups were like wolf puppies: once they were done nursing, they moved on to partially digested meat regurgitated by packmembers.

"Of course."

So I hadn't been swallowing the ocean in my dreams, I'd been swallowing—

Gabel sighed as I crawled to the edge of the bed and puked up fish-mush.

He waited until I was done, then shifted into human form—heedless of the blood trickling out of the gouges in his thigh—and dragged my bed to a different part of the deck. He cleaned everything while I lay there, weak and panting.

...Gianna...

I flailed onto my belly and managed to get my legs under myself.

I panted, then summoned the strength to shift forms. Joints cracked and creaked. Muscles protested.

I somehow dragged myself up into a sitting position, propped up by the deck railing, with my back to the ocean.

...*Gianna*...

The weight of him pushed me against the wall of the house, how he crushed me, his salt-and-snow scent suffocating me, his lips moving against my ear, his breath soft, vicious, his resolve a stone in the Tides.

...*I will stop at nothing. I will pay any price*...

My soul twisted and tore as his claws were back, only this time, *inside me*, ghostly and pulling through me like silk gauze.

...*I did it out of love. Love of you, love of my pack, love of the future for our species*.....

My fingers traced the raised scar. I couldn't bear to look at it, but I knew the design: *instrument*, bisected with *balance*, and adorned with the final rune for *courage*.

He'd carved it into me so slowly, so cruelly, with such fervor, and it had ended, but it was endless.

I sobbed once. "It's not gone. It's not gone."

The Moon had betrayed me. After everything I had endured, how I had questioned nothing, how I had given up *everything*, and what I hadn't given up, She had let Gabel *take* from me. Aaron couldn't have known those runes. The Moon had guided his claws as he'd carved this into me.

I heaved another sob. It'd healed. It hadn't festered.

"He's very dead," Gabel's voice rumbled.

"He's still here." My heart broke over and over, I wanted him here, I *needed* him here...

I hated him. I *hated* him and I had not *wanted* to hate him.

Suffocating need for Aaron strangled me and drowned out everything and his howl grew louder, pulling me to the other side.

Gabel dropped to one knee. One big hand stole across me to clasp my naked hip. In human form, the glorious blue-gloss of his Mark reflected the ocean itself. "No, he's not. *I* am here. And you are here with me and we are together again, and *no one* will ever separate us. Not again. Never again."

I breathed hard and opened my eyes, fearing who would look back at me. Our bond twisted and pulled, drawing me tighter as Aaron tried to pull me away.

"I am here. You are with *me*."

"Why is it still there?" I rasped.

"You are healing. It will fade to nothing, for whatever that is worth. It is not stained blue-gloss, as ours is." He glanced towards the daylight sky.

"I hear him," I whispered. "I hear him, I *feel* him, he wants me to go to him. I want to go to him. I do, I do—"

"He has *made* you want to go with him." Gabel gripped me tighter.

I laughed, crazy and wild. "Oh, irony! You telling me that."

Gabel's voice was the ash and the storm. "I will not let him have you. I will find a way to free you from him, I swear it, even if I have to destroy the Moon and place *you* in the sky to rule in Her place."

"Don't talk madness." I keened as the pain twisted my entire being. Aaron's soul *pulled* at mine, and Gabel's claws sank deep, and I was just the knot caught in the middle of it all, I was the fulcrum. I was the scales in the storm.

I inhaled and caught Aaron's scent on the salty air.

Gabel crushed me against him. "Hold me, buttercup. I won't let the Tides have you."

The storm lashed through my mind. The eye, the *eye*, stared back at me, and *my* eye pounded with my heartbeat.

Some part of me had loved Aaron.

He howled from the other side.

It was unfair, it wasn't right, he hadn't been a monster, he shouldn't have died like he had.

He shouldn't have done what he had done to me.

I arched against Gabel's grip and screamed to the sky.

...Gianna!...

"I will never let you go." Gabel's voice was a growl and a storm, "I let you go once to humor the Moon, and I will never make that mistake again."

"We had to." I writhed in his grip. "We had to, Gabel. We had to do it!"

"No," he said darkly. "We did not. And I will regret every day for the rest of my life, and every moment of my existence after that, that I let you go that day. I am done howling for Her pleasure."

CHERISHED ISOLATION

The SaltPaw house was small and on legs that kept it ten feet off the sandy dunes. Opposite it, not far away up a crumbling asphalt road, was a line of trees that turned into a forest. A constant breeze pulled off the ocean.

The house itself had been abandoned months earlier, and the sand had blown through the house, covering everything in a swirling grit. There were dried bits of leaves and forest floor too, and the remains of whatever the SaltPaw hadn't taken with them.

He'd found some flowery half-robe of a satiny material among the left-behind possessions. I clutched it around my breasts as we stood on the front porch and the sea breeze tugged at everything. He had on a pair of too-large cargo shorts that he'd bothered to zip up, but not button. His feet were bare.

I focused on Gabel, even if it felt like gathering pieces of cotton candy in wet hands. "Where did you go?"

He had disappeared for a while, trotting off down a path with a scavenged backpack in his maw, and returned several hours later pulling the bag, now laden with a random assortment of canned foods, bags of chips, and plastic-wrapped cupcakes.

He said, like it was silly, "Hunting, of course. Or, in this case, foraging. Since you object to my fishing skills."

"What did you do, ransack a gas station?" I contemplated a can of spaghetti in one hand and a wrapped cupcake in the other. "Because I know you don't have your wallet."

"You threw up the fish—"

"Technically, *you* threw it up first."

"I *regurgitated* it." He sounded mildly affronted.

I stared hard at the wrapped cupcake. "You didn't... maul anyone, right?"

He retrieved a can opener from the abandoned kitchen. "No."

The food refused to make sense. "Your leg?"

"It's fine."

"It isn't going to heal," I said, still feeling vague and distant. "You need to not be running miles on it."

He took one of the cans. "Haven't I proven by now I can take care of myself, buttercup?"

I didn't know how to respond to that. It was too difficult.

He opened the can of spaghetti. I recoiled at the smell, and my stomach tried to heave. Without comment, he set it aside and opened a can of chili. This didn't turn my stomach, but that's all I could say about my reaction.

I took the can from him and stared at the contents.

I heard myself say, "You came for me."

"Of course I came for you."

"But you left your army behind. You don't know what happened to them."

"I swore I would never let another take you from me," Gabel said, voice cold. Then his lips curled in a cruel, small, bitter smirk. "Or do you not remember the third vow I made to you that night?"

Tears slipped down my cheeks.

Gabel glanced briefly at my arm, then back to my face. "I will refresh your memory. I swore to cherish and love you so no other would ever be worthy of your glance. That bastard Aaron had a bit too much of your attention and could smell your lure-scent. Lucas told me to tolerate the situation as you would not want rescue. I spoke with Aaron, who rubbed my face in the vows, on how I had failed all of them, and if I truly loved you enough, and cherished you as you deserved, *he* would not smell your scent, as he was clearly worthy of your attention."

Each word became more and more edged with fiery, suffocating rage and a dark, black fury that conjured ash and burning and the consuming roar of an angry ocean filled with burning glass.

"And I *humored* the wolf," Gabel hissed, "I *humored* him because what if he was *right*? You did refuse to return to me, and our Marks are blue-gloss. Aaron told me I was not your mate, I was your *pet*, and the Moon had given you my soul in penance for what I'd done to you."

Aaron had told IceMaw the same thing: that our Mark wasn't a true Mark, but that the Moon had bound Gabel to me to keep like a snarling dog on a chain. That I was the Balance-Keeper, with the Moon in her eye, and I was tasked with keeping the escaped Hound on his lead.

But the fact Gabel had spoken to Aaron at all spun my mind around. The fact that Aaron had said *anything* to make Gabel hesitate spun me a second time. I had to catch myself on the table. Aaron's presence in my soul grew more intense.

Gabel growled, softly. He touched my face. "Then I felt him take your soul. I felt—"

"He tried to convince me you'd never leave the front and give up your conquest of SableFur for me." Tears bubbled down my cheeks. I couldn't say Aaron's name. Saying it would summon him across the river of death back into this world.

Gabel rubbed his thumb over my lips. "You did not believe him."

The tears came faster. The sky seemed to darken. There was a storm on the wind. "I knew you would come. I told him you would. He did not believe me."

"Oh, some part of you believed him. Did any part of your soul believe I would abandon you to him?"

I gulped down a sob. "I don't know. I don't know anymore."

"Why did you want me to kill him? I could have broken him. We could have kept him alive and in the basement. You didn't have to endure this."

My soul twisted. "You would never have broken him."

"Oh, yes, I would have."

My tears stopped long enough for me to laugh. "I had a vision of you two fighting. Over and over, actually, I have had visions of you two confronting each other. In the final one, I tried to stop you both, and the sky rained glass and stars and the oceans boiled. She showed me how I am the fulcrum, and if I kept trying to keep the scales balanced, there's nothing but the storm."

Gabel frowned slightly. "So, who won in your visions? You risked your life having me kill him. You knew, even if you survived, what it'd do to you."

"What it would do to *us*."

"I fear no pain save yours," Gabel said darkly. "And I *will* free you from this, even if I have to hunt Aaron's soul into the void itself and devour it. I swear to you, it may take the rest of our lives, it may take eternity, but I *will* free you."

"Your conquest of the Moon's Realm will have to wait. We have a more immediate problem."

"Yes, yes, I know, you want your crown," Gabel said, a wild light in his eye. "So tell me. Who won in the end?"

I smiled miserably. "That's just it. I always drowned in the Tides before it was over. *It* didn't end. *I* did."

Gabel's expression compressed and the Bond between us shifted and rumbled, seething and shot through with smoldering cracks.

I changed the subject. "I have to go back to SableFur. Kiery... Lucas... you spoke with Lucas—"

"Only the once, and not since Aaron absconded with you."

"You know what Adrianna will do to him!"

"She has likely already done it. Especially considering Adrianna's taste for Oracle blood. Why would you care about Lucas? He failed you."

"Bernhard," I growled, the world snapping into focus. "I trusted that wolf! As much as I could trust any SableFur. He was there when Magnes was destroyed!"

"Ahhh, the Second Beta. I wonder if it played out the way he expected. Perhaps he isn't dead yet. I would love to ask him some questions. Here. You need to eat."

The weight of all my thoughts bore down on me like a wave. I was in an abandoned house eating chili out of a can. "Why did we come here, Gabel?"

He shifted his weight slightly to favor his injured leg. "No one will look for us here. Let them believe Aaron wounded me, your soul is torn in two, and we have crawled off somewhere to die."

The jangling in my mind got worse. "Is that what we're doing? Hiding?"

"I do not *hide*, buttercup. Nor do you."

"Then what are we doing here?"

"Enjoying the ocean."

"Gabel. We need to go back."

"To what?"

"IronMoon. SableFur. The world!"

"No," he said simply. "Let it all burn, as you've foreseen."

What? What was he talking about? He didn't *want* to go back to IronMoon? He was... done? My brain clouded and flailed, still too addled to wrap itself around thoughts. Gabel took the can from me before I dropped it, then captured me around the shoulders to steady me. "You need to recover."

I'd never recover. I'd been doomed the moment Gabel had walked into the house at Shadowless. I'd been a pawn in the Moon's infernal game the moment I'd been born.

I was the Balance Keeper, the point on which light and dark turned. But from where I stood, it was all just darkness.

And it seemed everything had played into Adrianna's hands: the IceMaw were without Aaron, so that southern alliance of packs? It would fall apart. IronMoon was in shambles. SableFur had been splintered, but now with Gabel not at the front, his forces were likely on the retreat, and everyone who had supported me was going to be put under the axe. How many were dead? How many packs had Gabel slaughtered? How many warriors had died for Adrianna's lies?

And now Adrianna would crown herself Queen in that awful temple of bones deep in SableFur, and the Moon closed Her Eye.

All the dead acolytes. My dead sisters.

I looked at the back of my scarred hands. "Maybe you *should* have refused to let me go to SableFur that day."

Gabel shifted again. "You mean it was a test for me, and I failed."

I didn't respond.

He lifted my scarred hands to his lips. "I regret *every* moment of every day going along with the Silver Sky Bitch's whims. If I had it to do again, I would refuse. I would rather be punished with your fury the rest of eternity than see you suffer one bit of pain."

He kissed my fingers gently. Licks of pain went through the warmth of his touch, and Aaron's agonized, angry howl twisted something in the back of my mind. "So now, I am refusing to participate in *Her* designs further, and I am not allowing you to either. We are done, my love. We are done and we can watch the world burn itself down."

He kissed each scar in turn, his blue eyes never leaving mine as he found the wounds with unerring accuracy. "I swear, Gianna, that nothing matters to me save freeing you from him. I *will* cherish you so dearly no other ever occupies your thoughts again, and I *will* be enough that your soul wants for nothing else."

Real Places

I looked down the beaten-up pathway that led to the main SaltPaw house. It stretched across the sand-swept, sawgrass-dotted land up to a narrow strip of equally sand-swept asphalt. The breeze pulled at my hair and the dress Gabel had found for me, and bent the trees at their tips. The sky was bright, brilliant blue, still speckled with gorgeous puffy white clouds, and the ever-present sound of the ocean sloshing against the shore.

The coastline was dunes and sand, but quickly became rocky, mist-laden forest. Even in summer, a mist came through every night, disappearing as soon as the sun was fully over the horizon.

"What are you about?" Gabel asked from halfway down the stairs.

"Don't you have some fish to catch?" My brain felt like it was wrapped in feverish cotton. My body felt like I'd been scraped raw on the inside, then my soul stitched back into it, and if I thought about it too long, Aaron's incessant pacing pulled me down into the currents.

"Not if you won't eat them."

"I'm going over there."

"Over where?"

"The trees."

He started down the steps.

"No, you stay here," I said.

"There is zero chance you are going alone."

"Your *leg*, you stubborn wolf."

"I am not bleeding." He glanced down at his cargo shorts, then twisted his bad leg to glance behind his knee. His muscles shifted under his skin. The summer sun and beach had burned him to a glorious bronze, and with his sandy blond hair and blue eyes and beaten-up surfer tee featuring some weird faded neon airbrush painting of a shark wearing sunglasses, he looked every bit a prime-grade beach bum.

"Not actively bleeding is the *minimum* standard."

"No, the minimum standard is *eating*."

"What am I going to do? Run away?" I closed my eyes and exhaled, then headed off towards the road.

"You? Perhaps."

"We have to go back. We can't just...just...abdicate!"

"Says who?" he asked simply.

"Gabel, all you have ever wanted is to be King."

He looked towards the north, then back at me. "And I still will be. On my own terms. In my own time."

"So you'd rather rule over *ashes*?"

"Buttercup. Remember who you're talking to. And your vision that you drown before I finish my conquest means I will *not* be pursuing my conquest until we change the future. I have lived life twice without you. First when I let you go, then when I let you stay away. I do not require a third lesson."

My head hurt, and whispers in the back of my head from Aaron were wind inside my skull. I headed down the path.

He followed.

The road ended in a sand dune about ten yards to the right,

and there wasn't another house in sight. The SaltPaw had had some prime oceanfront property, that was for sure. And they'd just... abandoned it. There was a dock a way off, but it was small and clearly private, nothing special. There were no boats on the water. To the left the road stretched between dunes and horizon, crumbling asphalt and swept with more sand, and ahead of me, more dunes and the treeline.

Gabel silently steadied me as we walked up the dunes, which revealed that the sand ended another hundred feet or so ahead of us, where the treeline began, and the trees ran along the beach up another mile or two, gradually encroaching until the beach no longer existed, and it was only rocks and trees.

It felt like it should be quiet, but between the ocean, the birds, and the buzzing of bugs, it wasn't quiet at all.

Gabel slid his hand down my spine. "You're too tired for this."

"I'm fine."

"I will forgive the lie."

I shuddered all over as a wave of anguish and exhaustion hit me. I took a few minutes to gather my brain together, then marched off across the pine needle forest floor. "I... I know this place."

"You didn't even know the SaltPaw existed before you met me, and I know you have never been here without me."

"I—I—" I closed my mouth. "I can't tell you."

I'd seen this place. I'd been here: the Petitioner Wolf who had come to see me at IronMoon. He'd been the one who had asked about the line in the forest.

It'd been the first time I had seen Aaron.

Back then, I had only known him as the MeatMan.

The memory of meeting him blasted into my mind, that shocked feeling, the stricken, struck, the *gasp*, the *who is this*, the horror of coming face-to-face with a vision. A vision that had claimed to smell my scent, a vision that had *known* my scent, given it a name. A name not even Gabel had whispered to me before then: that my lure-scent was the night-blooming cereus.

...Gianna...

I spun around.

My arm burned, throbbed, *pulled*, like my skin was splitting open again. I clapped my hand over the scar. It rose up to meet my palm, every line and ridge of it. Like he'd carved it into my bones and it'd anchored itself there.

...Gianna...

"He's not here," I whispered. "He's not here, he's dead, he's gone. He's not here. *You aren't here.*"

Gabel paced closer. "A vision?"

"Yes. Someone else's question. Someone else's answer," I whispered. "But... the first part of the vision I saw... there were things meant for me. It was..."

"Focus on me." Gabel's voice bore into my hazy half-reality.

I trained my attention on him, pressing out the haunting whispers and visions like I'd been trained to do as a child.

Gabel said, "The Petitioner Wolf. The vision where you saw Aaron for the first time."

I laughed. "You always did have a way of wrecking my vow of secrecy. That's how the SableFur got me away."

"Simple deductions aren't remarkable."

I danced along the edge of breaking my vow of secrecy. "All the visions I've had since... since we met... have had something in them that was meant for me to see. And I've... I've been here. I know this place. Aaron was... he was right there."

I pointed to the small place where Aaron had been standing in the vision. I remembered the shape of the dunes, the way the pine needles lay, the sound of the ocean in the distance.

And I remembered with a horrible pang that seemed to split me in two that I had lost my bowls *again*. Gabel hadn't known to get them from IceMaw after the fight, and they were still there.

Gardenia had shattered my tools, Magnes had shattered my stones, and now I'd lost the beautiful bowls Aaron had had made for me. How could I call myself an Oracle any longer?

I sobbed once.

Gabel's hand closed over my wrist, slid down to take my hand. "But you've been to real places in your visions before."

"But it hadn't been *my* vision, and what I saw happen didn't happen here. It couldn't have happened here. So why show it to me *here*?" The actual exchange between the MeatMan and the MeatTaker had not happened here. The deal had been struck somewhere else. Why had the Moon showed it happening *here*, in a real, wholly unrelated place?

Yes, the SaltPaw had been in Aaron's pocket—either directly, or indirectly—and they'd been abandoned when Gabel had come calling. They'd fled and were still missing. But they hadn't brokered the deal. They'd just been pawns in Aaron's game.

And there had been no reason in the vision for the Moon to show me the table, the stones, or the runes. Those things clearly weren't here.

So why *here*?

Not that I could have asked even if I'd had my tools. Oracles couldn't scry for themselves.

"There were other things too. Things that had been meant for me, not the petitioner. The petitioner's question had been so meaningless I was surprised the Moon entertained it at all. "Things I keep seeing, in all my dreams and visions, no matter if it's a vision or I end up swept away beyond the Tides, over and over, everywhere, I see..."

...Gianna...

"We have to go back, Gabel," I said. "We have to go back to IronMoon."

"No. I am not participating in the Moon's designs any longer."

"These Marks *are* Her design! What about this *isn't* Her design?! You don't get a choice about if you participate or not."

"Then I choose to participate no more than I currently am." Gabel's fingers ran along my palm as he felt the fresh scars from handling mirror shards. "Oracles, and visions, give us a chance to see the path we are on, and *perhaps*, change it. But not avert it completely, correct?"

I nodded, eyes leaking tears.

He spoke low, calm, and so, so cold. "A year ago, you saw this place. And now we are here. I am done giving you to Her designs, to be abused and mauled like a warrior in battle. We have done that. We have responded, we have acted, and we are still here."

"No." If we *hadn't* acted, we might have ended up somewhere else.

"The only thing I have *done* as Destroyer," Gabel said simply, "is destroy you."

FISHING

Gabel bounced in the surf.

I watched from the house porch. The constant ocean breeze tore at my hair and the hem of my dress. Three days since my outing to the forest, and Gabel refused to consider going back to IronMoon, or anything resembling our previous life at all. Instead, he seemed more than content to dwell in the abandoned SaltPaw house, with our beautiful but desolate surroundings.

...Gianna...

I bowed my head and gripped the railing. "Go away. I don't want you. I never did."

...lies. If that were true...

I shook my arm as *his* Mark twitched like he'd touched it. It was just the breeze and my hair in the wind. It wasn't him. My imagination.

...if it were true, my Mark wouldn't stay. You love me. Some part of you...

"Stop it!" I said through clenched teeth.

Aaron's presence receded, but the deepest recesses of my mind rang with the echoes of his howls.

Gabel stalked fish in the shallow water of the surf, periodically bouncing into the waves, ducking under them like a bird, and half the time, came up with a wriggling, flapping fish in his maw. He then trotted onto the sand, bit the fish's head off so it didn't suffer further, and returned to the waves. He dug clams out of the wet sand and found the occasional oyster. He'd eat his fish raw in wolf-form. I preferred to cook mine until they were charred and bore no resemblance to how he'd "fed" me. I made him take the clams and oysters *far* out of sight. Even thinking about them made me retch.

"This isn't the island at the edge of the Tides." I came down onto the beach as he brought in his newest fish. "We *can* leave whenever we want."

He wagged his rat-tail. It slapped his flanks. He deposited his fish, nipped off its head, spit out the head, and left both parts on the small pile he'd accumulated. Then he shifted back into human form. "But I do not want to leave."

"I do."

"To go back to what? Let it all burn, buttercup. Just let it burn. It will burn with or without us."

"I don't *want* it to burn," I snapped. I had not been living this life to just *let it burn*. I had been actively working *against* things burning down. "You don't get to quit."

"I have not *quit*."

"Really? Because it seems to me like you've quit. This seems like quitting by a different name."

"I have quit playing the Silver Sky Bitch's game." Gabel gripped me by the hips and tugged me against his soaking wet and naked body. A layer of salt crusted his hair and face as he dried in the blinding sunlight. "Yes, *that* I have quit."

I growled, "You can call it whatever you want, and you can justify it however you like, but you've *quit*. You can't win, so you're just not going to play."

"Why should I? Why should I risk you in a game that I

cannot win, and the only thing I stand to lose is you? Oh no, my love, we've played *that* game. We have played it many times in many forms, and each time, you return to me more battered than the last." He caressed Aaron's Mark, his eyes burning blue.

I yanked my shoulder away. The Mark burned hot enough under my skin I clenched my jaw against the pain while my soul twisted. "Because it's the world at stake, and we're obligated to keep getting up and wading back in. That's why."

He almost sounded gentle when he spoke. "But I am the Destroyer. You know what's going to happen."

"And I am the Balance Keeper, the point on which light and dark turns. I can't be out here watching you catch fish!"

"But I am very good at it."

I rolled my eyes and let out a long, slow breath.

He smirked. "Admit it."

"Have you ever considered using a *net*?"

"What is the fun in that? You are grouchy. I will go catch you something woodland-esque."

"You don't have to—"

"Of course I do. You need warm, fresh prey."

I sighed. "Your leg. You shouldn't even be in the water. You will probably get a parasite or such."

He glanced down at the still-healing gash on his thigh, crusted with thick scabs. "I am fine, while you are not. I will see if today the hunting is better."

"I don't need prey." I sighed again. I *needed* him to go back to IronMoon. And while I didn't much care for fish or the canned goods, food held little interest anyway. My stomach felt on the urge of revolt half the time if I thought about food. In fact, even thinking about Gabel and oysters made my throat tickle with a gag right then.

"Yes, you do. You are..." he paused, rummaging for a word that eluded him, then said, "you need something warm and bloody. I will go find it."

"Gabel." I turned as he released me and headed up the beach, shifting into wolf form. "Gabel, I want to go back, not prey!"

He barked and loped back up the beach towards the wooded area across the sandy road.

"You're just going to leave the..." I looked at the mound of fish parts.

Couldn't just leave them there to rot in the sun. Because he'd eat them, no matter how smelly they got, and while he hadn't managed to make himself sick yet, he would one day succeed and I didn't want to find out how sympathetic a puker I was. I got a bucket and scooped up the fish. Might as well toss them on the fire, and if he complained about them being cooked, he shouldn't have wandered off to go hunt things with fur.

The SaltPaw had left a fire pit and firewood for said fire pit, so I stirred up the ashes and tossed the fish and fish heads onto the heat to char while I contemplated how to make Gabel see reason. He and I couldn't stay here in the SaltPaw house while everything else went to hell around us.

Gabel returned about an hour later, just as the fish were well and truly *cooked*. In his maw was a fat summer rabbit. The wind blew the scent of the rabbit away, but the thought of fresh rabbit kicked my stomach into sudden starvation and I dropped into wolf-form as he approached. I darted forward, clamped my jaws over the haunches dangling from his mouth, and snatched.

He released it with a huff of amusement.

I dropped to the ground right there and began to chew on it.

It was *delicious*. The best thing I'd had in as long as I could remember. I growled around mouthfuls.

Gabel sat and watched me eat, rat-tail wagging slowly against the walk. *"Do you plan on sharing?"*

I barred my teeth. *My* rabbit. Not his.

I returned to my aggressive devouring.

By the Moon, I had been *starving*.

His tail wagged a bit harder.

I gulped down the rabbit in record time and flopped over onto my side to rest my engorged belly.

Gabel settled down beside me and licked my ears, and then the blood from my muzzle. *"Shall I get you another?"*

"No." My belly was full enough. *"I did not realize I had been craving rabbit."*

"I thought you might."

"Oh?"

A playful nip on my ear. *"I told you you needed warm prey."*

The sun baked my belly. I let it, and I let myself drift. I was stuck in this form for a few hours now while I digested the raw meat, but it wasn't so bad. The sea breeze through my fur, the hot sunlight, the sound of the ocean, my chosen mate with me, and a full belly. Although Aaron was silent. Ominously silent.

I rolled onto my chest. He was *too* quiet.

I growled. He *wanted* me to stay here with Gabel! I slicked my ears down and barred my fangs.

I know what you're doing!

No answer. No movement. Silence.

Flint had warned me that the agony wasn't just the death, but how your mate howled in pain at the separation. The way the Bond stretched thin and awful, the never *ending* pain.

Gabel nipped my ear. *"Buttercup."*

I rolled back onto my side and focused on the hot sunlight and breeze and how *not* like the Island at the Edge of the Tides this was. Gabel licked my ears. His breath smelled of carrion and ash, which was not pleasant, but *was* him. I pulled my mind onto focusing on each breath and *him*.

Aaron's soul paced, then slunk back, watching.

"Breathe," Gabel told me, sidling his leathery body along my pelt as close as he could manage. It was far too hot, and that was

perfect. My belly was uncomfortably full as well, and that helped. Helped keep me *here*.

Aaron's Mark throbbed.

Gabel bit me again. Harder. *"And you want me to take you back, buttercup? I can't do that. I have to protect you, as I failed to do so often before now. I will hunt warm prey for you. I will fish for you. We will watch the world burn into ash, together. You will not drown. My Kingdom will not crumble to dust."*

I rolled back to my belly and panted around a twist of pain in my soul. *"But that's what he wants."*

"HIM?" Gabel rumbled, shooting up to his paws. His massive yellow claws tore at the sandy turf.

"I don't know why. But when I start to enjoy being here, he goes quiet. He haunts me when I try to leave. He doesn't want us to leave." But I did know that I trusted Aaron to have a very good reason why Gabel going on vacation suited Aaron perfectly. And when Aaron got what he wanted, he would hunt me until I threw myself into the water to escape him—which I never would. *"We have to go back. I know we have to go back. We have to!"*

Gabel growled. His claws tore at the turf. Then he bent and licked my muzzle, breath smelling of death and burning. *"Then we will go back, buttercup. Then we will go back."*

Not What I Meant

"It doesn't look like it's changed." A wave of disorientation washed over me. A year ago Gabel had brought me to this very house, with a Mark slashed into my arm, and my soul twisted.

And here we were again: Gabel bringing me to this very house, a Mark I didn't want on my arm, and my soul twisted.

Gabel might be right about how it was all futile from the beginning. Then why did the Moon *drive* both of us? Why had She told me to go to SableFur? Why had She given me the starlight wolves?

Why a lot of things.

Gabel said darkly, "It shouldn't have. You weren't gone for long."

I stared at the facade of the house. "I guess... you're right. It's only been... four months?"

"It has been eighteen weeks. I have counted each day."

The landscaping didn't look quite as manicured, and determined weeds had come up through the gravel of the drive, and grass was a few days late on being cut, and there were some left-over leaves in the gutters and clustered around the chimneys. Gabel had always been strict about keeping the grounds pristine.

It *smelled* the same. I inhaled, it caught in my chest, and I gulped on an unexpected sob.

I needed to get myself together. I felt like a mess, all ragged and moth-eaten and chewed up and spit out.

Gabel surveyed the house with a frown. On the other side of the house were the thumps and clacks of the warriors training. "You will forgive the lack of ceremony. I told Flint you weren't in the mood for songs and displays of prowess."

"Am I ever?"

His lips curled in a grin. "You preside over it so naturally, though."

"I doubt IronMoon will appreciate their Luna coming back." Quite a difference from the way IceMaw had welcomed me with so much enthusiasm.

Gabel bent his arm into a tighter crook, squishing my hand between the muscle of his forearm and his rock-hard bicep. "Their appreciation of you is no longer a concern."

"What are you talking about?"

He pressed his palm into the top of my hand. "Have I not made clear these last four months that you are my mate, and I will tear down the world itself to have you back? Any wolf foolish enough to challenge that deserves to have his bones added to my tower."

That hadn't answered my question. Not at all. But Gabel just had a twisted little smile lurking under the surface of his otherwise flat expression.

Right as I set foot on the bricks leading up to the front door —which had been replaced in my absence—Flint came out onto the brick path. He wore his usual kilt, body sweating from working out in the summer sun, and his gold hair flattened to his head in a bronzy sheen. His tattoos shone with a brilliant blue gloss. The one for *duty* drew my eye more than the others.

Eroth—battered and also wearing a kilt, but not sweaty, and marked with various healing scabs—also came out the door. With him was Cook, wearing his apron and—

"Ana!" I exclaimed.

I shuddered on guilt and held onto her *tight*.

"Ooof, settle down there," Ana chuffed around my grip.

I held Ana's arms in a death grip. "What happened to Kiery and Lucas? What's happening in SableFur? The last I heard from Lucas—"

Her face fell. Fell harder than I'd ever seen it.

"Oh no," I said softly. "I hoped Lucas could..."

Ana spoke like a doctor giving grim news. "I don't know. I was expecting shit to hit the fan when Aaron took you, but Lucas sold the lies about you going to negotiate an alliance before Beltane. IceMaw's pretty popular with the southern SableFur, and I guess everyone in the central part was actually kinda okay with the idea of you making an alliance with Aaron and his southern allies and everyone being on the same page. Lucas really sold how powerful it would be, and it'd basically lock Adrianna and Gabel in a room and the Moon could figure it out."

Brilliant ploy on Lucas' part. I'd expected SableFur to rip into pieces, and Aaron had seemed fairly confident that would happen, but Lucas had held it together. Damn good First Beta.

If I'd been the death of another First Beta, and another Oracle...

Ana sighed. "I think a lot of wolves don't believe Adrianna was in league with Magnes, but they *also* don't think you *aren't* the Luna of SableFur. They all believe Gabel is Magnes' bastard son and the SableFur owes him something, but they don't know what. Nobody wants to be the first to say something."

Gabel shifted like a hot, banked coal. His voice sounded like the rumble of distant thunder. "A very interesting insight, Doctor."

Ana shrugged and kept talking to me. "Yeah, well, all that went to fuck when Aaron Marked you. Lots of witnesses and that got back to SableFur in like... an hour. And the news just kept coming and—you know what, you were there. You don't need me to rehash it."

My Marked arms thumped, the blue-gloss one carrying Gabel's mark sharp and so cold it burned, while Aaron's felt like he had carved it into my bones. I managed to keep my voice steady enough to ask, "What happened?"

"Lucas was furious, but there was no keeping it from the pack. Aaron sold out Bernhard and shit got bloody. I hid in my room, packing my stuff, intending to head south. Aaron called me as I was hitching down the highway. Told me to come keep you company. But by the time I got to IceMaw, you were already gone, and he was dead, so I figured you'd show up here eventually."

Aaron had betrayed Bernhard? Why? Why give up his most useful SableFur spy?

Carlos' name conjured a memory of his hopeful face staring *right* into me like needles of silver and ice, how all the IceMaw had howled and looked at me with such fierce, hungry, hope. That *finally* their Alpha had a Luna worthy of him, who could and would see under all those scars, who had the Moon in her eye.

I let out a shuddering breath. "Did Carlos say anything about how I told Gabel to kill Aaron?"

Ana released my arms and stepped back. "Well, about that. According to them, you told *Aaron* to kill *Gabel*. That didn't sound possible to me, so I played the Gee Whiz, I'm Just A Dumb Human card."

"*What?*"

Gabel shifted, his scent curling into something dark but oddly amused. "In the chaos of the storm and the fight, they must have thought you were shouting for *Aaron* to kill me, not the other way around."

But that didn't make sense. Why would IceMaw want to promote a version of events where their Alpha had not just been defeated, but had failed his Luna? Had I misremembered? Had it been a vision?

The memories were storm-laced, and a jumbled, veiled mess, like looking at them through a thick layer of silk. Pain washed over me, excruciating pain wracked me. The lines between vision and IceMaw blurred. I clutched my head and dug my fingers into my scalp.

Gabel stepped close. "Gianna."

"I'm fine," I said hoarsely, waving him away with my other hand.

Eroth shifted his weight. "So Aaron tried to make her the IceMaw Luna?"

Ana shrugged. "No, big guy, he *did* make her his Luna. And crazy as it sounds, they were giving me the vibe they think she's still their Luna and Gabel abducted her."

"And they are not chasing her down like Hounds unleashed from the Void?" Eroth snorted. "She is *our* Luna. They shed no blood to keep her. They have spent not even paws to follow her."

"Catastrophic wars have been fought over less," Flint stated, his blue-gloss tattoos seeming brighter and the halo diffusing further around his skin.

Eroth, almost impatiently said, "What pack just randomly decides to tell a she-wolf she will be their Luna?"

"Well, to be fair," Ana said, "She *does* have the Moon in her eye *and* commanded the starlight wolves. She's pretty obviously The Chosen One and all that. If I had a vacancy I was recruiting for, she'd be a top candidate."

I straightened and turned to Gabel, "Wait, they don't know? You didn't tell Flint?"

"I told *him*. He apparently did not tell the pack."

Flint, serene, merely said, "It was not my story to tell."

My throat choked on Tides. Or maybe I almost threw up.

"Luna?" Eroth inquired as the other warriors that had shown up with him looked at me with unbidden curiosity. Cook seemed concerned.

"What's he talking about?" Ana asked.

"The IceMaw didn't tell you?" I choked, feeling like I was sinking into the stones.

"Carlos and I talked for about ten minutes before I booked it the hell out of there. I wasn't going to ask a lot of questions beyond *where is she* and after he said *Gabel took her* I was like whoa, time to get the fuck out of here like *right now.*"

Slowly, Gabel pulled my light cardigan over my shoulders down to expose both of my arms. The fabric pooled around my wrists.

...Gianna!...

I closed my ears to his howls. I clenched my jaw against my own howl of anguish. My ears rang with the jangling of scales.

Eroth inhaled again. Flint said something under his breath. Cook blanched and covered his mouth like he was going to vomit.

Ana was the only one to use words. "Oh, honey. Oh, no. Oh no."

Flint's lips drew into a thin, terrible line, and his jungle-green eyes reflected the things he'd told me.

"It hasn't faded, has it?" I asked Flint, unable to look anywhere but him.

"It looks fresh. It is just not blue-gloss like your other."

Eroth found his voice. "How is that possible? Two bonds? Two mates?"

"Well, one's dead," Ana reminded him tartly. "Try to keep up with basic math. If a human can do it, you can."

Gabel lifted my sweater back over my shoulders.

Flint turned his attention to Gabel. "So Adrianna needs us destroyed to redeem Magnes and secure a future for her sons. And IceMaw wants their Luna back, because she is their future. Quite a mess that has been made."

"I don't regret telling Gabel to kill Aaron," I snarled at Flint. "He *did* this to me. He ripped me open in front of IceMaw and then—then—"

I clenched my jaw against the spike of fury that made me dizzy.

"I never said you should regret anything you've done, or any choice you made," Flint replied.

"Sure sounded like you did," Ana growled at him.

Flint raised a brow like he couldn't believe she was real. Eroth coughed.

Gabel's the one who chuckled, and his scent was a bit wild and feral. "No, Master of Arms, this is an *opportunity*."

The other wolves exchanged a doubtful look. Even Flint looked skeptical. Eroth finally asked, "How is it an opportunity?"

Misery tried to dissolve me.

Gabel ran his palm over my hand, smiling at Eroth. "I'm disappointed, Second Beta. Everything is falling apart, which means everyone is busy trying to put it back together."

My skin got cold, and even Aaron's howling paused. He listened from beyond, and my soul vibrated with his cold violence.

Gabel, almost airily, said, "I am not interested in putting anything back together. I am going to destroy it all."

GET OFF MY LAWN

I ran a brush through my hair and tried to take inventory of my reflection. I had on a lacy shrug to cover my Marks.

The Scythe-Moon has fallen, and the Sun has set.

Except the Moon hung in my eye, so as long as I carried it... the Moon didn't fall on the world's neck.

Right?

"Buttercup."

I looked towards Gabel's voice.

"Breakfast." There was a wild light in his eyes, and his usual scent of burning seemed more intense. He was also wearing a kilt and nothing else. Gabel normally wore pants to the table.

His hair had bleached to an even paler blonde from our time at the SaltPaw house, and now his eyes appeared brilliantly bright blue, like a robin's egg, and the blue-gloss Mark shifted like it had its own silky heartbeat.

Making him... *brighter*... seemed to make him more terrifying.

"The pack is expecting us," he added.

I glared at him. "My first day back and you want to show me off to the pack?"

A cruel, wicked smile. "You misunderstand."

"What part of this am I *misunderstanding*?"

"I am not showing you off, my love," he said. "You are mine. You are not theirs. And they need to understand that."

"What are you talking about? We're pack. And yes, I've had four packs in the course of the last lunar year. IronMoon twice, actually."

"And been Luna of three of them. And you say you aren't ambitious."

"I'm a lousy Luna and an even worse Oracle."

He smiled and his eyes danced with the same wicked light as the Tides. "And you wish to continue this string of failures by not showing up for breakfast?"

"Gabel, it is *too* early for your games. I hate you."

He chuckled, and the bond surged with his wicked satisfaction at my annoyance, savoring it. "I am so glad you are back to tell me such terrible things."

"Damnit, Gabel."

His eyes darkened to a more familiar stormy-Tide hue. "Come."

"What are you up to?" I asked as he pulled me after him.

"We are in the middle of a war. I am always up to something. I must be unrelenting and ever-vigilant, lest I lose you again. And I will *never* lose you again."

The anguish refreshed and Aaron's pull tugged like a little hair caught in a clip. "I thought you said you weren't participating in the war anymore."

"I'm not. But a wolf has to keep himself entertained, as entertaining as you are," he paused to caress my cheek, "spending every moment in bed with you is not a practical plan."

"Gabel, what are you *really* about?"

He brushed the knuckles of his other hand against my cheek.

"Are you saying after everything you do not trust me? I came for you, did I not? I kept my promise, did I not?"

What was this pseudo-romantic over-attentive mate routine coupled with the deranged *I've finally lost it* vibe? The wild light in his eyes reminded me of the first time the Moon had dragged me down through the Tides: how the blue had also seemed filled with its own light, even when the blue had turned dark and murky and freezing cold. "I trust you to be *you*, and I don't have the stomach for bloodshed to go with my biscuits this morning."

"This is IronMoon. I can't promise there won't be bloodshed at any given meal, but I have no plans to kill anyone. Quite the opposite, actually. Now, you really must attend breakfast."

So they wouldn't think I'd crawled in a hole to die. Because in IronMoon, weakness was death. I needed to put on a good show that I was still sane, and strong, and capable, and not a broken shell. If Adrianna was off leading armies by herself, then I could manage to eat breakfast.

Except breakfast did not smell the least bit tempting. But a wolf who didn't want to eat was a dead wolf, so I couldn't let the pack think that. Especially IronMoon. IceMaw would have fawned all over me and offered me the choicest bits off all their plates.

The IceMaw had hoped for so much. They had believed so deeply in their Alpha, and even in the end, could I say that Aaron had failed them?

Except they had known what he'd done to me, and he'd let them believe he'd done far worse.

Gabel still held my fingers tight enough the sharp wire of pain cut through the fog that threatened to cloud my thinking further.

He led me down the stairs through the repaired foyer—koi pond still devoid of fish, though—and past the dining room. It was empty. Like empty, as in all the furniture was gone.

"What—" I started to ask, but he pulled me towards the kitchen.

Cook and his crew bustled about, slinging pots and such. We wove through the chaos to the backdoor and out into the courtyard. All the dining room furniture had been placed outside in neat rows. And there were extra tables. A *lot* of Iron-Moon were here. More than the usual number by a good bit.

And the thing about IronMoon festivities? Every single time, *someone died*. I tugged on his arm and growled, "You told me you didn't have *plans* to kill anyone. This looks like a plan!"

"I don't." Gabel pulled me towards the Alpha's table, which was set apart on the stone patio overlooking the grassy lawn itself. The flowerbeds and arrangements were overgrown and some disobedient ivy had gotten ambitious and started to creep over the stone wall. I tried to take all of it in, confused for a moment about where I was, and where Aaron's Mark said I should be.

...Gianna...

The males all momentarily paused in their eating, and a hush fell over the yard, as they glanced at me in that *how much should we care she's here* way. A lot of the faces I only vaguely recognized, and I think I spotted some GleamingFang and a Shadowless in there. There were even two female warriors mixed in.

But the intensity of the stares told me something else: they knew. They knew about my second Mark.

I braced myself against the inevitable howl from the abyss, and the grasp of a dying hand pawing at my soul.

...Gianna...

GO AWAY.

...IceMaw will love you...

I didn't *need* a pack's love. I'd never had it, and I wasn't off hunting for it now. I just wanted...

"It all to stop?" Gabel whispered in my ear as he offered me my chair.

"What?" I jerked my head around to look at him. "What did you say?"

He caressed the offending Mark hidden under my lace wrap. "It will stop."

"You can read my thoughts?" I whispered.

"I can hear your soul howling songs. I can feel your pain. I drink it in, I am attuned to it, I know all the curves and edges of it. I know when your soul pleads for rest and stillness. Because *he* grasps for you. I feel that as well."

Did that make me feel better or worse? Gabel somehow made me sit down with a gentle hand.

"Morning," Ana drawled, as if the entire yard hadn't gone quiet. She was seated between Flint and Eroth at the Alpha's table.

The seat across from me was empty: Hix's seat. The First Beta's seat.

My ears rang with the jangling of those damned scales.

Maybe this was why Oracles rarely took mates... if we survived, we didn't remain sane.

Gabel hadn't broken me. He'd fought me to a draw. If the Moon's Own Destroyer couldn't break me, Aaron didn't get to cheap-shot me over the edge.

My anger curled around my bond to Gabel and pulled me out of the fog, but it didn't wake up my appetite. He poured me a cup of coffee from the carafe on the table. I sipped it with a grateful sigh. Gabel made terrible coffee, and this brewed-by-anyone-but-him tasted divine.

"Good?" Ana asked me, saluting me with her own cup.

"After a few weeks of drinking whatever that is that Gabel calls coffee, excellent."

Ana chuckled, and Eroth looked mildly uncomfortable at the revelation that his Alpha made inadequate coffee. Gabel offered no comment and kept one eye on the room, which had gotten back up to its previous noise level as he portioned out eggs and bacon and toast.

Gabel placed two eggs on my plate and neatly cut them.

"I can cut my own food." I wanted to sip my coffee and think about nothing.

"I will draw the line at feeding you bite by bite."

But he hadn't drawn the line at feeding me like I'd been a sick puppy, which was even worse than bite by bite. "I am not an invalid."

"What a nasty word to accuse me of thinking." He used the fork to scoop a bit of egg onto a triangle of toast, then presented it to me.

A she-wolf who refused to eat was pretty much dead, so I'd have to choke it down. I managed to gulp down a bite, but more than that, my jaw was just too tired.

He picked it up and offered it to me again. "That is not eating. Food. Eat."

What did he call swallowing, then? Not eating?

...Gabel has no idea how to keep what he has, up to and including his own head...

It was like Aaron's lips whispered in my ear.

Gabel picked up the triangle and presented it to my lips. I snatched it out of his hand and bit into it just to make him stop.

Ana commented, "He's gonna be real good at getting a fussy baby to eat."

Flint sighed, mortified for her. Eroth gave her a shocked look.

"What'd I say?" Ana asked.

"Only runts don't eat well," Eroth said under his breath, emphasizing the word *runt* slightly.

Ana gave me a smirk. She knew I knew she hadn't meant it that way, and she also didn't give a fuck. Human privilege had its perks. Still Ana, and I still loved her for it.

Gabel tapped my plate with his fork.

I growled at him.

He responded by positioning a sliver of wriggly egg on a triangle of toast and cutting this into an even smaller triangle.

"Will you quit?" He was making a scene, feeding me like this.

Gabel put the prepared triangle down on my plate. Then he nodded at it.

I choked down the rest of my toast and two eggs and a piece of bacon just to make it not be an issue. With the way things were going, Gabel would puke in my mouth again and tell me I should enjoy it.

Gabel waited until I had eaten and the courtyard had become mostly chatter. Then he stood, coffee cup in hand.

The morning sunlight was already hot, and his beach-tanned skin seemed to glow a deep, peculiar shade of bronze, like scorched metal. "Wolves of IronMoon! Our work in SableFur was successful! My wretched father is dead, and my stepmother remains wandering the north, hunting her ambitions in a forest of bone and ash."

Eroth jumped up and howled. The other warriors howled as well, and fists pounded the tables. Silverware and plates jumped.

Gabel waited for the howling to settle down. "Luna Gianna has completed the task the Moon set before her and has returned to my side."

This was greeted with considerably less enthusiasm. In fact, it was met with zero enthusiasm.

...IceMaw loves you...

I slammed a mental fist into that voice.

Flint twisted around in his seat to look at the room. His blue-gloss tattoos glowed in the sunlight, while Gabel's seemed to shine, limned with that soft halo of blue.

"Wolves," Gabel's voice curled with silky violence, "Luna Gianna is the one who destroyed Alpha Magnes of SableFur and made herself Luna of SableFur by right of conquest. I take your silence to mean you are shocked there is a female as dangerous as I am."

The wolves shifted and shot looks at each other.

"Or are you threatened by her cunning?" Gabel inquired, pacing to the edge of the patio. The sunlight chased shadows down the carved muscles of his back, giving him a burnt appearance, like he was a creature of charred bronze and ash. Trickles of sweat sluiced down the shadow-cast shape of his physique, and his grown-out pale-blonde hair, dampened slightly by sweat, haloed his head like a tangle of wheat... or bones.

Gabel grinned. "I expect an answer, wolves, or someone will be adding their bones to the tower I am building."

A few more awful heartbeats of silence, and finally, one wolf decided he'd stand up. It was one of the ones who had challenged Eroth for the position of Second Beta. "She doesn't carry your Mark. She has Aaron's Mark!"

Pain cut through the bone of my left arm.

...IceMaw loves you...wants you...

My marked eye pulsed and throbbed, and I bit down a gasp as it felt like something tried to cut through the bottom of the globe.

Fierce glee from Gabel lifted me in a warm, bloody current. This was what he'd been expecting. So much for his promise nobody would die at breakfast.

Another warrior found the courage to stand. "She's covering it thinking we don't know! It's too hot for her to wear that sweater!"

"Hey, she's so damn pale maybe she doesn't want skin cancer," Ana said like he was stupid.

"Maybe she also shouldn't want a pet human," the wolf sneered back.

"Man, you are salty about not getting some of this, aren't you." Ana waved a hand at him like he was a fly.

"While your inclination to fight is commendable, now is not the time," Flint muttered to her.

Ana ignored Flint and wriggled her pinky finger at the mouthy wolf. "Now's the perfect time when they're coming at Gianna like they know a damn thing about anything. I was there. I saw what happened. I put stitches in what happened. I've never seen you get beat up bad enough to even need a kiss on your boo-boo."

Snickers from some of the other wolves, and the new female warriors laughed out loud. But more wolves glowered and snarled and practically bristled.

"She does not have to explain her choice of attire to anyone. Including me." Amusement coursed through Gabel's voice.

"If she is your mate, why does she have another wolf's Mark on her arm?" the first wolf growled. "Why is your Mark blue-gloss? Is she even your mate or are you her pet?"

Ana sucked in her breath.

That was what Aaron had told IceMaw: that the Moon had given me Gabel's soul, and that the blue-gloss Mark was not a Mark at all, but just the mark that Gabel was my pet, to do with as I pleased.

"We could have defeated the SableFur, and you'd be king now!" That wolf carried on. "Instead you told us to come home with our tails shoved up our asses so you could run off to get back the female who let some other male put a Mark on her! She already betrayed you once! Are you sure that Mark on your arm isn't a mark you're a thrall!?"

There was not a chance an IronMoon had come up with that *it's not a real Mark* nonsense. Not with Flint having his blue-gloss, and him never telling anyone why or how he had them, and nobody in IronMoon even seemed to realize what they actually were. The gloss that had gone extinct. The gloss that mortal wolves had lost the knowledge of, and only the Moon had left.

49

So all this? This shit was from Aaron's playbook.

Aaron had gotten to IronMoon wolves before. Multiple times. Hell, he had introduced himself by proving he could get a wolf alone with me.

Gabel casually sipped his coffee.

Eroth shoved his chair back. "She is your Luna and the Moon Herself consecrated that Mark!"

"Because she's let males carve their Marks into her arms twice!" the wolf shouted back. "We could have the SableFur on their knees in front of us now and Gabel on their throne and we'd be howling songs for our king! She couldn't even keep her own arm safe from Aaron!"

It cut like metal lashings around my bones and into my soul. I couldn't breathe. If I did, the Tides would rush in and fill my lungs.

Howls, growls, louder shifting at the tables and exchanged wary looks.

"We didn't even want you to take her as a mate," the wolf ground it deeper. "You could have taken the warrior female instead. She fought bravely when we cut through Shadowless. You could have offered her a deal! Her body for the pack! Leave this scrawny, pale thing to whatever pack would have her!"

Gabel's grin turned especially cruel, and his soul pressed against the bond with feral, wicked glee. "That was a fool's prize. The Moon offered me the night-blooming cereus. The flower that blooms only one night a year."

"She's still an Oracle and deserves your respect," Eroth growled.

"Is she? I see no tools, no bowls, no runestones!"

This wolf was either very good at guessing, or someone had told him a great deal of dangerous information.

Either way: he needed to be quiet. Permanently.

I stood and shrugged off my wrap, baring my arms to the sunlight. "Come have your fill. Drink it down and choke on it."

Gabel's violent fury smoothed to something like velvety pride.

I walked around the table, putting no one between myself and the wolves. "You want to look, wolves? Then come *look*. That is all you will do is look. And perhaps bark like you think I or the Moon cares about your yipping."

The sunlight shone off my Marks and baked my skin and made me dizzy as *he* giggled ...*Gianna...* in my mind.

The wolves at the other tables shifted and roiled like an unsettled ocean. They glanced between each other, each one waiting for the other to be the first to approach to inspect my arms, and as a result none did.

Cowards. Nothing but yipping.

Gabel pointed at the previously mouthy wolf. "I have humored you long enough. Your Luna invited you to inspect her Marks. Inspect them."

The wolf did not move.

Gabel pointed at the spot before my feet. "Grovel on your belly before your Luna for your cowardice and insults."

"Apology?" I schooled my voice into cool contempt. "I don't want his apology. I've no use for his words or his whimpers."

Gabel took another sip of his coffee. Then he set it down and walked past me into the courtyard. He smelled of burning and glass and amusement.

"Um..." Ana intoned, twisting around to watch the scene.

So much for Gabel's promise no murder at breakfast.

The wolf startled. Other wolves hurried to get out of the way, a few others held their ground and even growled very low under their breath. Gabel approached the rude wolf, seeming to loom like a creature of water-slicked charred metal in the intense morning sun.

"She has no use for your whimpers, and I certainly have no use for your growls. Show me your fangs, wolf." Gabel curled his fingers into claws. "All of you. Your fangs."

The tension split. The defiant wolf lunged at Gabel with a howl.

Ana swore and clapped her hands over her mouth. Flint grabbed her and practically flung her over the table onto my side, then surged up out of his seat, body taunt and blue-gloss moving like shadows on water. He placed himself at my side, shoulder turned towards the gore happening just at my feet.

More wolves poured onto Gabel like rats pouring over a wall. Tables and chairs splintered. Silverware fell, plates shattered.

Gabel twisted into war-form, nightmarish and his eyes green-yellow and the blue-gloss of his Mark ripped into his arm, like it'd been burned, healed, and burned again. He flung off the defiant wolf without difficulty, howled his challenge, and slammed into the wave of wolves with a fierce, violent savagery.

He threw his head back and howled, the scent of ash and burning mixing with the scent of coffee and bacon. He grabbed a wolf by the arm and flung him, then bit down on the shoulder of another wolf. His fangs punctured the other war-form's leathery hide with an audible pop. Gabel ripped his mouth free and tossed that wolf aside.

Blood splattered my skirt and breasts. Dripped down my shoulders over my Marks.

The wave of wolf-forms and war-forms broke, and he stood over them, clawed foot on one back, digging deep into the spine, the other holding the original defiant wolf by his skull, one clawed finger pressing into the wolf's eyeball, but doing no damage.

The blue-gloss Mark scalded onto his leathery arm glowed a pure blue light, which made the putrid yellow of his fangs and eyes even more vile. Spittle dripped over his fangs in long tendrils.

Gabel slammed the defiant wolf head-first into the table. The table snapped and collapsed. Gabel rode the wolf down, driving his knee into the wolf's spine as his hand kept a grip on the wolf's skull, yanking it backwards to expose the throat, claws digging into the delicate tissues below each eye orbit.

His ghoulish lips stretched in a gleeful grin that sent shivers of horror and fierce delight through me.

I hated myself in these moments.

Gabel twisted, mostly, into human form, his strong hand still securing the wolf with an iron grip. Only his Marked arm—glowing sacred blue against his grotesque hide—remained in war-form.

Gabel raised his claw up towards the sky. His voice cut through the chaos. "I think you have made enough use of this."

He swept his claw down and shoved it into the side of the wolf's mouth. Claws pierced the space between fangs and he twisted, popping the jaw open. He yanked.

Something bloody came with him.

A fresh arc of blood splattered Flint and me.

The wolf screamed and disintegrated into human form.

Blood poured between his fingers and he made horrible drowning-gibbering noises like he was a sputtering faucet.

"Luna," Flint said, shouldering me back towards the table.

Gabel rose to his feet, breathing hard in the sunlight. Sweat cut clean trails through the lines of his sinew and bone and muscle, erasing the layer of blood, gore, dirt. His wild hair clung to his head in a filthy halo. He glowed like white-hot metal in the sunlight, dark and brilliant at the same time.

He picked up his discarded kilt in his free hand and strode back to the table. He tossed something in front of me, then told Ana, "Doctor, I have removed the problematic part of his anatomy."

The wolf's tongue lay on the table.

Gabel turned back to the wolves, casually sashing on his kilt before picking back up his coffee cup. Blood dripped down his torso. The hand holding his cup was coated in gore. He sipped his drink while casually re-approaching the stunned breakfast crowd. He stood at the edge of the courtyard steps and informed them, all while sipping his coffee, "I am the Moon's Destroyer, the Instrument of Her Wrath, and now I will destroy that which *I* created: IronMoon. You eat because I choose to feed you. You are feared because I have made you fearsome. Begone, wolves. If you want a place atop my tower, you will beg for it. Until then, drown in the burning stars."

Stunned silence. Even from Flint, who was stock-still.

Gabel took a final sip of his coffee, surveying the scene with satisfaction. Then, casually, he said, for anyone who had missed his meaning, "Get out of my pack, and get off my lawn."

Sonnet 12

The wolves, absolutely confused and bewildered, milled about in confusion.

"What have you done?" Flint asked Gabel.

Gabel twisted towards him, one eye still on the milling wolves. "Dismantling all of it."

"Even your *pack*?"

"The pack still exists. I am simply dashing it against the rocks. I believe it is called the *conservation of mass*?"

I inhaled, while Aaron's scar danced and Gabel's scar squirmed and seethed on my arm, and the Moon loomed in the back of my awareness. My marked eye stung, and I blinked several times while the vision in it wobbled and dimmed before returning to normal, but the eye itself still hurt, like there was something lodged in it.

Eroth exchanged a shocked look with Flint, as if pleading for Flint to *make it make sense*, but Flint's shock was so thick it hung on the air like ozone. His blue gloss squirmed and shifted. "How can the pack still exist if you have dashed it against the rocks?"

"I'm not sure. I am curious to find out." Gabel looked at his gory hand and ran the cleaner one through his gore-covered hair. He was smeared in blood that quickly dried in the summer heat.

Curious? "Curious is why you Marked me to begin with!" I exclaimed.

"And that ended beautifully."

"This is not beautiful!" I pointed at the carnage. I gestured to the blood splattering me.

"Not yet. Buttercup, you were a trap." Gabel came around the table and embraced me, gore and all. "You were a beautiful test, and prize, the most wonderful prize of all. And it's not over yet. I have sworn I will free you from him, and I *will* find a way to do it. I will not find my crown among *these* wolves. I will find it elsewhere. Take it by other means."

"While the world burns?"

A wicked, cruel smile. "But wasn't that your warning? That the world was *always* going to end? It's why I exist. I will reign over what remains. I will remind them I offered them something better, I offered them the *truth*, and they rejected it. Invest no tears in any of them, Gianna. They've given you nothing, while taking everything you will give, down to your..." he caressed Aaron's Mark, leaving bloody smears on my lace wrap, "down to this. The world cannot have you. You are mine."

HIS OFFICE WAS THE SAME. THE BOARD FULL OF HIS maps and strings and markers and plans. Books lining the walls.

And the blue tourmaline on his desk.

It reminds me of you, buttercup. I think I'll keep it.

Below me were the training fields. Except this time there were no other wolves. It was just Flint and Gabel, one gold and blue, one charred metal, while lurking uselessly in the shadows of the trees and, at a distance, were the cowed wolves Gabel had no use for.

I'd shaken off Gabel's gore-soaked touch and tossed the

tongue in the woods for the scavengers. I wasn't about to pickle it and keep it on a shelf. Gabel had grinned and laughed at my rejection of the gift, then snarled at all the breakfast-wolves until they'd bolted. They hadn't gone far, but now drifted around like frightened wolves trying to approach a pack's kill.

Now I was in his office because I wasn't sure where else to be, and thinking about it was too difficult. My *soul* ached. If I thought about it too long, Aaron's howls started eating my brain.

...Gianna...

I focused my gaze on Gabel's form and grit my teeth against the ghostly howl, and the way the hair on the back of my neck moved.

"You're dead," I said to the air. "You're dead *because I killed you.*"

...Gianna...

"Shut up!" I snapped at the air. "Shut up, Aaron!"

His howl reached me like a noise I could just barely hear and felt compelled to investigate, and for a second, his scent wafted across my nostrils.

And he was carving me, again, and again, his body pressing against mine, pinning me against the house, all his strength and weight holding me, his breath hot against my throat, his scent desire and that flat, unmoving, rock-like resolve as he tore—

"No!" I gasped, my chest lifting. I wrenched myself out of the memory. The world popped, and I braced myself against the window. I gulped, tasting water full of burning glass and stars and gore, and through the hazy wash over my eyes, I saw Gabel with his crown of gore and bones.

...Gianna...

The door to the office opened. Ana poked her head around the door. "That asshole Donovan is here. He smells like a swamp. Whoa, you okay?"

"I'm fine," I said, straightening. "Why?"

"You look like you've seen a ghost."

I snorted. "Didn't see, but heard him."

"Do all Oracles see all this crazy shit? Just comes with the job?"

"Sort of. It's how most she-pups with the Seer gift die. Well, if they're *lucky,* they die. The Tides wash their minds away. Then a lot more lose their souls on the Tides while they train."

She blinked, then asked, "And now you're seeing stuff?"

My eyes saw the world, but my brain saw the temple and the jungle and heard the jangle of the pans in the storm and the wind pulling my hair. I gripped a handful of my hair and keened around a fresh crush of soul-pain. I gasped for breath, caught it, held it, before I said. "He wants me to go to him. He's howling for me."

Ana snapped her fingers by my ear. "Well, tell him he can fucking get in line."

The world crystalized again. "He cut the line."

"And I heard he was the one with manners. So what you want me to do about Donovan back there?"

"Let him in." I hadn't summoned Donovan. I didn't even know how.

"Sure thing."

Before she slipped away, I said, "Ana, you can leave. After this morning, I don't know what's happening. Gabel is... unhinged. He talked about not coming back here at all."

"That's not unhinged. I've *seen* him when he's unhinged. He's just had enough of the Moon's shit. Like up to here." Ana held her hand up to her temples.

"I don't even know what he did this morning. Nobody does what he just did. He didn't dissolve the pack, he didn't officially exile anyone." There was no name for what Gabel had done.

Ana shrugged. "Even stupid human me gets what happened. Doesn't need a name. We all seem pretty clear on it."

"If you're staying for the money—"

"The money's nice, but it ain't about the money." She turned and ducked around the door.

Donovan, filthy, bearded, and stinking like a swamp, walked into the office. "You get around, Luna. How many crowns have you worn this year?"

"Three, but the year's not over yet," I said evenly.

"Came to see for myself."

"Looking for new prey?" I asked. "Or did you come to see if I am, in fact, still alive for a different client?"

He grinned. A big pink wad of bubblegum was crammed between his teeth. He sat down in the chair across from the desk. "IronMoon's my only client. You don't ask questions."

I resisted the urge to tell him to get lost.

He shoved the wad of gum into his cheek. "Now that the Lord-Alpha's withdrawn a lot of his forces from SableFur, I'm reporting in to find out the next move."

Gabel had done a great deal more than withdraw his forces from SableFur. He'd cancelled his participation in the war. Not sure how he intended to make himself King if he didn't have an army and expected his crown to be delivered to the front door. But he seemed to have his own thoughts about how it would all play out. I cocked my head to the side. "And what about SableFur?"

"There isn't much to report. The IronMoon Gabel left behind are doin' a good job of harassing her forces, but she's pressing back south and east again, cautious, though. The wolves at the heart aren't howling for her return, either. Nobody's marching out to help her."

Not what I would have expected, given how unpopular I'd been as Luna of SableFur. I hadn't lasted long before my own Second Beta had betrayed me. "Do you know why?"

He shrugged slightly, shifting the wad in his cheek. "No. Wasn't sure how deep I was supposed to press on it, or if it matters. SableFur's a big pack. A lot of ground to cover. I just know that they haven't suddenly rallied around Adrianna. That could change anytime, though."

Perhaps Adrianna was playing possum. Perhaps not. This presented an opportunity. Either Adrianna wouldn't interfere, *or* she couldn't interfere. Time to find out which one it would be. Gabel might have decided that he didn't want any part in this fight, and he might have told his army to scram, but *I* wasn't done. "I need you to find Lucas and Kiery."

"You mean the SableFur First Beta and the Elder Oracle?"

"Yes. Find them or whatever happened to them. Adrianna is hell bent on killing off the other Oracles. She *will* kill Kiery if she hasn't already. If she's playing possum, she won't let you leave with Kiery. Assuming you get caught, of course."

"I won't get caught. Never do. But you're also assuming that First Beta didn't do something noble and get himself killed."

Unless that. "Find what happened to them. Kiery might be the last Elder Oracle. Unless you've heard of some elsewhere?"

"The only Oracle I know of that was outside SableFur or not named Gianna died of old age a year ago in Emerald Pelt. I know you're used to having your sisters nearby, Luna, but Oracles are *rare* elsewhere in the world. Everyone's heard of them, or has a story about one being here or there, but *she died years ago*. Same story everywhere you go, and packs have sent their Seer-pups to SableFur for training for a long time."

"I didn't know that."

"It's true."

"Have you ever heard of a pack called NightScent?"

"Barely. *Far* to the south, beyond even Aaron's reach. Is that where Kiery's from?"

"Yes. And if what you say is true, then the SableFur had been consolidating Oracles for at least thirty years. Anita's training was brutal and cruel, and it destroys souls. I have always thought that is simply how Oracles are forged, but now I wonder if she was... overly harsh."

"I see, I see. So the SableFur would weed out the ones they could not control, then have them all, the Voice of the Moon ate at their table, and takes food from their maw. But not you."

"But not me." Anita had known I had a hole in my soul, and she'd shipped me back to Shadowless when I was done training rather than risk keeping me around. "Find Lucas, Hunter. And don't whimper at me about having to go into the heart. I might start to think you're getting old."

A sly grin and a shrug. "Your money will buy whatever of my time you want. *And nothing gainſt Times ſieth can make defence/ Saue breed to braue him, when he takes thee hence.*"

"What?" I asked.

"Shakespeare, Sonnet 12." He shrugged again, as if that explained everything.

Great. Donovan quoting sonnets at me. I had enough obtuse mysteries in my life.

"Hunter." Gabel's voice sent a chill through the office. He stood in the doorway, dripping sweat. "I was informed you had arrived. Sonnet 12? What are you distressing my Luna with?"

As Long As They Feed

Donovan shifted his weight, suddenly wary. "Your Luna has given me a new quarry, Alpha."

"And what does Sonnet 12 have to do with the quarry?" Gabel asked with particular menace.

"A comment about the relentlessness of time, nothing more," Donovan said. "And how my time is for sale."

"Gabel," I told him, aggravated. Hadn't he had enough bloodshed for the morning?

Gabel weighed Donovan another moment, then went to his desk. He tossed a tight roll of bills to the Hunter. "See her task is completed as she has ordered."

Donovan shoved the rolls into his back pocket and sauntered out, taking the smell of the swamp with him.

Gabel inhaled the scent off my neck. I tried to push him away. "I'm fine."

"Then what upset you? And do not lie to me." He slid two of his fingers along the edge of my cardigan. His rough skin skimmed along mine. "It cannot be this morning. You might want to have disapproved, but you have ruled over far worse bloodshed than that. Or is that what troubles you?"

I pushed his hand away. "Leave it be. Just leave it."

Gabel growled, his soul pacing like it was at the end of a chain, but after a moment, he started to smolder instead of burn. "What did you set the Hunter upon?"

"Perhaps if you had not scared him away, he'd be here to explain it for himself."

"He is not still alive because he does not know when to leave a room."

I folded my arms across my breasts. "Well, I tasked him to find Lucas and Kiery."

He abruptly headed towards the stairs that led to the second level of his office.

"Are you going to tell me what your plan is? Adrianna will eventually deal with the IronMoon wolves who are harassing her, or the SableFur will get tired of them causing chaos. We won't win the war like this."

"Are you impatient for your crown, buttercup?"

"I don't *want* a crown and I never have. How do you intend to get a crown without an army?"

"So far, the army has not proven very effective in getting a crown." Gabel picked through his many books, skimming the spines for a particular title.

"*Gabel.*"

"Are you familiar with the conservation of mass?"

"What? What are you talking about?"

"It's a basic scientific law. That in any given isolated system, mass can neither be created nor destroyed. It only transmutes."

So he had smashed IronMoon against the rocks to see what it re-formed into? Did he hope that it would randomly re-form into a crown? "And you think *that* will make you king? Or have you given up on being king?"

He paused in his searching and turned dark attention on me. His answer passed over me like the heat of a furnace. "Never."

At least some things never changed.

"I am also not dancing the same dance, over and over," he said darkly.

"So what are you doing?"

"Getting my book of sonnets, I want to see what that wolf was quoting at you."

I sighed. That wasn't what I meant, and it wasn't what *Donovan* had meant either. "Gabel, it wasn't like that. You don't have to be so jealous and unreasonable."

"I am perfectly reasonable. I did not rip his arm off and beat him to death with it."

"Not enough bloodshed for one morning?"

"You said that wolf's mouth was no use to you. I didn't kill him, did I?"

"I suppose not."

"You wanted me to deal with him. I felt how afraid you were of him. He was not worthy of your fear."

"He was one of Aaron's spies. Aaron warned me he had spies everywhere." I wasn't afraid of that wolf. I was afraid of *Aaron.*

Gabel's voice dripped malice. "How do you know?"

"Because of what he said about the Mark. That's what Aaron told IceMaw: that our Mark isn't a *real* Mark. It's not a mate's Mark. And that this blasted thing on my other arm is a true Mark."

"Spies. Always with the spies. And that is why I do not trust a single wolf save Flint."

"What about Hix?" I asked waspishly.

"*You* could trust Hix."

"He couldn't trust me in the end." Hix had been the only wolf who had ever apologized for Gabel's actions. Not even Flint, although I understood now that Flint had been letting things play out. Hix had been the one who had stood up to Gabel.

Who, in the end, had defied Gabel to try to save me.

Who, in the end, had placed me above everything.

Who had suffered and died for it.

Of all the blood on my hands, Hix's was the blood that had left a stain.

Gabel came back down the stairs, put his hand under my chin and squeezed my jaw just enough to deliver a pinch of pain. "I thought Adrianna killed him."

I yanked my chin free. "She did. I guess you don't know any of this. How he died. What they did to him."

"No. I know he's dead, but I'm not clear on how he died. We never discussed it."

"He found the she-wolf spy who betrayed us," I said, still not looking at him. "He dragged her corpse to SableFur. He stood in front of the house and howled to the heart about how Magnes dealt in spies. They descended on him. Tore into him. Locked him in a dungeon below ground. Broke his jaw. Took out his eye. Tortured him."

Gabel's smoldering, ashen presence did not react.

"They let me see him. They let me see him and he was... I could have gotten him out. The keys were right there. We could have escaped. He wouldn't leave without me, and I told him I couldn't leave. He didn't know, Gabel. You never told him the truth of why I was there. He really thought you had given me up."

"The truth would not have stopped him, only goaded him. I told you that wolf was going to die for you."

My heart unfolded like a bloody flower. "I promised I'd get him out. I told him to hold on. I thought if I was fast enough... but I knew I was leaving him to be tortured. I knew what I asked. I knew what I did. I left my First Beta to die. For nothing, it seems. I am right back where I started, except this time there's more blood and bones."

The anguish was almost more than I could bear, and each word only twisted it deeper and further. "Lucas took me to

Anita, and that's when Adrianna struck. She knew Lucas would have stopped her. She butchered Hix like he was commonstock. Gave his life to a no-name warrior and the other SableFur were too cowardly to stop her. She told me he died howling my name."

Gabel nodded. "And that is a most appropriate way for a First Beta to die."

"Is it?" I demanded, voice hoarse and tears falling. "I was his Luna. He helped me pass the Second Test. I couldn't have done it without him and I just abandoned him!"

Gabel rubbed his thumb over my cheek. It smeared tears in salty trails. "You were his Luna, and you asked him to sacrifice his life for you. If he hadn't done it, I would have taken the life from his chest for failing you."

I shouldn't have expected anything else from Gabel. At least he wasn't berating me for crying. In Gabel's world, wolves died. They also lost their tongues at breakfast.

"Sit."

"I don't want to sit."

He growled and herded me to the couch. "I said sit."

I did what he wanted just to humor him, then realized my fingers were trembling.

Gabel glared at me. "You barely ate breakfast. You are an Oracle—"

I laughed bitterly. "I'm not an Oracle anymore. I've lost more tools than I can count."

"And now you are speaking madness. You *are* still an Oracle. How many times have you rubbed it in my face that eating and sex root you in *this* world? I came here because I felt a wolf's claws around your throat—now I realize it was Aaron. That wolf is going to try to pull you into the abyss with him, and I will *not* let it happen, even if you seem inclined to!"

"I don't want to be with him," I snapped. "I told you to kill him, didn't I?"

"And that bond is still there," he growled.

No shit the bond was still there.

Gabel snorted. "Tell me what the Hunter quoted at you."

"I don't know. Something about time and taking thee hence."

Gabel flipped through the small volume. After a second, he frowned. "Well, he certainly was not trying to woo you with this one. It's a sonnet about the passage of time, and how all things fall apart. Unremarkable."

"He just told me it was my money for his time and threw a line about time at me. Is he normally that strange?"

"Yes. The line in more modern language is *And nothing 'gainst Time's scythe can make defence/ Save breed, to brave him when he takes thee hence.*"

My gut fell. "Wait. What... read that again."

He did. Then he snapped the book shut.

I touched my marked eye.

Gabel loomed over me. "Gianna."

"The scythe-Moon has fallen, and the Sun has set," I whispered, not sure if I was talking to him or me. "It's a poem about everything fades. That's what you said, right?"

"And you are trying to tell me you *aren't* still an Oracle?"

"Can we not argue about that? Just answer my damn question."

He scratched his chin in two harsh swipes. "Yes, that's what I said. Reminds me of when you told me that my kingdom would crumble and fade when I am too weak to defend it. But poets write about death and fading all the time. An Oracle I'd heed, a poet I'd tell to take it elsewhere."

"I know, I know, but it's... it's the scythe. Why did he choose those two lines to quote at me? The Moon I keep seeing is a scythe-Moon. I know it as a scythe."

"Donovan's a Hunter with a penchant for dusty old poetry, not the first male Seer with some wild untamed gift."

My paranoia was too high—was that Aaron's influence?

Even if the Moon *had* used Donovan to drop a clue, it was just more of the same: *I'm pissed and about to destroy the world.*

Yes, old news. Thank you very much.

There was nothing left for me beyond the Tides.

"I'm going to Shadowless," I told him. Or what was *left* of Shadowless.

"No, you aren't."

"Yes, I am."

"*No*, you aren't. I am *not* letting you go." He gripped my arms again.

"I'm not some nightingale you get to keep in a gilded cage. Don't you dare start talking like Hix—"

"Hix might have had things right."

"It's high summer, but winter's coming, and we need to know who is alive and who is dead, and how many the pack may have to provide for. You destroyed your vassal-packs, but you didn't free them. I'm going to start with Shadowless since it's the closest to SableFur."

"Are you *hearing* yourself? Go *close* to SableFur? And I didn't destroy a single pack that didn't betray me. Shadowless betrayed me. I know because *you* told me. We are *done* with catering to IronMoon's whims. I do not care anymore, Gianna. I care *only* about you and those who *wish* to be loyal to me. The rest can rot into the ground at my feet!"

"Do you even hear yourself!" I shouted.

"Yes, yes I do," he snarled.

"Just go finish the job and kill every last wolf so you can be the lord of blood and gore. You know, I've seen you wearing a crown of blood and gore as you come across the Tides to destroy everything. But you know what I've never seen you do, in *all* the visions I've had? I've never seen you *rule*. The only person I have *ever* seen wearing a crown before her pack is Adrianna. And it was a crown made of *your* bones. Oh, and your arm as her scepter. Wonder which arm it was."

Gabel's jaw tightened.

"I have seen crowns *over and over and over and over* again. A crown of bloody bones, a crown of gore and glass. A crown made of your skull. I've seen you wear a crown. But I've never seen anyone *rule except* Adrianna. And the wolves howled their victory, and they welcomed her even as she was coronated in a hall of bones and corpses, and she wore my fur as a cape, and your skull and fangs as her crown, and Aaron's arm as her sceptre. You have never been King in any of my visions."

...will you make him king...

Gabel's jaw twisted into a deranged grin. "But, my love, you are missing one key thing."

"Which is?"

"Those visions are old. Those visions are from before. Before, when I craved triumph to go with my crown."

"You think you're changing the *rules*?" I exclaimed. "You think if you change how you're playing the game, it will change the outcome?"

"Won't it?" he asked matter-of-factly. "Aaron was so confident I'd never abandon the front line to retrieve you. He was the fool, wasn't he? And now, we are together again. You've told me yourself that the future is not set in stone, and that the Gift exists so we can glean knowledge to change outcomes. Well. This is me, radically attempting to alter the outcome."

My marked eye throbbed, and I rubbed it to try to make it stop while I boggled over what he'd just said. I whispered, "What do you want now?"

"A crown, and a reckoning."

My eye throbbed like something tried to burst out of it, but only for a second. Aaron howled, his cry echoing through my soul, and down the bond to Gabel, making him snarl, and his cold, horrifying violence soak into me.

I yanked myself free of all of it, gasping. "I am going to Shadowless. If you refuse to feed who is left, they will find someone else to feed them. You started it, you finish it, you don't get to abdicate. At least Aaron had meat in his hands. Meat that the hungry wolf was glad to take. The hungry wolf that came into this very den having already betrayed you, and *intending to do it again*."

You'd Think That

"Oh, hey," Ana said.

"You aren't expecting company?" I asked in reply.

"Nah. Not in the mood. What you want to talk about? Sending me back to my human life?"

"Why *didn't* you go back to your human life?" I asked as I sat down on the one spare chair. I couldn't understand why a human would willingly get involved in this drama.

She plunked herself down on the edge of her bed. She tucked her hands between her knees.

Her scent was pure unhappiness. "Ana, you don't have to stay. We had a business arrangement."

Ana rolled her eyes. "Yeah, I know, okay? I'm sad that I ditched Lucas and Kiery. Not that I even *knew* Lucas and Kiery, and not that they'd have left SableFur, but I still don't like that I noped out, and *don't* give me the *you aren't a wolf* line. They were the only people in that entire shit show interested in doing the right thing. Which probably means they're dead. I know you sent Donovan to find the bodies."

"We don't know if they're dead."

"Come on, we both know they're dead."

"And I don't want you to die, too. Go back to your human life. You don't have to stay here for the money. We'll just give you the money. Pay off your loans and stop getting paid in hams."

"That an order?"

"No, of course not," I said softly.

"Good, because I'm not going back."

"Well, why the *fuck* not?" I snapped.

Ana shrugged. "My family wanted me to be a doctor, and it was bad enough I became a vet, but when I got fired from *two* prestigious hospitals and had to open up my own little shithole practice where I got paid in hams? You see how many friends I have? You see how many people have come looking for me or called me to ask where the fuck I am? Or showed any concern about my practice getting tossed?"

Nobody had ever tried to contact Ana. I'd never heard her talk about any friends or family, or seen her texting anyone, or overheard her talking to anyone on the phone. Wolves changed packs, they changed ties, and that was that.

But humans stayed in touch for years and years.

Ana shrugged again. "According to my family, I'm a complete and total fuck-up and utter disappointment. You saw what my life was before you showed up. Why would I want to go back?"

"Because it's safe," I said softly. "Because you might die here. And what you do *does* matter. You came here for money. Well, we can give you the money, and you can go, and build a new life and shove it down your family's gullet. You don't have to stay here."

"And I'm staying for the man-beef and the angry deities. Oh, and the money."

I sighed.

Ana gave me a look like she was my big sister. "You aren't going to understand this, because the past year has been the shittiest time in your life. But I've had the *best* time of *my* life since you and Lord-Alpha Nutso there rolled into my life. I get to stitch up bloody bits while feeling like I'm doing something important. That's the whole damn reason I *became* a vet. Why the *hell* would I want to go give that up to do discount spays on cats with a belly full of near-term kittens or working graveyard in an ER while management tells me to upsell treatment on an animal that's going to die anyway while my own family reminds me what a disappointment I am on the rare occasion they *do* invite me to the holidays just so I can be there to play the urinal cake everyone pisses on? Yeah, I'm good."

Hard to argue if she'd thought it through like that. "You can leave anytime."

"Yep, I know. Maybe one day I will, but not right now. I know where the door is."

That was oddly comforting. "I need to go to Shadowless. I want you to come with me."

"Why you going to Shadowless? Or anywhere, actually." She wrinkled her nose. "You haven't seen what... well, what he did."

"I know what he did, and I can imagine what it looks like. I have to go because Gabel didn't kill everyone and if he isn't feeding them, someone else will."

"Solid math, but dangerous. Why do you care, though? They abandoned you. Adrianna is on the run, it sounds like, so why not just put your feet up and let it fall down around you?"

"Because Gabel is still on the hunt for his crown. He wanted to keep me hidden, he *still* wants to keep me hidden. But he also wants to be King."

"So let it end however it is going to end. You don't have to keep fighting. You aren't going to undo what they did to you.

Isn't that what Kiery warned you about? You don't know when to quit?"

I heaved a sigh.

"Just a thought," Ana said soberly. "I'm not you, and I'm not in your dreams. But... you know... how much of this is the trauma talking?"

"Adrianna isn't going to quit." I knew that. Adrianna would *not* quit. She couldn't quit. She had two sons, and she *needed* Gabel turned into a trophy for her mantle. "Her soul is forfeit. She *has* to secure her sons' futures, and the only way she does that is defeating Gabel. I also know for all Gabel says he's done, he's not done. He's up to something. He's just radically changing tactics trying to change the future, because every single future I've seen of him where he wears a crown also results in my death. And I never see him reign. The only one I've ever seen reign is Adrianna."

"Ahhh..." Anna nodded, her head bobbing up and down slowly, like a dashboard doll. "Now *that* makes sense."

"Except it isn't going to change any future at all," I said. "Or, at least I don't think it can, because Adrianna can't change what she wants. And Gabel isn't going to change what he wants. She needs us all dead. Gabel wants triumph. Sort of mutually assured destruction. Since I'm done being an Oracle, I need to focus on being a Luna. I may even be the last Oracle, but did I make the choice to give up that mantle when I chose Gabel?"

"Do you really think you're all gone?"

"Donovan was telling me how Oracles in the rest of the world are *really* rare. I knew we were rare, but according to him, some packs don't even believe we're real. It sounds like Sable-Fur's been collecting them for a long time and limiting access to them enough other packs aren't even sure they actually exist."

Ana rolled a peanut between her thumb and forefinger. "Huh."

"Alphas have *always* tried to use Oracles to their political advantage," I added. "We're trained to resist Alphas who would use us. But what if the SableFur figured out a different way to control Oracles?"

"If you've got the direct line to the gods, you hold a lot of cards. Someone wants access, they've got to trek all the way up to your door and ask permission. Which can't be *denied*, but come on, we all know Alphas get off on someone coming to them and asking *please*."

I managed to keep my throat still against the sudden urge to gag.

Ana sighed. "This all sounds like some Tower of Babel shit to me."

"What?" I cocked my head. "The tower of what?"

"Ancient story from the human Old Testament. It's a story about how all the people of the world once used to speak the same language and were all friendly with each other, so they decided to all get together and build a tower to reach heaven. Which they *totally* weren't supposed to do, but did anyway, and God watched for a while waiting for someone to say *hey, guys, this probably isn't what we should be doing*, but nobody did. God was not amused."

I sat up straighter. "So He destroyed the tower and crushed everyone?"

She laughed. "Yeah, you'd *think* He'd have destroyed it, right? That'd have been the *easy* thing to do, right? Just smash the tower and say *fuck you, don't do that*? Nope. He left the tower, but scattered all the people through the world and gave them all different languages so they couldn't work together again. SableFur's here trying to build their own Tower of Babel, and the Moon *could* just smite the offenders or whatever, but She hasn't and doesn't. Instead, She sends Gabel to see if anyone's paying attention, but they're not, even after She literally turns his dad into a stain. The Moon's probably on Her throne eating popcorn while Gabel tries every which way to prevent what's coming, but the truth is, the Moon's down with however it ends, because it's only going to end very badly."

Lucas, do you think we'd recognize a new dark age as it was coming on us?

ONE OF US, ONE
OF THEM

Gabel had torn Shadowless' heart into pieces.
Piled the remains into a tower.
And set fire to it.

All that remained of the Shadowless house and surrounding structures were pits in the earth, some pipes, concrete. Nothing else remained except scorched earth and burned-out debris.

It was, ironically, a gorgeous summer day, complete with bright blue sky and puffy white clouds. But the scent of death and burning clung to the grass, to the tower, to everything around this place. It still smelled of the Comet's impact.

I nudged another pile of ash. My toe turned over some bleached-looking shards.

Bones.

So, so many bones.

I knew what Gabel was. I had chosen to take those vows. I had chosen to tell him to kill Aaron.

I had chosen the Destroyer.

And this was what I had chosen.

"Some of them still have to be alive," I told Renzo, the hunter I had brought along, and one of the few wolves Gabel had permitted to stay in the IronMoon tower. "Even at his most insane, Gabel doesn't butcher the helpless. He has his limits. The survivors wouldn't have left the territory."

There were still pockets of houses and structures up and down the remote, winding roads of this rural area, and two small towns populated mostly by humans. Shadowless' heart had been burned to the ground, but Shadowless had to still survive.

I stared at the ash.

Ana slid up beside me and looped her arm through mine.

"I can't even cry," I whispered. "I don't feel anything."

"You're in shock," Ana said.

"I don't feel shocked." Even my Bonds felt far, far away.

Ana said, kindly, "That's how you know you're in shock. Your brain shuts all the emotional parts off so you can get through."

I touched my eye.

"It's called trauma for a reason, and you've had a lot of it recently."

Renzo re-appeared out of the brush. "Luna, we've found them."

"BE MINDFUL, LUNA," RENZO MURMURED AS WE stepped into the clearing.

Some pups scampered away into the small cabins and bungalows. So this was where they'd fled: an old campground at the base of the foothills, dangerously close to SableFur's northern border. Still the scent of charred leather and coal, but minus the fetid stench of corpses. Despair and grief permeated all of it.

A female emerged from one of the cabins.

"Amber," I whispered as she strode towards us, face full of fury and mad enough Renzo half-stepped in front of me.

Gabel had said he'd killed her, and she'd fought bravely to the last.

She was thinner, gaunt, with a gash on her scalp that had peeled off half her hair, and half-healed wounds on her arms and legs. She seemed otherwise in good health, smelled of hunger. And shocked anger. Mostly just shock.

"I thought you were dead," I said, astonished and hope assaulting my heart for a second. "Amber, I thought—"

Her scent changed to dark anger. "Your mate *left* me for dead."

"Amber—"

She spun around and shouted to the woods, "It's Gianna! Come to see how her mate keeps his promises!"

Keeps his promises? She had low standards for *promises*. "You have a bad memory. You're the one who told me that Jermain made a deal with Magnes to steal me back. Shadowless made a false promise to Gabel."

"And he burned everything and shattered bones? Did you see? Did you see what he did to us!" She pointed back towards the south.

"I saw," I said flatly. "What did you *think* would happen when Gabel discovered the lie?"

She snorted. "What do you want, Gianna? You look like shit. Did IceMaw throw you out? Did Gabel tell you to crawl home to Shadowless? If so, there's no soft landing for you here. Go peddle your pale Oracle ass and your pet human somewhere else."

"Oh, so you heard about Aaron taking me from SableFur and making me his Luna by force, hmm?"

"Why those Alphas fight over you, I have no idea," Amber hissed.

Interesting that she'd heard that bit of news so far north in this Moon-forsaken part of the world.

What was left of Shadowless had emerged from the cabins.

Females, mostly, holding pups, older pups, some half-grown males, a handful of older males, and a few adult males with obvious injuries. Didn't take much creative thought: Gabel had butchered everyone who had fought. Their bones for his tower. And the bones of their mates, who had died with them.

I cocked my head slightly. "I'm not here to crawl home and I'm not here to make speeches. I'm here to take inventory. You're Luna here now, I take it?"

She grimaced. "I'm the dominant female. I don't call myself Luna."

Interesting choice. "Lord-Alpha Aaron of IceMaw is dead. Lord-Alpha Gabel of IronMoon lives."

She eyed me. "Aaron is dead?"

"You haven't heard?"

"No," she said darkly. "We're isolated up here."

So *that* news hadn't gotten this far. I kept my tone flat as my heart did weird, anxious flops. "Gabel killed him."

Something shifted in her eyes, but I only caught a whiff of her scent, and it was hard to tell what she was thinking. Time to focus on what I'd come for. "Ana."

Ana bounced to my side. She had on a short white coat with *Dr Ana* embroidered in rainbow thread and an overly cheerful smiley face on it. She always broke out a white coat when she needed to impress someone. "Want me to take stock of the running noses and stitches?"

"I want a complete report of every scratch and bruise. Treat what you can."

"Right." Ana hefted her bag over her shoulders and sauntered towards the biggest group of pups and females to her left."Oh hey, folks. Point me at the blood and scabs and broken bones!"

Amber gave Ana *that* look, then asked me, like it was a year ago and we were still females sharing an attic room. "Is she serious?"

I smiled. I'm sure it was a ghoulish expression. "Renzo, hunt something to eat."

"You aren't going to make things better with some rabbits and rash cream," Amber told me.

"Were you really hoping Adrianna's army will breeze through and throw you some crusts of bread?"

She didn't reply.

"So the latter, then. Or weren't you paying attention that the Moon turned Magnes into a puddle?" I asked.

"And yet *she's* still alive," Amber said.

I sighed. "Amber, I've seen what happens if she wins. She crowns herself with bones and skin, but the coronation happens in the SableFur tombs where the Moon cannot see. Gabel is the Moon's Dark Comet, the Instrument of Her Wrath, the Destroyer. There are no good sides here. There is no version with a happy ending. It's just *how* it ends: it ends in a tomb or it ends..."

Come to think of it, I didn't know how the *Gabel Triumphs* version ended. Because presumably, it did end, and he was victories, even if I was dead. What would that even look like? Bone-and-ash obelisks lining the road up to IronMoon's heart? My corpse laying in permanent state on a massive obsidian and iron platform?

Better not give him any ideas.

"Or?" Amber demanded.

"I don't know," I admitted, "I'm Gable's mate, so I can't have visions that involve my own future."

That was something of a lie, obviously.

I added, "But I can tell you that I know Adrianna's victory means a literal tomb full of bones underground while wolves sing their happy songs, thinking everything is as it should be, but above ground, the Moon's Eye is dark and angry. I'm not sure what's worse than that, so I'm fairly confident in choosing the path that *doesn't* result in Adrianna's victory gives the best outcome."

Her fingers knotted and unknotted into fists. She turned around to face the pack as Ana rounded them up to look them over. "It was supposed to be me."

"I know."

"I would have killed him."

In the worst moments of being with Gabel, I'd never considered killing him. Destroying him, hurting him, ruining him, dismantling him, but never killing him. "You would have wanted to."

Amber snorted. "I would have done it."

She had no idea what she was saying. "The Bond wouldn't have let you. Gabel would have destroyed you. You're a warrior, and Gabel knows exactly how to break warriors. You'd have fought him with your fangs."

"Damn right I would have! And none of this would have happened!" She shoved her hand towards the sad cluster of cabins. "You didn't stop this! You could have! I'd have put my goddamn fangs right into his throat! You didn't! You let this happen!"

Oh, I had done more than let it happen. I'd told him to attack Shadowless. I'd only asked he give my father a clean death.

"I," Amber snarled at me, "would have put my claws through his throat while he slept! Bitten off his cock! I would never have become his whore."

How wonderful that she thought she knew what she was talking about. So nice to know that they just thought I was some mush-spined idiot who left her claws at home. "You think being a warrior would have helped you? That's how Gabel would have destroyed you. He'd have relished the fight and goaded you for more. The more angry and violent you became, the more you'd have excited him. The Bond shares when you please your partner. Even as he tortured you, you'd have enjoyed pleasing him.

He loves pain because he craves the triumph of defeating it. He wanted a mate so he could torment her and endure the pain of the Bond punishing him. He wanted a challenge no mortal wolf could offer. So, clever warrior who thinks she knows how to defeat the Moon's Dark Comet, how do you defeat the monster that dines upon fear?"

She knotted her hands into fists and her whole body shook with raw fury. "So how did you tame him? You're just an Oracle."

Just an Oracle. *Just* an Oracle. Gabel had broken her, and she hadn't even realized it.

She drove onward. "That's right. You didn't. You just spread your legs for him. You saved your own pelt, and you probably enjoyed his cock!"

"You *gave* him my pelt! You made a promise in bad faith to IronMoon and you're surprised when he punishes you? You threw away *my* soul and *my* life to perpetuate a lie! You *abandoned* me to him, then judge me for how I survived? I owe you *nothing*." I turned away before I raked my claws across her face and gave her a new scar.

She advanced towards me, one of the warriors blocked her path. Amber spit on him. "Hiding from me now? I challenge you, Luna!"

Why couldn't any of them *see* what was right in front of them? Gabel was the symptom, not the disease! "Challenge me for what, female? IronMoon? Is that what you want? My throne of blood and bone?"

"Yes!" she howled.

She wanted the death Gabel had denied her, not the mutilated shreds of the life he'd let her keep. I, not being a warrior, would have to defer the challenge to Gabel, who would kill her easily, and she knew it.

The wolves of the enclave crept closer to listen.

My blood slowed to a smoldering simmer of anger. "Oracles are trained to look into the pit and see hideous things on behalf of the wolves we vowed to serve. And you call me *just* an Oracle? You're a warrior too cowardly to look the truth in the eye. You don't want to avenge anyone or anything. You want to die so you don't have to live this life anymore, and you want me to kill you. No. I am not giving you a selfish coward's death. Go give it to yourself if you want it that much, but I know you won't, because Gabel's broken your spine and you're too gutless to even realize it. I won't give you a selfish coward's death. I refuse your challenge."

"You can't refuse! You have to answer me!" she screamed.

She wanted an answer? I'd give her the only one I had. I pushed the sleeve of my shirt up to expose Aaron's ragged Mark fully. "You were there when Gabel Marked me. You know this isn't the arm he took, nor the Mark he left. Nor is this one." I presented her the blue gloss arm.

I walked towards her and let her get a really close, good look at both.

"But..." she said, "that's impossible. It's all impossible."

I grabbed her chin and yanked her face right up to mine, giving her a close-up view of my Moon-marked eye. "You want answers? You think you're entitled to something from me when *you are how it all started*? The answers are carved on my body. They're in that tower of bones. They're a stain on the floor of SableFur's hall. They're in the corpses of my Oracle sisters. Those are your answers, and if you can't look them in the eye, don't think you're worthy of challenging me. Instead, tuck your tail and be grateful I can do what you can't, I can face what you won't. You stay here and take care of these wolves who need you, and you pray to the Moon I don't fail."

She seemed to really see my eye for the first time. "Your eye. What—what—"

I released her. "Kill her if she so much as growls."

"Yes, Luna," the warrior, this one Flint had prevailed on Gabel to keep, said quietly, tone hushed.

"Quickly," I added. "Cleanly. Efficiently. Lord-Alpha Gabel may enjoy some ceremony and showmanship with his executions, but I do not. You are capable of neat and tidy?"

He bowed his head. "Yes, Luna!"

I gave Amber a final warning look before I turned away. If she died, it'd be by her own choice.

Two By Two

"You should not have gone," Gabel said, voice taut. "It was dangerous. You knew they wouldn't welcome you."

"It was necessary," I said, annoyed. We'd already had this fight, and I was no more interested in having it *now* as I had been *before*.

"That could have become a very bloody conflict very quickly."

"Are you afraid I'd have drawn you off your tower and into a bloody war?"

"Why do you reject me protecting you?" he demanded just as tersely.

"Because we both know it's not about you *protecting* me."

"Of course it is!" He grabbed my hands, blue eyes wild, and he tugged me close. "All of it is about protecting you. You are exhausted, raw, hurting in a thousand ways. But you keep running back into the fight! Is that the only way you don't hear him? Is it to punish him, or me? To inflict this upon yourself as you used to, to punish me for how we began?"

"No," I said quietly.

"Then why are you so driven?"

"Because it is the end of the world and you are not Hix! And even if you were, I'd escape that gilded cage and beat you with it."

"Buttercup, when you are fierce like this, I am not sure if I should bite you in rage or bite you until you submit to my lust."

"Is there a difference?" I shot back, even though my body shivered at the prospect of his dominance dissolving my senses.

"Shall we find out?" He advanced, reeking of prestige and sex and aggression and knowing damn well I was about as resistant to it as sugar in a rainstorm.

Aaron howled and scratched, but the bond to Gabel dilated and warmed.

The sex would have to wait. I couldn't get distracted—or let him (or Aaron) distract me. "Not until I'm done arguing with you about how you *didn't* tell me Amber is still alive."

"I left her for dead. That's not the same as sparing her life. I burned that place to the ground for a reason. The survivors can rot in their misfortune. Like all the rest."

"Gabel, you *can't* ignore the world."

Gabel nodded towards his office window. "But have you not been happier since the others were banished? That the ones who remain are ones you know by name, feel safe with, and *trust*? The others cling to the firelight, and they deserve to cling there."

Yes, it had been pleasant not having to watch my back in my own den. "But they're still *there*."

"Shall I kill them?"

"No. I am asking you what you intend to do when the other survivors come here. The ones who survived your bloodbath are the ones who did not participate. They might have known, but they weren't the designers. They weren't the wolves who created the situation. You *killed* all those wolves."

Gabel eyed me. "I have no interest in what happens beneath our tower."

"They are not rats or crabs in a bucket. They *aren't* going to devour each other. Adrianna will scoop them up before that happens, and they will be grateful to *her*, and she will create a tower of her own. She lives *only* to destroy you and build a future for her sons from our bones."

He scratched his chin, a smile lurking on his mouth. "Buttercup, so *feisty*. Talk to me some more about this kingdom and my failings."

"You're getting turned on." I rolled my eyes.

"We have already established I was aroused. And whenever you rage about this kingdom of mine, that you *claim* to not want but clearly *do* want to succeed, you have compelling observations." He slid his hands over my hips, expression feral and devious, scent ash and burning glass.

"Hmph."

"Tell me more."

"I don't want to talk about it. I want to *do* something."

"Yes, yes. Keep going."

I slapped his chest with my palms. "You maddening wolf!"

Gabel smirked, then straightened the cuff of his shirt. He was actually wearing jeans that night, not a kilt, and looked very much the part of the well-to-do human beachbum with his sun-bleached hair and deep tan. His hair had grown out a bit to be a trifle roguishly shaggy. The Bond curled with his deep, satisfied enjoyment of my anger, sipping it like it was his favorite drink.

Aaron had not liked my anger. He also hadn't hated it as far as I could tell. He had just accepted it existed and ignored it, as unmovable and uncaring as a cold stone.

...Gianna...

Gabel tugged me hard against him, the pain of his grip cutting back through us. I gasped as I smushed into him, and my tits felt like they squished against his chest. I threw my arms around him in response and held tight.

"I will never let you go," he told me, his tone low and rough by my ear. "Never. Never again. *Never.*"

Emotions overwhelmed me and my throat spasmed like I was drowning on mouthfuls of water that wasn't there.

He actually pushed me back, studied me, and said, "You haven't been in your workroom since you came back. That means you have not been meditating. I know your tools are lost, but you can still do that, yes?"

My mouth went dry. "I... I've given up being an Oracle."

"You've *renounced* your Oracle vows?" He didn't believe me for an instant.

"I can't talk about this." My throat was so strangled I couldn't get the words out. I didn't dare think about Aaron and those bowls, or that night in that little room under the shed, or what had happened afterwards. "Do you want me less if I'm not an Oracle?"

"Of course not."

"My bowls are *gone*, Gabel. All of them. All my tools, gone." I dug my fingernails into his shoulders. "And *he's* waiting for me. We always knew I'd have to choose. Look how it's been used against us once already! It'll keep happening. I will *always* be the weak point as long as I'm an Oracle. It'll just take Adrianna figuring out what to exploit *this* time."

Gabel shifted his shoulders under my grip, sampling and weighing the minor pain my nails caused. "You're afraid you're the last Oracle, but you're telling me you've *given* up being an Oracle? *You* would never leave the world without Oracles. You wouldn't do that to whatever Seer girls there are still out there. You love your sisters too much, no matter how many times they've failed you."

And he didn't even know about how I'd lost the tools I'd left back in IceMaw. Like the terrifying tektite bowl that Aaron had gifted me. Gabel didn't even know about how *badly* I'd failed as an Oracle.

"What aren't you telling me?" he demanded.

My mental defenses shattered and I, like a total fool, crumbled into whimpers against his chest.

What the *hell* was wrong with me?

What had Aaron taken from me?

...nothing, I have taken nothing, I sought only to free you, to give...

I clenched Gabel's shirt in my fingers and held in a scream while Aaron's bond tried to wrap itself around my mind.

Gabel squeezed my hands until my bones creaked. I gasped, and his lips were there, against mine, hot and painful as burning glass. The bond to Aaron writhed, horrified at Gabel's touch, punishing me for accepting the touch of another male.

He shifted to holding both my hands in one of his, and moved the free hand to my hair, yanking me up to him and kissing me hard and ruthless, twisting his fingers into my scalp until it stung and pain lashed through our bond, sending it writhing and twitching as pain/pleasure twisted through it.

My secondary agony eased, leaving just the unpleasant pain of his too-tight grip. Gabel released me, but stayed close, and he said, in a low voice. "We aren't keeping secrets, buttercup, and you also won't be telling me half-truths. Tell me."

My soul felt fragile, when I spoke, it felt like I was testing out an injury expecting to feel searing pain. "I've lost multiple sets of tools. I need to take the hint that my services are no longer required."

"But it does not change you are still a Seer." He twisted my hands over and kissed each of the bright red scars in turn. "And Seers need to take care of themselves."

Gently, he pushed me down onto the couch.

...Gianna...

His eyes trailed over my form. "The combined might of SableFur no longer exists. SableFur doesn't realize how weakened they are. I will merely ensure they don't realize it until it is too late."

"Don't be so sure about any of that."

"I am certain that Adrianna has the same problem you say I have. Her top lieutenants are dead or were in the hall when you called down the starlight wolves. She has to lead her army herself. She can't be in multiple places at once. SableFur is porous and exposed." His smile was wicked and cruel.

I looked down at my hands, half-expecting to see the shards of the old mirror there, reflecting something back at me. "So you're going to try to force them to pick a side?"

"In a fashion. I am going to ensure every wound I cause to Adrianna does not heal, but it festers, and the infection spreads. So that it settles into the bones. I am going to infect her pack not with hunger or fear, but with despair. I do not need an army to claw together a crown, and I will not be distracted from my *true* concern." He smiled, and it was ghoulish.

My spine tingled. I sat up straighter, but couldn't shake the gnawing, crazed-badger horror/excitement at the base of my tailbone.

He caressed my face again, and looked down at me with a strange, too-intent gaze that also seemed curiously unfocused. "Losing you taught me what it is to dread sleep. To dread the dawn. I will never lose you again. My crown will mean nothing with Aaron's claws in your soul. I *will* free you from him."

He dipped his fingertips and his nails scratched my skin lightly.

"We did this together," I told him roughly. "No, I *begged* you to let me go. You don't have to make it up to me. *I* did this. *You* should hate *me* for doing this to us."

"No," he growled, fingers tight.

Renzo appeared at the door. He coughed and averted his gaze.

"Come inside," Gabel rumbled, his voice like those dark

clouds and for a second, I was back on that terrible island and getting lashed with rain.

Renzo obeyed, closing the door behind him with a soft click.

Gabel picked up the blue chunk of tourmaline and juggled it in his hands for a moment while he smoothed out the last of his thoughts. "I have an assignment for you, Hunter. As Donovan is currently on a hunt for Luna Gianna, you will have to suffice."

Renzo's lips pulled back. "I am always eager to hunt, Lord-Alpha."

Renzo seemed pleased as punch that he was getting a chance to be the Alpha's go-to predator. I rubbed my nose. I couldn't smell much of anything. Great, just what I needed: a summer cold.

"Go to SableFur. Hunt four sets of adult male wolves for me. They must be from different parts of the pack. Do not take from the southern parts. Each pair must be related in some way. A father and a son, lovers, brothers, twins. Find them, and bring each pair to me, one by one, undamaged. Be as gentle with them as possible."

As Gabel spoke, his words dripped like liquid glass, scalding and cruel, and the charred feeling curled through the Bond. My soul drank in, drowned in the searing sting that was *him*.

Renzo's grin widened. "I will be as gentle-mouthed and efficient as a human's bird dog."

"Excellent." Gabel's grip tightened on the chunk of tourmaline until his knuckles whitened. "Take the prey quietly. I want them gone in the night with as little trace as possible. You can accomplish this, or shall I wait for Donovan?"

Now Renzo practically trembled with eagerness at the challenge. "I will accomplish this, Lord-Alpha."

Gabel pointed to the door.

Renzo bowed to him, then bowed to me, before scampering out the door like a pup told he could have another piece of candy.

Gabel's soul's dark, ashen fingers moved over the Bond. He set the tourmaline down and his fingers played over the sharp pointed tip. He dug the pad of his index finger into it.

I didn't ask what Gabel was going to do to those wolves.

I already knew.

Further Improvement
Needless

No storm on the wind for that day, and the bugs hummed in the trees. A few gnats tried to take a swig of my sweat. Still couldn't smell much of anything, that was clear, because usually I could smell the training warriors by now.

Then again, maybe I wasn't missing anything.

And then there was also the fact most of the wolves of Iron-Moon had been kicked to the curb. Gabel hadn't specifically exiled them, but he'd also told them to find somewhere else to be since they couldn't behave. It had taken a few days for them to learn they weren't getting *anything* from IronMoon except a very bloody lesson.

Now they wandered around the base of the hill and in the forests.

...Gianna...

"Shut up," I hissed at the obnoxious voice haunting the back of my mind.

This had worked once before, time to see if it could work again. Aaron probably wouldn't care as much as Gabel—because Aaron refused to let *anything* affect him—but it might buy me thirty minutes of silence. If I was so busy feeling Flint beat me up, and hearing my brain scream *stop it, stop it,* then I wouldn't be able to hear Aaron.

Flint stood on his crate. He stopped everything as I approached and bowed low, his kilt swinging around his knees. "Luna Gianna."

"Master-of-Arms." Out of old habit, I glanced up at Gabel's window.

Flint had several wolves with him. The ones who hadn't been sent to the woods were fortunate enough to get Flint's undivided attention. I didn't recognize any of the wolves by name—they were the same ones that I had seen before at that breakfast.

The Master-of-Arms gestured to the assembled warriors with his blue-gloss wrapped arm, then jumped down off the crate to stand next to me. "These are some new wolves you had not met before you left us."

Flint snapped his fingers, and they squared up into orderly lines. Only two or three were IronMoon originally, the rest were some combination of other packs, including two SableFur. The two SableFur bowed to me. Off to the edge of the treeline, underbrush rustled, and a few lupine-form heads watched from the woods, and whined.

Flint snarled in their direction. "*Silence.*"

They fell silent.

"They haven't moved on," I said under my breath, bewildered. The IronMoon had never struck me as especially loyal to the pack.

Flint moved close, keeping his tone low. "They won't."

"Why not?"

"Because they are broken wolves," Flint said in little more than a whisper, his green eyes troubled. "Gabel took wolves that no other pack valued. He gave them a sense of purpose and value, that what made other packs reject them is what made them valuable to him. He gave them glory and violence and gore and food. He fed more than just their bellies. He *made* them. And some of them realized this and became more."

Flint flicked his gaze towards the handful of IronMoon still present, and I understood his meaning to mean names like Eroth and Renzo.

"And others refused to walk further up the stairs," Flint added.

The jungle temple flickered in my mind, and for a second, I saw it in his green eyes. Even Aaron had gone quiet, listening with interest to Flint. "They stayed in the water as the flood came."

"Precisely. So Gabel has kicked them from his tower—"

Temple. Gabel had kicked them off the temple into the rising water as the storm lashed the world.

"—and now they are broken. Gabel *made* them. They were nothing before him, now they are nothing after him. When they have debased themselves and groveled before him, they will be permitted to lick scraps from under the table, and they will be grateful for it."

Aaron's presence shifted with a wash of cold amusement and a wash of ...*clever*...

Flint stepped back and folded his hands in front of himself. The blue gloss on his skin squirmed and slid, the glyphs for *duty* and *love* seeming especially glossy. "What brought you to my domain, Luna?"

"May I watch and perhaps join in at some point? I need to clear my head."

He hesitated a split second. "You may watch, but you will not train today."

No surprise, but I wasn't just going to roll over. "Master Flint, I—"

"No," he said, more harshly than I expected. "You may watch."

"You have supported it before." When had Flint gotten squeamish about this? He'd been the most ardent supporter of me *improving myself*.

Before Flint answered me, Gabel's voice cut between us. "Gianna!"

Gabel shoved his way through the lines of warriors and stopped dead right in the center of the ring. "What are you *doing*?"

"She was inspecting the warriors, Lord-Alpha," Flint said, voice measured.

"And trying to get a workout," I added. Flint didn't get to leave out that little detail.

"Absolutely not," Gabel snapped.

How *dare* this arrogant jackass wolf talk to me like that. "You have always made your objections to this *very* well known. I'm not interested. Go back inside."

Gabel's expression darkened. "You are *not* going to permit this, Master-of-Arms."

Flint resettled himself, his blue-gloss tattoos shifting and slipping over his torso. "I was not inclined to do so."

"You were the one who endorsed it last year!" I exclaimed.

"You're not in the right frame of mind, and I have sent you away before when you're not in the right frame of mind."

I narrowed my eyes. Flint didn't so much as blink.

Gabel's blue-gloss reflected intense, mirror-blue in the sunlight, and my marked eye seared with pain as it seemed too bright to look at. The vision in that eye blanked out. Gabel's anger intensified, but he wasn't going to budge: he was just a hot lump of coal camping our bond.

I swore under my breath, batted his hand away, and stalked to the backdoor, burning with humiliation and anger.

Gabel slid his hand over my back. I smacked it away as I stepped through the porch door into the kitchen. Right back where I'd *fucking* started. I stalked down the hallway.

Gabel pulled me around to face him. "What were you *doing*?"

My shoulders bumped into the wall and he loomed over me. His fingers held my wrist, but I felt Aaron's weight against me, his breath on my neck, and I was back there, while he tore the Mark into my arm—

...Gianna...

...come to me...

The scales jangled in my mind as rain drenched me.

I screamed and *shoved*.

This time, the weight fell back easily, and I was free.

Gabel stared at me, charred and metallic in the shadowy light of the hallway, his eyes bright blue.

...Gianna...

I hugged myself and raked at the Marks on each of my arms. The pain sliced through the swirl and anguish as the Bond to Aaron writhed and twisted, stretched thin by death, and his ghostly claw tried to shove its way towards me, while the one to Gabel howled and snapped and dilated.

Gabel grabbed my hands. "Stop!"

I howled in pain.

...Gianna!...

Aaron howled with me. The scales jangled madly, rune-stones falling everywhere, while the Moon watched and the rain fell, and fell, and fell and the water rose—

"Stop!" Gabel pried my hands off my Marks and yanked them onto his shoulders. My fingers *dug,* and I expected rain-soaked stone, but felt only iron muscle covered with a thin layer of yielding flesh.

I pulled out of the spasm.

"Buttercup." He looked at my left hand, then my right. My nails were dug into his skin. Blood stained his shirt under my fingers.

I yanked my hands back. "I—I'm sorry."

He shrugged slightly.

I ran my hands over my face and sagged against the wall. "I—I—"

"Aaron," Gabel growled, the Bond churning with smoldering, fresh violence.

"He... he held me against the wall while he did it," I said helplessly, holding a handful of hair. I was losing my grip on reality. The visions were bleeding into memories and waking moments. "I...I need to clear my head."

Gabel's expression turned very dark. "Training with Flint was a bad idea then, and it is a terrible idea now. You don't belong in that arena, and you never have."

"The hell I don't. I've been on battlefields. I've *killed*, or do you not remember that, Lord-Alpha?"

He seethed. "I remember. But the place for you is your *workroom*, not the training ring."

"I am not going to live in some gilded cage where the most sweat I work up is fucking you!"

"You're still a Seer." He grabbed my hand and kissed the scarred palm, but his eyes never left mine, and his fingers gripped me painfully tight.

Still a Seer, even if ruined as an Oracle. Like a goddamn silver collar around my neck.

"You don't get to pretend you aren't still a Seer and don't still have the gift. Being an Oracle and serving the Silvery Sky Bitch's whims was so important that you traded *our bond* for it."

"Is *that* what you think? That I traded *us* for that?"

The crazed pain—maybe it was his, maybe it was mine—clawed at our Bond like a trapped badger. "Isn't that what happened?"

"No!"

He traced our blue-gloss Mark with the index finger of his other hand. Aaron's Mark throbbed like a deep bruise. "If you aren't going to tend to the matters that concern an Oracle and

Seer, then you can sit with me while you work on matters concerning a Luna."

"I am doing exactly that," I managed to grit out.

"You are not a warrior and never will be. I won't let you endanger yourself *or* waste Flint's time."

"Fine. I won't waste yours either."

"That isn't what I meant."

"I know exactly what you meant." The shards in my throat were sharp, and the Tides bubbled up to suffocate me.

"We aren't doing this," he growled.

"Damn right we're not. Let me go."

"My office or your workroom. Those are your choices. I will free you from Aaron. I have sworn that to you. I won't see you abusing yourself. We both know it's only temporary."

"Do *not* speak to me like that. You don't own me."

"No, but I do love you." He traced the blue-gloss on my arm.

He flipped over my hand and moved his thumb over the red marks from the wounds I'd suffered handling the mirror shards. They were still a bit sore and sensitive. He closed his fingers over my palm.

I let him pull me upstairs to his office.

Of A Place & Time

I didn't bother asking Flint for an explanation. From the looks *fucks given: zero* on his face at dinner that night, an explanation wasn't forthcoming.

"I don't mind if you want to be salty about it," Ana told me the next morning.

"Thanks," I said. "I'm trying not to be. I trust Flint."

"They didn't have to be dicks about it, though. But you *are* kinda... scrawny looking."

"*Ana*. Don't call a wolf *scrawny*."

"Well, you *are*. That silver did a number on you. Silver and werewolves, no joke. It's why your hands didn't heal fast. That and the doctor did a shit job, *and* you kept playing with broken glass."

"I don't feel scrawny." I patted myself down. Still had my tits and all.

"Tell Cook to make you cookies or something. Eat all of them."

I yawned and laid my head down on the table. Ana tossed a crust of bread at me. Then another.

"Come on, slacker." Ana lobbed a third crust at me.

The table felt divine. Lovely table. Wonderful table...

I jerked awake as Ana flicked water on me. "Hey! You didn't hear that?"

"Hear *what*?"

"You've been asleep like an hour and not even *that* woke you up?"

"I haven't been asleep—"

Howls. Loud howls. And it was the song announcing the arrival of visiting wolves. No IronMoon howls.

"Yeah, I just let you sleep," Ana said, "but I think we gotta go now."

Oh hell.

Someone had come for IronMoon. And because Gabel had pretty much told most of IronMoon to sod off, whoever had just showed up had strolled right on in.

The scales jangled in my mind. My whole body felt the cold rain lashing into it, and I shivered, pain seeping into my bones. A needling pain began at the base of my spine, sending more pain down the back of my legs and across my hips, as every muscle and nerve tensed and tightened.

I coughed, but instead of coughing up water, I tasted spit and blood.

...the Tide is coming in...

Aaron's voice curled around me, cold and soft. My marked eye throbbed, the vision blurred, darkened, like gauze falling across my face.

I arched as the pain around my hips reached a crescendo.

I gasped and broke free of the vision.

"Fuck," I gasped. "Fuck."

Ana grabbed me. I stumbled down the hallway with her.

Flint stood at the front doors, golden and menacing. I approached and got a view over his shoulder. Gabel had already arrived. I tried to duck under Flint's arm, but he grabbed my wrist, grip tight enough to startle me.

On the walkway were thirteen warriors in kilts, each one wearing a white cloth tied around their upper arms with a weapon in their other hand, paired with another thirteen in wolf-form, wearing white cloths tied to war-collars.

"The hell..." I recognized the warrior at the front of the line right away: Carlos, the First Beta of IceMaw.

...the Tide is here...

"This is an honor guard, Luna. Thirteen men, thirteen wolves, one for each moon of the year."

I tried to focus on him. "If they're here for revenge, this is a strange way to go about it."

"They aren't here for revenge. They're here for you," Flint whispered, then he let me join Gabel out on the steps.

Gabel glanced over his shoulder and extended one arm towards me. "Go back inside."

I pushed his hand aside as I took my place.

"Gianna," Gabel hissed.

"Unless you plan on throwing me over your shoulder and putting me in the basement, do *not* presume to tell me this isn't my business."

A wave of dizziness hit me.

Strong hands caught me again.

The wave passed. Flint held out a hand to stop Gabel mid-lunge and his other hand steadied me. I quickly extracted myself from his grip and gave Gabel a glare. He practically bristled, face dark, and he snarled at Carlos. "What do you want, wolf?"

Gabel didn't need to be a jerk, and plenty of reasons for him not to be. "That is Carlos, he was Aaron's First Beta."

I had no idea if I should refer to him as *Alpha* Carlos, if he was still First-Beta, if IceMaw had caught on fire and fallen into a hole. I also had no idea why he was even here.

Carlos swept one hand in front of himself and half-bowed, but didn't take his eyes off Gabel.

The thirteen wolf-form wolves extended one foreleg. The human-forms remained upright, but heads bowed.

Gabel snorted. "I know who he is. I remember his face when I killed his Alpha."

Carlos curled his lip at Gabel. "And I permitted you to limp away. How *is* your leg, IronMoon?"

"My leg has healed, not that I care for the opinion of a First Beta who permitted his Alpha to barbarically rip his Mark into a mated female's arm."

"So you are either a hypocrite or have a short memory. As I recall, you ripped your Mark into a female who you demanded be given to you as tribute. She was a war-prize, but no blood was shed for her. Lord-Alpha Aaron shed blood for her when he defended *her* honor in front of *your* father."

Gabel's expression schooled to stone.

"You did it to prove you could, to amuse yourself." Carlos ground it deeper, clearly having run out of fucks to give, although I wasn't sure why he was even here. "You took because you could, he took because he must. I followed his example when I *permitted* you to leave with our Luna out of fear of doing her greater harm after you killed her mate. Now we are here for her, that she has had adequate time to regain her strength from her fragile state, so she does not think the IceMaw have forgotten her, or that she has no choice but to remain here and reign over these... degenerates... or suffer your presence."

Our Luna?

Wait a hot damn minute.

I'd *told Gabel to kill Aaron.* I'd betrayed Aaron. I'd given IceMaw the biggest two-fingered *fuck you* I could have.

What was it with these First Betas with zero ambition!

Gabel laughed. "Over my dead body. I humor this... honor guard and parlay. You try my patience. Leave. We will meet again when I decide to add your bones to my tower, unless you want to bend your knee now."

"Luna," Carlos turned his attention to me, "we are here to return you to IceMaw. We may leave when you will it, regardless of what this wolf says about it."

I tasted salt and brine and blood and burning stars on the back of my throat.

Gabel pointed at the IceMaw. "No one is taking her anywhere. She is the Luna of IronMoon, she wore my Mark before any others."

Carlos's fingers curled into fists, and the thirteen wolf-forms growled. "She is the Luna of IceMaw, and you will not hold her prisoner!"

"She is not a prisoner. This is her den!"

"Then she is free to leave at any time. Luna Gianna, IceMaw awaits your return, we are here to escort you. It would seem that IronMoon lacks any real ability to resist us." The thirteen wolves remained bowed over their forelegs, eyes lowered, while the other dozen human forms remained standing.

Gabel snarled. "I see Aaron didn't tell you the truth: that I gave up Gianna at the Moon's command, that it was all a farce, and my Mark re-appeared as soon as Magnes was paste on the hall floor. Gianna wore my Mark long before she ever wore Aaron's."

Carlos' voice reminded me of a sword pointed at Gabel's throat. "I know all about your Mark, and I also know that Alpha Aaron's Mark did not fester. I saw myself how it started to heal. I know that my Lord-Alpha's Mark rivaled yours, and because you had her first does not mean you will have her last!"

Aaron had already started seeding that with his most trusted wolves, starting with Carlos: so Carlos was here believing that the Mark wasn't a Mark, but a leash, and *Aaron* was my only legitimate mate.

"I defeated your Alpha and claim his Luna as my own, then," Gabel said with dry, feral humor. "Our business is concluded. Leave."

Carlos returned the grin. "You know that is not where such wars end, only where they begin."

Gabel's smile disappeared.

"My Alpha swore to me he smelled her lure-scent." Carlos ground on, as the wolves around him growled. "That she smelled of the night-blooming cereus. That *was* her lure-scent, wasn't it?"

Gabel's anger bore down like a comet pressing out of the sky.

"He swore he smelled it, even through *your* Mark, even through that blue-gloss. That it was a test from the Moon, a test of faith, just as challenging his own family to save IceMaw was a test of his soul. He smelled her scent, he chased her into the abyss *you* put her in, he Marked her, the Mark was healing and would have taken." Carlos stared right up at that comet hurtling out of the sky.

Gabel's bronze human skin split down the length of his spine, folding back to expose leathery hide as he snatched his kilt at the hip and flung it away, twisting like molten bronze and leather into war-form.

Carlos fell back exactly one-half step.

"Iiiii sseeentttt youur Alllpha to Hell, and youuu will beeee next," Gabel growled. Spittle dripped from his yellow fangs onto the stones and they sizzled in the summer heat.

Carlos sprang backwards, twisting into his own war-form with a speed the IronMoon would admire, exposing a tawny gray wolf with a long coat that swayed with his movements. The honor guard scattered. The wolf-forms threw their heads back and howled the Luna's call to battle.

...Gianna...

My brain filled with salt and rain and the mad jangling of chains in the storm.

Gabel's claws cracked the stones and crushed the gravel. He grinned at Carlos, his leathery, putrid coat drinking and consuming the sunlight. The scent of ash and burning was overwhelming. Some of the IceMaw coughed as if they'd inhaled smoke and tried to spit out the ash.

Carlos barred his impressive fangs and curled his claws inward. *"Iiii willll notttt killll you, IrrronMoon. Forrr heeeerrr sake."*

"Hoowwww kinnnddd." Gabel sprung.

Carlos caught him but dropped to his knees under the impact. Gabel seized the First Beta's shoulders in his claws, puncturing the Beta's hide, and Carlos snarled in pain. Blood bloomed against his coat. The IceMaw clumped back together behind the First Beta as he and Gabel tumbled across the gravel and stones.

Carlos hooked one foot into Gabel's belly to brace himself while Gabel snapped at his throat. *"Ddiiiid it takkke? Does sheeee have hiss Marrrkk?"*

Gabel snarled and pushed forward, thumb-claws digging deep into Carlos' upper chest. Spittle seared fur off Carlos' chest.

"It'ssss nottt fadded! Itttt perssisssts!" Carlos howled, and the IceMaw sang the song to summon a Luna's champion.

The pounding in my arm was like hammers on bone, and Aaron was carving it into me, again, and again, and again. I gulped, about to vomit brackish water and salt.

I shoved past Flint and stumbled out to the edge of the walk. *"Stop! Stop it!"*

Gabel drove forward, grinning wildly as Carlos' claws dug into him. Fear flashed across Carlos' face and the IceMaw coughed on their song as the ash suffocated them.

"Stop!" I screamed, but the storm of songs drowned me out.

Flint sprang forward in a golden blur. He dove between the two war-forms, wedging himself with one claw braced on the gravel as he drove both feet into Gabel, kicking him off Carlos, then flipping and rolling with Carlos and tossing the First Beta a good distance away.

Flint spun to his feet, as bright as the sun, except for the blue-gloss cutting its way through his pelt like a river through a golden thicket.

Gabel rolled to his feet.

Flint pulled his lips back to expose gleaming white fangs. *"Sssheeee saaayysss ssstoppp."*

Carlos, much slower, got back to his feet. He bled from punctures just below his shoulders. His skin was burned off over his chest and down his abdomen. He took his gaze off Gabel for a moment to look at Flint.

Gabel returned to human form. Blood trickled from minor scratches. One of the IronMoon wolves darted forward and returned his kilt to him. Gabel casually sashed it around his hips. "Leave, IceMaw. You have no business here. I will deal with you when it suits me."

Carlos spit out some blood. "We don't answer to you, IronMoon."

He jerked his head towards the wolves that had clumped together. They separated again, and this time four human-form wolves came forward carrying a beautiful wood box. It had been stained a bright cherry red.

Carlos swept low in another bow, and all the wolf-forms did as well. "Your tools, Oracle. As you were unable to bring them with you, we have returned them." He glanced sideways at Gabel, then at me. "The tools Lord-Alpha Aaron provided for you."

Gabel's expression didn't change, but the Bond darkened with fury. Flint corralled him with a golden arm. *"Saaaayyyy noottthinnnggg."*

I was back in that small shed, with all those stones, for an instant, with Aaron, as he watched every tiny reaction and movement and counted each of my breaths.

...Are you sure, Balance-Keeper, there is only room for one of us in your soul?...

I felt the memory of my body reacting to his presence, the warmth pooling between my thighs, the way my nipples had hardened, the reaction to *him*.

...If you were his, you wouldn't smell like this...

I dug my fingernails into my scarred palms hard enough to draw crescents of blood. Oh, he'd answered his own question: I apparently had a very big soul, and he'd *made* room for himself in it.

But Gabel had done the exact same thing to me... and for a lot worse reasons.

I turned and walked back into the house without another word.

Unintentional Secrets

I stumbled down the hallway towards the sun room, putting as much distance as I could manage between myself and the wolves outside. My control fractured and re-fractured.

I couldn't let the pack see me like this.

I caught myself on the wall and retched, tasting bile and salt. Tears squeezed out of my eyes, and my Marks tore at me. My control shattered, and I sobbed, slumped against the wall.

"Not here." Flint's voice cut through my weeping. He hooked me under my blue-gloss arm and hauled me to my feet, and half-dragged me down the hallway towards the parlor, where I had originally humored the Petitioner Wolf and my entanglement with IceMaw had begun.

I pawed at tears and tried to reconstruct what was left of my fragile control, but the damn jangling in my ears wouldn't stop, and I felt soaking wet and cold and all I tasted was salt and burning ocean as my soul howled in anguish.

Gabel barreled through the door. He descended on me, his hands seemed to be everywhere.

Flint shoved him so hard he almost sent Gabel tumbling into a corner. "Stop."

Gabel snarled. "I—"

"You are not helping. You are making things worse."

"Why do these fools still believe you are the Luna of IceMaw?" Gabel growled from his place in the corner. "You can't tell me any of this makes sense, Gianna!"

"Gabel, *please*."

...*Gianna*...

"You never told me. You never told me he replaced your tools. You never told me *any* of this!"

"Stop it!"

"You *lied* to me!"

"I never lied to you!"

"What else haven't you told me?!"

Flint snarled at Gabel. "Shut *up*!"

Finally. Some damned silence.

He glared at me from the corner.

I spoke carefully. "Because it wasn't important. Magnes had summoned Aaron to SableFur to demand the IceMaw take action against IronMoon. Kiery planted me in the conversation. Aaron refused. A fight broke out when Magnes insulted me. It's how the rumors that Aaron and I were courting got started. It was something Kiery did to protect me. It was all a set-up, and Carlos is just goading you and it's working."

Gabel raised a brow. "You didn't tell me Aaron had given you new tools. Did you scry for him as well?"

"Oh, I'm sorry. I didn't have a chance to *tell you all this before you showed up*," I snapped.

"You know he was manipulating you! What did you see? Or you can't tell me?"

"I knew *damn* well he was manipulating me, but I also couldn't refuse," I retorted. "And his question, his answer. And you wonder why I'm not an Oracle anymore? *This is why.* Because I'm *used*!"

"If he used you to try to gain an advantage over me, it did not work, did it," Gabel said with a feral hiss.

"He Marked me after I scryed for him," I said softly.

"What did you see?" Gabel snarled, advancing again.

"You know I can't tell you that!"

Flint shoved his palm into Gabel's chest. "*Enough*! Remember what I warned you about, pup! What I said about your Mark? It has just played out on your front steps! What more proof do you need that the truth isn't what you *know*, but what *they* believe?" Flint pointed towards the front of the house.

I had never heard Flint raise his voice. Not even a little. "What did you say about our Mark? Do you believe it's not a true Mark, too?"

Because the Bond was very, very real.

"I believe the Moon scorched it with the blue-gloss for a reason. That is sufficient for me. But I warned Gabel back at SableFur that those looking to discredit your union would prey upon your Mark. Aaron was not the first to have that thought."

Eroth crept around the door, trying his best to look calm and like he had a grip on whatever the fuck was happening. Gabel spun on him. "Get those IceMaw out of my territory."

"What? No! I'm tired of you being rash!" I exclaimed.

"Rash? Was I rash when I came to get you from IceMaw?" Gabel demanded with a snarl.

"Of course not. You always promised you'd come for me. I knew you would keep that promise."

"Exactly. And I am not being rash banishing those wolves from my territory."

"Oh, you're not? Those IceMaw still think I am there Luna, even though I told you to kill Aaron. Why the *fuck* are they here now?"

Gabel resettled himself with an effort. "Because they're desperate, for some reason. You were Aaron's Luna, and you named a male champion to deal with an Alpha you found beyond redemption. The pack didn't weigh it as a betrayal or abdication. The agony of enduring his death and the risk of your life is sufficient collateral."

Flint looked sideways at me. "The fulcrum, Luna."

I shook my head. "But I never mated Aaron. He named me Luna, but I never mated him."

Flint's green eyes were full of pity. "You know it is the Mark that makes most of the bond, and the rest is little more than a formality. Only you can say why the IceMaw cling to you."

Gabel raised an expectant brow.

Because the IceMaw had loved Aaron. He had been their savior. He had brought them out of a nightmare, and they did not want to return to it.

Aaron had known he was playing a dangerous game. He'd named me Luna to cement his legacy. The wolves loyal to him clung to that legacy like a mirror surfing the Tides, knowing that if they let go, it'd all go back the way it had before.

Carlos had been right: this wasn't where wars ended, only where they began.

I took a breath. "I want to speak to Carlos. Alone. Only him."

"No," Gabel growled, and everything in my soul told me *that* was not negotiable.

This was exhausting. "Fine. Fine. Flint, would you mind chaperoning?"

Flint nodded.

Gabel set his jaw. Then he turned and headed towards the door. "Second Beta, tell the IceMaw Beta that his Luna will see him."

I raised my voice after Gabel. "Eroth, tell him I will see him as an Oracle. My question, his answer. He is not to speak of what we discuss."

Eroth paused. "Yes, Luna, and if he declines those terms?"

"He won't."

Gabel's expression was practically charred. "I will be in my office."

Flint Speaks

I touched Aaron's Mark. Wolves saw that Mark, which was the sort of Mark they were used to, and they instantly doubted the nature of what was on my other arm.

All must believe. Even you must doubt.

Flint closed the double doors to the parlor and then took up a place at my side.

Carlos cataloged Flint's blue-gloss tattoos with a First Beta's usual vaguely scornful doubt. Flint gave him his usual serene *I could rip you into two pieces and not even feel a drop of sweat* look.

Before things got bloody, I said, "Carlos, Flint is the Moon's Servant. He will not speak of anything we say."

"I am impressed you untangled yourself from the beast to speak to me alone." Carlos' voice was more concerned than dry.

I suppressed a macabre smile. "Gabel's not the mindless monster that people like to believe he is. But it's very convenient to let people continue to believe that. Why are you here? You know I have Gabel's Mark on my arm."

"A blue-gloss Mark from the Moon. I wouldn't call that *Gabel's* Mark. But I also know you have Aaron's Mark, and it is still there."

"You are two badly chosen words away from Flint throwing you through that door."

Carlos wasn't impressed or even put off. "Aaron told all of us after he met you at the GleamingFang party that you were his future mate. That he had smelled your lure-scent, drawn blood on Gabel, and he swore you'd be his consort yet."

"And you believed him. What wolf has ever taken another's mate that way?"

Carlos' eyes had a frightening intensity. "I believe you would call it faith. Even after that second Mark, he swore he could still smell you, the scent was stronger than ever. He vowed to us ranked wolves he would yet succeed, that he had had dreams of being on the top of a tower in a jungle, and there was blood and ash all around, you stood in the center of it, with your arm flayed open and bleeding blue-gloss blood while you carried thousands of fangs on threads tangled around your wrists and neck, holding a crown of bloody bones set with three stones in your hand, and a scythe with a blade like the crescent moon in your other, and all around you were night-blooming cereus flowers, and petals rained from the ashen sky. He told you to come to him, he would take you somewhere safe, and you refused, because you couldn't leave the fangs behind, and there were too many to take with you. He saw all the threads of fangs extended over the edge of the high tower into the flooded jungle below."

I stared at him for a few moments in total non-comprehension. "And Aaron relayed this dream to you?"

"Yes. He felt it was important enough to share it."

I almost asked if Aaron had discussed it with an Oracle, but Aaron had been too paranoid for that. It was strange for males to have dreams from the Moon, but not completely without precedent. "And when did he have this dream?"

"When he returned from SableFur bloody on your behalf. I'd never seen him like that. He was certain you would be his. He told me *Carlos, she is mine. The Moon has answered our prayers. I have to find a way to save all of us if I am to save her.*"

The Moon had showed Aaron the jungle temple beyond the Tides. She'd left something for me in Aaron's dreams, just like every vision I'd had for Gabel had been as much for me as for him. The Moon had *led him to me.* The Moon had all but told him *take her.*

We'd been set on this path long ago, and *nothing* had changed.

Had Aaron, the Moon's Instrument, tried to yank me onto the correct path? Or had this all been exactly as it should?

And why had he seen me holding all those fangs? I did not fancy the idea of being a soul collector.

Carlos cricked his neck. "As for your blue-gloss mark? He was not deterred when he found out. He swore he could still smell you. He told most of us ranked wolves and assured us *his* Mark would triumph and erase your lure-scent permanently. He ordered us to pretend we had no idea you had the blue gloss."

My stomach twisted. Not because of what he said, but because I could hear Aaron's voice saying it. It made so much sense even I wanted to sort of believe it, and I knew it was bull-shit. "Surely, though, IceMaw realizes that a blue-gloss Mark is not to be taken lightly."

"If it was a true Mark, Aaron's Mark should never have held," he said this with a strange and final certainty. "Your lure-scent should never have been in his snout. And yet, it was, and here we are. We are not convinced Alpha Gabel is your true mate in the... classical sense."

Just like SableFur wasn't convinced Adrianna was guilty in the *classical sense*? "You mean, Aaron said the Moon bound me to Gabel for some other reason than as a conventional mate."

"I can see Aaron's Mark, so white it shows up even against your Moon-touched skin. It should have faded, but it hasn't. It's remained in a place of glory on your arm. You still sense him, don't you? You have the scent of soul-blood on you. Just like the Servant there. That's what gives the blue-gloss its gloss."

He'd shocked me so numb I'd regained my composure. "That's a very interesting way of thinking of it, First Beta."

Carlos met my gaze and said with the usual direct bluntness of a First Beta, "So you understand why all of us are skeptical. A Mark should not be mingled with blue-gloss. It should not glow and shine. Those who know how the blue-gloss gets its shine can see how much blood and anguish and pain created that Mark. That is wrong. That is anathema."

Now he sounded like an Oracle. I'd figured out by now the true blue-gloss tattoos weren't from mortal hands: they were consecrated by the Moon Herself, and the key ingredient was blood and suffering. "Flint, is that true?"

Flint paused, then nodded grimly. "Yes, Luna. The true gloss is from the blood and anguish that caused you to take the gloss at all. Blue-gloss tattoos are always born from soul-deep pain."

So that's why he doubted my Mark was a true Mark. Shouldn't an Oracle know that? On the other hand, I wasn't surprised Aaron had a rare bit of knowledge and passed it around like a strategic breadcrumb when it suited him. Aaron collected scraps for all the same reason he'd had glass walls in his office: absolute, total, and complete paranoia.

Carlos kept talking. "We also know you told Aaron Gabel repudiated you in name only to suit the Moon, and your bond was not sundered, just constricted. But She erased your Mark, and did not restore it. Instead, She gave you that. She didn't erase your lure-scent. You still have Aaron's Mark, and I know you can still feel him. You still hear him, don't you?"

Now he was getting too personal. "Get to your point."

"None of it changes that the bond between you and Aaron was real, which means you did love him, and he was meant for you, and the Moon approved. Aaron's Mark endures and looks like a Mark, Gabel's Mark looks like..." He glanced at Flint. "We let Gabel take you because we knew you are bound to him, and we were afraid in your fragile state any other stress might harm you and the pup you may be carrying. I knew Gabel wouldn't let any harm come to you. We protected our Luna by permitting this to play out. If you had thought we had abandoned you, I apologize."

Carlos dropped to one knee and bowed his head almost to the carpet, exposing the back of his neck. He curled his spine to offer me a choice of vertebrae.

I rolled my eyes. "Oh, get up. You *also* heard me tell Gabel to kill Aaron."

Carlos uncurled. "Yes, I heard that, as did some of the others. Some believe you told Aaron to kill Gabel. Others believe you told Gabel to kill Aaron. Many more simply weren't there to hear it or couldn't hear it through the chaos."

"So you know Aaron is dead because I *wanted* him dead."

Carlos' gaze only flickered a bit, and for some odd reason, he barely smelled of anything at all. Was there icewater in this First Beta's veins? "He warned me you would despise him. He loved you desperately, and he told me he was at peace with whatever small part of you loved him, even if the rest of you despised him. I stood by him in life, and I will stand by his purpose in death. I do not believe he made an error, and I do not believe he failed."

"And why should I believe IceMaw isn't looking for revenge and all this is merely a clever ruse? Why are you so determined to have me be Luna after everything?"

"Why are you still with Gabel after everything he's done? He is a monster. I have seen the towers of bones he has left in his wake."

"So have I," I said flatly. "He is the Moon's Dark Comet, the Destroyer. You seem to think that I have *not* seen him at his worst. I asked the question. Answer it."

Carlos pointed to his eye. "He told me you are Luna, and I

am to be your First Beta. IceMaw will remain loyal to his design. Everything he did served the pack and the greater good. He was never selfish. He never took anything for only himself. He didn't know how."

The Scythe-Moon in my eye felt sharp and heavy, and the pans on the scales jangled in my mind.

Carlos paused, then added, "You might think he took you for himself, but he didn't. He took you for us. It cost him his life, and it cost him your love. But I know he did it without hesitation. Aaron did not know how to be selfish."

It explained Aaron's iron resolve. Gabel had always been sort of malleable, shifting, seething. Aaron had been an unmoving rock.

"I am more certain than ever that you are the Luna of IceMaw. Come back with us. Leave your blue-gloss pet behind to rule his kingdom of ash and bones."

"Carlos, don't be delusional." I sighed.

"You don't have to stay here, Luna." He sounded worried and fierce at the same time. "If that monster won't let you walk out the door, we will help you escape. It does not have to be bloody. We can spirit you away in short order. You might be bound to him, but we can take you to a place so far away he'll be dead of blood loss before he ever finds you."

I wasn't even tempted for an instant, but I was so shocked by his ferocity my brain had to hurry to catch up.

Carlos mistook my shock for hesitation. "You have no midwives here. No other females to help you rear the pup, no pups for it to play with. This is a place to raise an army, not a pup. Gabel will never accept Aaron's pup as—"

"Gabel swore to me when we took our vows that he would take the pups I brought to him." Pups this, pups that. Aaron's pup! What the hell was he about! Hix had kicked it off with nonsense about pups my first dinner at IronMoon. Gabel had been on my ass about pups since almost the start. Even Lucas had been like *you need to pretend to find a mate because everyone is going to ask about pups.*

Did nobody notice the piles of bones and the angry Moon? And they wanted to talk about pups? I had no time for pups! There might not even be a world by the time we were done!

And there was zero chance I was carrying Aaron's pup, although Aaron had let everyone believe he was a next-level monster, and willing to cross a line that even Gabel refused to flirt with.

I glared at the First Beta. "So *that's* why you're really here. The possibility I'm carrying his spawn."

"If there is a chance any piece of him survived—"

I snarled. "You don't care about me, you just want—"

"No, Luna, I *swear* that is not true!"

Flint stepped forward. "Luna Gianna is still very weak from the events of the past year. If she wishes to make IronMoon her den, then she has earned that right, and you must abide by it, First Beta. Even if you disagree with her reasoning."

"With respect, Master-of-Arms, this is no place to raise a pup," Carlos growled.

"What, you object to the weeds on the front walk?" I said sarcastically.

"I object to the lack of midwives, to start. You were silvered at SableFur. You shouldn't even *be* pregnant, I told Aaron he was trying for nothing, and all the damage he was doing, but he was determined. You *need* a midwife, the risk you're—"

"*You* are entertaining a great deal of risk," I snapped.

Flint stepped so that he was halfway between us. "You will not be returning to IceMaw today with her, First Beta. She will summon you when she is ready to consider your request."

"Do not, Master of Arms," Carlos growled. "That is my Luna."

Flint cocked his head slightly, unimpressed. "You plead with this wolf to be your Luna and give her pups to IceMaw, yet you disrespect her choice in dens, insult her blue-gloss, and question the covenant that has sealed it. You are not an Oracle. You are not the Moon's Chosen Balance-Keeper. Even First Beta Hix apologized for his Alpha's disgraceful actions, then sought redemption at the cost of his life. I have not heard you apologize for your Alpha's *abhorrent* conduct, which by your own admission was not just abhorrent, but pointless, given the recent silvering."

Carlos set his jaw and stared straight at Flint.

"Why would she want to inherit a First Beta who makes nothing but excuses for the Alpha who brutalized her? First Beta Lucas and First Beta Hix both lost their lives to defend her from Alphas they believed had become unworthy. Aaron is dead because she ordered his death. You sound like some slavering thrall serving a dead master instead of a First Beta she can trust to be *her* First Beta and enact *her* will. You have proven *woefully* unworthy, and the *easiest* price you can pay to redeem yourself is your life, so don't think that is worth very much to her." Flint was going *off*, even if his tone was mild as if he was instructing a pup on why chewing someone's tail was rude.

Flint continued, "You insult Gabel but admit you trusted him with her safety. You insult her intellect and demand she leave her den like she is incapable of making good choices. You make nothing but excuses to justify the actions of a dead wolf. A wolf *she condemned to death for his crimes against her*. Think *very* carefully on that."

Carlos' jaw moved but he didn't speak.

I pointed at the door. Time to play along with Flint. "Go. I will summon you when I care to deal with IceMaw. You may not speak of the words you and I exchanged, but you are free to tell IceMaw what Flint said to you."

"Luna—"

"I don't want your damned apology. Get out."

Carlos bowed deeply. "Yes, Luna. IceMaw will await your will."

A NAME WITH NO
MEANING

I watched Carlos go, pondering Flint's speech. Then I asked him, "Why did you step in?"

"I apologize, Luna, but it seemed prudent."

Prudent? *Prudent?* "I'm allowed to be aggravated, Flint."

"The situation was escalating. The scent on that wolf was telling."

"He didn't smell like anything." Males had sharper snouts than females, but Carlos hadn't smelled of much at all. "That wolf has ice-water in his veins. I doubt he really cares about anything other than the pup he thinks I'm carrying."

"You did not smell him at all?" Flint asked.

"No. I haven't really been able to smell much for a few weeks. Some rotten summer cold, I think."

"Not to argue, Luna Gianna, but the wolf smelled of quite a few things. I am sure your scent was goading him too. You cannot disguise your scent of anguish when you speak of your time in IceMaw."

I bit my lower lip and ignored the pulse of pain in my arms. Just like I hadn't been able to hide my body's traitorous reaction to Aaron, and oh, how that wolf had gloated over it.

"Thank you, Master Flint. I'm sure your snout is better than mine. But why didn't you tell him my Mark is a true Mark? I pretended in SableFur Gabel wasn't my mate when he was, but there's no point in persisting with that now. It was always just a stupid and temporary ruse to put off the inevitable."

"Exactly. Putting it off. Sowing confusion and offering nothing to our adversaries to put their teeth into. So turn this," Flint gestured to me, then to our surroundings, "back on IceMaw as their fault, it buys time for us to establish clarity."

As soon as we *found* some clarity. "Aaron's Mark should be gone, Flint."

He seemed old again. "The Moon Herself is sowing confusion. I think it is best if we play along for now."

Good point. "So you're saying that once I can offer them something concrete and real, they will latch onto it."

"I am saying that the *first* person to offer something concrete will be the one to win. Just be wary that rescuers often have to protect themselves from those they're rescuing. The desperate have a tendency to flail and panic, and then everyone dies."

Yeah, he was right, but what the hell was there for me to use as a cosmic sledgehammer. Nobody questioned Magnes' was the Moon's Despised. The starlight wolves had taken care of that. But it seemed like I'd need a pack of starlight wolves and the Moon Herself to get through to everyone about Adrianna.

Where the hell could I get another pack of starlight wolves?

I rubbed my head. "Thanks, Flint. Your quick thinking saved my fur again."

A tired, tormented smile. "Of course, Luna Gianna."

I could still see the shadows in his jungle-green eyes. "You're tired, Flint."

He nodded again.

"You can go," I said, trying not to get choked up. "Surely you've earned your redemption by now."

His blue-gloss seemed to shift as if something had moved

over it, causing the light and shadows to change. "My beloved would never forgive me if I told her I took my leave now. She would send me right back."

I cracked a smile. "She sounds feisty."

"She has to be, to endure me in my first life, and wait for me all this time," Flint said, permitting himself a bit of a fond smile. "You are quite tame compared to her. She is... more like Ana, if I am to be honest."

"Your mate is like *Ana*?" Well, let's file that under things I wouldn't be telling Ana.

"Not nearly as uncouth, but as sharp and willing to tap-dance on my entrails while singing her favorite song."

"I was imagining her to be some sweet and gentle she-wolf with halos around her paws."

Flint raised a bushy blond brow.

Dually noted. "Thank you again. Now do you have any ideas for a cosmic sledgehammer?"

This time he shook his head with a heartfelt sigh.

"I keep hoping that finding Gabel's mother's name would do something but I've lost faith in that idea. Nobody at SableFur even knew she existed, and those that do are either dead or silent."

"Is it possible she was a SableFur herself?"

I sighed. "No. In my visions of her, I always understood she was not-pack. I think it was all just a way to get me into SableFur to strike at Magnes."

Flint glanced up at the ceiling. "And that is more than you seem to appreciate. You should go speak to your mate. I am certain he is very worried. Shall I have your tools set outside your workroom?"

There was nowhere else to put them, although I wasn't sure if I was going to use them. "Yes, thank you. But just *outside*. Not inside."

"Of course." He half-bowed to me. "I will see to it myself."

GABEL - EYES OF RIVER STONE

He stared at his map, periodically reaching to move a pin or string to adjust for all the changes in his domain.

Eroth opened the door to his office. "The IceMaw have left, Alpha. The scouts are monitoring them."

"If they so much as glance behind them, Second Beta," Gabel said with a growl. "If they so much as glance."

Eroth grinned and ducked back around the door.

Instinct nagged him to go check on his mate, but that would be "fussing" over her, and she despised that. Still, her swatting and growling at him was entertaining and reassuring. The alternative was her howling in pain, or worse, just laying there waiting for it to be over.

She had not told him Aaron had replaced her tools. She had not told him she had scryed for him. An unfamiliar prickly-hot feeling started under his ribs. Stones he could have obtained, but he had no access to the appropriate stonecutters.

What else had happened between her and Aaron?

He turned back to his contemplation of the map.

These were not wolves who wanted answers. They did not

want to see their own reflection in an Oracle's scrying bowl.

He summoned the memory of the first time he had beheld his human face in a bowl of water. The painful shock, the horror. He had seen his mother in human form, he had even seen other humans from a distance. He had known, because Mother had explained it. But that moment of seeing himself as one of them still hit him with its jolt of world-bending confusion.

These wolves needed to kneel. They did not need to understand. They did not need to look in the bowl. They needed to submit.

And he would *make* them submit.

But none of it would matter if Gianna slipped away from him again, or Aaron spirited her soul away.

Her scent, soft and floral, with a hint of spice, graced his nose. It conjured images of autumn-faded rose petals, the quiet of night, the distant burn of stars, the halo around a winter moon. It matched her Moon-touched skin and the careless tumble of loam-dark hair, her eyes the same color as a quiet pond, not quite blue, not quite brown. She was taller than average, and her body showed her warrior pedigree, but was more like marsh grass than supple strength, and the past year had carved hollows and lines into places that should not have hollows and lines.

She smelled tired as she sat down in her usual place on his couch. She had on a soft pink sundress, and had removed her cardigan, giving him a clear view of both her Marks: the strange blue-gloss, and the raised bone-white nightmare flayed into her other arm. It was a distinct bone-white color, completely different from her Seer skin tone, and impossible for him to ignore.

Flint had warned him, more than once, to be more careful. Aaron's barbs lingered like the damned wolf's claws were still in his leg.

She stared out the large window to the daylight beyond.

The ache in her soul echoed through his: she hurt, and she was tired of hurting.

And as much as he delighted in pain, *her* pain was beyond his control, the source beyond his reach, and he could not make her pain stop.

"You've sent the IceMaw on their way."

"Yes." She sighed and rested her cheek in one too-thin hand. She closed her eyes.

I am telling you that you could have done more, and done better, and done wiser. She loves you, despite all your hideous flaws and the pain you've caused her. Do not confuse meeting the minimum standard with doing well. You set the bar very low in the beginning.

Flint had told him that. Aaron had more or less told him the same thing. And Flint had also warned him that the Mark would be denied as a true Mark because it was convenient and easy. It had all come to pass. "And?"

"And what?" She opened her river-rock eyes and looked at him, sort of unfocused and far away.

"And will I have another war on my southern border?" This was the wrong conversation to have, but he could not figure out the words for the one he wanted to have, so this would have to do.

She sighed at him. "No. According to Carlos, I am the IceMaw Luna. But they've gone away for now. Flint convinced them I was angry at them and they had no right to dictate where I made my den, so sod off."

He waited for her to tell him more, but she stared at nothing. She seemed untouchable and remote, like part of her was still somewhere else. She made love to him (so fiercely that if he'd been in wolf-form, his ruff would tremble with excitement at the prospect of more), and he had felt her closeness in those moments, but now she was withdrawn again.

No further clues, save for the strange earthen spice scent she'd had since returning from IceMaw. It smelled of weariness and stillness and reminded him of summer earth, not unpleasant, but instinct told him it was *very* important. "If they are going to upset you, then they are unwelcome here."

They were unwelcome in general. But if they wanted to occasionally show up and howl sad songs beseeching their Luna to return to them, he'd humor it as long as it didn't upset her too much.

"You want to be King-Alpha and think you can just ban people from coming here because they upset me? They have the right to ask their ruler to attend their concerns. Or have you abandoned your ambitions to be King-Alpha?"

Of course his ambitions had not changed. His ambitions would *never* change, only the reason and the route by which he obtained them. His previous method would only result in calamity, but there was an even darker, crueler path to triumph, and the Silvery Sky Bitch had revealed it. The prospect of a triumph so vast and complete it seared his nerves with excitement. Conquering SableFur had always been the final step in his ambitions, but he had anticipated doing it with blood and gore, and then having a decade or so of entertainment in dealing with minor rebellions and unrest until finally the pack accepted they had been defeated.

Now he would *break* SableFur. He would chew them out from under Adrianna until she fell into their grip and devoured her for him, and then they would crawl on their bellies before him. They would *submit*. Completely. Totally. And it would be exquisite.

The matter of Aaron's grip on his mate was something entirely different. Aaron had proven maddeningly out of his reach, forcing him to watch Gianna suffer as Aaron haunted her.

Aggravated, he asked, "Why did you even humor the IceMaw?"

Adding *when that First Beta watched him brutalize you* seemed very unwise. Hix had watched him do worse to her. Hix had watched him torment and humiliate her. He had been an idiot that day with Anders—and Flint had taken him aside and all but begged him to reconsider, and Gianna had lashed into him with that exquisite, righteous fury but that sickening, humiliating contempt where she'd all but spit on him. He'd been an idiot, drunk on the exotic agony of the bond and the fierce challenge Gianna had presented.

Her fury had been glorious and irresistible, but her contempt had seeped under his pelt like water running into the den so all his fur was soaked, and there was no way to be dry. He'd grossly underestimated her, then had done it again, taking her to run off the RedWater, and then again and again, and again. No one else had ever challenged him like she had, and he'd wanted to twist it into every possible shape and form because he had not been able to fathom how she kept getting her teeth into him. Her contempt and disgust had been raw acid, her laughing had humiliated him, and the way she'd faced the violence and cruelty and gore of IronMoon had not so much as made her knees tremble. Even those few times when he'd made her weep she had refused to surrender, and her tears had been a fascinating, yet empty, thing he would never call victory.

She had never shown him her belly. She had capitulated a few times, she had wept a few others, but she had never come close to submitting. Eventually she had stopped showing him her rage or her fury. She had simply given him her contempt and disgust, taunted him, laughed at him, and smiled fiercely when she told him so very, very sweetly she'd be by his side to watch his kingdom crumble into ash. She'd been happy about that, and it'd felt like she'd picked her teeth with his bones.

The instant she had stopped respecting him was the instant she had taken his power, like she'd taken a rabbit from his mouth and frisked away with it.

He had been impossibly aroused at the same time he had been infuriated.

Surely there had to have been a limit, something that would break her, like all the others. Like a blood-blind fool, he had pursued a prey that did not exist. He had dragged her into his darkest actions, his most brutal delights, and she had given him a river-stone cold gaze, as distant and disdainful as the Moon in the winter sky. *She* had not been the one who had been forced to look into the Oracle's bowl.

And he had spilled the contents of the bowl in his flailing, and now he'd never be dry again. He had even shattered the bowl, because he was the one, ultimately, who was responsible for feeding Gardenia's ambitions, and fueling Gardenia's rage. He was the reason she had felt she had to give up being an Oracle. It was almost like Aaron's mocking laughter ripped open the wound in his thigh so that he was wet with his own blood.

You destroy everything you touch. You have no idea how to keep what you have... up to and including your own head.

She raised her head off her hand and gave him an annoyed look. "Don't tell me you're worried I'm going to run right back to IceMaw."

The swipe of her aggravation against their bond tugged the corners of his lips. "No."

"Then settle down. I am not going to just slam IronMoon's door in their face. You can't be some lonely king on some high mountain and expect your subjects to quietly pine after you while asking for nothing."

He poked with another question. "So what did he tell you? What was said?"

She glared at him and their Bond met his own seething annoyance. "I met with him as an Oracle."

"And you were the penitent. Your question, his answer. It was your question, his answer."

"Is that a command, Alpha?"

The prospect of her fiery anger sent a quiver of excitement through him. "I could make it one, if you like."

"I don't want to talk about it."

Her scent transmuted into raw anguish and her voice took a tense note as her aggravation dispelled and she withdrew, their Bond shuddering like she had curled up inside herself. How could she expect him to ignore that? "Is the southern alliance still intact?"

"I believe so."

Will you cherish me and love me so that I know no other male will ever be worthy of my glance?

She does not flinch when I touch her. She tells me to stop, but I sense her skin accepts my caress in those stolen moments.

That dead wolf's words still twisted in his kidneys like the damn mongrel was whispering in his ear. The *do something* deep in his brain stem got to a fever level.

What had happened between her and Aaron? Had she accepted his touch? Shared a kiss?

No. Thoughts for another time.

Gianna ran a finger over her lower lip. "The IceMaw believe I am carrying Aaron's pup."

He jerked all over, and horror pooled inside him, like all the waters of the Tides had just rushed into a tide pool. *Pup? Pup? Pup?*

PUP?

His throat constricted. His teeth sharpened, and his fingernails itched in their beds as the hair on his arms stood up. "Did that wolf *hurt* you, buttercup?"

He had already asked her once before. She had denied it.

Gianna paused a heart-wrenching second, expression very far away. Her fingers almost touched the bone-white Mark, but stopped short before returning to her lap.

The Silvery Sky Bitch would *pay* for this... he'd strangle Her with Aaron's soul. He would rip Her out of the sky and place Gianna there and put a crown of stars and gore on her brow.

"No," she said softly, and he definitely did not believe her, "but he let IceMaw think he was."

Was? That it had been *ongoing*? How long had Aaron fed the lie to IceMaw? What had he subjected her to? Had he terrorized her, so she'd smell the right way to beguile the pack? Perhaps smeared her with his fluids? Tormented her until she had screamed at him even if he'd never laid a hand on her?

Gabel pointed at the door and forced his legs to stay rooted. "And that wolf dared to come here and ask anything of you? He stood by while he believed his Alpha raped his Luna and thinks he has *any* right to ask you for anything except your claw removing his testicles? He questions why you'd rather keep your den guarded by the Moon's Destroyer than remain in IceMaw with your *rapist and his thralls*?!"

Those stone-blue eyes of hers were back to being remote. "He did offer me his neck. I didn't take it."

"Why not?" The strange twisting anxiety and fury knotted into something that made his fingernails itch in their beds and his teeth burn in his jaw.

She shrugged. "Flint interceded and told me it's best we let IceMaw remain confused."

Flint had *intervened*? Twice in the same day? "Is there a chance? Even the slightest one? The *slightest* one."

She actually laughed. There wasn't much to it, but she did. "No. Aaron very blithely informed me he wasn't dumb enough to put his cock within easy reach."

Relief poured through him. That was his Luna smiling at him, and her wicked shine gleaming under his heart.

And so long as IceMaw believed she was their Luna, and she was angry with them, they'd remain withered and docile. Especially if they believed she was carrying Aaron's pup.

Neither ruse would last forever, but they'd last long enough.

PEE ON THIS

"Fuck," I muttered to myself as I stood at the top of the narrow stairs, staring at the door and that cherry-red trunk.

"You can just leave it in the room," I told myself. Was I talking to doors now?

I opened the door, stepped over the box, and walked inside.

Everything was exactly as I'd left it, except for the layer of dust, but it felt like I was walking into a life that wasn't mine anymore.

I set the box down on one of the lower shelves, then paced the circumference of the room, noting the dusty piles of salt in the corners. But the room itself was barren, except for a few vials of oils that I'd left behind.

"Hey."

I snapped out of my wit-wandering. Ana leaned against the door frame. "You okay?"

"Yeah, I'm fine," I said. "Just... I'd given up being an Oracle."

"Why?"

"Because I lost my tools three times," I said. "The first time they got shattered, the second time Magnes stole them from me, and the third time I left them behind at IceMaw. I thought it was the Moon telling me I was done as an Oracle."

Her brow furrowed. "Why the hell would you think that?"

"Being an Oracle and being a Luna aren't really compatible. Anita used my Oracle vows like a crowbar. It's a way to get me alone, or to put me in an impossible position, or to just accuse me of things. They've done all three already, actually."

Ana looked around the room. "Yeah, and three times your tools got shipped back to you. You sure the Moon's saying *quit*? Sounds to me like She's saying *don't you dare bail on Me*."

"It's not the Moon bringing my tools back to me. The IceMaw brought them here as a bribe. They *should* have sent them the instant they knew where I was."

Ana shrugged. "Okay, fair enough, I guess."

I sighed. "You want something, Ana?"

"Yeah, Ink-Daddy asked me to check in on you. He's so hot. It's just not fair. Gotta give the wolf credit for being brave enough to knock on my door."

Damn. First Flint had confessed Ana reminded him of his mate, and then he'd shorn up the courage to go knock on her door? Flint wanted off this carnival ride before it took him back to hell. "Ana, don't creep on him."

"I'm not creeping! I *admire*. From a respectful distance and in silence. If he can smell my panties, sorry, can't help that."

I shouldn't have snickered, but I did.

"Anyhow, ol' Ink-Daddy told me I should probably ask you to pee on this here stick." Ana flashed a thin white plastic wand.

"Flint did what now?"

Ana waved it back and forth. "Well, he didn't ask me to ask you to pee on *this* stick, or a stick at all, specifically, but this is how we're gonna do."

"What are you even talking about?"

"Honey, I'd ask you when the last time you had your period

144

was, but I know you wolves don't get your period and man, can I just say I am *so* jealous. Fuck."

"I am still lost."

"He thinks you're pregnant."

"Because Carlos ran his mouth about a pup? I am *not* pregnant with Aaron's pup. Aaron wasn't that stupid."

"No, because your ass is dragging, he knows you banged Gabel back at SableFur—"

"I also got exposed to silver in the last six months. SableFur put me in restraints."

"...and he tells me you've got that scent to you, Gabel's acting more rattled than usual probably because he can smell it but can't identify it, *and* your own sense of smell is shot, which he tells me is a pretty classic symptom a she-wolf's knocked up. Just go pee on this."

I stared at the stick.

She waved the stick. "Go pee on this and come right back up here."

"No," I said suddenly, "I don't want to unsettle my wards. Let's go to your room."

"Sure, whatever you want. Gonna pee in my potty too?"

"Yes."

"Asserting dominance. I'm kinda into it."

"More like if Gabel thinks we're up to this, he will lose his mind and be underfoot."

"Exactly why Flint told me to take care of it discreet-style. I *am* pretty good at being discreet when I wanna be, and nobody pays attention to what I do around here."

Ana's room was on the second floor. Actually, it was a two-room suite near the stairwell, putting her in a good spot for late-night emergencies. I hadn't been in it, and I sort of expected a chaotic homey decor with lots of posters of naked men on her walls and an unmade bed, given her apartment when I'd first met her.

Instead, it was neat, tidy, and she'd done absolutely nothing to decorate it. It looked exactly the same as when she'd moved in. She hadn't even added a plant to her window sill.

"What? It's clean," she said indignantly.

"Yeah, that's what shocks me."

"Hey, I'm a *vet*. I like things clean. Was my clinic dirty?"

"Well, no, but... you don't even have a plant."

"Why would I want a plant?" she said, her tone suddenly defensive.

"How about fish? They're like swimming plants."

She rolled her eyes and pointed at her bedroom. "Piss, please."

"I can't believe you had this."

"Bitch, I've got a stash. Look, I'm not here trying to have some hybrid puppy, so I am *extra super careful* and on top of that situation."

"There are worse things than having a hybrid."

"Sure, like being a single human mom in IronMoon raising a hybrid. Give me thirty seconds and I can think of like ten more."

"I'm going, I'm going."

"Not on my carpet, you're not."

"You want me to bring this back to you soaked in pee?"

She sauntered over to her nightstand, yanked open the drawer, and pulled out a glove. She pulled it over her hand with a snap and wiggled her fingers. "Leave it on the back of the potty."

"What... you know, I'm not even going to ask."

She grinned.

I did what she asked and returned to her front room to wait, like a bewildered penitent. "You know what you're doing, right?"

"Of course I know what I'm doing."

"I mean, you are a *vet*."

She rolled her eyes as she returned carrying the stick. "If you really insist, I'll give you a blood test."

"I had a silver exposure, Ana. That's going to make it hard for me to get pregnant for... a year. It makes you bleed."

"Well, I guess you'll have to be careful then and keep an eye out for spotting and maybe you have the baby in a human hospital and I test your clotting factors to make sure you don't bleed to death." She flicked the pee-stick in her gloved hands. "Because two stripes."

"Meaning?" Damn, I was not nearly this dumb.

"You're pregnant." She chucked it in the trash and sat down next to me.

"You're sure," I said slowly.

"Well, let me put it this way: if this was my pee-stick? I'd be panicking."

My brain couldn't form a thought.

She tucked her hands between her knees. "Any chance it's Aaron's? You can tell me. Won't tell a soul. Just need to know how far along you are."

My lips parted, but no words came out.

Anna nudged me with her knees. "Hey. Just nod yes or no."

Still dazed, I shook my head. "No, no, no. He wasn't that dumb. It must have been when Gabel visited SableFur."

"Damn, Ink-Daddy knows his shit, doesn't he?" Ana said, half-grinning. "This is why you've been kind of a mess. That and the whole angry Moon goddess stuff and soul parasites."

I stared at her rug. "That must be why Carlos insisted I was carrying Aaron's pup."

"Say what now?"

"He made it sound like he knew I was pregnant. He's mated and has a pup of his own. He must know the smell." I'd had no idea that males could smell it so early! Although it wasn't that soon. I'd seen Gabel about a month before Beltane, and now it was high summer.

147

"And everyone here is a kissless bachelor who wouldn't know what end of the pup to feed." Ana still was grinning, her eyes dancing with mischief.

I shook off the shock. "When am I due?"

She pulled out her phone and tapped on it, then shoved the screen at me. My due date was around Solstice.

Oh no. Oh no. That was no time at all! I'd be losing the ability to shift very soon, once the baby was too big for a wolf-form body to support. I clapped a hand over my still-flat belly. The world was falling apart, and the Moon decided to complicate things with a baby?

Whatever Gabel and I were going to do to end this, we were going to have to do it fast.

And IceMaw was going to think it was Aaron's. And when I told them I knew for a damn fact that it wasn't, what happened then?

But first... I had to figure out how to tell Gabel.

Because whatever plans he'd had? They were about to get trashed.

THE SUMMER NIGHT WAS HOT AND HUMID, WITH BUGS and moths dancing around the lights dotting the courtyard. A light breeze kept the heat from being unbearable and the bugs from crawling in the corners of our eyes while crickets sang and cicadas did their incessant drone.

I wished I could smell the flowers. I kept my hands behind my back so he wouldn't see my fidgeting.

"You have been nervous since dinner, buttercup. Which you also barely pecked at. Are you turning into a bird?"

"The opposite, actually," I said, unsure how to tell him or what reaction I needed to be steeled for. Because if he started acting triumphant like he'd won some prize, I'd brain him. I took a deep breath. Oracles get taught to just say the words. "I'm pregnant."

Gabel froze for a split second. Then he spun so fast his kilt brushed my knees. He grabbed both of my arms in his hands.

I stiffened. "If you dare get angry, I will gut you."

"Are you sure? Are you sure?" he said, leaning terrifyingly close, his fingers a soft pinch but veins popped out against the skin of his arms and his muscles clenched so hard they twitched.

My throat was too dry to say anything but, "Yes. Ana's absolutely sure. Flint suspected it, she confirmed it."

He gave a quick, almost crazed look at the house, then around the courtyard, then back at the house, then finally to me.

I knew the feeling.

"Is the pup... healthy?" His words echoed through the Bond with concerns about everything that had happened since he'd dragged that buck through SableFur.

"I suppose so. Aaron didn't seem to..." I breathed a silent sigh of relief that Aaron Marking me hadn't ripped a hole through *all* of me. "But Carlos—he's got a pup. That's why he was so sure. Because he must know the scent."

He moved to carefully touch my hair, fidgeted with the strands, then touched it again, tracing his fingertips along my temple, down my jaw, over my lips, down my throat. I closed my eyes. His fingertip traced one line of my collarbone, then the other, and he slid his palms over my forearms to lift my hands to his lips. His fingers found the raised scars on my palms and fingers.

"You haven't been bleeding," he said quietly, like he was sorting through his own memories.

"No."

"Because I would have smelled that."

"Yes, and I would have noticed. Probably before you smelled it."

Gabel smiled—one of those rare smiles without any malice

or mischief. It was a smile I loved and didn't see too often, and gave me hope. "Buttercup. When did—"

"When you came to SableFur."

"And Flint told me I was being presumptuous. Well. I suppose I was, impregnating the Luna of SableFur. What a scandal." He purred and kissed my forehead, then ran his hands down my arms, taking care to avoid the sore spot of Aaron's Mark.

Aaron's soul was quiet, but he paced, slowly, listening for each word.

LIE TO EVERYONE

O nce my workroom had been my sanctuary.

I pushed open the door. No scent of salt or oils rushed out to meet me, because surprise: I couldn't smell anything.

I ran a hand over my lower belly. Was it a bit softer, and I hadn't noticed? Was I imagining it? I wasn't imagining the tender breasts, or the spike-like pain in my back, or anything else. I'd just ignored it as damage from the past few months. Getting chained up in a SableFur dungeon and made to wear a silver-laced collar like a mad beast would do that to a girl.

I touched the faint silver scars around my neck. I *shouldn't* have gotten pregnant so soon. Usually even a small silver exposure kept a she-wolf from getting pregnant for about a year, or she had a miscarriage when the baby became too large and her insides weren't healed enough to form a good placenta.

"I guess we will just have to trust the Moon, runt," I told the pup affectionately.

I could almost hear Gabel telling me what a stupid idea *that* was.

Not that I had any evidence at all that the Moon *wasn't* trying to crack me and drive Gabel truly insane.

I didn't want to be a monster. I *wouldn't* become a monster.

The bowls sat in their velvet wrappings. The bag of tektite runestones sat in its velvet pouch. No familiar obsidian bowls this time. Not even the frightening tourmaline spears. My choices were the bowl made from the meteorite, or the bowl made from tektite.

I ran my fingers over the rims. The slightly sharper, sleeker meteorite. Then the thicker, vaguely warm, seething tektite. The tektite took me beyond the Tides, but I'd never used the meteorite bowl. It might take me somewhere I did not want to be at all. On the other hand, it didn't feel angry.

And on the *third hand*, the only runestones I had were tektite, so it was going to be tektite either way.

I pulled down the meteorite bowl and the bag of runestones. I knelt on my familiar little mat, sneezed at some dust, and spilled out the beautiful runestones onto the floor. The Thomson structures on the polished surface of the shallow bowl tugged on my Seer gifts. I wouldn't need to add water.

I picked over the runestones. There was a complete set, including obscure ones like *waterfall*. I selected *balance* and *protection*. It was a bad time when an Oracle didn't even feel safe enough in her Gift to meditate.

"Interesting." In the mix of runestones was one for *comet*. There was no official rune for *comet*. There was just the old sigil that most had forgotten. I had not even known it before Flint had told me what it was. Aaron must have told the stonecutter to include it.

I added it to the bowl. The world wasn't going to forget about the Moon's Dark Comet again.

Just to remind the Moon, I added *pup*, and finally, and reluctantly, *instrument*.

"No visions, Moon. Just a nice refreshing meditation." I settled myself back on my heels and took a deep breath.

~*~ Meditation Over A Meteorite Bowl ~*~

I WALKED OUT OF THE GROTTO.

The Tides rushed against the rocks, stormy and churning, while the storm itself came in the distance, with the Scythe-Moon's blade dipping just below the horizon, cutting into the world on the other side of the Tides.

A silhouette of a man waited on the rocky shore.

Aaron.

Was it Aaron, *or a specter?*

He turned and looked at me over his shoulder.

I choked and grabbed my chest like my heart had stopped. Everything rushed back as the Bond between us dilated and re-formed, no longer stretched thin by the span of death.

"How did you get here?" I rasped. "You're dead. *You should be waiting at Judgement!"*

He looked exactly the same, appearing before me in human form, except for white fur sprouting from all the scars on his back and torso, shining a clear, pure luminescence like starlight in the otherwise faint, demented light of the Scythe-Moon. His Mark was carved into the flesh of his arm, deep and ragged and dripping blood onto the rocks below, which drained into the ocean. The kilt he wore was ragged and strange, and it dawned on me it was made from pelts.

The pelts of the family he had killed to become Alpha of IceMaw.

He was glorious, and he was hideous.

He could have been so much more...

Perhaps he had been? And I was too ruined to see it?

"Gianna," he said my name, speaking with the voice of the ocean and storm.

The pain of his loss—and that I could have loved him—twisted me. I straightened as best I could. "Is it you, or just a specter?"

"You know it's me." He approached.

I backed away. "Don't touch me."

"Still so angry? You know why I did what I did."

"You're a deranged monster."

He laughed. "I've always been what the greater good needs me to be. Ask yourself who the true monsters are."

"If that's what you want to tell yourself, go ahead."

Another chuckle. "We both know it's true. Have I ever been more wicked than circumstances require?"

"You enjoy an excuse to be the savage asshole. You just hide behind some sad excuse of the devil made me do it. You abducted me from SableFur and Marked me by force."

"And Gabel took you like chattel from your father's hand and did the exact same. I will always have that card to play against you, and the only reason you hate me for it is because it's true."

"Better to be with the devil who says he's a devil than the mutt who blames his evil on everyone but himself."

Aaron merely smiled that sharp-edged smile that made me want to rip it off his face. He ground it all deeper into my soul. "Oh, I haven't been called a mutt since I was a pup. By my own kin, no less. Such an ironic insult, don't you think? And what a change of tune, Gianna. You didn't judge me when I told you how I killed my own family to take IceMaw in a bloody coup. You have no idea what it's like to live under the thumb of corrupt, deranged leadership. You have no idea what it's like to watch a pack wither and suffer. I took up the mantle of monster to save my pack. You were sad that I had had to, you were sad I had broken my body and consigned myself to loneliness because no she-wolf would take a broken, bloody wolf like me."

Aaron leaned close, his scent salt and snow and Aaron *and my heart wept for all of it. He lowered his voice to something like the froth on the wave caps. "You have blood on your own claws. You have it on your breath. You destroyed Magnes and will destroy Adrianna, leaving her pups to a miserable future. They are only children. But you will make them orphans, as you've made so many others orphans. And you might spare it a thought, but only a thought. It's necessary, so you will do it."*

I said nothing.

"You have killed. You have ordered wolves to their deaths, knowing they will die. You have watched Gabel torture and maim and execute wolves. You ordered a she-wolf to suffer and die." His voice was so soft. "What was her name? Gardenia?"

I wanted to tell him to stop. He wanted me to scratch and claw at him as he spoke the list of my crimes.

"And you left Hix to die." The final accusation washed over me like the froth of waves. "You could have escaped with him. You chose otherwise, knowing he would die. Then you left him to die alone, humiliated and degraded and broken and maimed, howling your name and loyal until the end."

Now tears rolled down my cheeks and my heart tried to break with each beat, the agony and pain and guilt suffocating all of me until it felt like it was going to burst out of my ribs.

"He is the only one you've wept for, isn't he? He's the only one that haunts you. The only one you wish you could take back—but you know you wouldn't."

Aaron did love his speeches, didn't he. Death probably didn't have a lot of people to pontificate to, so he was getting it in while he could.

"But you did it for the right reasons, didn't you? All of it, yes? Did you enjoy *your triumph over Gardenia? Even a little? Will you enjoy your triumph over Adrianna, even if you know what it will cost? You aren't horrified. I'm not even sure you're* hesitant*."*

"You should be in Limbo, before Judgement. How did you get here, shade?"

He smiled, but it had a cruel, sharp edge. Clever. Wicked. "This is the Place Beyond The Tides. I cannot cross the Tides back into the world, but I refuse to go beyond the Gates of Death to Judgement until you are with me again. So I linger in Limbo, and I, being the very clever wolf that I am, found a way here. This place. She knows I am here, She can see me perfectly well."

He pointed at the scythe on the horizon. "The Moon let you come here. Perhaps She even brought you here. Perhaps your thoughts of me led you here."

"Fuck off."

"If the Moon wanted to protect you from me, She could." Aaron's smile didn't waver.

"So you want revenge because I betrayed you?" Aaron might be dead, but I knew my way around the Place Beyond the Tides at this point. He was an amateur.

"Betrayed me? You say that as if I wasn't aware you wouldn't have sunk your claws into my neck if you could have. In fact, I believe you warned me on more than one occasion to watch myself. Only a fool would love you believing your pale skin and moonlight coat make you a gentle soul. You did tell Gabel to kill me. Ruthless." He seemed very amused.

No doubt this was Aaron. Running around the not-world like he owned it. Probably pissed on everything he could find, too. "What do you want?"

"Good things for you. Good things for our species. Gabel is still an idiot, who has no idea how to keep what he has, including his own head."

"Correct me if I'm wrong, but you're dead, Aaron. He strangled you with your own guts."

"But didn't take my head."

"I'm not quite sure what difference that makes. You're still dead."

"I don't mean literally. *I mean IceMaw did not fall apart. IceMaw continues on. Carlos came to see you, did he not? Restored my gifts to you. Restored you to your place on IceMaw's throne."*

"So you can spy on me. Grand."

"IronMoon, though—look how the pack fragments and frays and is barely held together. How much does he rely on Flint to guard his back?" Aaron studied his fingernails and picked flesh out from under them. What had he found to kill out here? *"You know that the pack will crumble the instant he is old and infirm. It might not even survive that long with Adriana out to secure a future for her sons. I built IceMaw from the broken remains of an abused pack and it has survived without me. It will continue to survive. You and I both know that IronMoon will crumble without Gabel."*

By the Moon, I hated it when Aaron and I agreed on anything. *"Could you hurry up with what you want? I don't actually enjoy chatting with you."*

"I could simply let him get himself killed, which would get you *killed, and I could be with you once again—"*

"Not a chance. We will never *be together again, not even in death."*

Aaron chuckled. *"—but I know you would not be happy with either of us, and ultimately IceMaw would be destroyed by Adrianna. I do take my obligations quite seriously."*

"Right. That's what we're going to call your demented idea of yourself."

"What sort of reward would it be for hundreds, thousands, of wolves to join you in paradise and tell you how they died when the world burned to cinders after Gabel's death and the end of his reign?"

"I hate you."

"I know."

"Get to the point."

"You're pregnant."

My blood sparkled with anger. "Yes, I know, and I'm not surprised you know, you eavesdropping louse."

"You need to tell the world I am the one who sired it on you."

I laughed. "Fuck you, no."

He pinched the bridge of his nose. "How will the world react to Gabel's spawn versus mine? What mantle will you place on the pup's shoulders before its eyes are even open? You have the option to give your pup my legacy, or to give your pup Gabel's legacy."

His words churned up my old worries about Gabel as a father —because while I loved Gabel, how was I supposed to also think I didn't want our children to be just like their father? My doubts, my deepest, most private doubts, had haunted me.

The bond between us, dilated and churning, betrayed my uncertain and knotted emotions. "You want me to lie. You want me to tell Gabel to lie. That you got me pregnant."

Aaron said, matter-of-factly, "You have the IceMaw throne, all you have to do is sit on it. The pup you carry, if the world believes it is mine, has a claim. You and Gabel each have a claim on the SableFur throne, him by birth and you by right of conquest. You have the IronMoon throne by right of mating. When in our history has a single wolf ever had so many jewels so firmly set in her crown?"

Three stones in the crown: white quartz, blue tourmaline, obsidian.

The crown had always been for a Queen's head.

But Gabel had also worn a crown: one of burning glass and gore.

Aaron glanced towards the Scythe-Moon as it sank into the flesh of the world. "I have given you the final jewel, and made you a Queen."

If I had been in my real body, my heart would have stopped beating.

"May I also add, I swore to you I would call no wolf King and..." He grinned. "So I won't."

"*I absolutely* hate *you,*" I said.

His eyes shone with starlight. "*If only that were true, my love. If only it were true. The Moon does not need to condemn me to Hell. I will suffer all the same for an eternity without you.*"

Ninety-nine percent of me didn't care. "Good."

"*If* you *do not make him King, consider what will happen to the world in his efforts to forge a crown on his own. Because I believe he* will *become King. He will* never *stop, and you will* never *stop him. He is the Destroyer. You will not change his nature. You've already seen him crowned in burning glass and gore, and you told me yourself the future is unchanged.*"

I looked at the Scythe-Moon. Fair enough.

Aaron said, "*You are the Balance-Keeper, the point on which light and dark turns. This isn't about* if *Gabel becomes King. It is about what happens* when *and* how *he becomes King. So, Gianna, the Scythe Moon has fallen, and the sun has set. Will Gabel make himself King, or will* you *make him King?*"

... EVEN HIM

I gasped for breath. I coughed, tasting brine and salt. Something wet tangled around my legs. I flailed in the total darkness while something hot and large moved in the shadows beside me.

"No!" I snapped an elbow back. It impacted bone and flesh with a *thump!*

I scrambled and fell off a ledge. My arm smashed into smooth floor, then my hip. The wetness tangled around my legs. I kicked, squirmed, and crawled forward as the wetness relinquished my thighs. A sliver of gray light beckoned me as the large thing in the dark sprang after me.

I screamed as claws closed over my hips. I twisted over in the grip and swung at it. My knuckles struck something like a jaw. The shade didn't stagger.

"Stop!" The hot shadow shouted.

"What—" I panted.

Gabel?

The hands released me and the dark shadow moved, and an instant later, the lights flicked on. Gabel stood by the light switch.

I tried to talk but just coughed around the taste of salt, brine, and blood in my throat. I was soaking wet.

Gabel yanked the blankets tangled around my ankles, then flung them back over the bed to expose the soaked sheets. He spun on me and dropped to his knees. He snarled and shoved *my* knees apart.

"Hey!" I smacked him away. I scrambled backwards.

"You smell like blood! Stay still!"

"I'm not bleeding!" I coughed again. Choking, yes. Bleeding, no.

He ripped through the bedsheets, then turned me on my hip to confirm I wasn't sitting in a puddle of blood. I tried to push him off me again. It didn't work. He just shoved his nose into my hair before reluctantly sinking back on his hip. "Your hair smells like blood."

"Well, clearly my hair is not soaked with blood, so I am not bleeding." This inability to smell anything was getting old, *fast*.

He shone with a light sheen of sweat, and his carved abdomen moved with deep, controlled breaths. He had on just a kilt. What time was it? How had I gotten here?

Fucking Moon. I'd been *meditating,* and I'd ended up Beyond the Tides.

Without a word, he tore every sheet and blanket off the bed, then stormed out of the bedroom.

Fine.

I hauled my muddled self to the edge of the naked mattress.

I sniffed my wrist. Nope, couldn't smell anything. I drew a fingernail along the back of my opposite hand.

A little bit of... salt?... came up with it.

"Oh, come on, this isn't playing fair." I patted myself down and checked between my naked thighs. No, no blood. Belly didn't hurt. Felt soft, though. Pudgy. But the Moon dragging me off to the Island at the Edge of the Tides to converse with

Aaron couldn't be good for my pup if it was torturing my body like this.

...Gianna...

"Shut up," I snarled at the ghost. "Go drown yourself."

Where was Gabel? Did I care? No. Time for a shower.

I slumped against the tile as the lukewarm water ran over my skin.

Gabel re-appeared, yanked open the shower door, and stared at me.

"What are you doing?" I asked petulantly. "It's three in the morning. Let me bathe and go back to sleep."

"Making sure you are not going to faint."

"I've been in here for five minutes. Would have done it by now."

"I was getting fresh blankets."

"You *moved* me while I was on the Tides!" I snapped. "Are you crazy?!"

"And leave you on the *floor*? You were supposed to be meditating. Not scrying."

"I *was* and you should have just thrown a blanket over me."

"You are *pregnant*. I was not leaving you on the floor!"

"You could have dislodged my soul!"

"It would seem the Silvery Sky Bitch did that. *Again.*"

"You *wanted* me to meditate."

He curled his upper lip and snarled something under his breath.

"Gabel, please. I am tired." I banged my head against the tile. He shoved his hand between my forehead and the wall.

With his other hand, he picked up a fluffy towel. "Then the shower is not the place for you to be. Wait, where are you going *now*?"

"To find something to eat." I wasn't hungry, but I didn't want to fall back through the hole in my soul into Aaron's grip.

Spending *any* time talking with that undead wolf was not high on my list of things to do.

"Excellent. I approve of you eating."

How lovely I had his permission. It was almost four in the morning. The kitchen was still and warm from the summer heat. Cook wasn't here yet, but he'd be along with his helpers soon. There was a bowl of hard boiled eggs. At first glance, the eggs looked disgusting, but then they looked like the most wonderful thing I'd ever seen.

I grabbed four and smacked them into the kitchen counter.

Gabel melted out of the shadows. He watched while I peeled the eggs and devoured them one by one.

"How long was I gone?" I asked between the third and fourth.

"Since yesterday."

Not too long then. "Why the hell did you move me? You know that's dangerous."

"I felt you slip away, that's why," he said. "Where did She take you this time?"

"The Island at the Edge of the Tides." I picked a few bits of shell off the fourth egg.

"And?"

I picked a moment longer. "Aaron was there."

"Aaron, or a vision of Aaron?"

I shifted my butt to one of the stools. "He escaped Limbo and is traipsing around the Moon's domain."

Gabel said nothing.

I fished the globe of yolk out of the egg. Gabel stood like a stone. He had a bruise forming on his cheek and another on his jaw. I rolled the yolk around.

"What did Aaron want?" He asked in a too-reasonable tone, while his presence in my soul was him prepared to be *very* unreasonable.

"To talk. To... to talk. It was him. It was his soul. He wanted to talk politics. He... he knows what's happening in the world of the living." I gave up on the yolk and shoved it at Gabel.

The shadows of the early morning made his bronze tan seem like he was charred metal. "He told you, as usual, I have no idea how to keep what I have?"

"More or less."

"And you *believed* him."

"Aaron isn't an idiot. He never was." When I'd had the vision of Adrianna as queen, she'd been wearing Aaron's pelt. In my visions of Gabel and Aaron, I had always been helpless to stop Gabel. In the visions where I'd tried to stop him, I'd died and the world had burned.

But the three crowns had never been in the same vision.

There were three distinct outcomes: Adrianna's crown, my crown, and Gabel's crown.

But Gabel was my mate. We shared the same destiny.

I took a shaky breath. "I don't know what to believe, Gabel. And I don't trust Aaron. He... he... he wants us to say the pup was sired by him."

Gabel shoved back from the counter. "No. *Never.*"

"I told him that!" I said quickly.

"That louse does not know how to stay dead," Gabel snarled. "I am going to find him, and I am going to eat his soul. Claiming *my* pup as his? Never!"

"He tried to tell me you had vowed to take whatever pups I brought you. What is his obsession with your promises?" I asked.

Gabel shook his head once, his expression terrible.

"His argument was—"

"I do not care what his argument was."

"Then don't ask me what I saw if you don't want to hear it."

"I have compromised on many things, Gianna," Gabel growled. "I have humored the Moon, I have played by the rules. I will *not* compromise our pup."

"I know. It's not as bad an idea as..." What was I saying. I *wasn't* going to consider this.

"*No.*" Gabel put his hands on the kitchen island. "*No.* We aren't even discussing it and I am going to make a *decree* that it's mine. Tonight. I am sending a messenger to IceMaw *today.*"

"Don't you dare," I snapped. "Will you stop and think? Our pup is in *danger*. As long as IceMaw believes there is a chance it's Aaron's, they will stay tame, hell they might even be willing to be allies!"

"You even want to *toy* with this?" He seemed aghast.

"I'm not toying with anything. I'm telling you there's no reason to *do* anything. Let IceMaw still think what they think. They're useful meek!"

"I have no use for Aaron's *scraps!*"

"They aren't *scraps!* It's a powerful pack and an alliance you could use to your benefit if you weren't being such a prideful, stubborn fool!"

"You would use our *child* as some kind of political *pawn*?!"

"No, but someone else will!"

"So we should be *first*?!"

"I didn't say that!"

Gabel growled, "It is *my* pup."

"Of course it is! It's also not your *fucking* trophy. It's not your *fucking kill* that you won't share with the pack until you get feted for it, like you dragged that buck into SableFur and demanded I eat it."

"It is *nothing* like that. Don't compare our child to a deer carcass!" Gabel raged. "I can pile a hundred deer on the back lawn for you, but there is only that *one* baby! I might be able to sire more on you, but they are each our *child*!"

I shoved back off the stool. "And what happens to us if you die tomorrow? If I survive, *if*, what about our pup and its future? You think I can stay on the iron island you've built? You think I will *fucking* survive? I have to raise our child *alone*?

Flint's old and tired, he's not going to be around forever. Renzo? Eroth? They'll try, and Adrianna will run through them!"

Gabel's nostrils flared. "Not that the IronMoon rabble would have made you any safer."

"That's true too, so you know what my plan is? I take my ass back to IceMaw, tell them whatever they want to hear, and let the entire world think this baby is Aaron's get. I found the strength to kill one mate, I'd find the strength to forget you. That's what I would do. And I wouldn't even have to think about it."

Gabel's eyes widened, and the bond seemed to freeze.

I ground it deeper. "I need you to secure the den against the storm, because right now we're drenched and standing out in the middle of it. This is no place for a pup, it's barely a place for a Luna! You are out of time to play games, Gabel! We're both out of time and we're out of options and choices!"

Gabel came around the island. His presence bore down on me, hot and smothering and seething. "Do not let Aaron do this to you. I swear, I will free you from him, do not fall into his maw."

"Trying to brush over my opinions by telling yourself no, that's *Aaron's* influence?" I spat.

He ran his thumb over my cheekbone. The pad of his thumb scrubbed along the skin, pulling and tugging. His grip tightened. The smoldering heat started to churn and tumble. The Bond dilated and warmed as the knot of emotions strangled it. He slid his other hand along my belly.

"Fine," he said, curiously strangled. "Fine. We will say nothing. We will let the world wonder. For now."

GABEL - SOUL OF TWO PIECES

"*Has it occurred to you that the Moon gave you the Mark you have now so that wolves would not instantly know it was a Mark?... She will have questions to answer now. And for what? Your impatience. Your belief you are owed. You have learned nothing.*"

Gabel contemplated the two wolves kneeling before him, distracted by the fight with Gianna before dawn.

"As you have requested, Alpha," Renzo said with obvious pleasure. "A father and a son."

The son was a young adult, perhaps nineteen. The father twenty or so years older. Gabel shook off the echo of Flint's lecture. "Excellent work, Hunter. Your next quarry is known to you?"

"Yes, Alpha."

Gabel flicked a hand at him. "Go hunt."

"*You push her into danger with your games and ambition. You'll do the same thing to your pups...I would never have given her to the Oracles. I would never have repudiated her. But you've constantly traded her safety and happiness and your own damn vows against your goals and what you want.*"

The father and son were dressed in human attire, blindfolds on, bound ankle and wrist, with another rope tied like a noose around their respective necks, and a long tail dangling down their spine. Gabel picked up the father's noose-tail. The wolf stiffened and inhaled.

Excellent.

The son looked like perhaps he had been in warrior training, and the father as well. Renzo had brought him warriors. Even better.

Gabel crouched down next to the older wolf. He reeked of fear but defiance. A deep, unusual sort of defiance. "Will you do anything to save your son, wolf?"

"Anything," the wolf replied instantly. "Let him go."

"No, I think not." In his experience, *anything* did not actually mean much. Especially when it came from the mouths of fathers.

He straightened and looked to the warriors behind him. "Take them to the basement. Do not maul them. Lock them in the same cell. They may remain together."

The wolves' scents shifted to confusion and almost a *hint* of relaxation that the abuses weren't going to start promptly. Good. Let them relax. It would be better this way.

He went up to his office to mull over circumstances. He would wait to deal with the pair of wolves until his mind was in the proper place. They would otherwise be able to sense his distraction and would misinterpret it as reluctance or weakness. His prey must always believe he moved without hesitation.

Gianna had retreated to her room—the one he'd given her when she'd first arrived—to sleep. She was angry with him, and not the sort of angry he enjoyed, which often resulted in her charming little swats and snarls becoming her panting against his neck and her nails clawing his shoulders while he made love to her. It was the sort of angry where their Bond was vaguely nauseated with her contempt and disgust for him. Now there was also some additional anguish that held her just out of his reach, and he felt as though she was prey about to slip his grasp.

He had her, but every moment felt on the brink of losing her to a predator he could not chase away.

Flint was waiting for him, tucked into some beaten up book on fly-fishing. "You have a great deal on your mind today. But Gianna is back from her scrying, so all is well."

"Meditating. She was meditating, and the Moon took her. I would not ask her to scry in her condition."

"She is pregnant, not fragile."

Gabel glared at him. "Do not, old wolf. Do *not*."

Flint returned the glare.

She'd been using some strange hammered metal bowl/curved mirror. And very strange runestones that had not been obsidian, but something else. What had Aaron given her? He had been too worried and angry to ask. Worried enough he'd risked moving her back to their bed, drowning in her flowery scent, which had intensified as it always did when she was... *away*... Then the rush of salt, and finally, she'd burst awake, gasping. Then there had been a rush of blood-smell, and he'd torn the sheets away expecting to see her gushing blood.

But there'd been no blood. There had been that layer of salt over her skin, and it had chapped her lips.

Flint's voice was hard. "The Moon returned her to you unscathed."

"Exhausted and distressed and covered in salt is not *unscathed*. The Moon led her to the Island at the Edge of the Tides. *Aaron* was there. He refuses to go to Judgement without her and is cavorting around the other world, and the Moon permits it."

"But she *did* return to you."

Yes, with her head full of... whatever it was full of. "He told her to tell the world our pup was sired by him."

Flint shifted and leaned forward on his knees. "Ah. And she thinks this is a good idea."

"It sounds like *you* think it's a good idea."

"I hold absolutely no opinion on the matter."

"She tells me she doesn't, but she wants to let IceMaw continue to believe it."

"Because she is the Luna of IceMaw and if IceMaw believes that pup is Aaron's, it solidifies her hold over the pack. Basic succession politics."

"I do not need an *infant* to secure a pack! She *listened* to the mongrel. After..."

Human words failed him. Human words were such a chore for things this large.

"...after everything he did to her." Flint finished the sentence.

Her belly had been softer under his palm. She'd been gaunt when he'd gotten her from IceMaw. She was still thin, worn down, but that little bump. The life *they* had made when she'd come to his room in SableFur.

"...which may or may not be worse than what *you* did to her." Flint's mild tone twisted in his spine.

...you've constantly traded her safety and happiness and your own damn vows against your goals and what you want...

Thoughts tore at him in a tangle of human words and wolf-thought.

...not your fucking trophy...

Gabel swam through the confusing swirl of human-form word-thoughts and lupine-instinct-urges. "She needs her den secure. I did make that promise. I thought I had provided it, but I do not think I have."

"You have failed spectacularly. I am glad you see now how much she relies on you to protect her from her own pack. What a miserable situation for such a Luna to be in. She bears it with far more patience than is appropriate. You are fortunate she has not moved her den to IceMaw or even asked Ana to shelter her among humans."

He pulled open one of the drawers of his desk and extracted a small, cream-colored envelope. Inked in a neat hand was *Gabel & Gardenia of IronMoon*. The invitation to Anders' Solstice party from a year earlier.

He thumbed one of the softened corners. If Gianna knew he still had this, she would set him on fire. Perhaps he should show her just so she'd favor him with her anger. He turned the envelope over in his hands, over and over and over. "I believe she secretly thinks it's safer for the pup if the world doesn't think it's mine."

"And I imagine you refused to humor it in your usual fashion, but your third promise is haunting you: to love whatever pups she chooses to give you, and to raise them as your own."

"I hate it when you read my mind, old man."

"I don't need to read your mind to know your thoughts, pup. I've told you that before. Is it really the lie that irks you, or that it'd mean you wouldn't win?"

Gabel stabbed under his thumbnail with the corner of the invitation. "And if there are more pups, do we let the world love one and despise the other because of that lie?"

The blue-gloss on Flint's body swirled as the sunlight from the large window slid over it. "An Alpha should never humor rude, prying questions about immaterial matters. Your mating vows answer the question with absolute finality. There is a *reason* the vows are as they are."

"I know the reason the vows are the way they are."

"You just did not think *you* would ever be the one benefitting from it? Pup, your howls and insistence will *not* change the truth, and the *truth* is not what matters. Haven't you figured that out by now? Starlight wolves destroyed your father's soul, and *still* the SableFur are willing to accept Adrianna as their Luna, because it is *easy*. Questioning who sired that pup is *easy*, and tempting, because it humiliates you and hurts Gianna. You even entertaining the question invites a conflict you will never win, and you cannot squabble with every wolf that baits you with the lowest-hanging fruit possible. There will *always* be a cloud of doubt as to the exact details of the pup's conception, and you will *never* dispel it. Even *you* doubt what really happened between her and Aaron at IceMaw."

All must believe, even you must doubt.

When the Moon had separated them, he had *known* she was still his mate, even if the world had believed otherwise. And sometimes, he had caught himself wondering if he was deluding himself and his mind had fractured. "I believe her when she tells me there is no chance it is Aaron's."

"Of course there is no chance. Because it is yours."

"That is not what I meant."

"I know what you meant. And you tell me you believe her, but if she suddenly changed her story and revealed he had assaulted her, you would believe that too. And you'd forgive her the lie."

Human words were too difficult. He nodded.

"So you don't *fully* believe her. Even *you*."

All must believe, even you must doubt.

Human words twisted his tongue. Nothing could come out.

Flint said, tone cool, "You know she scryed for him. You can never know exactly what happened between them."

It had been years since the last time he'd found himself rendered frozen and mute.

Flint waited, giving it a long span of moments before he filled in the gap. "I can always see it when you can't use human speech. Maybe that's what you're seeing on her. That she cannot convey what happened to her. It's too hard, too painful, too confusing, the words won't come or maybe they don't exist."

His thoughts settled like snow. He turned the invitation over in his fingers, then set it back in the drawer. "Do you believe there is still a way to be the wolf that fills her gaze?"

"Doubt. Interesting. Have you realized that freeing her from Aaron's grip might not even be something she wants, or is possible?"

"It has to be possible," Gabel growled.

"And if it isn't?" Flint asked. "You have sworn to free her, but you've made no progress on the front. You have, actually, made no progress on any front that matters. And knowing you as I know you, I suspect it has more to do with you avoiding battles you'd rather not have, hoping to make progress on other fronts that will result in victory elsewhere."

Gabel closed the drawer. "So you don't believe I can keep my vows to her."

"I can't answer that, but I will tell you this: she is in true, real danger. Her den is not secure, and there is a pup in her belly and a war over the hill. Don't get distracted by small wolves who want to badger your pride with things that do not matter. Don't let them bait you into squabbling with your mate over things she can't explain and then be angry when the words you force her to shape are inadequate. Recognize the traps that are being laid for you and avoid them."

The human words flowed through his mind again, mingling with the wolf-thoughts of foxholes and burrows and roots of trees, and overlaid with it all, the memory of when he'd first met her, and the scent of Gianna mingled with the scent of Amber.

He picked up the blue tourmaline spear.

His resolve would not fail him.

It would not fail *her*.

TEMPER, TEMPER

Gabel wasn't at breakfast. He also hadn't come to bed.

"I believe he's in the basement." I lied to Eroth, since Gabel not being around was not at all like him. Eroth nodded. "I think so, Luna."

Lies. Both of us. Was I going to have to chase him all over the house? Had he gone off to lick his paws?

"It ain't like him to not be around," Ana muttered under her breath as I checked the empty parlor.

"I know," I muttered back. "I've got a bad feeling about this."

"You think he's run off?"

"I can't believe Gabel would run away from *fatherhood.*" It didn't seem possible. Aaron's soul paced and he snickered, distant and ghostly, like dead branches clacking together.

We checked every room in the house as discreetly as we could, but Gabel was nowhere to be found. Even the basement was dark, and he wasn't in his office. We huddled in her bedroom.

"Nah," Ana said. "*Nah.* Not *him.*"

"Maybe he's just gone for a run to wear himself out." Gabel

did not just *disappear*. He had *never* spirited himself off somewhere, then strolled in like a smug tomcat. Gabel had also never gone for a run to wear himself out. "But he's not here. I know he's not here."

It was an eerie, uncomfortable feeling.

"What do we do?" Ana whispered, a bright and nervous light in her eye. "I'd rather not be stitching up my own tongue, you know."

Without Gabel around, things would get rowdy with the males. "Flint's still here, and Flint can rip a war-form in two. It's not the first time I've had to mind IronMoon on my own. He wouldn't have gone far."

"Gianna, I've seen him snap. I've *seen* it."

"He *wants* the baby."

"Except you didn't tell him you weren't going to tell the world who the daddy is and isn't."

"*He's* the father. He's the father like my father was my father!" I had no patience for that nonsense. "And anyway, I never said we'd go with Aaron's version of events permanently, just that there's no point inviting more trouble."

"Hey, you don't have to tell *me*."

I scowled. "If he's really run off because he's dick-hurt, he can keep running. I can't believe he'd do it, but if he's turned into a cretin, fine. I'll let the world keep believing whatever they want. Don't worry." I softened my tone. "I'll keep you safe. Promise. And I don't believe he's actually run off."

Ana grimaced. "I hope you're right, but I've seen him lose his mind. If one thing's going to unhinge him, it'll be the Moon using Aaron to fuck with him."

I swallowed the salty lump in my throat. He had abandoned everything to come for me in IceMaw. He wouldn't have let me go. He'd sworn he'd never do it again.

"Maybe he's gone out to find a deer or something." I didn't believe it, but who knew what went through his head sometimes. He did love bringing me prey. No reason to think my being pregnant wouldn't give him some drive to bring me something fresh and bloody.

"Hey, lies we tell ourselves."

"I don't like this," I agreed. "I *really* don't like this. But just pretend everything's as it should be. We'll be safe as long as Flint's around."

GABEL STILL HADN'T SHOWN UP BY LUNCH.

He wasn't in our room, my blue bedroom, the sunroom, the sitting room, or the basement. Time to go to his office to see if his map would hold any clues.

The office lights were off. He had not been in here since I'd stuck my head in after breakfast.

"The hell, Gabel." I stalked over to his map. "Where the hell are you?"

The blue tourmaline he kept on his desk was missing.

Aaron's ghost perked his ears.

I slammed a mental door on his paws, then ignored his pacing. I smoothed my hand over the place where the spear normally was on his desk. Pulled open a few drawers, not that it would have fit into them. Nothing but papers and random envelopes.

Skeletal claws tapped up my spine.

Where... where... where...

SHUT UP.

I spotted something through the railing of the second floor.

I gasped, grabbed the railing, torn between if I needed to scream in terror or beat the snot out of my mate for being dumb.

"What are you doing?!" I dropped to my knees and crawled over to him, reached to grab him, caught myself.

He was in lupine form, on his chest, snout on his forepaws,

with the tourmaline spear clutched between his claws. His eyes were shut.

He'd used the blue tourmaline to visit me in the cherry grove while I'd been in SableFur. He'd come for me in deep visions before. Ana had said she'd found him clutching it and comatose. Except this time *I wasn't on the other side.*

"Am I going to have to come find you, you stupid wolf?"

I picked myself back up and headed out of the office, upstairs to my workroom, and retrieved the metal bowl, despite the smoldering hum of the tektite.

Moon, how could *You let him through the tourmaline without me on the other side!*

I marched back to his office, then set my bowl down with great care opposite Gabel's prone form.

Even like this he looked dangerous.

...Gianna...

GO AWAY!

...Gianna...

Aaron's ghost paced, whispering my name as I tried to calm and clear myself and focus on the Bond. But *his* Bond was there too, and he twisted himself around my awareness.

LEAVE ME ALONE!

His skeletal claws slid over me, his fur twisted around me.

...I love you. I would never leave you...

LEAVE ME ALONE!

... No...

HOW CAN YOU DO THIS! YOU CAN'T DO THIS!

I jerked my spine in an arch and opened my eyes, a howl in my throat as the stupid wolf paced the Tides, refusing to let me in.

Keep giving me reasons to hate you. One day I will hate you so much you will be forced to accept it!

...never...

Gabel's office was lined with old weapons and armor, along

with a few pieces of art, antique rugs, and books. In fact, on the wall just behind him, was a set of bladed claw weapons with twinkling sharp points.

I took a deep breath and put the meaty part of my forearm, just below the elbow joint, against the blade's tip.

One. Two. *Three.*

I stabbed myself on the tip of the blade.

The blades were so sharp my skin parted like wrapping paper under sharp scissors.

Blood welled up from the slice and ran down my forearm onto my wrist to cover my hand.

I shoved my bloody hand in front of Gabel's snout.

His nose twitched.

Then his leathery maw wriggled, his stumpy little leather ears twitched, and he made a thin, crackly growl.

"Come back." Blood dripped onto his snout. "Come back, Gabel."

A few more twitchy moments, and his eyes opened, strange washes of fetid green-yellow pierced by dark pupil.

"What the *fuck* were you doing, you stupid wolf?" I asked sweetly, still dripping blood onto him.

He surged back, or tried to. He flopped and scrambled as his body creaked and wobbled.

Well, hell, the Silvery Moon Bitch really *had* let him go through the tourmaline.

...he will destroy everything he touches...
NOT INTERESTED RIGHT NOW.

I snatched the blue tourmaline out of reach. His claws raked the polished wood floor, he flopped into a half-sitting position, panting, then abruptly regained full control of his body and twisted into human form.

I recoiled in shock.

"What did you *do!*" He lunged at me. I yelped and scrambled backwards, he tackled me and pinned me to the floor. The tourmaline rolled away.

"Gabel, it's me!" I shouted. "It's *me*!"

"I know it's you!" he snarled, "What did you *do*!"

"What are you talking about! I didn't make you use the tourmaline!"

"I mean *this!*" He grabbed my hand and pointed to the gash on my arm.

"Get off me, you stupid wolf! You're scaring me and I'm pregnant! Or did you forget about *that* fight!"

He scrambled back off me, coiled like a serpent for a moment, then hauled me to my feet.

"Hey! Wait a second!"

"You're still bleeding. This needs stitches."

"Will you stop!" I wrestled my way free. My arm was all bloody so it was easy to slide out of his grasp. I snatched up the spear and brandished it. "What the fuck were you doing!"

"Will you focus on what's important!"

"I am going to stand here and bleed until you answer me! Where were you? What were you doing!"

"I don't know where I was," he said tersely. "And I didn't see anything specific."

"You got lost on the goddamn Tides! What the *fuck!*"

"Shouldn't you be howling at the Moon then?" He noticed the bowl on the ground. "Were you about to scry*?*"

"Aaron blocked me!"

"Have you lost your mind?"

"Have you lost *yours*? You know what this thing can do!" I screamed. I flung the spear with a howl.

It arched through the air and smashed through the large window. The pane shattered.

Gabel blinked.

Oh, hell.

"Buttercup," Gabel said, although he sounded like he was trying not to laugh. "Really. Temper, temper."

I let out all my breath. "At least the whole window didn't break?"

"I do not give a damn about the window." He grabbed my bloody hand. "You're bleeding. The more you bleed, the less blood there is for the pup."

"Actually, I'm making extra blood—"

"That's just more for you to bleed. Let's *go*."

"What the hell were you doing with that rock?" I demanded as he pulled me down the hall in pursuit of Ana. I dripped blood on the way.

"Does it matter? I wasn't successful."

"You were trying to get to Aaron! You idiot, you can't do that! The Moon shouldn't even have—" This was too crazy. This was all insane.

"I've used that stone before to find you, why couldn't I find Aaron?"

"Because I've always been on the other side!"

He snorted.

"Gabel, you can never do that again," I pleaded. "I don't even know *how* you're doing it, or where we go when we do, but you can never do that again. You can't!"

He ignored me as he tapped on Ana's door.

"Promise me you'll never do that again."

"No."

"*Promise.*"

"No."

Ana pulled open the door, a length of red licorice sticking out of the corner of her mouth. "Heard the crash. Oh, hello. You're bleeding pretty good there."

"Gabel decided to try to scry in that fucking spear to chase Aaron's soul and I cut myself on something sharp so the scent of my blood would get him back," I told her, annoyed. "He was up on the second floor of his office this whole time Moon-knows-where."

"Yes, She probably does," Gabel said flatly. "Doctor, I will leave her to you. I have a spear to retrieve—"

"You better throw that thing into a deep pit," I snarled.

"And a window pane to replace. And blood to clean up."

"Gabel, I mean it. Get rid of that thing. You aren't going to get to Aaron!"

...no, he won't...

Aaron howled his laughter. I cringed and clutched my head.

Gabel walked away and left me to Ana's tender ministrations.

A Particular Gift

I was getting a little tired of being yanked out of work by howls—this time; the howls summoning the Alpha, but not the rest of the warriors. Not howls that sang *invasion!* Just *unwelcome guest*.

"What now?" I tossed my pen. It bounced across the table and onto the floor, and for some stupid reason, I nearly burst into tears before falling asleep on the table again.

Being pregnant *sucked*. This was not fun, nor cozy, and I definitely was not *glowing*.

"Does it always have to be so dramatic?" Ana asked with an eye roll. "Stop shouting up the stairs, for fuck's sake."

I snickered. "You mean barking there's a squirrel on the lawn?"

She guffawed.

"If I thought me saying we don't need it to be howls all the time wouldn't get me side-eyed for being a petty bitch, I'd suggest it." But it would, and the wolves would probably howl louder in a *I'm not touching you* way and then there'd be more tongues at breakfast.

We headed in the direction of the howls. This better be

good. A few new fat koi swam around the repaired pool in the foyer—Gabel had abruptly shown up with three of them a few days earlier.

The heat of the day hit like a fist. Then our new arrivals hit me again.

It was Lucas. And Kiery.

I ran forward a few steps until a warrior stopped me. "Luna, wait."

"Don't touch me," I snarled. He yanked his hands back and glanced nervously towards Gabel, who was on his way around the side of the house, with the other warriors he'd been training with in tow, including Flint.

Lucas and Kiery had two wolves with them. And by "with" them, I mean wearing heavy leather collars around bloody necks. Lucas had on a kilt, his body battered and bruised, but his head thrown back in defiant pride, his now-healed Mark clear on his arm. Kiery, looking exhausted but also defiant, stood at his side, wearing a tee-shirt she'd cut the shoulders off of to expose her own matching scar and pale, Moon-touched skin, and she also had a red silk cord around her neck. Looked like she'd stolen it off some drapery. Over her back was a red backpack she probably had stolen off a human.

Holy shit, they'd gotten here under Oracle protection.

But why the *fuck* weren't they at SableFur? What had happened at the heart? And who the hell were the wolves with them? And why did they look like they'd been on the receiving end of a very bad day? They'd been beaten into soft, puffy pulps and were on their knees, shoulders bent, heads practically on the gravel, and trickled drying blood like wax melting off a candle.

"Luna Gianna." Lucas swept low in a bow to me, showing me the length of his muscled spine. He had a deep claw-mark cutting into the beef.

"Lucas." Was he still First Beta? Was he a rogue? A lone wolf?

...Gianna...

I kicked Aaron's soul away.

"Elder Oracle." Hoped I didn't sound like I was choking on my own throat.

"Luna," Kiery said in kind.

The scouts that had been on duty and brought Lucas and Kiery to the house circled around Gabel. One shifted into human form and practically groveled at Gabel's feet like he'd brought the Alpha a choice price. "The Oracle said we had to let her pass. She was wearing a red cord."

Gabel glared at the scout and he scuttled away. He took a single step forward, head cocked, as he eyed Lucas. "Oracles do have right of passage, but I very much doubt *this* Elder Oracle is here on Oracle business, or she would have left her pet at home."

Kiery met Gabel's gaze directly, her tone unimpressed. "He is not my *pet*. He is my mate."

"So a male hiding behind a female's prestige. Do you feed him from your plate as well?"

Lucas moved, but Kiery smacked her hand into his chest. "He is an Elder Oracle's mate, and due tolerance for that fact alone. And as to why I am here, that isn't your question, and it's not your answer."

So the Moon had re-opened Her Eye to Kiery?

Gabel's lips curled and his tone took on a terrible, amused warmth. "What brings you to IronMoon, Elder Oracle, that you would grace my pack with a second Oracle? Or do you simply need me to feed your pet?"

"Gabel." I stepped to the edge of the walk.

Lucas smirked and made a gesture like he was putting on a collar.

Kiery smacked his chest again.

Gabel gave me a look, then flicked his chin slightly, and turned his attention back to Kiery, visibly arranging his posture to communicate grudging reasonableness.

Kiery lowered her hand, and Lucas stepped past her. He kicked one of the collared wolves in the back. The wolf fell forward onto the gravel, gibbering and weeping as he ate rocks. With his foot on the wolf's back, Lucas told Gabel, "I know you're taking prey from SableFur. So I brought you prey you wouldn't have known about or found on your own. Twin brothers."

Gabel weighed Kiery, then turned his attention to Lucas. "And why, SableFur, would you have brought me prey cut from your own belly?"

"These were cut from Adrianna's belly. They are from the northern reaches." Lucas delivered a kick to the second wolf. "I know you are hunting related males. Fathers and sons. Brothers. So I have brought you twins. They have not been seriously damaged. Merely restrained. They also have other siblings. Family looking for them."

What the hell? Since when was Gabel hunting families? "Why are you *here*, Lucas? You should be in SableFur's heart!"

And where was Donovan? He wasn't getting paid for this.

Lucas swung his gaze to me. "There's no blood left in the SableFur heart. We decided to see it abandoned rather than destroyed. We nailed Bernhard with silver spikes to the door of the Hall and left. The heart was pierced, the blood drained, and congealed."

That was an Oracle's speech if I'd ever heard one. "So there's no one in SableFur's heart right now."

"No," Lucas said. "Adrianna can have it. No one will greet her except the damned."

My mind spun. I fought it down and grabbed onto anything to keep my mind level.

...Gianna...

Ana grabbed my arm and pushed me upright again.

Gabel turned dark anger on Lucas. "And yet you come here, bringing me these gifts, when you abandoned your Luna to

Aaron of IceMaw? You were content to just let him keep her and maul her?"

Lucas bowed his head.

Gabel paced closer, and this time Kiery didn't try to intervene. "What did you do, First Beta, when you heard what he'd done to her? You abandoned her, then you abandoned your pack, and you come here hiding behind an Oracle? You aren't even the first Beta to come here, groveling, and you aren't doing it *nearly* so well. First Beta Carlos of IceMaw brought her IceMaw, you haven't even offered her your spine. Your life dangles at the end of that red cord around your mate's neck."

Gabel's disgust was cold and barren, like the dampness of the basement against my skin.

"Are you going to be the one to cut it? So you can have the last Oracle?" Kiery asked Gabel.

"You mistake me for my father. I don't build my strength from stolen divinity."

I stepped down off the walk. "Is it true, Kiery? We're the last in the world?"

Her voice cracked with grief. "Our sisters are dead or worse, Gianna. The Moon has shown me we are the last. All that remains aside from us are a handful of scattered Seer girls too young to train who may never come into their gifts. The Moon's Eye threatens to close forever."

Gabel crossed the distance between us, sliding one arm across me, head turned to keep one eye on the others. He pushed slightly. I didn't budge. "Thank you, Lucas. Your gift is appreciated."

The *gift* probably didn't appreciate whatever Gabel was going to do to them.

One of the brothers raised his head. "Luna, no, please! Please!"

A chill stole over me. "You called *Adrianna* Luna, wolf, and you *dare* switch your allegiance just to save your neck?"

Gabel clicked his teeth.

"I have no use for wolves like you," I told them.

Gabel smiled cruelly. "But I do."

The Bond twitched like a muscle clenching, but then it clenched harder as if he had stopped himself from moving. "Before I feed him, Flint, make certain he won't find a swift end once his mate leaves him unattended. And make certain he knows his manners. Given he *still* has not apologized, I don't believe he's been well-raised."

"And if he is lacking?" Flint inquired.

"She will have to keep him on a little red leash. I wouldn't want to damage the last Elder Oracle's soul. Gianna would find it distressing."

Lucas grinned. "And may anger the Moon."

Gabel's smile reappeared, smoldering and cruel. "It already has, wolf. I *am* the Moon's Wrath."

DROWNING

Kiery looked around my workroom, careful to avoid the salt circle that circumscribed my workspace.

Flint had taken the red cord from her and led Lucas out back.

She seemed haunted. "Will Flint kill him?"

"No. You can trust Flint. But this isn't the pack for a male to hide behind a female," I said. Flint would force Lucas to show he wasn't a wolf to pick a fight with, and it wouldn't be pretty. But it would be effective.

"No other choice. I'm the only one with prestige right now." She hugged herself. "I'm so sorry. We didn't think Aaron would..."

I shook my head.

"SableFur was... shocked. It's hard to explain. You weren't... popular, I guess, as a Luna, but... you were still the Luna. It was devastating. I'm sorry, I can't imagine what it was..."

I gulped.

"Lucas wanted to go get you... I'm just going to stop talking." She hung her head.

"I wouldn't have wanted him to leave SableFur to rescue me. He knew that. *You* knew that."

She sort of breathed out a single sad laugh. "He wouldn't have had to do a lot of convincing. Wolves were pissed. Mostly embarrassed, if I'm being cynical, which I am. Then Aaron sold out Bernhard and the shit hit the fan."

"Is that when the Moon opened Her Eye again to you?"

"I had a dream, and Lucas interpreted it to mean it was time to abandon the heart. We nailed Bernhard to the hall, and everyone... headed out. Lucas and I were the last to go, and we sort of wandered around, lone-wolves but not. Then I had another dream about twin wolves in the north—and that they'd be keys."

I frowned. "Keys."

"It was a strange dream. I dreamt of a large charred heart smashed into a hillside, and on it was a door, and the wolves in my vision were marked with the rune for *key*."

"A heart like a dark comet?"

"A heart like a dark comet. All charred and smoldering and smashed into a crater."

"So what happened when you... put the keys in the door?"

"Well, the wolves turned to large fangs in my hand, and the keys slid into the lock, and the door didn't open, but the charred, bloody heart started to sink into the smashed earth, and water started to rise then spread outwards in rivulets."

The scab-island at the Edge of the Tides. The one where all the blood ran into the water. And how I always came to it through the grotto that either led to the jungle temple or the forest with the ruined shack.

"Anyway, I figured we might as well find these two wolves and bring them to the only comet with a heart I know of: Gabel. Lucas knew exactly who I was talking about, and the dream showed me exactly where to find them, and when I saw them I said those are the wolves. So we made off with them."

"And all the other wolves of the heart..."

"Went south, some said they were going to find you," Kiery said. She added, "I guess they didn't make it."

Or they weren't here yet.

She changed the subject. "When's the pup due?"

I felt my waistline. Definite swell now, not just pudgy from enjoying Cook's food. "You can tell."

"Lucas smelled it instantly. Is it... Aaron's?"

"It's Gabel's," I said flatly. "And Solstice."

She barked a laugh. "Seems appropriate."

"Seems like it's coming too fast."

"Chop chop, Balance-Keeper, we've got a schedule." She tapped her wrist.

Clearly. The Moon wanted this matter mopped up before the new year. "I guess you never found anything at the heart about the Oracle of Mirrors."

"You know I didn't."

"And what about your family? You told me before Magnes died to head south to NightScent."

She tossed her hair back. "My mom didn't want me to go to SableFur to train. Too many rumors of girl-pups never coming back. There was a distant cousin who would have been about the right age and maybe ability."

"Can we call her? Ask?"

"Already did. She didn't remember the cousin's name. She'd never actually met the cousin, just heard the story lumped in with all the others. That and she told me not to call her anymore because apparently I'm a renegade."

"Nice."

"Isn't it though."

"I wonder how much of this was Anita. Weeding out the weakest ones to limit supply. I've started to wonder how much she *didn't* tell us. Like how blue gloss gets its gloss. The *IceMaw* knew, how did *we* not know?"

"It was how she controlled us. I see that now. Hell, I am an Elder Oracle and that bitch still pulled my strings. Moon, I feel so *stupid*." She dragged her hands over her face.

I picked up the bag of tektite runestones. I shifted the runestones, then reached into my pocket, and after a moment, called Carlos.

"Luna," Carlos said instantly, tone too crisp and eager.

"Carlos, my tektite runestones."

"They are all there, Luna, exactly as you left them. No one touched them."

"Yes, yes, I know. But do you know the stonecutter Aaron sent them to?"

"Of course."

"Can you ask the stonecutter if the request Aaron sent included a stone for *waterfall*, *comet*, or *blessing*?"

A pause, then, "Of course."

"Right now, please."

"But all your stones are there—"

"Carlos." I growled.

"Yes, ma'am."

"There's no runestone for blessing or comet," Kiery said. "And what the fuck is a tektite?"

"Look it up, and know I have a bowl and set of runestones made from it. And yes, scrying in it is exactly as terrifying as you would expect."

Kiery pulled out her own phone and consulted it. "*What the fuck*. You have a *bowl made from that*?"

"Yes."

"Glass made from an asteroid impact."

"Yes."

"That's *millions* of years old."

"Yes, and still pissed about it."

"And you *use* it?"

"Yes."

"And Aaron gave it to you?"

"Aaron had a whole stockpile of bowl-appropriate gems and a stonecutter. He didn't trust SableFur."

"Which means *you* now have a stockpile and stonecutter." She tapped me on the head. "Hello. *Hello.*"

"Oh," I said intelligently. "I guess... I do. As long as the IceMaw think I'm still their Luna."

Kiery raised a brow. "Because the SableFur stonecutter's dead, you know. Adrianna killed him. Well, that's the assumption."

I sighed. "That bitch..."

"Except he was in the south and the southern part of the pack didn't really like that very much. Gabel's not considered dumb enough to head south to kill some random stonecutter."

Interesting.

My phone rang. Carlos.

"No, Luna," Carlos said, voice heavy with apology. "The stonecutter says the list from Alpha Aaron only included *waterfall*. He said he doesn't know the runes for *blessing* or *comet*, but if you send a design, he can make them for you."

"And have an unmatched set? That's dangerous, Carlos." I hung up on him. Best he not think he was in my good graces again.

"What are you about?" Kiery asked.

I found the runestone for comet easily enough and grabbed a random other one. Normally, I'd never show my tools to anyone, but other Oracles were an exception.

I ran my finger over the sigil. *Comet.* Exactly like the others of the set. Nothing unusual about it. I set it in my palm and held them both out to Kiery. "Aaron ordered the set, but the stonecutter confirmed he never made one for *comet.*"

The tektite was distinctive. It was not like obsidian or anything else, it was clearly something *else*, and these two stones matched.

"They match," she agreed.

"I have to find Gabel."

I ran down the stairs, the hallway, spun my way down the twisting staircase to the first floor.

"Gianna, slow down," Kiery said behind me.

"I'm pregnant, not an invalid." I passed the hallway door to the basement. Two wolves stood outside it.

"He said he didn't want to be disturbed," one wolf told me as I approached.

As if I'd ever taken orders from Gabel. And it wasn't like I *wanted* to go down there anymore than he wanted to be disturbed. I'd call it a hellhole, but that'd be an insult to Hell. "How very nice for him. I don't care."

"He said no." The other wolf extended his arm across the door.

"And the Lord-Alpha cannot command *me* to do anything. Open the door," I told the smarter-looking of the two.

After a moment of hesitation, he twisted the knob and pulled the door open. The darkness of the staircase awaited, and unholy, cold, dead air rushed up. Even through my pregnancy-dull nose, I could smell the bleach and despair.

"What is that place?" Kiery whispered over my shoulder.

"A place the Moon does not care to look. Stay up here." I set foot on the first step, then the next, then the next.

The door closed behind me.

"You should not be here, buttercup." Gabel's voice came to me in the dark.

The agonizing stillness was punctuated with a soft male gibber-moaning.

A single chair sat in the center of the clean concrete floor, while a sturdy wooden table with a trough cut through its slightly angled halves was on the far wall that housed the shackles bolted into the walls. A human-form wolf—the son of the first pair Renzo had brought—lay on his back, spread-eagle and strapped down.

Of the cells along the walls, two were occupied. The moaning came from one of them, where the lights were dim. In one, one human form huddled, and in the other, two wolf forms huddled in the farthest corner. The human form gibbered sounds of utter anguish. The wolf forms—the twins—were so still they might have been dead.

"You should not be here," Gabel said again, voice a restrained rumble, even though he looked furious, and the Bond burned with his anger.

A curious stillness stole over me. I paused as my hand felt along the back of the simple metal chair. My bond to Aaron.

Just... stillness. Quiet. Peace. Just Gabel. His own little pocket realm. A place *really* beyond the Tides.

I pulled myself back together and tried not to look at what Gabel had done to the son-wolf. There was something in his mouth, but the basement seemed full of his terrified, rasping breathing. His skin had raised lesions all over it, and his fingers and toes and the soles of his feet looked swollen and misshapen. Ironically, Gabel had not stripped him naked, but afforded him the mockery of modesty with a clean kilt that did not appear to be sullied with blood.

Gabel, wearing a crisp button-down shirt and pants, with just his sleeves rolled up to his forearms, had no blood on him either, not even on his bare feet. "You *cannot* be down here."

How odd, because I clearly *was* down here. The pup burned like a little golden gemstone inside me. The bond to Gabel, on the other hand, writhed with his aggravation and worry. "We're fine."

Gabel spun on his bare foot. He went to the utility sink on the darkened wall and scrubbed his hands and arms with a dark, raw soap, carefully cleaning under his nails with a little brush.

"What was so important you came down *here* in your condition?"

My *condition*? "It won't wait. Leave your...project... for a moment."

Gabel flicked water off his arms. "Upstairs."

Fine. *FINE.*

Jerk.

As I stepped back over the threshold into the upstairs, the *din* of everything spun me around. My bond to Aaron slammed back into me and his howls rattled my skull, and my Seer gifts threatened to explode in my head as the Tides rushed over me with whispering and churning.

Gabel grabbed me before I dropped to my knees.

"*Stop!*" I rasped as I choked on the Tides burbling up in my throat. "*Stop, stop...*"

A Ring, Discarded

... G *ianna...Gianna, I lost you...where did you go...*
His touch was like a dying, grasping hand,
his howls panicked.

My throat tried to answer his howls.

Gore and glass rained from the skies.

...NO, NO, I PREVENTED THIS...

...Gianna, come to me...

And I was smashing something against the stone altar as the
burning rain soaked me and I sobbed and I *smashed and I
smashed and I smashed* and it was so bloody and wet and I was
there, and it *burned...*

...no, no, I can't keep doing this, no, no...

Dark heat burned through the rain, the howls, the storm
and tore it all apart, set it all on fire, evaporated it.

MINE

Something like teeth lunged at the other Bond. Jaws
snapped over me and sank into me and *yanked*.

I think I screamed.

I shook off the hold, the gurgling, and fought to push all of
it away.

I was on my knees, staring at the floor, one hand cradling my stomach, the other braced on Gabel's shoulder. His leathery, war-form shoulder, and his maw was closed over the nape of my neck.

Nauseating salt and brine coated the back of my throat. The storm and din drenched my mind and Aaron howled and howled and *howled*, eroding my brain like the ocean wore a beach.

"No," I gasped, "I stopped this... I stopped it... I chose. I *chose.*"

Gabel's growl rattled like bones, the razor-sharp tips of his fangs *just* breaking my skin with a sweet, gentle pinch. He could have bitten right through my spine. "*Miiinneeee.*"

He growled with the weight of burning sky.

I grabbed hold of him and hauled my brain out of the Tides. He shifted back into human form in my grip, releasing my neck and replacing the grip with one hand buried in my hair.

The storm didn't ease, but the shock of it roaring up on me faded. I coughed and gagged once on the thick brine choking my throat.

Gabel still had his hand on the back of my head. I headed (slowly) towards the kitchen with him still holding my hair. What was he going to do, catch me by it? I was afraid to swat at him in case I jarred something loose.

Kiery moved ahead to pour me a fizzy drink and ransacked the pantry until she located a few crackers. She slid the sleeve at me while I sipped the drink and it burned away the rotten gurgling feeling.

Aaron continued to howl and pace like an angry junkyard dog that had caught a whiff of a cat, while Gabel burned like a bug lantern too close to my hair.

"The basement is *no* place for you," Gabel growled.

I laughed miserably. "Don't you remember showing it to me, waiting for me to flinch?"

"Now you're *pregnant*."

"The pup was safe."

"The pup shouldn't be anywhere near it. You aren't thinking clearly."

"Don't tell me what I'm thinking."

"*Sit*." He all but shoved me onto one of the stools. "What were you doing down there?"

I shoved my hand in my pocket and slapped the two runestones on the counter.

"Runestones?" Gabel asked warily.

"From the tektite set *he* had made for me."

"And?"

"The IceMaw stonecutter didn't make one for *comet*. There's no rune for *comet*. Just some old sigil that barely anyone remembers."

Gabel picked up the *comet* runestone. "It looks quite real to me."

"Of course it's real! That's the point! Everything the Moon's showed me has been *real*. Real places, real things, not visions!"

Gabel gripped the stone. "You think the Moon created this and put it with your set?"

"I know I sound crazy! But do you remember when we had sex in the cherry grove vision? How you used the blue tourmaline to find me? Well, I woke up with *you* on my thighs."

The smoldering Bond shifted with his doubt.

Kiery said, "That is true. Lucas was unnerved. It made for some awkward conversation."

I grabbed Gabel's forearm. "We've been to where I saw *him* for the first time. I don't think your mother's tools were thrown into that thicket. Adrianna and Magnes were too meticulous. The Moon *put them there for me to find*. And a dream led me there. Oracles live in fear of the line between our visions and reality blurring, because we can get lost on the Tides. We're also taught the Tides are *very* real, but the visions aren't. They're reflections, or glimpses, or messages. *Visions aren't real*. That's what you get taught so you stay sane: *it's not real*."

Gabel didn't seem to blink.

"But this is real!" I pleaded with him. "I was made with a hole in my soul. When you Marked me, something changed. I started to see myself in visions. I became *part* of the visions. Everything in every vision and dream I've had since then has had something for *me* in it. A clue. Something. And I've gone Beyond The Tides. I think we've even been to Hell when you found me. I keep choking on the Tides. They're coming through the hole in my soul."

"Gianna, you should eat a few more crackers." Kiery pushed the sleeve towards me.

Gabel picked up a cracker.

I pushed his hand away. "Listen to me! The veil's thin and the Moon's passing things through it. Can you find your old home in the northern forests? Where you lived with your mother."

Only the heavy pulse in his neck and the throb of the bond said Gabel was still in there. "Why?"

"I want to look for the pup-ring I saw," I said. "If I can find it, if it's *real*, then it's proof of... I don't know, something! Everywhere else I've been has been *real*. I've been to that burned out shack numerous times. It opens up onto the grotto on the Island at the Edge of the Tides."

"Gianna," Kiery said in her best teacher voice, "slow down. Eat some food."

I smacked at her hand as she tried to touch me, then whirled back around on Gabel. "We go to the northern forests. You and I. We have to do it before I get anymore pregnant. I can still get there on my paws."

Gabel glared. "My mother didn't have a ring, and she didn't have a box."

"We'll find one!" I said stubbornly.

"No, we won't, because I am not taking you for a hike through the northern forests."

"I am fine. I feel fine."

"Do you not remember the past twenty minutes?"

"That wasn't the baby. That was... the noise."

"There was no noise. I am done discussing this."

"I can't feel Aaron when I'm down there," I blurted out.

He paused before he walked away. "But you can feel *me*?"

"Of course I can feel you. But I can't feel *him*. It's outside the Moon's domain. Just... it was... still. And then it wasn't again. He was panicked that he had lost me. He... grabbed."

Gabel's annoyance settled, and he seethed, but in that satisfied banked-coal way that he always did when contemplating something. He slid his hands down my arms. Picked at my bra strap to resettle it. "You cannot feel him down there. Not at all."

"No, it's a tomb."

"That is interesting. And no, we are not going to my childhood home. There is nothing there."

Nope. Not taking that for an answer. I would call Carlos and pack up Lucas and we'd tear that forest apart if we had to. I was going while I could still be in wolf form scrambling over pine needles and rocks. "*Every* vision I've had since meeting you has had some part of it meant for *me*. The only vision I haven't found reflected back at me is the shack in the forest containing that box and the pup-ring. I haven't found it yet. I *have* to find it."

He ran his thumb over my lips, pushed past them, raked my gums. "Even if there is a ring, it proves nothing except the Moon is tossing things at us like we're ducks in a pond. I am done running after crumbs."

"But it could be important!"

Gabel dropped his hand. "No."

"Are you afraid we'll find it?"

Gabel's eyes narrowed and hardened to tourmaline. "If She

wants you to have the ring, tell Her to deposit it in your work-room. This is a trap, and an obvious one: take my pregnant mate forty miles overland in high summer to chase a ring that means nothing. I am not taking the bait. Not this time. And I am not letting *you* take it, either. End of conversation."

GABEL - HEART OF
FOUR CHAMBERS

He crouched on his belly, snout on his forepaws, and stared at the tourmaline spear that he'd placed on the floor at the tip of his claws. It seemed foolish to be up in his office at all, and even more foolish to have retreated to the second floor, in one of the corners tucked in among an old globe and the bookshelves.

Was this what *sulking* was? Or was it being *pensive,* as an adult was permitted to be?

His spine tingled from the base of his skull to the tip of his tail and something gnawed on his brain urging him to do *something*.

And that something was *not* going to be to give in to Gianna's demand to go to the forests.

To hunt for a ring that didn't matter, even if it did exist. Did she not see how foolish this was? Why couldn't she demand he give her prey or water or *anything* but this? Hadn't she learned a damn thing about what happened when the Moon dangled something in front of her?

That goddess had *taken her and not given her back.* He'd

gone against every instinct She had given him, every promise he'd made in Her name, and he'd taken it on faith that wouldn't be betrayed. But that was *exactly* what had happened, and worse: Gianna had been besmirched, tortured, silvered, held prisoner, barely fed, abused, and made to suffer over and over and over and *over* again. And even *then* she'd been trapped by Lucas giving her the crown of SableFur while the Moon laughed and blasted the blue-gloss Mark onto them.

And *still* he had humored his mate's request to stay away.

And *still* they had been betrayed.

And *still* the Moon had allowed Aaron's Mark to remain.

And *still* the Moon used her.

Over and over and *over*.

Even the baby! It was a miracle she'd gotten pregnant. He was not such a feral idiot that he didn't know it took time for a female to recover from silvering. *Gianna* did not realize it was a miracle. She was too wrapped up in the other stupid miracles of the Moon conjuring runestones and chasing rings. It was as if she did not *care*.

Of course she cared.

She was also a fierce hunter. A wonderful predator. She did not hunt rabbits or deer, she hunted dreams and souls and secrets. A divine hunter, relentless and fearless. She wanted to stop the war. She wanted to defeat Adrianna.

So fierce. So ambitious. So demanding. So insistent that these things be obtained, and that if he would not provide them, *she* would wrestle them from the Maw of the Moon herself.

He licked his chops.

So fucking *infuriating*.

And there was not a goddamn chance he was going to let her chase the Moon again.

She picked at her food and turned most of it away as too nauseating. Her barely-healed hands would not be paws tough enough to handle fifty miles over rough forest terrain.

It was impossible. Letting her try was dangerous.

The Silvery Sky Bitch was just *daring* him at this point. The taunt would not go unnoticed.

So Gianna would have to be angry with him, and not the *fun* angry. The bad-angry where she refused to even chew on him and curled up on her side of the bed and gave off that scent of *leave me alone*. The fun-angry was when she wanted to bite and scratch him and draw blood but didn't permit herself.

That was the most fun.

No, the *most* fun was goading her into giving in to her anger. Then she turned it on him in a sweet, fiery storm that danced over his soul like lightening strikes.

He wagged his rat-like tail. *That* was the best kind of anger.

This was not that anger. This was the bad-angry. This was the *chasm* and the *shadows* and *the cold needles*.

He slicked his ears as his whole body clenched.

He had passed the first test: he had not given in to the temptation of the warrior she-wolf. But he had failed all the others. First with Gardenia, then with Anders, then dragging Gianna to the RedWater fight, letting her go to SableFur, letting her delay returning to him.

And her visions had become more nightmarish, more extreme, until now he wore a crown of gore and she died.

She had seen it as a test of faith, but why would the Moon test *their* faith?

When he'd first started to gather wolves to the IronMoon pack, Flint had taken him aside and explained an Alpha did not test his wolves' loyalty without reason, and that demanding much of a wolf meant an equal reward.

This was *not* a test for Gianna. Gianna had passed all the tests. She had answered every call.

This was a test for *him*. *He* had failed all the tests. The Moon was taunting *him*, and using his mate to do it. Perhaps revenge for how it had all begun, or goading him into being the very best Destroyer he could be.

...you destroy everything you touch...

"No." He snarled at the echo of Aaron's voice. No, he would *not*. His kingdom would not crumble like Gianna had foretold! His pups would not inherit a pile of bodies and bones. *No.*

He struck the tourmaline. It didn't oblige him by toppling.

"I will find a way," he hissed. *"You think I do not hear you, IceMaw? I heard every word you said."*

He would not fail.

If it goes on forever, then I will be endless.

And there was a glimmer of hope: Aaron could not reach her in the basement.

...so no other wolf is worthy of your gaze...

He had not realized the din she lived with—she'd been hiding her torment from him. Perhaps from herself. Inured to it because she was an Oracle and trained to the constant noise.

There had to be a way to free Gianna. There had to be a way to protect her for more than a few moments at a time.

He would not destroy his family. He would not fail his mate.

And he wouldn't fall for the Moon's tricks again.

———

GABEL GLARED AT THE DOOR. IT REEKED OF KIERY AND Lucas.

He settled himself and deigned to knock. It was polite, after all, to knock. Proper etiquette. Flint had taken too many shots about him not using proper manners. Time, perhaps, to display that training. It would keep everyone guessing.

The door opened. Kiery was on the other side.

"Alpha," she said in the distant, respectful-but-not manner of Oracles.

"I am here to speak with your mate," Gabel said.

She stepped aside for him. "He's in the shower."

Flint seemed to appreciate having a good replacement for Hix as a training partner, and Lucas had been able to demonstrate what the SableFur First Beta position had been about.

Gabel stepped past her and to the open bathroom door. The wolf stood under the shower through the clear curtain soaping his dark hair. This wolf had served his father. What had he known? Suspected? What useful information could he perhaps betray?

"Your scent precedes you," Lucas said.

The First Beta's scent saturated the steamy air, revealing a number of things, including his annoyance at being interrupted. He had had other plans that had not involved anyone but his mate.

Too bad. Such things would have to wait. "I have a task for you."

"I do not answer to you."

How entertaining. "You are an Oracle's mate and I suffer your presence on her account. Unless you prefer me to think of you as a First Beta who fled the heart he was sworn to defend to bring prey to your pack's mortal enemy. In which case I would suggest you move along, as I have no use for such a wolf."

"From what I have seen, you very much need me."

"Given you served my father not realizing he was a monster, and then failed your Luna, I am certain I am not interested in your counsel nor opinion. The standards for IronMoon First Betas are quite high. But you'd know that, as you watched my step-mother have my First Beta butchered like livestock." Gabel permitted himself a small grin. Lucas' blood would be delicious.

Gianna would be upset about Lucas being mauled into living paste, but these things were necessary at times.

Lucas turned the water off and shoved the shower curtain back. "What is this task?"

"It involves this matter of the ring and her visions."

Lucas scrunched his hair with a towel. "Not a chance I'm taking her."

"I am glad we agree on this. That is why I will tell *you* where to find my birthplace. If there is a ring there, bring it back."

"Even if the ring exists, it doesn't matter."

Irritating wolf. Surely Kiery could be without him a few nights. "It will be something when I am offering her nothing."

"Bring her a deer."

"She does not want a deer. She wants the ring." But perhaps he would bring her a rabbit. She did enjoy a fresh rabbit, and he could find a summer-fat one now. It would be good for her. Or perhaps fish. There was no reason his mate could not have both the ring *and* prey.

"She also didn't want the deer you brought her at SableFur, but that didn't stop you then."

So much gnawing on his authority, and with such precise skill. Usually his wolves were more direct and crass, but Lucas slid those barbs in so neatly. "How convenient that this is *now*, and I am not *asking*."

Lucas lowered the towel from his head down to his shoulders. Good, this wolf was not afflicted with human modesty. And his scent was not cowed either. Even better.

"Lucas," Kiery said out of the corner of her mouth.

Lucas ignored her. "You have hunters who know the terrain."

"And they are busy elsewhere." Busy as in *dead*, probably running for their souls from the Moon's Hounds, but... busy. Definitely busy.

Lucas didn't move.

How quaint. And how *novel*. The wolf did not crumble like all the other ambitious toads that had croaked at him. He pulled his lips back in a feral, amused grin as his fingernails itched in their beds.

Lucas did not budge. Not so much as a twitch of his jaw or fingers.

Gabel closed the distance between them. Lucas was *very* slightly taller. Smelled of a strange resolved defiance: he wasn't going to do this without a fight. He would not obey. He would be *compelled*.

They understood each other quite precisely.

Gabel struck first, twisting his left arm into a war-form claw as he did, breathing in the pain of his body twisting and breaking to be two things at once. The pain seared its beautiful song. He struck Lucas by the human-form neck, his claw closing neatly over the wolf's thick throat.

Gabel slammed him back into the nearest wall, clenching down on the wolf's throat. Shock flashed across the wolf's face. The same shock every other wolf had: *what the hell are you?*

It was always what came next that told him about his adversary.

Lucas grinned. And in the next second, Gabel's claw was around a war-form neck.

A battle-shifter. Well, well, his father had had *all* the toys, hadn't he?

Lucas smashed him backwards with a clean strike of his dark gray claw and sent Gabel flying out of the bathroom and over the bed.

Gabel neatly landed on his feet. The wolf had had the advantage staying naked. The cunning sent its violent song through his veins.

How exquisite. Wicked delight sent tingles along his bones.

Lucas walked out of the bathroom, back in human form, this time his scent and expression dark. The cocky defiance was gone. The former First Beta had recognized he had picked a fight with something he had never faced before.

But he was not deterred.

What an *excellent* way to start the morning.

And Lucas had even shifted so he wouldn't destroy the floor. How courteous.

"You will do this, wolf," Gabel taunted him, "because you are otherwise useless."

"I have my own mate that requires my presence."

"Mate? You've fallen so far you barely qualify as her pet. She should tie you to a fence at the dog park with a sign *free to good home.*"

"Go find some other male to please your mate," Lucas said. "Wait. He already exists. You couldn't even kill him."

Deep, bloody fury sparked in his gut and Gabel held onto it by a shred. He would answer the taunt with brutal calculation, not blind rage. He twisted his body to the side and gestured to the hallway. "Outside, wolf. Or shall I drag you through the house?"

"I don't think you will be dragging me anywhere."

Gabel dropped into wolf-form and lunged at Lucas. The bigger wolf jerked in surprise. Gabel's fangs closed over his throat just as Lucas' shifted into war-form again, and Lucas flicked his hips, sending them both tumbling into the coffee table.

Excellent. Gabel shifted as they spun, ending up on the bottom, with his hind claws tucked into Lucas' belly. Lucas realized the mistake, twisted into wolf-form, and squirmed away. They tumbled into the hallway.

Gabel shifted again, and grabbed Lucas' ruff, dragging him forward. His war-form claws tore up the floor. Lucas snapped and snarled and managed to twist himself into position to bite Gabel's leg. The wolf's fangs drove into his leathery hide, sending blooms of mediocre pain through him.

"*Unnnnimmpresssivveee. Harrdderrrr.*" He shoved Lucas *into* his leg to drive the fangs deeper. Lucas' jaw stretched and creaked. The SableFur curled into a little ball to brace his hind legs against Gabel's calf and his claws dug through the leathery hide. He squirmed and bucked, becoming impossible to hold, and slipped from Gabel's grip.

Lucas rolled away and sprang up in war-form.

Such lovely shifting, but such sub-standard pain. Surely this wolf was capable of better. Gabel shifted his body position to feign an opening. Lucas took the bait and sprang, and they wrestled, biting and snapping through the foyer (had to avoid the koi pond, it upset Gianna to not have the fishes around), and through the front door. Gabel tossed Lucas onto the stones. Lucas barely seemed to hit the ground as he bounced back up.

So impressive, but still, such *mediocre* pain. His thigh barely stung, and the little bites he'd gotten barely bled. *"Moorreeee."*

Lucas beckoned him with a claw.

Gabel drove one claw forward, Lucas dodged, Gabel bit his shoulder. He could have clamped harder, but resisted the urge to break through the wolf's clavicle. Gianna would not appreciate him seriously wounding this wolf. It also wasn't necessary. He could break Lucas quickly... or slowly.

Slowly would be entertaining.

Kiery emerged through the front doors, along with some other wolves who had heard the fight.

Blood washed over his tongue. Lucas drove his own claw into Gabel's side, grasping for his liver. Liver-pain was unlike anything else, and this wolf's skill at finding the soft, vulnerable spot sent spasms of happiness and agony through him.

"Yesssss," Gabel growled as he twisted his jaw back and forth like a snake consuming prey. Lucas' hide tore, frayed. The liver-pain made it hard to breathe and Lucas' claws skillfully found the *exact* point to press to provoke grinding, brutal pain.

Lucas stomped on his foot and raked his claws through the skin.

Pain burst through every joint in his foot. His claws felt like they would explode off.

Clever. Very clever.

Gabel grinned around the blood flowing over his maw. He wrested his jaw free, then shoved *into* Lucas, driving the pain higher. Lucas staggered in surprise. The normal reaction would be to get *away*.

Lucas' scent bloomed with that shocked surprise. The scent of horror at *what are you.*

Gabel threw him to the ground.

Gianna, her dark hair a storm around her pale face, burst out the front doors. Kiery grabbed her. His Luna whirled on the Elder Oracle. "What the hell is happening?"

Gabel grinned at Lucas and dug his claws into the wolf's neck and leaned down onto Lucas' belly. *"Riiiightttt whereeeee weeee starrrrtedddd."*

The dark gray wolf barred his fangs anyway.

He lowered his lips to Lucas' furry ears. *"Sssuuubbbmittttt."*

A snarl. Lucas' scent said *earn it.*

Adorable. He had already earned it. Lucas just hadn't real-ized it. He twisted his vocal cords so he could whisper. *"Orrrr I willlll breakkkk you whillle ssshee wattcchhesss, thennn rettturn youuuu to her. Yooouuuu willll be tooo brookeeen to eeevven wwiisssh for ddeeaatth."*

Lucas' gaze burned with rage and his scent too, but under it: the fight had been broken. He went backwards into the ground, spine going limp, and raised his chin to expose all of his throat.

Gabel twisted down into human form. His spine snapped into place last with a sweet metallic sting.

"What were you doing?" Gianna demanded, the Bond furious with her anger, hotter than the summer sun.

That storm of dark hair and her stone-colored eyes, and the sweet little swell under her dress, her scent pure and wafting around him on the hot breeze. The things he loved best, espe-cially commingled with the stench of blood and the sweet sting of pain that elevated the triumph. "He picked a fight he could not win."

"Lucas? Picked a fight with you?" She didn't believe him. She was angry. It had the scent of *fun* angry.

Except with the little pup so obviously in her belly, such fun struck him as increasingly inappropriate. The little one had ears, after all.

Behind him, Lucas rolled to his feet and dusted himself off, bleeding from a number of scratches and bites.

Gabel looped a filthy arm around her waist, and tugged her against him. "I am in one piece, my love. Have no fear."

Her nose wrinkled. "I was not worried about you."

"And now you do not need to be worried about Lucas."

Kiery had on the usual composed Oracle mask of interested-but-not-caring. They'd just been waiting for the right time to pick a fight with him. Cunning. Very cunning. Oracles were dangerous adversaries.

Cruel, hot delight baked his insides. Gianna pushed away from him, he tried to hold onto her.

"I told you, buttercup," he teased, dancing in his heart under the little licks of lightening against his soul. "I will never let you go."

"I believe you." She placed both hands on his chest and shoved.

"What do I have to do to win you back to our bed?"

Her adorable little glare didn't ease. She was *just* about to growl at him about bloodying up her pets when Lucas sauntered by and flipped him the finger. Blood trickled down the other wolf's back and ass cheeks.

Gianna turned her glare on Lucas. "For fuck's sake."

"I told you he started it," Gabel whispered by her ear, then he nipped her.

She pushed, her scent bloomed like a flower, but this time he released her. Her lightening-lash anger peppered him like raindrops.

She brushed her hands over the dirt he'd conveyed to her clothing. The red scars on her palms flashed in the bright light against her pale skin. "You are such an ass, Gabel."

He couldn't hide his grin. "I will expect you in our bed tonight, my love."

Go To Sleep

I made good on my threat to sleep in my own room again that night. I was being petulant, but damnit, I *felt* petulant.

This bedroom had a window, and I had it open for the summer breeze, which was a nice change from Gabel's no-window situation and Aaron's paranoid glass cage. The view over the shadowy hills and forests was beautiful, and the light of the half-moon overhead gave everything a slight blue-white wash.

The door opened. Gabel, spectacularly naked, stood on the other side.

I pulled the sheets up around my breasts. If he said anything about being in *our* bed, I was going to bite him.

He got onto the bed next to me. "It occurs to me that since we are mated—"

"Where did Lucas go? He wasn't at dinner, but Kiery was," I said shortly.

He had himself braced on his Marked arm, and the blue lines curved perfectly around his chiseled muscles, and the soft blue halo around the darker glossy edges flickered like candle-light. "Off licking his wounded pride, I imagine. But as I was saying—"

"Bullshit." Lucas wasn't the sort of wolf who slipped off to nurse his wounded pride. "You didn't throw him in the basement, did you?"

"Of course not."

"Then where is he?"

Gabel drew his legs up onto the bed, mischief in his expression, and something impish in the Bond. "As I was saying, it occurs to me that since we are mated, this bed is *also* our bed."

Oh, for fuck's sake.

He used his other hand to pull at some loose hairs by my ear. I batted at his hand. "Lucas better not be in the basement."

A chuckle. "I promise he is not in the basement. I would not put one of your pets—"

"He isn't my pet."

"Fine. He's Kiery's pet then, and I would not offend an Oracle by putting *her* pet into the basement without telling her where to find him."

"But you aren't going to tell me where he is."

"I don't know where he is." Gabel slid under the sheets, but gave the open window and fluttering curtains a look of distaste.

"I like fresh air," I said sweetly. "Does it make you nervous?"

He moved closer so that his body pressed along mine. He kissed my bare shoulder, then slowly traced my blue-gloss Mark with his finger. Then he traced his finger along my shoulder, my collarbone, down my breast, over my nipple, lower, until his hand settled over my belly. He kissed my skin again. "Can you feel the baby moving?"

"It's too early for that."

"Why does me asking make you embarrassed?"

More like squirmy. "I'm not used to you being... squishy."

"Fine. I expect you to birth me a strong male pup fit to lead armies."

I rolled my eyes.

Gabel brushed at my hair. "After breakfast tomorrow, I will be setting my plan in motion."

"Plan?" Plan? What plan? Nobody had told me he had a *plan*.

"To breed despair in SableFur. I want all of IronMoon to see what I have done."

The little hairs on my arms stood up. He smiled down at my belly, his expression uncharacteristically soft while the Bond curled with sated, bloated violence. He then raised his hand to caress my cheek, turning my face to his. His blue eyes were like the tourmaline: strangely bright, but unmoving at the same time.

He kissed me gently. "Are you sure I cannot convince you to return to our other room?"

"No." I found my voice.

...he destroys everything he touches...

"Buttercup?" he focused on me again.

"I'm fine." I twisted away from him and took a slurp of the water by the bedside. Some ran down my throat and between my breasts. "How about we do something else instead?"

Sex always made Aaron disappear from my awareness for a minute. Then he came howling back, but it was worth it to be free for even fifteen minutes.

His hand remained on my belly. "I know the midwife says it is fine, but it must be my lupine nature. Males don't cavort with females who have a belly full of pups. And you obviously have a pup in your belly."

So I was going to have to go the rest of my pregnancy being denied? But his scent was unusually serious and actually squeamish—he was adverse in a way I'd never known Gabel to be averse to anything. Or shy.

It was almost adorable.

Except Gabel didn't really do *adorable*.

"I am sorry," he said again, "I don't think I can."

He looked troubled, like he was leaving me to Aaron's haunting.

Which he kind of was.

But I'd forgive him for it. "Then sleep here and don't complain about it. I like the breeze."

He gave me another troubled look. "Sex clears your mind?"

"Gabel, I'm not going to force or beg or nag you into doing anything."

"It was a yes or no answer."

"I can't hear him when we're fucking. But I get it ah, ah, *no* —" I put a hand on his chest as he moved towards me. "Nope. We're not doing pity fucks, Gabel."

He frowned. "I can try to put it out of my mind."

"Ew, that's gross."

His frown intensified.

"Go to sleep." I cut him off before he could say something else absurd because this was math he couldn't do. He was kind of adorable. The midwife had warned me that a pup was a challenge no Alpha was actually prepared for. She was proving right.

Gabel watched, then looked at the window again, and twisted into wolf-form. He shifted to wolf form so he could press his lipless, leathery cheek to my belly, and just before I was about to shove him off me, he shifted to my feet and put his chin across my ankles, attention on the window.

Gabel was sadistically pleased with himself at breakfast. Which meant I was too anxious to eat.

I'd fallen asleep almost immediately after our little *Lupines Don't Like Pregnancy Sex* conversation, which meant that Gabel had probably stayed awake plotting his next move, because he sure as hell wasn't going to let Aaron live rent-free in the back of my mind.

I managed to choke down some dry toast, but even bacon looked repulsive, and the oozing yellow yolk of an egg, which I normally loved on my toast, made me gag once. Lucas was absent from his place at the warrior tables, but Kiery was in her usual spot and didn't seem the least bit distressed.

Lucas was off doing something. But even *thinking* about talking threatened to make me retch.

"Here, try these." Ana passed me a red and white candy shaped like a disc.

"A peppermint?" I asked.

"Yeah. They're great when you're feeling pukey."

"You are rather green," Kiery commented, sipping her coffee.

I shoved the mint into my mouth. It didn't immediately make me want to puke, so that was promising.

Gabel stood. "Wolves of IronMoon."

All attention swung to him. There were far fewer faces at the tables, but Gabel still addressed them formally.

"After the meal is cleared, please go to the front of the house." Gabel sipped his coffee, casually glorious, his expression smoldering malice. "I have something I wish to show all of you. How we will weaken the SableFur until they struggle to so much as growl."

Palms hit the table and silverware jangled.

Kiery blinked, and Ana whispered, "When'd we get a super weapon?"

... *Is this the legacy you want your pup to inherit?* ...

SHUT UP, AARON.

"I want to do this before the day gets too hot." Gabel winked at me.

If he said anything about my *delicate condition*, I'd bite him.

Although he'd probably enjoy that. He was enjoying my being pregnant a whole lot more than I was. Probably because he could still drink coffee and eat bacon.

Ana leaned across the table. "Should I wear my fancy coat?"

"Sounds like it's going to be a formal occasion," I said. So time for me to find a dress and brush my hair and try to settle my stomach.

FLINT OFFERED ME A HAND.

I stepped up onto the stone edge of one of the flower beds. Kiery, myself, and Ana stood with Flint, while Eroth stood opposite us. Ana had put on her white coat with the rainbow embroidery, and Kiery had found a pretty green dress to wear, her hair swept up from her shoulders, and like me, her pale skin on full display.

"Do you know what he's up to, Flint?" I muttered to him.

"You would know better than I, Luna."

I knotted my fingers together and tried not to seem nervous.

Flint nodded soberly. "He will keep it fast. He is concerned the summer sunlight will be too intense for you."

The sunlight *was* intense, and the day was going to get hot, but right now, it was tolerable. Soon we'd be baking.

The assembled IronMoon craned their necks and looked around for whatever Gabel was going to show us.

The front doors opened, and Gabel appeared, wearing nothing but a formal kilt, except around his hip he had what looked like a silver chain, and... holy shit, had he taken my tektite *comet* runestone?

He *had*.

Before I could even get angry about him thieving my runestone, two human-form wolves walked after him, but they were so bent and twisted they seemed to crawl.

Ana sucked in her breath.

They were the father-son pair. Bent at the hips, backs in arches, heads bowed. Their gaits were awful, shambling, jerky motions. They had tucked their hands up against their sides, but their fingers seemed purple and floppy. They both made awful gibbering noises. They watched Gabel's feet with the rapt obsession of a trained dog.

Even the bugs stopped their hum.

Gabel led them to the edge of the walk. They positioned themselves in that bent, hunched posture by each of his legs as if imitating shattered stone statues.

Gabel looked down at the older one. He was marked with little oozing slits and cuts and bruises. He flinched at Gabel's gaze, sensing it even though his head was bowed, and he made a terrible, *terrible* noise. Gabel said, "Go, wolf. Lead the way home for your son."

The wolf shivered all over. He shuffled forward, finally raising his head once his feet hit the gravel drive. Blood stains marked where he stepped. His eyes were awful. Whatever he saw, he saw through flame and nightmare.

Gabel looked at the son-wolf now. "Go. Follow your father. You are free to go. Both of you."

The son-wolf's fingers flopped like grotesque, loose sausages attached to swollen hands, while he staggered on whole feet but broken toes. Blood drained out of the corner of his mouth. Silver burns blackened his skin, deeply mottled and bruised.

As both wolves shuffled on the gravel, they revealed Gabel had used a blunt silver object—a spoon, perhaps—to carve out the rune for *dark comet* on their arms, defacing the father wolf's Mark. The pressure had caused raised, thick scabs so black they seemed blue and shone in the sunlight.

Every part of me screamed, and the Tides rushed through my throat, tasting of brine and blood and burning glass.

The father-wolf made terrible gibbering noises as he looked at his son. The son did not seem to see. His eyes were bright, tormented marbles retreated far back into their sockets.

"That way." Gabel indicated the direction. "Follow the path to the road."

The father-wolf's gibbering increased, and he waved broken hands at Gabel.

Gabel's smile seemed almost sweet, and the Bond coiled and quivered. "As I promised: when I was done, you would be returned. I will not bother you again."

The son-wolf made a noise that froze even Aaron's soul in its pacing.

Gabel handed Renzo a scroll tied with a black ribbon and sealed with black wax into which he had scratched the sigil for dark comet. "See them escorted to the border of their home. Be quite gentle with them."

"Yes, Alpha," Renzo said as he tucked the scroll into his bag.

Gabel seized the father's broken jaw. "Always remember, wolf. *Always*. That I gave you a choice. Remember what you chose." His voice took on a terrifying silken quality like the low, distant drone of hornets. "What you tell his mother is *also* your choice."

Gabel dropped the broken wolf's jaw and nodded to Renzo. Then he turned neatly on the ball of one foot. "My Luna. Perhaps this bright sunlight is too much for you."

Through the horrified chill coating my soul, I asked, "What choice did he make? What will he have to tell his mate?"

Gabel smiled as he smoothed his palm over my belly. "I have infected the bone so it will not heal."

"And Adrianna can't stop you," I whispered.

His smile spread across his face and through the Bond like dark, congealing blood. With his other hand, he caressed my temple. "I am the Dark Comet, but it's not the impact that destroys life and ecosystems. It's what comes after the impact. Like the tektite and its lingering rage that does not forget the moment of its birth."

"What are you talking about?"

That smile just spread more and his teeth shone in his mouth. "The impact throws up dust and debris. It creates a wave of fire and quakes that incinerate everything and what doesn't burn collapses for miles. And all that fire and smoke and dust goes into the sky. It blocks out the sun. It becomes winter darkness for years, the rain is poison, the oceans die, plants cannot grow, so animals that eat plants starve, then animals that eat animals starve. The *lucky* ones are the ones that die in the explosion."

The dream of Adrianna and her crown and cloak and scepter in the tomb seared into my waking mind.

Lucas, do you think we'd recognize it if we were entering a new dark age?

*But it is over, little wolf. Because you ended it. This **is** the end.*

The scythe-moon has fallen, and the Sun has set.

"That is what you have seen, buttercup. That is why the sky rains glass. It is not glass. It is tektite." A shadow moved over his handsome face, his eyes turning to the same color as the stormy Tides. His hand was hot through the fabric of my shirt, and something shifted in my belly like the pup recognized his touch.

He swept low and kissed me.

I softened for him as he pressed closer, his tongue meeting mine, something savage and raw in his kiss, his fingers curling into my cheek, his nails scratching me lightly.

Aaron's Mark burned into my bones.

... Gianna ...

My soul spasmed with pain. I broke off the kiss and threw my arms around Gabel instead, shivering in the sunlight.

"You can hear him?" he whispered.

I sob-mumbled *yes*.

His fingers dug into my skin. "I will find a way to free you from him. And I will give Adrianna her crown. I will fashion it for her myself, and set it before her to wear, and all will see her crown, and all will behold it. We will see if she has the will to wear it."

A Look Inside
the Box

Gabel held up a tie. "Is a tie required?"

"I have no idea."

He pondered several ties, then contemplated his reflection in the mirror. He had jeans and a button-down shirt in a pale shade of pink check, which somehow only made him look even *more* beach bum. His hair had grown out into slight, loose curls, and his beach tan hadn't faded, and while it was not especially dark, when the light hit his skin, he still seemed charred and metallic.

Taking him amongst humans seemed... risky. Gabel wasn't exactly... domesticated... at the best of times.

But Ana and the IceMaw midwife had insisted that I *needed* to go see an actual *doctor-doctor* given the worries about my silver exposure. There apparently were a few doctors the IceMaw worked with, but they were far to the south, and I was pretty much an idiot about this kind of thing, so the midwife had arranged for us to see a doctor several hours south of IronMoon, about halfway between us and the Gleaming Fang pass.

Ana appeared in our doorway. "Come on, kids, we've got a hike."

Ana had agreed to come along, both as support and so she could learn something. I said, "Gabel is debating if this requires a tie."

She laughed. "Trust me. No tie."

"I wish you could do this," I said.

"I have *no* idea what I'm doing with human babies. Or human-shaped babies. It is going to be human-shaped, right?"

"It was conceived in human form, so should be human," I said.

"But what happens if it's human and some *other* form?" she asked, giving me the eye.

I shrugged, because I had no idea. "Gambler's choice, I guess."

Gabel, having overheard no tie was required, unbuttoned the top button of his shirt and tossed his ties onto the bed to sort later. He pinned Ana with a stare. "Is there anything else to know?"

"Yeah, don't growl. Just let the professionals do their job. The midwife's already sent over everything and set everything up, so they know what they're looking for."

"I am not sure about a human being involved in this," I said warily. Which was a very dumb thing to say, because werewolves didn't eschew medical care, especially for things like a pregnancy or a sick infant. Clearly, the last year had made me a little too paranoid.

"You like *dying in childbirth*?"

"No," Gabel said firmly. "We don't. We're going."

"Of course we're going," I said, but my nerves jangled. Mostly, I was afraid of something *other* than a normal baby being on the ultrasound, or Aaron tearing at my mind at the worst possible time. Or being told my placenta was too thin or hadn't formed correctly, which was very common after silver exposure, and there was no treatment and no good end to that.

Ana patted me between the shoulders and pushed me

towards the door. "Just like the midwife said. Make sure your placenta is right, you're right, all that nice stuff. If there are going to be problems, best to know now so we can move you to IceMaw. As much as Gabel hates that idea."

Gabel's eyes narrowed. "If that's what needs to be done to keep them safe, I will not hate the idea."

The doctor's office was in a tangled complex of a medical center with multiple buildings all flanking a large hospital. I kept my hand on my belly and tried not to worry too much. Aaron paced in the corner of my awareness, waiting, watching.

If that wolf interfered while I was around humans...

Ana went to go find coffee and wander about.

Gabel in a room full of humans—entirely women—was a... thing. I wasn't sure if I should laugh or cry, because Gabel seemed to take up a great deal of space in the room, and even when he was flipping through the parenting magazines on offer, he was a smoldering presence.

He slowly made his way through an article on breast feeding tips. Another woman had a toddler with her, she looked exhausted, and the kid headed towards a large basket of toys and started tossing the toys out of the basket.

Gabel paused in his reading to observe the brewing chaos.

The toddler's mother made an exhausted attempt to round up the toys and plead *one at a time*, but the kid was having none of it, and descended into howling, red-faced tears. This sparked an infant that was present in another, even *more* exhausted woman's arms to wake up and start screaming. Attempts to round up the toy-toddler escalated to toys being flung and the toddler suddenly going boneless and noodling onto the ground to scream.

Oh no. What had I gotten myself into?

In the back of my awareness, Aaron seemed to shift, then observe, quietly, watching for... something.

Gabel observed the howling, toy-flinging, shrieking, tear-shedding toddler. Then the mother holding the wailing infant started sobbing.

My nerves grated like fine cheese.

The toddler was left on the floor in a sobbing heap while their mother picked up the toys, and one of the office staff magically appeared to console the other mother and the infant. I sensed Aaron's caustic disapproval of something, and Gabel seemed unusually pensive as he watched the sobbing heap of a child on the carpet while the exhausted mother plunked herself back down with a massive sigh.

We got called back before the tears ended. I was so busy not getting lost in the reflective, bright, polished surfaces of everything I barely heard what anyone said, although I must have given adequate responses. Not having my sense of smell was so disorienting in this new place, with these new people. No idea how to read any of them.

"You're nervous, buttercup," Gabel said as we waited for the ultrasound tech to come in for the last thing—the thing I was *really* frightened of.

"That's charitable," I replied. "More like terrified."

He slid his hand into mine. "I noticed I was the only man in the waiting room."

"Oh, everyone else noticed you too."

"I was behaved."

"You have a presence." That and Gabel was damn good looking. He had the dangerous appeal of a wild animal coupled with effortless good looks. The sort of presence that instinctively warned everyone in the vicinity, regardless of species, to not take him lightly.

"And I meant that it is obvious small hu—*children* are *far* too much work for one person." He frowned with disapproval.

"I'm already intimidated."

"Intimidated by a small child. Tsk, tsk."

Before I could tell him he was a jerk, the tech came in. Goo was promptly smeared over my belly, and she started to talk, but I didn't hear her because I focused my mental effort on not panicking at *this is really happening*. Gabel had some kind of conversation with her involving if we wanted to know if it was a boy or girl. He seemed completely mystified by the question.

"You can tell?" Gabel asked.

The tech, to her credit, didn't look at him like he was a moron. More like she spoke to morons on a regular basis and Gabel was just the most recent moron on her roster of morons. "She's far enough along we can probably see, if baby's in the right position."

Gabel glanced at me, then back at her, recovered quickly, and said, "No, we decided we'd rather be surprised."

"Surprised it is," the tech said pleasantly.

It seemed to go on *forever*. The baby fluttered at the cold on my belly, and the prodding from the tech. Gabel watched the tech, and once she glanced at him and hesitated, instinctively unnerved by an Alpha wolf watching her with the quiet, composed intensity of a predator. Until the tech turned the monitor around and gave us the grainy, black-and-white view into my insides. She pointed out the long bright white line of the spine, the shadowy white silhouette of the skull that reminded me of the moon behind clouds, the vague outlines of little arms and legs.

Gabel's lips moved, but he didn't say anything as he stared intently at the monitor.

Holy fuck, it was a *baby*. Like an actual *baby*. We had made a baby-baby.

The tech apparently was also used to dealing with overwhelmed morons. The doctor who came in also didn't treat us like morons, but seemed familiar with dealing with over-whelmed *this is actually happening, what have we done* parents.

Talking with a human who was blissfully unaware that she was speaking to the Moon's Dark Comet and the Balance Keeper and *werewolves* was also surreal. I barely processed what she said beyond the important thing: my placenta looked fine. Baby looked fine.

"So the placenta is fine?" I asked, barely daring to believe it.

"Looks fine," she said. "Why, were you concerned?"

"Reading too much on the internet," I said evasively.

"Don't do that. Everything looks picture-perfect normal. Even the anxiety is normal."

Even Aaron had shut up in his pacing and just watched.

Everything else drifted along. Gabel said some things, I said some things, and Ana rounded us up as we wandered back downstairs to the lobby.

"You guys look like you've been hit with the same stick," Ana said. "Is something wrong?"

"No, it's just... we *saw* the baby," I said. We'd declined copies of the images, which had earned us some sideways looks, but neither of us wanted to have something like that lying around within reach of our enemies. It could put the human doctor and her staff in danger.

"There is a baby, yes," Gabel said.

Ana twirled the keys around her finger. "Mission accomplished. You two are a riot. Come on, divine-chosen-ones, let's get back home."

As we walked out into the sunlight across the crammed asphalt parking lot, we passed two more women, one with two children in tow while being pregnant, and the other carrying a crying baby, Gabel told me, "Still no partners. I have always known how dangerous and difficult it was for my mother, but I see that different circumstances do not seem to generate less difficulty. How is it in packs?"

"Depends," I said. "My own father adopted me when I was still a baby when my parents were killed, and I know it was hard for him too. I don't really remember how it was for other pups."

Once I'd hit an age where maybe I'd have noticed such things, my Gift had started maturing. But I remembered my father being busy and always pulled in a dozen directions at all times of day or night.

Gabel watched the one woman managing the children. His eyes narrowed slightly. He turned back around. "Human-form children are just as feral as pups."

"Probably more," Ana said. "Or maybe it just seems that way because they're like that longer than a puppy."

Gabel's brow knit together. He gripped my hand tight. Almost too tight. "*I* will be with you, buttercup. No matter what."

... And so will I...

Too Many Stuffies

"You're falling asleep, buttercup."

"Yep." I snuggled into the couch cushions. He'd added pillows to the couch in his office, and they called me to sleep. All the time. Constantly. The couch was not especially comfortable, but it was more comfortable than getting up and finding somewhere else. My hips *ached*.

"What are we going to do about IceMaw, though?" His voice had a teasing prod to it.

I sighed and dragged one eyelid open. I'd managed to put off Carlos again when he'd called, but the midwife reported to him regularly. She'd taken up residence in IronMoon since it was such a hike between the two packs and travel for wolves was hazardous at the moment. IceMaw had more than one midwife though, this was just the one Aaron had chosen for me back when I'd been in IceMaw and he'd been lying to the pack about our efforts to conceive a pup. The trade-off was the midwife also was a snitch.

IceMaw, apparently, was waiting with bated breath for every pregnancy update, convinced I was carrying Aaron's offspring.

They also sent gifts. *Many* gifts. And every unique gift also included diapers. Gabel had been fascinated by onesies and snaps. He had, apparently, somehow, never encountered snaps. Zippers, buttons, clasps, frogs, laces, velcro. But snaps had fascinated him. Along with all the unique baby attire and gear like onesies and swaddlings and the rules of "safe sleeping" and "milestones" and everything else that went into human-form pups.

"This seems *far* more complicated and fraught than raising lupines." He almost sounded worried.

"Well, IceMaw isn't going away," I said wearily. In fact, sitting on the floor by the couch were the most recent round of gifts shipped from IceMaw: several adorable stuffed animals in soft colors and yet more diapers.

They knew something I didn't, apparently.

He contemplated the lines and pins he had painstakingly repositioned with the latest reports. "IceMaw presumably still has spies in SableFur."

"I'm certain Carlos does. A—*he* was always clear that he was prepared for his death and IceMaw needing a clear line of succession." My throat couldn't form *Aaron*.

"But you also said *he* was paranoid."

"His paranoia took a lot of forms. But you know the more useful I ask Carlos to be—and I am sure he's willing to be *very* useful—the more he's going to expect me to come back to IceMaw. And the less I talk to Carlos, the happier I am."

"You could always abdicate."

"At this point, I think Carlos would believe he has to break your hold over me and just march the entire southern alliance up here to *liberate* me. They will come up here to get our baby. *He* was a savior to them. He died an IceMaw martyr. You can't kill him."

Gabel looked at the map, expression and Bond dark. "And

you still aren't willing to publicly assert Aaron could not *possibly* be the father?"

"No one's going to believe me. They'll think I'm in denial, just like they believe I'm only with you because I'm afraid of you."

"And it cannot possibly be because you love me," Gabel growled.

"Well, there are plenty who believe that too, and that I'm a monster for it." I dragged myself back up to a seated position, emotions swinging to misery and anger. My Marks ached and Aaron's itched, but I recoiled at the thought of touching it.

Gabel left his map. He raked his fingernails along Aaron's mark, and I sighed gratefully, then he smoothed the same hand over my belly. The light fabric of my summer dress didn't hide the rough texture of his chapped, calloused palms. "Then if we cannot win, we will triumph. I am not yet sure how we can make use of the IceMaw, beyond what they are obviously useful for: the midwifery provided."

"That is something I am very grateful for," I admitted, then I had to tolerate Aaron's smugness clouding the back of my brain like a wave of nausea.

"Do not listen to him," Gabel said, still holding the rise of my belly in his palm while the pup squirmed, delivering little flutters.

"I'm trying," I told his troubled gaze. "I'm trying, but he's getting louder. He's getting better at being a... a haunt."

Gabel's expression tightened several turns. "I *will* figure out how to silence him. I will."

"There might not be a way." The only moments of relief I got where I couldn't feel or sense Aaron were sex, but Gabel had gotten squeamish and I wasn't going to mention it again. Or being in the basement, which couldn't be healthy for the pup. Or when I was feeling some kind of stinging pain intense enough to crowd everything else. *Also* not an option.

Gabel placed both hands on my belly and smoothed the pale pink-and-white fabric taut over it, and told my belly, "There is a way, little pup. I will find it. Before you arrive."

I ruffled his hair. He ducked away, and said, "Tell IceMaw that instead of these," he picked up one of the little stuffies, shook it, then tossed it away to some far corner, "they should send books."

"Books," I echoed.

"Yes, so I can read these pup-appropriate books. The baby is too little for prey anyway." Gabel chucked another stuffie.

"I'm not sure stuffies are meant to be *prey*..."

"Then what are they for?"

"Cuddles. Like a doll? A companion?"

Gabel recoiled. "Teaching our pup that *this*," he picked up the remaining stuffie, which was an adorable duckling toy, "is not *prey*? Buttercup, we can't traumatize them. They will shift and then feel the urge to hunt ducklings and ducks and think they are killing their companion!"

He threw that stuffie away too. "Trash. All of them."

I tried not to laugh. "Gabel, it's not like that. Kids know stuffies aren't *real*. At least by the time they're old enough to shift they know the difference between a toy duck and a real duck. Usually stuffies get torn apart when they can shift."

Gabel looked skeptical. "And this does not deeply traumatize them? That they are ripping apart their old companion?"

I had to work *very* hard to not laugh, because Gabel had been a lupine, so maybe a lupine pup would think of it that way. I shoved him on the thigh with a foot. "Go pick up the toys, put them in the basket, and I'll tell Carlos we have plenty of toys but need more books."

Gabel went to retrieve the tossed toys.

A rap on his office door, then it opened. Lucas and Kiery stepped inside.

"Lucas!" He was filthy, shaggy, and smelled so bad even I got a whiff of him. "Where have you *been*?"

"Luna." Lucas nodded politely.

Gabel walked over, clutching three stuffies in his hands. "Did you find anything, wolf?"

Lucas looked at the stuffies, bewildered, then smirked.

Gabel looked at the stuffies too, then asked Lucas, "Did you have these things when you were a pup?"

"Stuffed toys? Sure." Kiery picked up the pale gray lamb.

"Didn't it disturb you when you started to hunt that your companion," Gabel shook the fanciful green frog toy, "was one of these creatures? Was that not traumatic?"

Lucas and Kiery looked at each other, then back at Gabel. Then Lucas said, slowly, "No."

"And wolves say *lupines* are barbaric. Wait here a moment." Gabel stalked out of his office.

I glared after him. "What did he have you do, Lucas?"

"Stay sitting, Gianna," Kiery said.

"I am not an invalid," I snapped.

"Just sit, *child*," Kiery retorted in her best Elder Oracle voice.

I snarled at her.

She growled back.

The baby fluttered and twisted as I got angry. I breathed and settled as best I could.

Gabel returned without the toys.

Lucas put his hand in his filthy jeans' pocket, fished out something, and extended his closed fist to Gabel. Gabel held out his palm. Lucas dropped something in it.

Gabel stared at the small object, then picked it up between his thumb and forefinger.

"Holy—" I scrambled. Lucas shoved a hand on my shoulder.

Gabel snarled. "Don't *touch* her."

"What is that?" I gasped breathlessly. "You sent *Lucas* to find the ring?"

Gabel turned away, and the Bond retreated into stillness and pensiveness.

Lucas nodded as if to say *wait*.

Finally, Gabel turned back around. "Where did you find this?"

"Where it was expected," Lucas replied.

On his palm was the pup-ring from my vision.

The band had two marks on it. One, the sigil for *mother*, just like in my vision. But the coarse version of *luna* was absent, as was *dark comet*. In the place of *dark comet* was *oracle*. The entire ring was grimy, but beautifully done, with no signs of the blasting or ruin I'd seen on the vision-version.

"This... this isn't the same." This ring was scorched platinum, the ring in the vision had been gold. It looked like the runes were lined with something faint blue.

"I know *love* and *mate* and *mother*, but not the other," Gabel said roughly.

"Oracle. It's *oracle*. In my vision, it was *luna* placed over *mother*, it'd been added by a different hand. And the oracle rune was *dark comet* scorched into the band. And in my vision, the ring was gold, not platinum. And your mother wasn't an Oracle."

We *called* her the Oracle of Mirrors, but technically, she'd never even taken the final tests, much less the vows. And I was guessing the ring was platinum, because it didn't scorch like silver. In fact, it was icy cold to the touch.

Gabel rolled the ring back and forth between his thumb and forefinger. "Where did you find this, Lucas?"

"In a charred metal box, buried under the ash and debris of the small shack, approximately where you told me I'd find the structure."

"Nothing else?"

"No, and it was not buried or hidden. Just under debris."

Gabel's voice remained rough and dark. "My mother was not Magnes' mate. You agree, SableFur."

Lucas' nod was crisp. "I was still a kid, but I remember the jokes about Magnes. That he liked to tomcat. He was high-bred, ambitious, desirable. They say he travelled around to the western packs for the best pairing he could sniff. The story I overheard was that he made a good impression on Adrianna's older sister while in EmeraldPelt, and *she* is the one who told Adrianna to give him a look. Adrianna was the *exact* opposite, story goes. There's no chance Magnes strung your mom along, much less chased her, or gave her a fake ring to lure her out of hiding."

Gabel nodded along with the story. "My father used my mother for sport, and nothing else. That's all she ever was to him."

Lucas flexed a finger. "But I also don't believe he had her murdered. He wasn't a fan of death as a way to solve problems. Executions to him were always a last resort. Adrianna was—is—more bloodthirsty."

"I don't believe either of them killed her. My mother was murdered by wolves also looking for sport. Oracle Kiery, I want to speak to you alone. I have a question for you to take to the Moon."

It felt like pieces of myself fragmented and fluttered off into the breeze.

Kiery nodded once. "Yes, Alpha."

Gabel turned his attention to the window.

Fine. Gabel was entitled to consult with the Oracle of his preference. With as much dignity as I could muster, I walked out the door.

Kiery closed it behind me.

GABEL FIXED THE ELDER ORACLE WITH A STARE. KIERY kept her body language *precisely* correct, neither deferential nor aggressive. Her gaze was neither too low nor too high. Her scent betrayed her worry and concern, and that she was not the least bit unsettled by any of this.

He'd never spent much time in the presence of another Oracle. She was six or seven years older than Gianna, very pretty, pale, and wore a pair of jeans and a plain tanktop in white. Her feet were bare, her hair in a simple ponytail spilling down her back.

Gabel circled her, eyeing her Mark. It was *normal*. Exactly like the first Mark he'd given Gianna.

Kiery tracked him with her gaze, the same as Gianna had done those first few months. "Your question, Alpha."

And the same maddening tone. The tone that held itself just out of reach.

Of course, *this* was the Oracle that had served his father. And whatever secrets she knew would go to her grave. "Two questions, related. I presume you can carry two onto the Tides?"

"I am not Gianna," Kiery told him. "And I cannot promise the Moon will open Her Eye."

"Exactly, you *aren't* Gianna. But you *are* here. You could have gone to IceMaw. You could have gone home. I'm sure you have your reasons for being here, and it's not your mate's ambition to be my First Beta."

"Lucas has no such ambition nor interest. He serves your Luna, not you."

The Moon had sent Kiery a vision of what to bring him as a gift: the twin wolves. Kiery was here because the Moon had sent her. "You won't discuss this with Gianna."

"Your question, your answer. There are no exceptions."

"My first question: how do we defeat Adrianna?"

Kiery nodded that mild Oracle nod.

"My second question: how do I free her from Aaron?"

She inhaled and held it. "As you inquire, Lord-Alpha. Your questions, your answers. But don't expect much."

Gabel permitted himself a cold smile. "I never do, Elder Oracle. I never do."

Adrianna - Wedding Gifts

"Mom."

Adrianna took her oldest son's hand. He squeezed tight, shaken, but trying to put on a brave show for the wolves around them. She nodded, because she couldn't think of anything to tell him that wouldn't be a lie.

Magnes' eyes looked back at her. Her heart twisted and the void where his soul should have been howled like an empty cavern.

SableFur's heart was empty. No one came to greet them. No one had stayed behind. The grass was overgrown. Weeds had sprung up.

She waited another minute, expecting *someone* to creep out of some shadows and welcome them home, but the only scent of wolves was weeks old. And there was the rancid scent of a corpse drifting up from the direction of the hall.

They'd abandoned the heart. Lucas, Kiery, Bernhard—all of them. Her scouts had told her the heart had been vacated, but she'd assumed *someone* would stay behind.

None of them had stayed.

All the ranked wolves, her *core*, the wolves who had helped hold SableFur together: gone.

For the first time, fear curled in her belly. Lucas and Kiery were lost causes, but the others! Yes, they'd seen what they'd seen, but they'd *left*? Just *left*?

No wolf abandoned their pack. Not unless...

"Find that scent of death," she told the uncertain warrior next to her. She'd need a new First Beta. She'd thought that she'd be able to tap a wolf from the heart on the shoulder for the job, but they'd abandoned her. The best wolves of SableFur, the ones she'd grown up with, played with, who had helped her birth her sons and counseled her, *scattered*. They were probably somewhere still *in* SableFur, but they weren't *here*, where she needed them.

Her oldest son tugged gently.

She'd promised him they'd go back to the heart in triumph.

This was not triumph.

"I don't want to go in the house," he said softly.

Neither did she. But she had to, and soon enough, she'd make the den her home again. And she would decorate the trees with Gianna's bones.

The scout returned, ashen. "Luna. We... it's Bernhard."

"Bernhard? Is he here?"

"He's... you should come see. But don't bring the pups."

Adrianna left the pups behind and went with the scout, along with a few other wolves, to the hall.

Nailed to the door, and rotted by the summer sun, was Bernhard. His face was still... sort of intact.

And he'd been nailed to the door with spikes, and a silver spike through his neck.

Under the body scrawled in his blood was *SPY*.

She inhaled.

"Spy?" the wolf with her asked.

She grit her teeth. *Fuck*. Fuck! "He was not a spy for Sable-

Fur, nor would Lucas have killed him for spying for Gianna. He must have been *Aaron's* spy. Well, that explains how that bastard always seemed to know too much. I knew he had spies, but he had my Second Beta! I *warned* Magnes about Aaron. I *warned him* and—"

It didn't matter now.

So that was why the wolves had left, that's why they'd lost faith. Because they had *spies* in the heart. Like worms.

She still had her northern army. She still had her sister in EmeraldPelt. The Oracles were dealt with. Aaron was dead. But now that she was in the heart, it was time to regroup and rebuild, so when Gabel returned... he would be swiftly butchered.

"Scrape that down," she ordered. "Scrub all of it. And send word to the outlying wolves that I am back in the heart. Do not summon them back here."

"But Luna—"

"Don't." She raised a hand to stop him. They hadn't come rushing to her aid when she was in the north, and they hadn't waited for her in the heart. The most senior wolves of SableFur had *abandoned the heart*. She would have to be careful, and not try to tax her authority. "I want them to know their Luna has not abandoned them, that is all. There's no other expectation."

She would see who came to the heart or sent their greetings. She'd start with the wolves closest to the heart, then go farther and farther out to determine how willing they were to fight for her. Gabel's forces hadn't harried her to the south, and the most recent reports were he had actually pulled them back to the Gleaming Fang pass.

The most recent reports she had from IronMoon were that Gabel had *banished* all the IronMoon from his presence except a select few. That seemed unbelievable. And even more unbelievable, the reports that the wolves howled and begged for a place in the pack again. It seemed absurd, but her sources also had been among those banished. So either they were lying, or something very odd had happened in IronMoon.

It might be the time to strike.

She looked at the hall. The old SableFur hall, that had stood for generations. But the last bitch who had sat on that throne had been Gianna, and now Magnes was a stain on the floor.

The problem? Magnes had earned his fate.

"Burn it," she told the wolf. "All of it."

"The entire hall, Luna?"

"The entire hall. The Moon has cursed it with a stain that will never be scrubbed out. I am not going to sit on that sullied throne again, and I'm not going to insult the Moon by pretending it didn't happen."

She didn't actually give a shit about insulting the Moon, but it'd be symbolic to the rest of SableFur that she was *purging* the old, sordid past and building anew. She needed a fresh start for her sons, and they couldn't sit in a hall where their father's stain was right at their feet.

She would build a new hall, and a new legacy. "Actually, dismantle some of the large beams, and the throne, and the board where *his* soul is a puddle. Ship them to IronMoon with my regards. Tell Gabel it's lumber for his tower."

THE END OF US

I'd never been the petitioner waiting for an Oracle to get back to me. At least Gabel was going to let us all hear the answer. We crowded into his office, including Carlos.

Wherever the Moon had taken Kiery, it'd been a rough ride.

Even though she'd been back two days, she still looked gray and gaunt. Lucas hovered nervously but overall kept his distance. Carlos lurked in a corner.

"Oracle," Gabel said, "my question, my answer. I presume you *have* an answer and we did not summon Carlos here for nothing."

"There is an answer," Kiery said, voice hoarse, like she'd been choking on the Tides.

"Then I am waiting. The question was, *how do we defeat Adrianna.*"

Bonus points to my mate for having the balls to just ask the Moon a blunt question—and getting an answer I couldn't provide.

A sense of foreboding crawled up my spine and stretched over my shoulders like skeletal claws. *He* breathed over my shoulder to listen.

Kiery coughed once. "The Moon showed me a stone temple in a flooded jungle. The trees had all been flattened and charred. On an altar was a set of scales made from a scythe, and in the pans were two crowns: one made of bleeding bones set with a blue, a white, and a black stone, and the other made of a skull. Gianna stood behind the altar, wrapped in a dress made of... fangs. Around her neck was some kind of very intricate burning glass collar set with gobs of gore. It had burned itself into her neck and melted the skin away so her skin mingled with the molten glass rain falling from the sky. Everything shone.

"Gianna's arm with Aaron's Mark was flayed down to the bone while Aaron, in a skeletal war-form, gnawed the shape of his Mark into her bones, and you, Gabel, in war-form but headless, tracing the pattern of her blue-gloss but you'd created deep grooves in it too, down to the bone. But you can't see or smell or hear what you've done, and since your claws are soaked with blood, you cannot perceive her blood from the rest soaking your hands. The sky was dark and smelled... terrible. Like burning and thunderstorms."

Gabel cocked his head. "Tell me about this skull crown."

"Specifically? It was *your* skull."

I had to sit down.

Gabel leaned forward slightly. "Interesting. Was there anything else? I asked *how* I could prevail, not if I *could* still prevail."

Kiery visibly swallowed and coughed again.

I licked my lips. The crown of gore and glass seemed to have become my collar... or jewels. Why was I wearing his crown around my neck? But the ornate necklace... I'd seen a necklace in that same temple. Just not made of gore or glass, but of silver and the three stones I kept seeing.

This was Gabel's question and his answer. I needed to butt out, this wasn't meant for me.

Carlos asked, "So was Gianna able to move her hands

towards the scales, or are they stuck that way? Are the scales in balance?"

"They were not in balance. They were swinging on their fulcrum while the weight settled. I couldn't tell if she could move. She seemed to... want to, but... perhaps was not able to?" Kiery shook her head.

"And what else? Nothing?" Gabel pressed, seeming to loom over her even though he was about ten feet away.

Kiery's Oracle mask fractured. "The Moon... appeared. She told me that there was a weapon that might defeat Adrianna, but She would only give it to Gianna, only Gianna can wield it, and... the price would be terrible."

Something felt like a *thud* when Kiery said *terrible*.

The cold, dead breath on my neck intensified.

Kiery swung her haunted gaze to me. "She said for you to take the tektite into the Tides. Without the weapon, the war *will* grind on for years, and there is no end nor answer to the question. But She also told me that this *is* the end, because you ended it."

Carlos scoffed. "How can it be the end if the war isn't going to end? If this is the end, why is it still happening?"

Flint's voice sounded hollow. "She meant it's the end times. The last days. She doesn't mean the end of the war. She means the end of *us*."

This IS the end, little wolf, because YOU ended it.

"No," I whispered. "*No*. No, no, no."

"Gianna could not have ended it because *she* is not the Destroyer," Carlos snapped.

Flint's voice sounded like an axe pressed to my neck. "She chose the Destroyer over the Instrument. Ergo, she brought about the last days. She is the Balance-Keeper. It was always her prerogative. Perhaps you should have been more of a Beta and less of a thrall."

I clapped my hands over my mouth to hold in the screams.

This IS the end, little wolf, because YOU ended it.
NO. NO!
...Gianna, come to me, it's over...
NO!

"But how can it be the end if I have a pup in my belly?" My voice cracked.

I refused to believe the Moon was *that* cruel that after *everything* I'd done, She'd see me get pregnant just for my pup to inherit a ruined world ruled by *Adrianna*.

Gabel snarled. "Fuck the Silvery Sky Bitch. She can keep Her weapon and Her secrets. If it's destruction She wants, I am happy to oblige."

"And what about our pup?" The sobs wracked my voice.

Gabel hissed and his fingers extended into claws.

"I have to go! If I don't, this is how it ends!"

"We are not risking our pup!"

"What the fuck do you *think* is going to happen if this war keeps going?" I shouted and was on my feet before I could even think. "You think the risk is going to be any less in a year than right now?!"

Aaron's Mark twisted and burned as my bond to Gabel twisted with his anger.

"Buttercup."

"I'm fine," I said around a deep breath. Cold sweat trickled down the back of my arms. I took another breath around the pain.

"Is it the pup?" His voice actually went up a note.

Carlos grabbed Eroth and told him to get the midwife.

"I can't explain this to you now!" The bonds twisted. My whole body felt like it clenched and pain seared through my torso and radiated down my limbs.

I swear by the Moon, if you two fighting hurts my pup, I will end both of you!

Dizziness spun me around. The pain hit a crescendo, and I

grabbed until my fingers found something. My throat clenched as everything inside me twisted and the bonds howled in pain, threatening to tear my soul into pieces.

Gabel grabbed me. His touch sent more pain through me. I snapped and slapped at him. "Stop! Don't touch me!"

"Gianna—"

"Go away! Go away!" Did this wolf not understand *go away*?

The searing heat felt like all of me was covered in burning glass and salty water.

No, I stopped them! This isn't happening! It's not still happening! I stopped that future!

I howled.

"Lucas!" I heard Carlos shout. He sprang out of his corner and grabbed Gabel. Lucas got the idea, and the two wolves wrestled Gabel back. Gabel snarled and struck, and the males tumbled backwards into his desk, scattering and shattering things.

...Gianna...

Deathly claws grabbed and *pulled* from within me. Living claws pulled back.

NO!

Two strong hands grabbed my arms. "Gianna!"

The voice, unexpected, bolted through the storm.

"It's the howls of the dead. He can't help it!" Flint said. "Turn away!"

I fought my way through what felt like water and burning glass and thorns.

"You *can't* answer him. Turn away! Walk away! *Walk away*!" He pulled me up and forward. I scrambled and got one foot under me, he hauled, I ended up on my feet. "*Walk away!*"

I pushed myself through all the water and glass and thorns. The claws sliding over my soul dug in, then released their terrifying grip. I staggered the final step and fell forward into Flint's chest as something shattered and books fell off their shelves.

His green eyes were cloudy, impossibly sad and too bright. "The dead howl. They can't help it. The silence of death, the *waiting*, it's excruciating. They can't help but howl. If you want to stay alive, you have to walk away and leave them to their howls."

His voice cracked, faltered, was hoarse. "Just walk away."

TUSSLE OF TWO MARKS

lint cancelled his afternoon sessions and retreated to his room. Ana appeared to stitch up Carlos and Lucas. Someone else went to go sweep up the splinters and glass and replace the books on the shelves. Gabel rubbed the debris out of his hair and ignored the scrapes on his body and tossed his ruined shirt into the hamper to be reused as rags. The poor beleaguered IceMaw midwife checked me over, had some sharp words that I was getting too pregnant to be falling or flailing about, that she was worried the silver might make the placenta too thin and prone to tearing so... you know... *don't* get between arguing males.

Right. Because that was easy to do when one of the males was a ghost, and the other was Gabel.

"What should we do with this, Luna?" Violet asked, presenting me with a small box of torn books and various debris.

I sighed. "Just throw it out, I guess. What a mess."

"They broke the shelves." She indicated the shelves on the second floor, which now had a Lucas-sized crescent smashed into them.

"Not sorry," Carlos, who lurked in the far corner with some

stitches in his scalp and bloody knuckles, said. He also had some stitches up the front of his shin.

"Just throw it out, Violet. If Gabel asks about them, I'll remind him his office isn't a battlefield."

"But it is, buttercup." Gabel strode into the office, changed and looking more or less like it didn't happen, except for the fury clinging to his shoulders. He shot a disgusted look at Carlos. "Are you still here?"

"My Luna has not sent me on my way, so, yes," Carlos retorted.

"I sense you enjoy bleeding for her," Gabel said coldly. "Does it make you feel as though you are earning her forgiveness with every drop you shed? Because finding wolves to bleed at her feet is not difficult and grows tiresome."

"And blood is only the beginning. Note that I am able to be *here* assisting her with this... diplomatic challenge... without worrying about what will become of IceMaw in our absence. It is a luxury IceMaw is able to afford."

Gabel's smile was ice and cruelty. "Yet you came here on your knees begging her to return to you, but *now* you try to convince her that her tolerating you at her side is a *luxury* she should appreciate. And you insult her as if she is too stupid to know what you're after: our child."

Carlos set his jaw. "I am her First Beta."

"And you serve IceMaw, just as Lucas serves SableFur. Who serves *her*? If there was no pup, you would not be here."

"That is not true. She is the rightful Luna of IceMaw."

Gabel dismissed Carlos with an aggravated flick of his head and turned his attention to me. "I will never apologize for defending you or our pups."

"I never asked you to apologize." Fuck, were we going to have this fight *again*?

"Good. Then I will also never agree to you going to the

Moon to petition for this weapon we don't need. I can prevail without it."

"You can't win it fast enough," I retorted.

"I am not arguing with you. This conversation is over."

"Good. I'm glad we agree."

He nodded, then realized we didn't agree at all. "You'd jeopardize our pup."

"Our pup isn't in danger from me scrying."

Gabel paced up to me and circled, and each word got angrier, darker, more vicious. "It's in danger from the physical strain scrying puts on you. And don't tell me to put my faith in the Moon. That's the only price She could want. And if She wants that, and you give it to Her, do *not* come back. *Stay* there. With *him*."

I couldn't even find the words to tell him to fuck off.

Carlos backed slowly out of the room.

"We are *not* negotiating our child," Gabel hissed.

"Our pup is *not* in danger from me scrying, and I have *no* intention of spending eternity with *him*. Stop being an idiot."

"I am tired of letting you walk right into the Moon's Maw. It is *not* happening. There is no weapon worth having. I have the weapons we need."

"This is the *end*, Gabel! There is no *winning* for any of us! The Moon can't foresee where this leads because it doesn't *lead anywhere!* That's what She's saying!"

"*No*," Gabel snarled. "I am the Dark Comet, and the impact doesn't destroy the world, it just forces it to adapt and survive!"

"After *eons!* My tektite bowl is *millions* of years old! Our pup is coming in *months*! You really think Adrianna's going to bide her time until I've had the pup and have recovered? Who's gambling our baby now!"

He turned his darkest smile on me. "I'm not the one presuming to humor some terrible price for a weapon that may or may not work."

"What if She wants *you*?" I flung at him.

"That is very simple: say yes."

"Even though it'd be an awful price that might tear my soul into shreds? Drive me insane?"

"That is not even a question. Give me to Her and take comfort in the fact I went willingly."

"So wait. You trust Her to protect my soul if I give *you* to Her, but you don't trust Her to look after me if I go talk to Her?" I rolled my eyes. "You are an *idiot*."

Flint stepped with delicate care through the door. He sidled close to Gabel, one deft spring away from tying Gabel's neck into a bow.

Gabel ignored Flint. "I do not trust you to not trade our *child*."

"You *fucking asshole!*" How *dare* he think I'd trade our baby for the world.

...but would I?...

I inhaled a sob. Tears fountained over my eyes and down my cheeks.

"You would *think* it," he hissed, leaning close. "Can you really swear to me you would never consider it?"

The tears blinded me and my chest shuddered on sobs. "No, I'd never do it!"

There I'd said it. I would not pay that price. I would not.

I was an Oracle: I looked over the edge. I looked into the bowl when others couldn't.

I'd had my peek, and that was enough.

"Are you *sure*?" he loomed closer.

Everything howled at me *run, submit, cower.* "Yes! I've served Her faithfully through all of this, but I won't serve Her if She asks that! I will come back and tell you to destroy it all! All of it! I'm not buying the world with our pup's soul! How could you think that?!"

He curled his upper lip. "Because I know you. You *resolved* it. You even *thought about it!*"

"How dare you!" I screamed. "You fucking monster, how dare you!"

"Don't deny it!"

"Enough!" Flint shoved between us. "Enough. Luna Gianna is entitled to contemplate all possibilities in preparation for going before the Moon. She is entering a negotiation. It is better to have her answers prepared ahead of time. It is *not* a sin to toy with a dark thought."

Gabel growled and eyed me. "I wonder, sometimes, if you want this pup enough."

I gasped.

Flint shoved Gabel back hard enough it sent Gabel flying. Carlos dove forward and pulled me out of the way.

"Luna," he said urgently, "we can leave. Go to IceMaw. Forget this. Leave them to their war. This is the second time today he's spoken to you like this! How much more are you going to put up with?"

Flint, voice unlike anything I'd heard, said, "*Never* say that, Gabel. Get down on your knees and grovel for that. You will regret those words as you have never regretted anything in your life. They will haunt you for eternity." Flint grabbed Gabel by the throat, yanked him down, face to face, and snarled, "*I know these things.*"

Flint flung him, blue-gloss dark and writhing, like a nest of snakes on his skin. Gabel impacted the wall. Some of the antiquities and books trembled.

We'd *just* cleaned that up.

Flint slashed at the air with one hand. "Have I taught you *nothing*? This is *fear*. This is the deepest fear there is: a fear born of love. And it will warp you and twist you and turn you into a coward! She's so afraid for the pup's future she can't enjoy it, so you think *that* dread means she doesn't *want* it *enough*? Maybe *you* don't want it enough if *you* are so unconcerned!"

"I do," Gabel retorted.

"Then you are the worst kind of fool. What if you had to choose between her and the pup? What if the price of saving her life was the pup's, and only *you* could speak for her?"

Gabel seemed to turn molten.

Flint raised his chin. "I thought so."

Gabel, defiant, said, "That is not the same."

"You'd consider sacrificing the baby for *her* life. *One* life. And she considered—for a *breath*—if she'd sacrifice it to save *thousands*. You're right. It's *not* the same."

Gabel's upper lip curled.

"*Grovel* for what you just said," Flint hissed.

"I don't want him to grovel," I snapped. "I want him to get out of my way. I'm seeking the Moon, and that's final."

Flint snarled at Gabel, "Perhaps you should occupy yourself with the Oracle's answer to your *other* question, wolf. I can guess what you asked, and I suggest you take her counsel."

Second question? How long had Gabel been having Kiery scry for him?

I turned and left the room before I started sobbing or screaming and flinging things. The pup squirmed under my heart. This couldn't be good for it. It had ears by now. It could hear us shouting at each other. Carlos followed on my heels.

"Gianna!" Gabel shouted after me.

I slammed the door to my blue bedroom behind me, but not before Carlos caught it on his palm.

"Leave me alone, Beta." Fuck, he was *always* underfoot.

"He is a *monster*," Carlos said flatly.

"He's the Moon's Destroyer. Being a monster is part of his divine mandate."

"You can't stay here. He was *menacing* you. You were afraid of him!"

"Like I was afraid of Aaron?"

Carlos stiffened and looked away. "Come to IceMaw. You have to punish him for accusing you of that."

"Who are *you* to tell me when to punish an Alpha?" I spat. "So I need to punish him for *that*, but I didn't need to punish Aaron for *this*?"

He looked at my belly, then looked away again. I had meant my Mark, but oh well. This was such a stupid game of keeping score. "I am going to speak to the Moon, Carlos. I want to know what this weapon is and the price She wants for it."

"Do you believe it's the pup?"

I shifted my weight to ease the pinch in my spine. "No, of course I don't! The pup's too obvious! Gabel once told me the art of torment relies on *not* beating the hope out of someone. If the Moon wanted Gabel to simply rip the world to pieces, I wouldn't exist. There are two outcomes on the scales."

Down from three, but I didn't tell him that.

Carlos watched my every breath. "The skull and the crown. And how many times did Aaron warn Gabel about losing his head? Seems it's already happened."

True, and it was a warning to Gabel if there'd ever been one. "The answer wasn't for you, Carlos. It was for Gabel, and it was for me. I've had similar visions since mating Gabel. Believe me: the Moon isn't after the baby, so everyone needs to calm the hell down!"

"Starting with you."

"I put up with you. I don't like you."

"It doesn't change She wants something terrible."

"And trying to guess the Moon's next cruel design is like trying to guess Gabel's."

"Fine. Come to IceMaw anyway. You can't let him think he can speak to you that way."

Well, that would be a stupid plan, wouldn't it? An infuriated

Gabel becoming even more deranged and paranoid and grabby. "Won't solve any problems, Carlos. Will just make new ones."

"He *cannot* talk to you that way! He cannot treat you this way! You can't cater to his anger!"

"Oh, how amusing that you found your fangs *now*. Where were you months ago? Gabel is the mate I chose. *Period*. He is the father of my pup. *End of conversation*. Now choke it down like a good wolf, or get the *fuck* out. Your choice, and frankly, I don't care what you choose."

"With respect, Luna, that blue-gloss Mark—"

"There is absolutely *nothing* about to come out of your mouth that is respectful. I am not some fucking *incubator*. I am not the vessel of your hopes and dreams. I am the Balance-Keeper, and I *chose* Gabel. Don't tell me I haven't earned the right to choose after Aaron *and* Gabel took those choices from me."

"I am just trying to advise you, Luna, even if I am insistent."

"Hilarious. Did you *advise* Aaron to *not* maul me with half as much candor and rudeness?"

He hunched his shoulders, miserable and contrite.

"*Out*." I pointed at the door.

He obeyed.

I ran my hand over my belly. The pup fluttered and squirmed. "You know I wouldn't jeopardize you. Not for the world."

Because I wouldn't. They thought I would, but I *wouldn't*. And the Moon knew it.

The baby shoved a foot into my side.

How was I so alone when I had so many damn wolves fighting over me?

LITTLE EARS & SONNETS

"**Y**ou aren't talking to me."

"I'm not *not* talking to you." I was allowed to be in bed nestled into an outrageous amount of pillows while reading some book of Shakespearean sonnets and I tried to get myself right for seeking the Moon.

Gabel stared at me from the foot of the bed, his hands twisted in his shirt. "I can *feel* you are unhappy."

"Of course I'm unhappy! How many times did we fight today?"

"That's not what has you unhappy. You are hurt. I can feel how hurt you are over something. I have done something wrong. By now, buttercup, I can tell. This reminds me a little of Gardenia. I have certainly not been neglecting you to... flit... with some other female." He sounded disgusted at even saying it.

Fuck this stupid Bond. "You accused me of not wanting our baby."

"Yes, and that made you furious. This has you wounded. Not the same thing. I know this feeling. I've felt it before."

I scrunched into the pillows.

He watched, his eyes as hard and sharp as the facets on the tourmaline spear. "And you are burrowing."

"I am not burrowing!"

"You have *eight pillows*."

"They're comfortable." There was exactly no chance I was going to confess to him what had me upset, because it was stupid: I had never felt betrayed by anyone choosing to consult another Oracle. And my mate had *every* reason to consult another Oracle because there were questions *I* simply couldn't get answers to.

But I still felt betrayed he'd consulted Kiery. It'd been hard enough to accept the first question, but now there was a second question? I'd thrown up from how wrenching it was.

And I could *not* tell him. It'd be grossly inappropriate for an Oracle to guilt a petitioner on their choice of Oracles. I should be grateful Kiery was here, and the Moon had reopened Her Eye and was willing to answer a question!

Any Oracle would tell me to get over myself. I would tell another Oracle to get over herself.

He flung his shirt aside. "You *know* I have not *looked* at another she-wolf."

"I know, and this isn't about the sex." He was a lupine. It was weird and uncomfortable for him.

He tensed, seemed about to speak, then visibly stopped himself, fiddled with his hands like he was turning something over in them, before trying again. "Then why are you burrowing?"

"I'm just emotional over nothing."

"Why aren't you telling me?"

"I can't. Oracle nonsense." There. That should do it.

"Oracles cannot coexist in a pack not named SableFur?"

"More like Oracles are never Lunas. She's an Elder Oracle, I am a Luna. I've got my pride." I was dangerously close to a lie and hated it.

Gabel half-grinned. "Send them to IceMaw and let them be someone else's problem."

"I'll just burrow and lick my pregnancy-thin skin. I'm mortified I even feel this way."

He gave me the side-eye. "I *mostly* believe you. I suppose that will have to do. The midwife has warned me about upsetting you."

"I'm not giving you details. I remember what happened the *last* time I gave you just enough information to deduce Oracle business. I ended up accused of violating my vows of silence."

He snorted. "Oracles. And no one is taking you from me this time. Not again. *No one.*"

"Please, Gabel," I begged, as Aaron shifted in the distance. Because Aaron sure as fuck was going to keep trying and couldn't resist the bait.

Gabel went to finish getting undressed, then got into bed next to me. He counted the pillows, noted I'd left him with one, then bent and pressed his cheek to my belly. "Little one, you probably hear your mother and I argue too much."

His eyes sought mine, his slightly-too-long summer-bleached hair slipping over his brow. I brushed the stray lock away. My fingertips moved over his cheek.

"You're determined to do this," he said.

"I have faith the Moon won't let anything happen to the baby."

"You frighten me with how...aweless... you are."

"Is that even a word?"

"Of course it is a word. It's an old human word. It means you have no awe for things you *should* be in awe of."

I brushed another lock of his hair. "This coming from the wolf who calls the Moon the Silvery Sky Bitch and threatens to punch out Her Eye."

He stroked my belly. "Do you hear how your mother speaks to me, little one? She is so fierce while trying to tell me she isn't."

"We're doomed."

He chuckled. "Watch our pup be calm and diplomatic."

"You have to love them even if they aren't fierce."

"I don't intend to leave a broken and warring kingdom for our children to inherit. A diplomat with a vicious silver tongue would be ideal, not another blood-thirsty creature. In fact, start reading some of that Shakespeare so they can begin words early."

"I am not reciting poetry. Good grief."

"Then I will." He reached for my book and took it, and flipped through the pages until he found one he deemed appropriate for a pup's ears, and started reading about trees decaying and things growing. He paused. "You *will* be careful. I would hate to have to come for you again."

"I know you'll come for me. I have no doubt. I'm not afraid."

"That's what worries me, but I also know I can't keep you off your prey." He flipped through the pages and chose another sonnet to read to my belly. "Little one, you and I will read sonnets while your mother is gone chasing the Moon."

Onward To Hell

~*~ The Way To Hell ~*~

I t was very hot. And quite dark.

No, not dark. It was red, and the walls glowed with heat.

I stood on a hot cobblestone road in wolf-form, curiously aware of an emptiness in my belly: the pup had not come with me, but my soul felt its absence within me. I slicked my ears down against the sudden jolt of worry and focused on staying within the vision. Under my paws I felt the smoothness of the tektite. I looked down again, and for a second, saw a flicker of the ancient glass.

Behind me stretched a dark cobblestone road disappearing into an acrid mist and darkness. Shades slowly walked up the road, shuffling, head bent, and they moaned.

The damned. These were the damned. They shambled very, very slowly to their final end.

Before me was a gate rising three humans high, made of twisted black thorns. The lock was made of shards of bone. Beyond the twisted network of wicked vines and brambles was a bleak, desolate landscape of sand and putrid sky.

I approached the gate. It swung open with a tearing, fleshy, bone-breaking groan.

I stepped off the road into the sand on the other side of the gate. A thousand little bugs swarmed—oh Moon, the sand was not sand; it was billions, trillions, some-unheard-of-large-number of little biting bugs.

And they promptly started to chew on the tender flesh between my claws and swarmed up into my fur like a stifling second pelt and bit everything. My ears, my eyes, my lips, tried to get into my mouth, under my tail.

Well, this sucked. So much for hoping the Moon wouldn't subject me to the full Hell Experience.

The Gate slammed, then disappeared completely, leaving me smack dab in the center of a desert-made-of-bugs.

No more shades, nothing—totally alone. Great. I'd been deposited into a remote corner of Hell.

I tried to ignore the bugs biting under my tail and crawling in my ears. There didn't appear to be a sun. The sky was just non-specifically bright and hazy and seemed gray and yellow at the same time. The only landmark was a shadowy black silhouette on the horizon.

That seemed as good a direction as any. I headed out across the squirming... sand.

A chorus of howls rose up from the sky. The Hounds. The Pack. The wolves that hunted the damned souls and devoured them.

And they were coming for me.

The shadows on the horizon wobbled with heat shimmer.

The Pack slowed to a lope, then a jog, and finally a walk. Each one of them was a nightmare: dark, leathery hides stretched over grotesque bones and joints, leathery stumps for ears, their faces like skulls left out in the sun. Patches and tufts of oily fur clung in places. They had huge, yellow talons and immense fangs, and *spittle that steamed as drops hit the bricks. Sick, diseased-looking yellow eyeballs sat deep in leathery sockets. Flies crawled over their skin, clustered around their eyes, lips, ears.*

And the stench. They smelled like ash and burning and... damnation.

They milled and writhed about, panting in the fetid air, yipping, rat tails wagging and slapping their desiccated flanks.

One separated himself from the others. He lowered his belly to me and wriggled forward. "Beautiful Oracle, who brings the gaze of our Mistress."

His voice reminded me of the little bugs swarming over my claws.

"Hound," I replied.

He wagged his tail and opened his maw, rotting tongue lolling between gruesome teeth. The rest of the pack whined with hunger. "Come with us, Oracle. The Moon bids us escort you to a certain location. It would not do for the Obsidian Oracle, the Wielder of the Scythe, to wander without escort."

My silvery-blue fur tingled with fear. Obsidian Oracle? Wielder of what?

The Hound spat something into the bug-dirt. The venom in his spittle caused the sand to curl up into glass beads. He approached me, and used his hind claws to scuff sand over the spittle, then said in his bug-hiss voice, "This way, Obsidian Oracle. Walk at my shoulder and ask me any questions you like."

The rest of the Pack fell in behind us, still whining and yipping. I ignored them darting at my heels and bouncing around me.

The Lead Hound set a brisk pace across the bug-sand until we came to a raised sandstone road. He set paw upon it and I followed, and the bugs instantly fled my coat.

"How long have you... been here?" I asked the Lead Hound.

A grin. "If I told you the name I wear around my neck, you might know it. A long time, Moon-Graced one. My pack is only the finest of the damned, the ones so terrible that we are useful. There are only thirteen of us, a wretched Honor Guard for the Dark Gaze, and when one arrives fit to challenge for a place, well. The loser is dinner. I have never lost."

"You seem rather... enthusiastic."

"Once you have been here a while," he giggled, "you realize how sweet this servitude is. They all believe they should not be here. The ones we devour, that is."

He licked his rotting lips.

"Have you ever eaten an Oracle?"

Another giggle. "We eat our own kind, Obsidian Oracle, of course we have dined upon Oracle."

"Recently?"

Another giggle and this time the entire pack giggled with him. "Soon. We are the end, not the beginning."

The pack giggled soon, soon, soon.

"This way, this way," the Lead Hound whispered, heading down the road until we came to a large, flat, open courtyard.

Damnation never looks like what you expect.

In the rather lovely courtyard was a bunch of wolves, all shaven like poodles. Really fancy poodles, like with the pom-pom leg poofs and hip poofs and all. They were lined up along all the sides of the plaza, each with a human handler. The human handlers were sort of see-through, like shades, but were clearly unique souls with blurred-out faces.

Somehow the Moon had acquired human souls. Those weren't constructs to facilitate the punishment—they were legitimate human souls. And each poodle-wolf wore a horrific choke collar where the prongs were like razor blades and the chains were fitted tight to their throats.

An "instructor" shade walked around calling out instructions for what each handler-shade was supposed to make each poodle-wolf do. When a poodle-wolf refused to obey or did not obey prop-

erly, they were punished with the collar and they'd scream and yip and the scent of burned flesh—

"Silver," the Lead Hound whispered in his creeping-bug voice. "Silver prongs."

The poodle-wolves were made to do all the usual things you'd expect, and were expected to obey instantly and perfectly. The poodle-wolves were all gaunt and starving, and if they were perfect, they'd sometimes get thrown a juicy bit of steak or clean, fresh water, which they were so desperate for they'd accept from human hands politely. Attacking the hands earned punishment.

Over and over and over, the instructions came. The poodle-wolves were expected to do many tricks, and sometimes a poodle-wolf would get singled out to perform for a cluster of human-shades, and the human-shades would suddenly manifest drinks and snacks, and they'd all have a little tea party while the poodle-wolf was commanded to perform tricks for their amusement.

The Lead Hound lowered his belly and whined to me as the rest of the pack yipped and writhed. "Obedience," he whispered, "they must obey, and they want to obey."

I cocked my head slightly, so I looked at him out of my Moon-marked eye. "And that is their punishment. They were disobedient in life."

"Yes, Mistress of Obsidian," he whispered. "In fact, you know such a wolf. He is over there, yes? Go see."

I wasn't exactly here for a tour of Hell and its occupants, but I couldn't resist either. I stepped over the perimeter of the plaza onto the blazing hot stones and somehow, from all the many wolves, spotted exactly who the Lead Hound had indicated. A big poodle-wolf who hadn't turned gaunt and starving yet, with a female handler with dark hair and pale skin, but no real face. He sat at the handler's heel, trying not to be sullen and failing. She jerked his lead every time she sensed his bad disposition.

"Romero," I said.

The poodle wolf swung his head around, and his lupine face turned into a mask of hatred. His handler froze but didn't punish him.

The Lead Hound paced to my side, giggling under his breath.

Romero pulled his lips back across his teeth. He spat at my feet.

The handler-shade lifted a hand but did not correct him.

"Stand quietly," the Lead Hound whisper-giggled to Romero, barring his teeth while the Pack whined and howled their hunger. "The Mistress of Obsidian would look at you."

"So you're in here with me?" Romero inquired with contempt.

"The Obsidian Oracle, Wielder of the Scythe, is a guest of the Moon," the Lead Hound crawled eagerly towards Romero, clicking his jaws. "We are hungry, soul. We are always hungry. But she is not for us. You, though..."

"Obsidian Oracle? Wielder of the Scythe?" Romero looked at the Hound.

The Hound wriggled more, eagerly. "Yes, yes, shade. So fortunate she recalls your name and favors you with it! Perhaps you will make a Hound one day."

"Not a chance," I said dryly. Gabel was a Hound. Romero was a low-grade scumbag.

The Lead Hound threw his head back with a howled laugh, and the entire Pack answered. The poodle-wolves, including Romero, cowered. Some submission wetted themselves.

"Punishment!" the Lead Hound howled. "Punishment! Only pups soil!"

The shade-handlers lashed into their charges.

The Lead Hound turned back to me and returned to his whisper-giggle-grovel. "This way, Mistress of Obsidian, this way."

The road became a huge, open avenue that ended pointing at the black structures that had been clinging to the horizon. All along the road were huge sandstone pillars, and on each one was a wolf bound in silver chains in varying states of... let's just say, torture. Some had spears in them, others had been cut open so their insides spilled out, others were bound and tied so tight the chains shook. Some were muzzled, collared—they were living statues that lined a lovely broad main road up to...

"What's in the... black structures up there?" I asked.

"It is where the worst souls are locked away for their own unique, custom-crafted punishments. And when the punishment meets its end, She sets them loose for us to devour."

I shuddered. "So, why are we here, Lead Hound? What is this... boulevard of the damned?"

The road seemed to stretch on forever.

"This is the place where those who betrayed their pack remain," he whisper-giggled. "The true menaces. The worthy betrayers. Not the small variety such as the one you called Romero."

A terrible feeling started.

"This way, this way, this way."

I tried not to look at the tormented souls, because each one was a different kind of nightmare.

The Hounds stopped in front of a pedestal.

His name was carved in some awful script that I had never seen before but could understand. Silver chains were taut. One front paw was broken, and his lower jaw hung loose and slack. One eye was missing. Flies buzzed around the oozing holes and wounds.

"Hix," the Lead Hound giggle-whispered, "you have a visitor."

THE TRADE

Below Hix were several runestones: loyalty, pack, love. Each blasted and upside down to denote their opposite meaning.

Hix had come to IronMoon when he'd been cast out of his original pack for trying to overthrow the Alpha.

Even after he'd given his life to help me in SableFur. It hadn't been enough for redemption.

"No," I whispered. "No. You don't belong here."

The sky washed from its fetid yellow to a blue, and all the souls cowered, and the Hounds groveled and howled the Song of the Moon.

The Moon stood in the center of the boulevard of the damned.

She had skin of many shades of gray and white, like the reflection of light on moving water. Her eyes were a deep field of darkness that waxed and waned in shape from full darkness to pure white, and her hair twisted in colors of gray and white as well. Long lines of fur traced in patterns all over Her body in Oracle-blue-silver, but like a blue-gloss tattoo. And on Her brow was a crown set with a moon that changed phases.

She gestured at me, and I twisted into human form, but did not kneel.

She tilted Her head towards Hix. The crown on Her head moved in the sallow light, now a sliver of a waning crescent.

"I'm here for the weapon," I said, my voice shaking. "I am ready to hear the price."

The Moon bowed Her head slightly, but only so She could grin at me, showing a mouth full of crystal, pointed fangs in a human mouth. When She spoke, Her voice was iron and stars. ** **The human Ana's soul.** **

"What?" *Humans maybe could sell their souls to their Devil, but not to the Moon.*

At least, I didn't think it worked that way...

The Moon's grin didn't waver, and instead spread. ** **Her soul.** **

"But it's her soul. I can't give it to you." *I wasn't normally this stupid, but I couldn't process what She was asking.*

** **How do you think the first wolves were made?** **

Well, yes, the first wolves had been chosen, and it was all sort of complicated and murky, but those wolves went willingly. She hadn't just reached down into the local village and plucked a couple of souls.

** **Far back in her lineage, she was a wolf. Her ancestors turned their back on Me. I want to reclaim what is Mine. Give Me her soul.** **

"But it's her soul. It's not mine to give."

** **You are not understanding. I can take any soul I wish. I am telling you that the price of the weapon is Ana's soul.** **

It finally dawned on me what She meant. "No, please. There has to be something else."

** **Your pup?** ** *She cocked Her head slightly.* ** **We could negotiate.** **

"I have done everything You have ever asked of me! I have

acted in good faith, how is this good faith? Why are You doing this?"

Silence, and the crown went dark, a wicked cruel sliver of the new moon, when Her eye was closed, and the ground of Hell trembled slightly with warning.

** You have come here, asking for a weapon to defeat Adrianna, and hold back the Tides. The Tides that others have sought to control, or ignore, and now they weep when the Destroyer comes. If I had wanted to hand you such a weapon at no cost, I would merely smite Adrianna in MoonFire and be done with it. **

I gulped.

** But that, ** She said in that iron and star voice, ** is not how it will be. I did not lead My wolf children to ruin. They did that themselves. You do not have to save them, Balance-Keeper. You do not have to save any of them. That is a choice you can make, too. You realize that, do you not? They will not thank you for saving them, just like most of the IronMoon are not glad to have you as their Luna. They do not respect you. They do not want you. They see you, at best, as their Alpha's toy, and at worst, something to be disposed of as a hindrance to their life plans. And that is your pack. The one you choose every day you do not go to IceMaw. **

Well, that stung.

** The only thing preventing them from acting against you is fear of Gabel and of Flint. They will, at best, fear you because of the company you keep. I have shown you this to prove to you that you are not like them. That you can look into the bowl, and they do not even try. You have no fear of this place. **

...was that a good thing, or a bad thing?

** You must understand that if you choose to try to save the wolves, they will curse your name, as They curse

Me, as you have cursed Me. You have only had a small taste of it. They will never be grateful. You may be remembered as great, perhaps, even, if you do things correctly, as one of the greatest she-wolves in history. Legendary, even. But you will never be remembered fondly. Your name will be whispered with fearful reverence. You will be the Obsidian Oracle, She Who Wielded The Scythe of Waning. **

I had not expected to die loved, but to be remembered as... that...I'd rather not be remembered at all.

** Or you can walk away. **

"Walk away?" I echoed.

** I cannot force you to pick up the weapon. I cannot force you to participate. I have shown you My anger and My wrath in all its forms.** She gestured to our surroundings. *** You can walk away. You can let come what may, and that too, is a choice. As Aaron told you, the planets will continue their doomed dance without you. You cannot stop it. It is inevitable, as this is inevitable for all who do not follow My Law. ***

"But I've seen what happens," I said. "You showed me. Adrianna crowns herself with bones and skin. Gabel's skull was on the other side of the scales. It's her or me."

** But not your bones or skin. Did you see yourself in that vision of Adrianna being crowned? Were you in that vision? **

My entire soul shuddered in terror. In all the visions I'd had since this began, I had always been in them, or there had always been something for me in them. But the vision of Adrianna in the bone chapel? Technically, I'd been in that vision.

Adrianna had worn my pelt, Gabel's skull as a crown with the fangs removed and turned upside down to crown the top of the skull, and one of Aaron's bones as a sceptre.

A sensation like the cool, silvery brush of fur against the nape of my neck sent a shiver down my soul-spine. Aaron. I looked around for him. Had he followed me through the Gate?

The Moon's crystal-toothed grin spread a little wider, and somehow, the waning moon of Her crown seemed even more dark and ashen, like part of existence had just been erased by its silhouette. **** You are the Balance-Keeper. You are the point on which Light and Dark turns. The Scythe-Moon has fallen, and the Sun has set. I offer you a shred of My power to grant mercy where I would simply let the Tides come, wash it all away, **** *she gestured to the bleak landscape again,* ****the tidal wave brought by the Destroyer. The storm caused by his impact. The barren, wasted, twisted land that will result. ****

Flint had been right: it was the end for us. "Is that why I have a hole in my soul? It's a keyhole."

** Not exactly. **

"What will happen to Ana?" *I asked to buy time or keep the Moon talking so I could figure out some option or alternative or loophole. She couldn't want me to hand over Ana's soul. I had to be misunderstanding.*

** She will become a werewolf. Nothing more, nothing less. You must decide, Luna, now. Will you take the power I have offered you, or would you prefer to fight with mortal claws? **

"It's not my soul to trade!" *I shouted.* "It isn't! It isn't! I never wanted Your power! I didn't even want to be an Elder Oracle! I didn't want to be a Luna, I don't want to be a Queen, and I sure don't want to become a goddess!"

** But you chose to be an Oracle. And you pursued My power your entire life. You have single-mindedly pursued the edges of your power, despite your teachers warning you you were too bold. You used it first for the purpose for which it was intended. Then you used it to fight the Destroyer. You used it to warp the Bond into a weapon.

You used it to survive, you used it to endure, you entered the Tides over and over, passed through My Eye, even walked through that Gate, all seeking to defy Me and My Design. You have never rejected My power. You have always wanted more, and I have always granted you more, Balance-Keeper, because that is how I made you. Just as I have always granted My Destroyer more of My power, as I turned My back on My Instrument so that when I howled for him, he obeyed without question because it was the only sound he heard. You have paid for that power, yes, but now the price of more is the price I have named. ** Her crown remained dark and unrelenting. Tendrils of smoke rose off the cruel tips, and it became even more ashen.

"I didn't ask for the starlight wolves," I said. "You gave them to me! I did that out of mercy! I never asked for that power!"

** *No, I did not give them to you. You took their lives, and you claimed their souls. You did nothing to return their souls to me. You did not enter the Tides to inquire how to give Me their souls. You simply kept them for yourself.* **

"No, that's not what happened. That's not what I meant to do!"

** *But you used them, didn't you, when I made them useful. You never questioned, you never inquired, you never doubted. I gave you power, and you used it. And don't you remember the terrible price you paid to wield them in SableFur?* **

"I wasn't *supposed* to..." I faltered.

** *You could have let Lucas challenge Magnes. You could have gone with Aaron. You could have stayed with Gabel. You could have fled with Hix. You could have chosen any of those things. I offered you the chance to* *change course* **many** *times, and you chose the divine* *weapon. You chose to chase My power.* **

I dropped to my knees and wept. "But You wanted *me to!"*

** **Wanted?** *Little wolf, I never* **wanted** *any of this to be* **necessary. I have offered you** *many* **chances at escape. The only thing I ever commanded you do is go to SableFur, and the only reason that came to pass is Gabel consented. You have had a dozen times you** *could* **have walked away, before or since. You even could have refused to let Gardenia stand at Gabel's side and chosen to use My power to humiliate him in front of Anders, but you used My power to punish him instead. You have** *always* **chosen to fight.** **

The cruelty of that crown felt like it crushed through my soul and sliced me into pieces. "I thought I was doing what was right."

** **I am not condemning the choices you have made. I am pointing out that you have had many choices, and you have always chosen to wield My power to try to thwart the Tides. The wolves have seen the Tides coming in for a long time. They have not done differently. Their choices have been made. Now they drown and cry to Me? The Comet will continue on his path. His purpose was—and is—to destroy everything. I did not send him to triumph and wear a crown.** **

I had thorns in my throat. I coughed and pawed at my wind-pipe, and fished in my mouth to try to get them out.

** **I sent Gabel to lay waste to that diseased patch of thorns. That is his nature, and his rage turned on Me? Exactly his purpose, and one he has pursued, as a puppy who learns how hard they may bite by biting their dam. Occasionally, he lost his way, drunk on his—My—own power, but you returned him to his course, because that is your purpose. He is blessed and I love him, because he is exactly as I made him. You love him too, because you see**

his beautiful, dark perfection, the nobility of his monstrous purpose.

**Adrianna I despise. I gave to her some of what I gave to you, and she defiled it and turned her back on it, she persisted, she set herself to be as inevitable as the Tides I suffer her wading in. I gave her Anita, but Anita failed in her purpose as well, and both are the sum of many things, and they chose to be those things, in the exact opposite manner Aaron did not. You see, little Oracle, this is the truth: Gabel, and Aaron, and Anita, and Adrianna... they are all phases of the same monstrous thing. And only you will ever see them for what they truly are, because you are the Balance-Keeper, the Obsidian Oracle, the Scythe of the Waning Moon, and only you dare look in the bowl that holds the world. **

I screamed to the putrid sky. "A weapon that might not work, for the price of an innocent's soul?"

** Yes. **

"You are a monster," I spat.

** I have My dark aspect, do not deny yours. You have never confessed to anyone, not even your mate, that you enjoyed—even a little bit—punishing Gardenia by putting her in Gabel's private playground, where I care not what he does. How you left wolves to suffer when they begged you for mercy, and how you sent your SableFur warriors to fight the IronMoon, knowing it was all a farce. Did you spend their lives and bodies cheaply, or dearly? You would say dearly, many others would be furious. How you left your First Beta to suffer and die, knowing that was the fate he'd endure. How you hid your Mark and misled packs. How part of you loved Aaron, and how for all your protests, you probably would have fallen in love with him eventually—how if he had done things differently, he could have won you. How you were

tempted, for an instant, in your room at SableFur, to go with him. How you did not tell your Alpha about the brewing betrayal in his kingdom. Shall I go on with my Judgement and the listing of your soul's dark secrets?

By the measure of the wolves who would behold you, Obsidian Oracle, you are *a monster, and you will never convince them otherwise. If they knew the truth, they would call you far worse. They cannot see through the Eye of the Moon. Gabel may be the monster that eats fear. He is debase, craven, a lupine who perhaps cannot be held fully responsible for what he is. But you? Oh, to all the other wolves, you are the monster who chooses to be a monster. Aaron was called, Gabel was born, but you were* taken*, and you've never had the good sense to escape, even when it would have been as easy as walking out the front door. Instead, you carry a monster's progeny. You* could *have run a dozen times. You even have an entire powerful alliance in the south willing to protect you from Gabel, but you still do not leave. That is what they will see. That you* chose *all of this when there was so much better waiting for you. *

The Moon touched Hix's paw, pushing Her crystal-tipped finger into the tissue between his claws. He yelped and trembled. She never stopped looking at me.

** Ana's soul** *the Moon said,* ***and there is no negotiation. I do not open the Black Thorn Gate lightly. Ana's soul for the weapon you—and you alone—can wield to smite Adrianna. ***

She wanted too much: I couldn't barter Ana's soul. "The hole in my soul is Your Eye? All this time... I've been seeing through Your gaze?"

She crouched down and tilted my chin up. *** **What do you think that Moon in your eye is, Oracle? Gabel was made to be a monster. I forged him that way. Aaron chose to***

answer my howls. You, you I forged in both forms. I gave you the capacity to be a monster and the sight to see the difference. **

My tears coursed down my cheeks and along Her finger and fell to the ground as crystal beads. My heart howled, it screamed in pain, and somewhere distant, Gabel howled in response, and Aaron's song tore through the rest of me. I wept while She held my chin and stared at me with those pitiless eyes, Her crystal-silver irises rotating with a sweep of light like the Moon moving across the dome of the sky.

I sobbed one last time. "There is nothing else You will take?"

** You have nothing to give. **

"But You won't promise the weapon will mean victory. Or what the weapon is. Or how to use it."

** You figured out the starlight wolves. I will tell you this: when the time comes to wield the weapon, you must not hesitate. You must not flinch from what results. **

"I already don't like the result."

A cruel smile.

"Will I at least know if it has worked or not?"

She nodded, the crown shifting from cruel crescent to full.

I could walk away. I could go to IceMaw, leave Gabel to the war, wall myself and my pup in the southern packs and hope it burned itself out. I'd endured Aaron's death, could I endure Gabel's?

But I'd abandon my pack, my wolves, my position as Luna, my chosen mate, my pup's father. How was any of that not damnation?

It was damnation by a different name.

I closed my eyes. The tears poured down my cheeks.

"Give me the weapon. Take her soul."

THE PRICE PAID

The Moon had kept me overnight. It'd felt like forever I'd been in Hell. I hadn't faced Ana yet. Breakfast was soon. I was trying to get up the resolve to walk out of the bedroom and face what I'd done.

"What did the Moon want?" Gabel asked as he sashed a kilt around his hips. "And what's the weapon?"

"She sent me to Hell to get it," I said, my voice hoarse like I'd been screaming. "I had to go beyond a gate made of black thorns and walk through Hell, and a pack of Hounds escorted me. I saw Romero."

"What's Romero's eternal punishment?"

I'd just told him I'd marched through Hell and he was like, *oh, really, how interesting*. Should I laugh or cry? "Eternal obedience training."

He chuckled, then turned serious again. "The weapon. The price."

I gulped. "I saw Hix."

"Hix is the weapon?"

I shook my head. "No, no, She... showed me. To show me how She... just... how it's the end. How She is past caring. She

285

didn't tell me what the weapon is. Just that I'll have to figure out how to use it, but I'll know if it's worked or not."

Gabel frowned. "And what did this... *weapon*... cost us?"

"Ana's soul," I croaked.

"Her *soul*."

"The Moon... turned her into a wolf. Like the First Wolves." I managed to croak it all out before I gagged on the thorns lodged in my throat.

"You sold Ana's soul and humanity to the Moon."

Everything the Moon had told me crashed down on me like a deluge of rain, but the rain and Tides would never wash away what I'd done. The mistakes I'd made. The times I'd chosen to fight when I could have fled. The times I'd taken the Moon's power as my own, not realizing what I was doing, what She *let* me do.

And now I had done the unspeakable.

And I had to go face Ana at breakfast.

And I wouldn't beg forgiveness, because how could she ever forgive me?

"So your pet human is now your pet wolf?" Gabel asked, disbelieving.

I pawed at my tears. "Yes."

"I haven't been woken to advise me there's a random warform tearing apart her room. Perhaps it was a trick of the Moon."

I raised my eyes to him. "You mean... She told me how I always reached for more of Her power. How I always called on Her power, how I always chased it. Do you think She did it to... prove something?"

"You are ambitious, buttercup. Tsk tsk, I have spoken to you about it many times."

"Perhaps I have to... use the weapon for the price to get paid."

"Or perhaps Ana just has not had her first cup of coffee."

"I would think she'd be *more* inclined to rage-shift pre-coffee."

He offered me his hand. "You did what was necessary, if that was the deal you struck. One soul to end this war sounds like an excellent price."

"How can you say that? She's *human*."

"Was, sounds like."

"Gabel."

He didn't even seem slightly contrite for his comment.

Ana was sipping her coffee. She was her usual sleepy-eyed self, and seemed no different, and I couldn't smell anything, but Flint was giving her the side-eye in the most subtle way Flint could give anyone the side-eye, and Eroth seemed exceedingly confused, but smart enough to not say a damn word. Kiery and Lucas gave me a look as I came in, and Gabel even hesitated as he took his seat.

Oh, no.

My stomach disappeared into some other dimension.

"You're back," Kiery commented.

"It was quick," I said hoarsely.

"Did you..." She stopped talking.

"She took me beyond the Black Thorn Gate," I rasped. "I... I paid the price."

"The Black Thorn Gate?" Kiery asked, tone hushed.

"The Gate to Hell, after judgement. It's black thorns. All thorns."

Gabel put food on my plate. The pup squirmed in my belly.

"I had the weirdest dream," Ana commented as she munched on toast. She stopped, looked at the toast, sniffed it, frowned, then kept eating.

"Oh?" Kiery asked. I think I went the same color as white paint.

"Had a weird dream about a woman with spinny eyes and a mouth full of crystal teeth." She sniffed her coffee, then sniffed her sausage, then leaned over and sniffed Flint. Flint regarded her like she was out of her mind. "She grabbed my head and took out her teeth and shoved her teeth into my mouth. Weirdest dentures *ever*."

"Your teeth look like teeth to me," Kiery said.

"It was so *vivid*, you know? Woke up convinced it had happened. Had to stare at my teeth for ten minutes to convince myself nope, no dentures. But it was *weird*. Even now it seems like. Bam. Can still feel her hand on my head. Scared the shit out of me. You guys smell that?"

"Smell what?" Lucas asked, head cocked to the side, although he was a shitty liar: they *all* smelled "that," but their "that" and Ana's "that" were not the same "that."

I tried to choke down tea, but my throat was full of thorns.

"I dunno. *That*." She sniffed her coffee again. Then raised her arm and sniffed her pit. "I am smelling something. Sorry if it's me. I swear I bathed."

Flint eyed me. His green eyes clearly said *what the hell is going on*. Eroth just looked extremely bewildered and a little freaked out.

"Smells like breakfast to me," Kiery said pleasantly, but I heard the notes of an Elder Oracle's training voice.

Ana sniffed her wrist.

Gabel watched her, pausing in his own eating, then said, tone calmer than I'd *ever* heard from him, "You're smelling what we smell."

Ana looked at him. "Say what?"

"You're smelling what *we* smell. I imagine you're experiencing something similar to what I experienced as a pup. Only in reverse, and not quite the same sensations."

"What are you talking about?"

"So... I'm not losing my mind," Eroth said softly.

"I'm not imagining that," Lucas said.

I closed my eyes and shook my head. "No. No, you aren't." I

forced myself to open my eyes and face Ana directly. "Ana, your dream was real. You saw the Moon."

Ana frowned. "Say what?"

"The woman in your dream was the Moon. The price the Moon wanted. It was you."

She stared at me.

I made myself stare back. Even my pup went still.

"So... I'm a wolf," Ana said, clearly not believing or grasping it.

"Made like the First Wolves were made."

Kiery gasped and put her hands over her mouth. "Gianna, you... oh..."

I forced myself to not bow my head.

"What did you do?" Kiery whispered in hushed horror.

Even Flint seemed appalled.

Ana frowned, tilted her head to the side, sipped her coffee. She frowned a bit more. Then she looked at me. "Can we go... talk about this in private? Because I am *really* confused and would rather not say something *really* dumb in public."

Kiery whispered, "Gianna, what did you *do*?"

WE WENT TO ANA'S ROOM, WHERE ANA WANDERED around for a second, sniffing random items and checking her teeth in the mirror before she finally sat down across from me.

We stared at each other. Ana said, slowly, "So I'm a wolf."

"Yes."

"Because the price the Moon wanted for the weapon was *my* soul."

"Yes."

"Why?"

"She said your ancestors were originally wolves, but along the way, one of them turned their back on Her. I guess they started interbreeding with humans and now you're human, but She said She wanted you back."

"K. Okay. That makes... no sense but..."

"I'm sorry. I'm so sorry, I'm so so, so sorry."

Why was I apologizing? There wasn't an apology that could offset the horrific thing I'd done. There wasn't an excuse for it either.

Ana cocked her head to the side. "So.... you traded my soul to the Moon for a weapon to defeat Adrianna?"

"Yes."

"And.... She made me a wolf? Like I know we just had this conversation, but I want to be sure I'm understanding."

"Yes."

"And that's why I can smell stuff. Not just because the guys haven't washed or Cook's trying new recipes."

"Probably."

"And why I'm not panting after Flint anymore."

"You can sense he's taken."

"Huh." She tapped her fingers on her lips.

She seemed to be taking it well, but how the hell was she supposed to take it? She just found out I sold her soul to the Moon for a weapon that I was supposed to use to defeat a would-be evil Queen. That was some fucked up fairytale bingo.

"So.... I should be able to shift, right?" she asked.

"Yes. I mean, you should...?" I couldn't really remember learning to shift forms. It'd just been something I'd been able to do when I was about eight or nine.

I couldn't smell much of anything, so it was impossible for me to know what she was really thinking. She drew her ankles up and gripped them with her hands, pretty face furrowed and lips puckered as she turned it around in her mind.

"So I'm a full wolf. Not a sorta wolf," she said again. "Like totally transformed."

"According to the Moon, yes. A wolf like any other, She told me. Nothing more, nothing less."

"So... I might get some guy creeping up on me telling me I've got a scent he likes and he'll mean the lure scent."

"I suppose so, yes."

"And I'm gonna totally be into prestige and all that. I'm gonna have to play by wolf rules now."

I nodded, hating how my tears redoubled. "You... you're still a doctor, so you still have your status that way. Like I have my status as an Oracle. But..."

I choked on the thorns in my throat and couldn't get out how she wasn't going to get her behavior excused. And she wasn't going to be free to come and go as she pleased, and she'd have to be careful what territory she was in. She didn't even know what she didn't know. And I'd done this to her.

She leaned back against her couch cushions and rocked a bit, staring at the ceiling.

"Should I leave?" I asked after a few long minutes.

She focused back on me. "What? Oh, nah. It's just a lot to take in. And I'm kind of distracted by how you smell. I was trying to figure out what you smell like."

There was a whole language she'd never learned to speak. "I guess you don't have... names for a lot of what you're smelling."

"Is that it? Because that's kind of nifty. It's sort of like shrooms. Everything gets really vivid."

"I'll leave if you need some time. Or I can go get Kiery."

"Wait, you think I'm mad at you?"

"Ana, I sold your soul to buy a weapon to save my species, and there isn't even a guarantee it will work!"

"annnnnd made me a wolf! Win-win!"

Win... win?

"Fuck yeah!" She fist-pumped the air. "Woo-hoo! Legit!"

"I sold your soul!" Maybe she was not understanding this part.

"And you knew I wanted to be a wolf, right? Like I asked you if the Moon was recruiting or took converts. Don't you remember that?"

"It's your soul."

"And I told you it was for sale. Sold!" She slapped her hand on her knee.

"But... I didn't consider you. I just—" Ana's feelings hadn't been part of my mental math.

"What was there to consider? You knew it was for sale. You brokered the deal. What do you feel bad about?"

"But you didn't choose your nightmare. I chose it for you, and you won't ever wake up from it. I've seen so many Seer girls refuse to continue their Oracle training. Once they got a taste of it, they didn't want it. You had to have seen it learning to be a vet, right? How other students thought they wanted this, but once they had it, they quit? Aren't you a special type of vet too? The one who sees the worst of the worst?"

For a second, her sparkle dimmed, and I saw the same cloud I saw in Flint's gaze.

Grief saturated me. "You're not okay with this. You tell me you are, but you're not. You're just telling yourself you are."

Her sparkle disappeared completely. "I knew hanging around you was dangerous and you were in some deep shit, and I knew if push came to shove, you'd throw me under the bus. I figured I'd just end up dead and I was good with that."

My heart broke. "I never considered you expendable."

"No, no, no, that's not what I mean. It's not like you didn't look out for me as best you could. I knew what you were about. I heard what you did to those RedWater wolves. I know what you did to Gardenia, I know you merc'd your own family, I heard about the runner wolves you told to basically stand outside and die. You waged a bloody fake war to keep up appearances. The Moon offered you a weapon that *might* end this war and the price was someone else's soul? Come on, Gianna. Of course you handed me over."

I willed myself to *not* cry.

"But I'm not mad at you. That'd be like working with big cats and getting mad because a big cat hurt me. Big cats are big cats. They always can be dangerous, even if you do everything right. I knew you were a werewolf, and I knew you had an angry goddess making use of you. You warned me over and over again how dangerous all this was. I saw it for myself more than once. You told me, over and over, *leave*. And I didn't. I always knew you'd protect me until the moment you couldn't, and I stayed anyway."

The anguish that washed over my soul felt like silver injected right into my veins. "This isn't your fault. It's not like you... asked for this."

"I kinda did, though," she said. "I put myself into a dangerous situation knowing it was dangerous. I knew I was hanging out with *werewolves* in the middle of some end-of-times situation. I'm not gonna go all shocked face that something bad happened to me. Did you have the right to sell my soul without asking? Fuck you, no, you did not. Do I feel like you *betrayed* me by doing it? Fuck, no, I am *zero* surprised. I'd be pissed if you'd come back and *not* sold my soul. I mean, didn't I say it was for sale? Didn't I look up at the sky once and say *take me, I'm ready*? Play stupid games, win stupid prizes."

After a long time, she said, "Yeah. I'm gonna go talk to Kiery."

Numb by the driving rain and half-deaf from the jangling of the scales in the back of my head, I nodded mutely.

Ana stood and headed towards the doors. She paused like she was going to say something, but then left.

THE COST

I wanted to keep crying, but my eyes had given up, and so had my chest. I'd fed the only friend I had, and really, the only friend I'd *ever* truly had, to the crystal-toothed Sky Bitch.

"You can't sit in this corner." Gabel stood over me, practically glowing with disapproval.

Seems I *was* sitting in the corner of the closet, tucked in with all the laundry and unworn shoes and a few ties I hadn't even known he'd had. I drew my knees up as high as I could manage while the pup squirmed under my heart. My spine protested. I ignored it.

"You *cannot* sit on the floor," he growled. "Will you get up."

I ignored him and stared at the hems of his shirts hanging over my head.

He breathed out, exasperated, looked around, and demanded, "How long have you been down there?"

Long enough to run out of tears, but not self-pity and grief.

He crouched down and shoved his arms around me.

"Put me down!" I snapped.

"Then get *up*!"

"Leave me alone!"

"No!" He scooped me up and hefted me out of the closet. "Don't make me throw you under the cold shower!"

"You wouldn't dare!" I snarled.

He deposited me on our bed. I grabbed a pillow and flung it at him, then squirmed up into them.

"Fine. Burrow as much as you want as long as you stay in *bed*," he grumbled, eyeing me. "I've seen you do far worse and shed fewer tears."

"Now you sound like Aaron." The monster who chose to be the monster. And the grossest part? I wasn't sorry. I'd do it again. Just like I wasn't sad about anything else I'd done up to now.

She'd said that I saw things with the Eye of the Moon— something other people didn't have. They wouldn't look into the bowl. "I have to make it worth it. But I don't know how. I don't even know what the weapon is or how to use it!"

"Do you know how to summon it?"

I ran my hands over my face. "No."

"Then what did you trade the human for?"

I broke into sobs. "I don't know! I don't know!"

He cocked his head to the side, expression confused.

The spasm of sobs relented. I sniffled and wiped at the tears. "Hix's also in Hell. She showed me Hix. Tormented him while I watched."

"I'm not surprised."

"He shouldn't be there! He earned redemption!"

"Did he? You don't know what he did before you met him."

"I know he tried to overthrow his Alpha."

"And you have no idea *how* he did that. Or why. Or what led to it. I am not surprised where he ended up."

I glared at him. "Before me, did *you* think you'd end up in hell?"

"I've never believed the Moon would weigh my life favorably." Gabel got up onto the bed.

I pawed at the tears. "She spent most of the time telling me how I chased Her power, so I couldn't cry about it coming to this. That I could have abandoned the path anytime. And I guess it's true, because do you remember how I always told you the future isn't written, and our visions are just driven by the most likely outcome based on what currently exists? The only time the Moon *told* me to do anything was to go to SableFur."

Gabel's expression darkened. "So She is laying the blame for this at your feet?"

"No, just that I could have always chosen something other than running right up the middle wielding the power of the Moon. I didn't even *realize* what I was doing, though." I hung my head. I'd fallen back on all my Oracle training to survive, except I had also ignored all the warnings Kiery had tried to put into my head. Even at SableFur, she'd told me again my greatest flaw as an Oracle had been my bravery. "The Moon even said I could still walk away."

"And go to IceMaw? The Moon might be telling you you can walk away, but as I have sworn to you, I will *never* give you up again."

"She also said I'd never be remembered fondly. The Hounds already used my new title. You are the Destroyer, the Moon's Dark Comet. And I suppose I have graduated to the Obsidian Oracle, She Who Wielded The Scythe of Waning. I'll never be beloved, at best feared and respected."

He smirked. "But *I* love you."

"Gabel, now's not the time."

"To point out the obvious?"

"Gabel."

"Better to be She Who Wielded The Scythe of Waning rather than She Who Ran Away."

"It worked for SaltPaw, didn't it?"

"Debatable. They went to ground like frightened rodents, so while they might survive the impact and aftermath, they remain food."

"You are impossible to talk to sometimes.

"My mother ran away."

"What now?"

"My mother ran away. She didn't go to the SableFur Alpha. She didn't announce anything to the SableFur. She didn't go home to her birthpack. She didn't howl for justice. She ran away to the northern forests. She gave birth to a litter of lupine pups in winter. It is no surprise my littermates died."

"You're blaming your mother?"

"No, I blame Magnes and Anita. But you are thinking you made a mistake every time you *didn't* leave when the Moon presented you an opportunity to do so. If *you* are the point on which light and dark turns, leaving would have been abdication of that. Everything would have continued on its course as if you did not exist."

The wolves have seen the Tides coming in for a long time. They have not done differently. Their choices have been made. Now they drown and cry to Me?

Gabel drew his finger along a faint, old scar that ran around his forearm. "You swore to me in the darkest moment that you would be by my side as my kingdom crumbled. You've chosen defiance from the moment we met. You are still defiant and chase the Moon across the Tides and into Hell itself. You refuse to accept the outcome that's been ordained since I was conceived. I think the problem is in your heart," he pushed his finger between my breasts, "you still think you can get it to end *nicely*. That was never possible."

He pushed his finger down my sternum.

"The Silvery Sky Bitch did not present you opportunities to escape. Those were *traps* for you along the way. Traps where the worst ending would snap over you like the jaws of a very large wolf. Just like She laid traps for me, and some I fell into, and I am not sure I scrambled out of them."

"What trap did She lay for you?"

His face darkened. "I am not sure I should have given you up to SableFur. That is a choice that haunts my dreams. But one trap I am certain of is Amber. The *obvious* choice. The *correct* choice, according to everyone. You think She is being merciful, pointing out all the many ways She gave you to escape? She's tormenting you by dangling hope in front of you, and now that you've gotten this far, She's grinding your snout in it to try to get you to break."

"Why would She want me to break?" I asked slowly.

He sighed like I was an idiot. "She's not sharing the hunt with you. If you want it, you're going to have to take it. This is just Her agreeing if you're determined enough, She won't kill you for your presumption. You're allowed to wait within breathing distance and take the scraps when She's had Her fill."

Bog, river, thicket: it was always going to end this way.

But it HAS ended, little wolf, because YOU ended it.

I understood that the Moon had sent Gabel to destroy everything, but that the *shape* of that destruction was in my hands. The two pans jangling on their chains, balanced on the scythe-moon-shaped fulcrum.

Gabel slid his palm under the curve of my belly. "You did what was necessary. Now we have an orphan wolf to look after, but she should be no more challenging than a lupine puppy."

"I wasn't expecting *you* to talk to her today."

"I talk to her every day."

"You know what I meant."

"I *very* clearly remember the first time I shifted to human form. Everything became very complicated and intricate. I knew my mother's human form and voice well, the physical nature of it was not a shock. It was this." He pointed at his head.

"Your mind?" I asked.

"And when I went back into wolf-form, it was not as it had been. My mind was not the same. When we shift into wolf form we retain much of our human mind. But I lost my wolf mind and it was *replaced* with a human mind, but I did not know this human mind."

"That sounds horrifying."

"Such a gift for understatement. I didn't have the words to ask my mother the questions I needed to ask. She needed to divine what I didn't understand and couldn't comprehend. I did not even comprehend enough to ask my mother for her human name until you needed to know her name. Do *you* know your mother's name?"

"Yes," I said, although it was just a name. She'd died before I'd even been a year old.

"Perhaps if my littermates had survived, I'd have understood the concept of names sooner. My mother was always *Mother*. Other creatures in the forests had mothers. I had *my* name, but to me it was... a designation. I understood my name the way I understood *mother, cricket, squirrel*. I was a *gabel wolf*, and I understood I was the only *gabel*, so of course when my mother called for me, I was the one who she intended to summon. It took a while to comprehend that I was a wolf, and Gabel was my *name*. Actually," he paused, and half-grinned, "it took a long time to understand that. So I am not... unsympathetic... to Ana's predicament."

"This baby is making you a softie," I said with a bittersweet smile. "First sonnets, now this?"

"I have been giving a great deal of thought to the rearing of offspring lately. I also lack books on it."

"There are no books on werewolf pups. Which also do not sleep."

"They don't sleep? I remember sleeping. I can assure you, lupines sleep."

"Only a little bit at a time. Then they start chewing on everything."

"But they don't shift until they are... perhaps six?"

"They start chewing as soon as they can put things in their mouths." Holy hell, Gabel had *never* been around pups or babies. I'd grown up in a pack with younger pups, so of course I'd done the usual amount of baby-minding and been around infants, and one of the first things you learned (after you learned never wake a sleeping pup, that they were *always* hungry, and *always* have a towel nearby) was whatever a pup could grab went *right* into their mouth.

"How soon can they manage that?" Gabel asked with a frown.

"Infants. Anything they can grab goes right into the mouth."

"This sounds incredibly perilous."

"It is."

"How do any human-forms survive?"

The last thing I needed was for Gabel to be even more protective and neurotic. Time to change the topic. "We manage. And I would feel better if I could figure out at least what this weapon *is*."

"But the Moon's already told you what it is."

"She has?"

"The Scythe of Waning," Gabel said matter-of-factly. "It's a scythe."

"What would a werewolf do with a scythe?"

"I am certain Flint would have some ideas on how to wield a scythe." He kissed me gently. "I have work to do. I'll be in the basement."

My skin grew cold.

He smiled, showing me very white teeth that seemed almost crystalline. "Have no fear, my love. The limb will be well-diseased when you are ready to swing your scythe."

A THRONE FOR A KING

"The hell is that?"

"It looks like..." Lucas watched the SableFur wolves who had arrived wearing white scarves of parlay carry a very large but battered-looking wooden chair across the front lawn towards the back of the house. "It looks like..."

Having SableFur wolves at IronMoon's heart was unpleasant enough, but they'd driven through the SableFur pass in a big box van that had large white flags strapped to it like some lost member of a non-specific human political rally. They'd slowly made their way up towards IronMoon's heart before being stopped about ten miles out, when Flint and Eroth had been sent to make sure it wasn't the most obvious Trojan Horse ever.

The report? The van was full of wooden junk. The nails had even been removed.

Gabel had chuckled. "Adrianna has sent me *trash*? This I have to see. Humor them and let them through."

I'd told Ana to stay out of sight—I absolutely did *not* want any strange wolves seeing or smelling her until she was better able to control her shifts, or at least recognize scents and body language. And I didn't trust the Moon to not have given Ana a lure-scent appealing to dangerous males, and she didn't know how to navigate prestige. These SableFur wolves weren't scrubs —these were some of Adrianna's trusted warriors.

Ana wasn't a timid or submissive wolf, but she was vulnerable. Especially to the crush of prestige. Luckily, her first prestige exposure was to wolves like Gabel, and Flint, and even Lucas and Carlos, who could teach her what *real* prestige was, and how it affected she-wolves. Her making a mistake or faux pas or missing a step around any of them was harmless, they simply explained the mistake. Other wolves would not be so kind.

Gabel was infinitely patient with her, and watching them interact was like watching a pup biting an adult's tail.

Imagine feeling safe around *Gabel*.

The Moon had a sick sense of humor.

Her attraction to Eroth, hilariously, had evaporated overnight. Even Flint no longer merited her admiring glance, very possibly because Flint was mated. Ana was bold, but Ana wasn't *stupid*, and even though she hadn't said anything to me (she hadn't really spoken to me at all), I knew she was lying low in the bushes while she got the lay of things.

Gabel assured me Ana had good instincts and would be fine. That the Moon wouldn't have minted a new First Wolf just to have her be a weakling.

I had a little less faith that that wasn't *exactly* what the Moon had done.

Flint supervised the unloading from the front lawn, while Carlos was in war-form on the roof.

Some more SableFur toted large, old, dark wood beams towards the back.

"Is this some sort of ancient SableFur fuck-you? Where you turn your adversary's territory into a landfill?" I asked Lucas.

Lucas shook his head, seemingly dazed. "I want another look at that chair."

I followed him through the house to the back, where the debris was being neatly piled on the lawn. Large, thick beams and that strange chair. I circled it, trying to place where I'd seen it.

Lucas stood back. "By the Moon. It's the SableFur throne."

"What?"

"It's the SableFur throne. From the hall."

Holy hell, that *was* where I'd seen it! And the large beams were part of the hall itself. "What... what is she doing?"

"I have no idea," Lucas said it like he had been hit on the head with one of those beams.

Gabel was now on the front steps, looking bronzed and spectacular in the sunlight. The blue-gloss squirmed on his arm. At his feet, hunkered over, were the twin wolves Lucas had brought him.

"What is this?" I asked.

"Oh, I am taking them for a walk." There was a cruel light in his blue eyes.

One of the twins was... mangled. Gabel had brutalized his body such that it was lumpy and butterflied and filleted like the petals of a flower. The other was abused and blackened, but not nearly so grotesque. That one hunkered at his feet, twitching and groveling and whimpering, while the other stayed bent and curled over his knees.

I walked up to stand on his other side, forcing myself to ignore the horror whimpering at his feet, and glad I could not smell them. "It's pieces of the SableFur hall. Including the throne of SableFur.'"

Gabel's lips curled. "So Adrianna gave us her throne."

"Adrianna's a Seer, so I suspect it's more symbolic that she's building herself a new throne."

"With our bones."

"Considering I've had visions where she wears your skull as a crown? Safe bet."

He grinned. "Flint was right: once a female is set on a fight, she is a force unlike any other. She goads me to be better, sharper. Like another Seer in my life."

He touched my Marked arm with a brush of his bloody hand.

The SableFur finished unloading the gifts, and then the most senior of them approached. Carlos leapt down off the roof, somersaulting neatly into human form, and Lucas glared at the SableFur.

The SableFur glared at him. One leaned over and spat on the ground.

Lucas just lifted his chin and sniffed once in disdain.

The most senior SableFur informed Gabel, "Luna Adrianna has sent you materials for your tower and a toy throne for your mate."

"And I have a gift for Luna Adrianna." Gabel looked down at the wolves cowering at his feet. The whimpering one squealed in terror, the other flower-shaped one did not. "Lift your heads."

They obeyed instantly.

The SableFur yelped.

"So you recognize your packmates," Gabel said pleasantly. "Since you are returning to SableFur, you may take these with you and return them to their families."

"What—what did you... do?" the lead wolf whispered.

"You won't take them? I thought surely you would want your packmates to return with you. I have become quite adept at taking and returning SableFur." Gabel's smile reminded me of the Moon's crystal-toothed malevolence. "These are not the first. They will not be the last. In fact, I have two more in my basement right now. But I am not done with them."

The SableFur twitched, then the lead one snarled, "Give them back!"

"You are under parlay, wolf. Do not attack. It would be

rude, and," Gabel glanced at Lucas, then Carlos, then Flint, then back at the SableFur, "unwise."

They were going to have to abandon their packmates to Gabel, or they were going to have to break parlay. And no matter what they did, they would be stained forever by it.

I know what I would have done... because I would never leave another wolf to a pack's "mercy" ever again. If Hix had lived longer, maybe he could have earned redemption.

These wolves weren't going to do a damn thing. They were thralls and nothing else.

Gabel offered me his arm, and we walked back into the house out of the summer sun.

"They'll take the prisoners." Lucas leaned back slightly so he could see out one of the windows to the front walk. "Yes, they are. They'd rather keep parlay than free their packmates."

"Of course. And that's my intention," Gabel said, amused.

"You are a cruel bastard," Carlos told Gabel with mild disgust. "You're taking those wolves and forcing them to choose who suffers and who doesn't. You're forcing a brother to choose against brother, father against son, and so on."

"How clever, IceMaw. That is *exactly* what I'm doing."

"What do you do, torment one a bit, then put him in a cell and really torture the other, while letting the first watch and telling him he can trade places, but you've already broken him so throughly he can't?"

Gabel chuckled.

Carlos' lips drew into a line. "Then you return them to the pack, where the shame and horror spreads as the story goes. And you take more, then return them, and Adrianna fails to stop it. Now those wolves are going to return in shame knowing they abandoned their packmates over loyalty to their Luna's order of parlay. You're robbing them of their nobility."

"I'm robbing them of nothing, because they had no nobility to begin with. I am forcing them to confront that fact."

"You have made yourself a beast of nightmares."

"I *am* a beast of nightmares."

Carlos said, tone sharp, "I would like this nightmare to end. So someone explain to me how having a non-existent weapon, a ring that shouldn't exist, and a human turned into a wolf is going to end this war and defeat Adrianna."

I put a hand on my belly. That part we hadn't figured out yet.

But in all my visions, I had always seen three runes: balance, courage, love.

Three holy "gifts": the weapon, the ring, and a human who was now a wolf.

I'd always seen three different stones: the tourmaline, the white quartz, the obsidian.

There had been three paths to the same destination: the bog, the river, the thicket.

I needed to get a better look at that ring.

HOLIDAY PLANS

I fished the ring out of Gabel's desk drawer. There was also an envelope in there, along with a bit of dust. How many drawers did this desk *have*?

"What *are* you?" Obviously, it was a ring, but why the hell did it exist? I slid it onto my fingers one at a time. No different from any other ring. No magic powers. Just a ring. So why had the Moon conjured it? To prove She could?

No. There was something important about this ring.

I put it back in the drawer and sighed. And then sighed again. The pup had squirmed into some position that felt like it was squishing my lungs. Which was marginally better than when it felt like it was laying right on my spine.

I had... three months to figure this out? The leaves were already starting to brown a little bit. I had a weapon to use on Adrianna. I'd bought it with a soul. I damn well needed to figure out how to use it.

...Gianna...

Go away, I wasn't asking you.

"Luna," Carlos said behind me.

"Carlos, I said *no*," I said irritably. "I'm not leaving Iron-Moon. *You* can leave anytime."

Carlos nodded to the ring. "He hasn't given you one yet."

"Carlos. The pup isn't here yet."

"And you're counting that he's going to accept the pup as his."

"It *is* his," I snapped. "It is his because I *say* it is his, and he takes his mating vows seriously."

"He hasn't kept them."

"Do *not* start parroting Aaron's bullshit at me," I snapped.

"Luna, he will—"

"He has given me his word," I cut Carlos off.

"That was a lifetime ago."

I threw up my hands. "What do you want, for us to have *another* mating ceremony?"

He grimaced. "I would prefer if you walked away and left him to his war."

The Moon couldn't have put a bigger "escape hatch" sign on Carlos if She'd done him up with blinking neon lights. No thanks, not taking the bait. "And *I'd* prefer if you stopped second-guessing my judgement. It's getting very old. Challenge me to be Alpha, or accept what I'm doing and tell me how to make the pack feel better about it."

"I have no desire to challenge you," Carlos said, "Not that I could in your condition. And you lack a champion."

"Bullshit I lack a champion. I have Lucas."

Carlos snorted. "I refuse to accept Lucas as a worthy champion, and the other wolves will agree to that. I am a First Beta. I am owed better than a packless wolf as my opponent."

He had me there: Lucas was a lone wolf who was surviving off his mate's prestige. "Is this a serious conversation?"

"No, of course not. I am just not going to stop urging you to consider alternatives."

"Fine, your protest is noted, and I don't care. Gabel is my *chosen* mate. Therefore, he is the father of this pup, and whatever other pups I give him. End of conversation."

It was so tempting to just tell Carlos, *guess what, this isn't Aaron's pup, it's Gabel's*, but he'd never actually believe me. Just like nobody believed the blue-gloss Mark was a true Mark. And so on.

Aaron would probably have a few ideas on how to wield this weapon, but like hell I was asking the asshole. I rubbed that arm as the Mark ached with the thought of him.

What was I going to have to do? Get up in front of the entire damn world and say *Gabel is my mate, fuck off*?

Hah. As if *that* would work.

I froze. "That's it!"

"Luna!" Carlos exclaimed, bounding towards me.

"I'm fine!" I snapped, waving a hand at him. "You gave me an idea."

"I did?" His brow furrowed.

"Well, you and that ring."

"What are you talking about?"

"It's a pup-ring. It's *love*. A symbol of love. And literally *love*."

"Luna, you aren't making much—"

I pushed past him and headed in pursuit of Flint. This time of day, Flint would be in his rooms. I hated bothering him, especially now, but some things couldn't be helped.

It was always so jarring to see him in human clothing. Battered shorts and a ratty tee-shirt today. His eyes were old, exhausted, but he said, "Luna."

"May I speak with you, Flint?" I asked politely.

The clouds over his green eyes shifted, but he nodded and stepped aside.

His room was the same as always. Three battered paperbacks

sat with pages spread, face-down on his coffee table. A box full of more paperbacks sat off to the side, and a few books lay scattered about. "Not finding anything to hold your interest?"

"Sometimes my mind is restless." He picked up the various books.

"Is she louder today?"

"I am tired today." For a second, he let himself slump, and I heard him sigh.

"You can go to her," I said softly.

"I can't leave Gabel now." He stacked the books into a small tower. "I can hold on a while longer."

"But you *can* go, can't you? You've earned your release."

He nodded.

"Don't risk damnation, Flint. Just go. You've done so much. She's waited so long."

He half-smiled at me. "Not yet. I want to see how it ends."

"It might end... badly... for all of us."

"Then that's my choice, isn't it? Now what did you actually come for, Luna? And sit."

I went back to my train of thought before pregnancy brain stole it away. "There's an old holiday in autumn, isn't there. An *old* one. Hallow, right?"

He paused in his picking. "Yes. But it's always... it's a dark holiday, Luna."

"It's the festival where the darkness is invited and hunted, and killed, right?"

He sat down on the coffee table. "Hallow is when the dark forces that have preyed upon a pack from the previous year are dared to come challenge the pack. It is symbolically to drive out bad luck by summoning it to you and daring it to fight you. Disputes and scores are settled."

That sounded just about perfect. "And then the year begins again at Solstice. And Hallow goes the entire month between that new moon and the Solstice."

"Yes. At Hallow, there were often bloody challenges, and if there were no challenges, the wolves would go on a hunt against dangerous prey, hoping to draw the bad luck out so you could devour it. It was seen as necessary, or else your bad luck would keep hunting you and taking your prey, and the prey over winter would be very scrawny because the bad luck ate it all. Your pups would be born weak and consumed. But Hallow stopped being celebrated a few hundred years ago."

Now there was usually a final autumn hunt to get some fat prey and anticipate the bright, clear skies of winter when the Moon shone brightest. Hallow was just an old derelict holiday from the old ways, a cousin of the human holiday Halloween, which always sported monstrosities (including werewolves) and Grim Reapers wielding scythes. Along with plastic skeletons and green monsters with bolts on the side of their head.

Gabel had always been about the old ways. And my pup was due around Solstice.

But this IS the end, little wolf, because you ended it.

"You want to celebrate Hallow?" Gabel asked, clearly familiar with the holiday.

"Yes. And I will challenge Adrianna. Winner takes all."

"Buttercup, you are eating jasmine-rose ice cream because you had a craving for flowers. The only thing you will be challenging will be a second helping."

"You mean... *yours*?" I set my empty bowl aside and lifted his off the table where he'd abandoned it. Challenge accepted.

"You will be very pregnant by Hallow."

"Even more than I am now," I agreed.

"You're still willing to gamble our pup. We agreed we do *not* gamble our pup."

"Adrianna won't kill me with a pup in my belly. She'll keep

you in silver chains until I give birth, then publicly execute both of us. Kiery will claim the pup as my Oracle sister and make off with it to IceMaw. The IceMaw still believe it's Aaron's progeny."

Gabel scowled, and Aaron's mocking howl reverberated from the abyss—and Gabel heard it. But my chosen mate didn't say anything sharp about it. Instead, he said, "The stress might be too much and make the pup come early."

I rolled my eyes. "The midwife—"

"Has her concerns."

"The challenge has to come from me. I'm the one who has the crown of IceMaw *and* IronMoon, and I was the most recent one of us to sit on the SableFur throne. You know it has to be me."

It also had to be me because I was the one with the scythe.

"You *cannot* fight her," Gabel said. "Although I am not sure why I am concerned. She will not simply come because you howl a challenge."

I turned my spoon in my ice cream. "No, I know. But Hallow is the answer. We have to figure out how to make Adrianna accept the challenge."

"You would gamble our pup on *that*."

I kept turning my spoon. "She told me how She will not save the wolves from the Tides coming in. She made *you* the reflection of Her wrath, but said I loved you for your dark perfection. I *have* seen that you *do* love, and you *do* care, and it's all twisted and thorny and warped, but it *is* there. You came for me in IceMaw. You gave up everything for me. Not because it was your duty, not because it was to your advantage, but because you love me. And I know you love our pup."

He said nothing.

"She made me the Balance-Keeper. She's always given me the choice to be compassionate or to fight. I think," I gulped the lump of salt and thorns from my throat, "I *believe* that She won't abandon our pup. That She will protect it on Hallow. Because there *is* still a tiny bit of compassion for us in Her. It's why you and I exist at all."

He glared, then turned to the big recently-repaired window, back taut. "I have never been accused of being an instrument of compassion."

"The alternative is to let the Tides come in." I looked down and ran my hand over my belly. "Compassion isn't always pretty."

Gabel tensed all over, then let out a grudging sigh and turned his attention to his map.

I ate another spoonful of ice cream. I was totally going to conquer this second bowl. "Since I came here, I've seen three runes over and over in every vision: *balance, courage, love*. I see three stones: blue tourmaline, obsidian, white quartz. Now we have a scythe, a human turned into a wolf, and a ring. I think the scythe is balance, Ana is courage, and the ring is love."

"My mother did not love Magnes."

"But you also said that wasn't your mother's ring. Come on, Gabel, it's *symbolism*."

Gabel frowned thoughtfully. He nodded, suddenly turning around inside the bond, like he was turning the ring over in his mind. "Then who is the blue tourmaline? Clearly the quartz would be IceMaw, and the obsidian IronMoon. The tourmaline cannot be SableFur."

"The Tides. And since the Moon's dealing in symbolism, let me point out some more: you're an old sigil everyone but Flint forgot. Flint's got blue-gloss that went extinct centuries ago. You insist on *old ways* for every ceremonial event here in IronMoon. So, in keeping with tradition, the *old* holiday of Hallow where we devour evil so it can't haunt us in the new year."

Gabel traced a finger down the southern border of SableFur,

clicking his teeth like he was hunting prey. "Fine, fine, buttercup. Hallow it is. I will make Adrianna answer your challenge. I have already seeded her pack with disease, but since our deadline is so tight, we will need IceMaw to hasten the process."

The spoon hung off my tongue. "What?"

...Gianna...

GO AWAY.

"We need to get the message of your challenge to Adrianna. Simply sending one of our wolves under parlay will not have the desired effect. Send an IceMaw to EmeraldPelt to deliver the message to Adrianna."

"But the Luna of EmeraldPelt is Adrianna's sister. She'll protect Adrianna."

"Of course. But have the IceMaw also spread the word in SableFur that you've challenged Adrianna to end the war. I will return my last project to SableFur. There will be two months for disease to fester and spread. And I will help it along."

"H-how?"

Gabel sat next to me, and he bent to kiss my belly while stroking the swell fondly. "Tell Carlos to bring himself and warriors he can trust to IronMoon. I am going into the field."

"Do you think that's necessary?" I asked.

"Why, do you want me here?"

"Of course I want you here."

"I will be here a while longer. There's something I need to do. If the ring is love, as you said."

Now he wasn't making sense. I made him look at me. "Gabel, what are you talking about? It's just a ring. Like that tektite comet runestone you keep on your belt is a stone."

He smiled, his blue eyes dangerous like the Tides. He reached over to the small book of sonnets he'd been reading from, chose one, and started to serenade my belly.

"What are you about to do..." I whispered.

...destroy everything, of course...

I flinched.

"Don't listen to him, buttercup," Gabel said, pausing in his reading to look at me with dark, *dark* eyes like the Edge of the Tides. "Hold on a little longer."

"Keep reading," I said. "Just keep reading."

GABEL - SOUL OF ASH & STARS

The door to her workroom was unlocked.

The workroom, like the door, was forbidden. She would have to be furious with him, and he would even weather the not-fun fury. If this worked, it would be worth it.

On the shelves were wrapped velvet parcels. Which one to choose? He brushed his hand over each. One felt distant and remote, cool and beautiful, instantly conjuring thoughts of Gianna's river-slate eyes and tangled, sweet scent. The other was hot, dark, strangely familiar.

Ah, yes, this one—from the vision where he'd carried her to a dark glass bowl.

Touching an Oracle's tools was forbidden.

He unwrapped the parcel. This one must be the tektite bowl, deep burning black, still oddly warm, and it reeked of destruction, polished to a wicked and exquisite shine.

Magnificent. Absolutely magnificent.

He carried it to the center of the floor, set it down, set the ring in the bowl. Then he shifted to wolf-form and peered over the edge into the burning darkness.

Males could not enter the Tides. Males were not Seers, and never were.

But he was the Moon's Dark Comet, Her Destroyer, and if the tourmaline could take him to Gianna... then this bowl and ring could take him, at least, to Hell.

~* Gabel's Vision *~

This must be the temple that Gianna had seen. There was the altar she had told him about, scattered with runestones and set with the scales, the pans empty. At the center of the scales was a living eye like river rock, with a sliver of moon in the iris. Gianna's eye. The fulcrum.

The sky was dark and stormy, and glass drizzle coated everything in smoldering, skin-melting glass.

Everything about this place was familiar.

He threw his head back and howled the Alpha's song of challenge.

It echoed over the empty treetops. No birds fluttered. The rain did not ease.

Then She appeared, melting out of the rain, wearing a dark sliver of moon on Her brow. She smiled at him, exposing crystalline fangs in a human mouth. ****Your mate will be displeased, wolf.****

"I am content to weather her wrath," Gabel replied, mind jumping and spinning.

** No tower was necessary to gain access to My domain, although I do admire your efforts and am most flattered. ** *The Moon taunted him with Her smile.*

"You did not answer Kiery's second question."

** So you are here to ask it yourself? **

It had been worth a try. "How do I free Gianna from Aaron? How can I be enough so no other is worthy of her gaze? The promise was made in Your name. There has to be a way for me to keep it."

** Except you made that promise on sullied ground, Destroyer. The root of your Bond is blasphemy. You took My power, my Gift, and you used it for your own entertainment. You defiled My Grace at every opportunity. **

"And I learned the error of my ways, and I ultimately made the promise with pure intentions and without compromise in my heart. You returned her to me. You have always returned her to me," Gabel argued. "She has done everything You have ever asked for. If it's suffering you want for how it began, then set it on me, not her."

The Moon paced over to the altar where the now-empty scales sat. She picked up a stray runestone that had been left behind. Flicked it away. **** I made you to take pleasure in pain. To find joy in triumph. You want victory over Aaron. I see no reason to indulge this request. ****

"I want peace for her. Her suffering is pointless."

** I am glad you agree, and that it sits like a thorn in your paw. There is part of her that will never forgive you. The part of her that loves Aaron. The part of her that hates you. **

No. This was a trap. "You dared me to come here. I am here. Tell me how to free her from Aaron's grip."

** You cannot free her from his grip. **

"Then set me loose so I can eat his soul. You permit him to wander around without going to Judgement, let me wander the same territory and I will hunt him and devour him."

** The destruction of his soul will leave a void in hers. The most you can do, wolf, is exactly what the vows say: to be so much that no other is worthy of her gaze. You are the Destroyer, the Dark Comet. There is yet another ancient celestial motion that caused fear: an eclipse. You can blot out the light. In fact, you already do it. You've already learned how. In the basement. **

An eclipse. Yes, a comet or meteor could mimic an eclipse. It could become so large in the sky the sun would not be visible. "How?"

** *You know how. Flint has told you a hundred times. You persist in not listening to his counsel.* **

He shook his head. "It is not enough. What must I do? Aaron is Your Instrument. You let him run free to torture Gianna. I can't allow that."

She grinned. ** *So bold, Destroyer, so bold. I would be angry if I did not know your nature.* **

"Why do You permit him to torment her? Why do You permit that Bond to exist!"

** *Because it* **suts Me.** ** She flicked a clawed hand and tossed him into a soft pile of glass. He howled as She held him and pressed him into the soft, molten glass.

He wrestled from under Her divine grip and dragged himself, burned down to bones in some places, back onto the rocks. "I made the vow in good faith! How do I eclipse Aaron so she no longer hears him or feels him? You sent the ring. That is how I know there is a way!"

She laughed. ** *I see she has taught you well to listen!* **

"What must I do? What do you want?" Gabel growled.

** *You snarl at her for daring to ask for the weapon, fearing I would ask for your pup, yet here you are. Very amusing, Comet.* **

"I lack Aaron's gift for silvery slavering. It apparently was not how You made me. Gianna is my mate. I love her. She does not deserve this torment. This is not justice. You sent the ring. I am here. What must I do?"

The Moon plucked another stray runestone. ** *What do you think I want?* **

Some of his burned skin melted off, leaving bones exposed. The pain seared him, exquisitely beautiful in a way that was almost beyond tolerable. He drank it in, absorbed it, turned the pain and

Her question over in his mind. The Moon crooned and twisted the pain higher, and higher.

** **What pain do you fear most, Destroyer?** ** She mocked him. ** **Her pain, or your suffering? You would die for her like the noble monster I shaped you to be, but will you** suffer *for her?* **

The agony, sweet and horrible, warped and tore his entire being, blasting away everything, burning away everything, skinning him down to his marrow.

The Moon's words slid over his bones, pulling up thin yellow-white slivers. ** **Will you SUFFER, Destroyer?** **

He watched as Her hand gripped his forepaw, his hide already stripped off to expose bone. She squeezed with crystal-tipped fingers to crush and punish the delicate tissues between his talons, then with Her other hand, She pulled up a wafer-thin sliver of bone from his stripped foreleg. Agony sang through his entire soul. The bone flaked and fell away to the ground, where it melted into glass. Dots of blood welled up, merged, trickled over the bone. Stained Her crystal fingers.

He howled in exquisite, perfect pain.

The Moon raked another sequence of pain through him. ** **BUT WILL YOU SUFFER?** **

The collar Gianna had been wearing in Kiery's vision—she had never worn a collar. And it was made of gore and glass, while his skull had sat on those very scales.

So his crown... sat around her neck, as a collar? Burning and scalding her, melting off her flesh. That was what Kiery had said. Kiery had said it was a collar, but he'd known it was a crown. His crown. She had worn it because he no longer had his head.

His first question for her she had seen Anders wearing many collars.

The crown of bleeding bones. The crown of living bone, that bled with an unknown heartbeat.

The exquisite pain pulled back, leaving him gasping and

heedless and bleeding and broken in the scalding glass sea on which the fiery remains of his bones floated.

** ***Yes,*** *the Moon crooned,* ***yes, Destroyer, My Comet. The Balance-Keeper always could change your trajectory. She has always been a challenge you had to respect, hasn't she? She has always forced you to choose, hasn't she?*** **

He tried to get back the clarity, the glimpse of understanding that the pain had brought him, but it eluded him.

** ***If you will set yourself to remaining in the sky rather than impacting Earth, and every day being the wolf who can be larger than Aaron's memory, I will help you keep your vow.*** **

Gabel pulled himself out of the glass, all his flesh burned raw, nerves exposed, but the sweet pain was nothing like what She had done. "So Aaron's role as Instrument is a whip on my flank."

** ***He will always be there, ready and able to take what is yours.*** **

"Then if it goes on forever, I will be endless."

** ***Such fine words, but not the answer I was looking for. If your mate wields her weapons and strikes true, this war will end, and the world will have no more use for you, Destroyer. I am curious if you will be able to turn your great power to something else, with corresponding great effort. Fatherhood, perhaps. Or will you simply fall out of the sky anyway, and destroy everything in your path?*** **

Yes. His pup. His tail wagged. The thought of the little creature in her belly lifted his heart. "I will suffer. Hang me in the sky by your claws for all to see, Moon. I will suffer."

Cruel, twisted laughter, and it mocked him, ringing in his soul that he was an idiot who did not understand. She seemed to swirl and coalesce to a single, cruel point, dripping with contempt. ** ***But you would enjoy that, Destroyer. I will explain clearly, fool, and perhaps you will listen. Surrender your ambition, your conquests, your crown. Turn your power*** *to defending your family and the wolves who look to you for protection and food. All this great power I have given you, and I will make it useless. You will look at the pack and see how your problems cannot be solved with blood and gore, but the statecraft Aaron was master of. You already see it now, how I goad your wolves to snarl and bite at your mate. Those are easy problems to solve, but they only soak you with more gore and glass. Again, I ask: will you SUFFER? ***

The clarity snapped across his face like a strike, and he understood what the Moon wanted. "I can never be King."

*** You must abandon your ambition to become King. ***

She pared another sliver of bone from his foreleg. Blood wept anew.

*** Falter, and smash into the ground, like the Comet you are. Succeed, and you will merely blot out the sky until your time passes. ***

For as long as he had been out of the woods, he had believed, he had known, he would be King. That he would not stop until he was King Alpha. The Moon had burned that into him.

But now, to save Gianna, he had to give up that hunger. He would have to become more like the wolf he despised. That he had been made to despise.

Now he understood. "I will suffer."

The Moon's eyes rotated with the motion of stars, a cruel smile on Her lips. *** Set foot upon the skyward path, and at the top, there will be a gate. When the gate shows itself, choose wisely, and I will set you upon that path with your mate. The denial will make Aaron a more fearsome, deranged adversary, and he will stalk the path, ready to hunt souls from it. Because why would I make it easy for you, Destroyer? When your dark nature is such a thing of beauty and gives Me such joy to see you mete out My fury. ***

325

"Why indeed," he agreed. "But she is the point on which light and dark turns. I choose suffering. My *suffering*."

** You will only have one chance, Destroyer. Once you fall out of the sky, I cannot set you back into it. **

The Moon had made him to conquer impossible odds. Just as Aaron had been made to do the same. Just as the Moon had set them opposite each other with Gianna the irresistible lure that drove them forward.

Everything he had worked for. Everything She had burned into his bones.

He must devour his mate's suffering. He must consume it and carry it across the heavens so she did not have to. The great power the Moon had imbued into him was worthless if he could not perform the most basic actions expected of a mate, father, and Alpha.

If this was what it took to keep what he had, then he would accept the burning glass collar.

He extended one charred foreleg, and bent the other, and bowed his head into the scalding, agonizing glass. "I will not fail."

The Moon laughed.

THE BEGINNING MEANS
OUR END

Gabel was missing, and he felt... far away.

But this time, he wasn't in his office hiding on the second level, cuddled up with that fucking tourmaline spear.

"Gabel, I am not chasing you to the Moon and back," I muttered to myself, hand on my belly as the pup did a very enthusiastic gymnastic routine.

That and I had this stupid ring, this stupid fight with Gabel, I'd sold Ana's soul for a mystery weapon.

...he has abandoned you...

"*Shut up,*" I hissed. "Shut up, shut up, shut up!"

... Never...

He howled for me. I dug my other hand into my hair.

"Luna?" Carlos' voice said.

For fuck's sake, was Carlos now my personal bodyguard? Didn't he have a pack to go run in my name? I glared at him. Well, he could make himself useful. "Tell Eroth to send out a few Hunters—discreetly—to see if Gabel has fucked off into the woods."

"He's missing?" Carlos' disdain wasn't hidden.

"He… he warned me he was going to do something. That the ring was going to make him do something. Or had inspired him. I'm not sure."

"The *ring*? Luna—"

"He's fucked off like this before. He can… He can get Beyond the Tides. I'm afraid he's done it again."

Carlos' eyebrows shot up. "He's a *Seer*?"

"No, let's leave it at his howls about building a tower to the Moon aren't far-fetched. He's off barking at Her, and I'm afraid wherever he is, his body is vulnerable."

Carlos gave me the side-eye. "Oh, really."

"*Carlos. Help* me. If his body is disturbed while he's out… wherever he is…his soul might never find its way back, or Aaron might find him or lure him, look, will you just go find Eroth and make sure Gabel's not wit-wandering where anyone can eat him!"

"Yes, Luna." Carlos half-rolled his eyes and muttered something I couldn't hear, but his tone of voice left no doubt as to what he'd like to do to a vulnerable Gabel.

Where *hadn't* I looked? I hadn't looked in the basement, but the Moon didn't pay attention to what happened down there, so unlikely he'd gone down there to mount his invasion of the celestial sphere. I hadn't looked under the beds. Maybe he'd go wolf form and was under one of the beds. Hadn't looked in Flint's room. Or Ana's. Or Kiery's.

"This would be a lot easier if I could *smell*." Being stuck with a human's sense of smell sucked. How did humans manage to do anything like this? I could barely taste food.

And how was I supposed to check under all the beds? The thought made my pelvis weep in pain.

"He *wouldn't*," I said to myself. There was one more room I hadn't checked.

He *wouldn't* have invaded my workroom.

If he was in my workroom, I was going to tie his leathery little ear-stubs in a *knot*.

I almost kicked in the door to my own room, but caught myself, and managed to open it slowly, quietly.

"You *asshole!*" I wheezed. He was there, in wolf-form, his head on the *shattered fucking remains of my tektite bowl!*

He cracked one yellow eye.

"How—how—" I sputtered.

He wagged his rat-tail at me. It slapped the floor.

"You know what? I can't deal with this right now." I held up both hands. "Nope. Not doing this. I can't believe you. I *cannot* fucking believe you!"

I turned and went back down the steps, slamming the door behind me.

"WHAT WERE YOU *DOING*?" I EXCLAIMED, NOW THAT Gabel had had a chance to eat and drink and sleep off his little foray into other-worldly hunting grounds. Because it didn't do any good to yell at someone who had just been on the Tides, even if they *had* managed to do it by hijacking a ride in *your bowls*.

The tektite bowl, perhaps not coincidently, was split down the middle, cracked into two pieces and now useless and broken. He'd brought me the pieces in their velvet wrapping like some sort of celestial roadkill. I'd told him to toss it all in the koi pond.

"You're lucky you didn't slice that neck of yours open on the broken pieces," I added.

"True. And to answer your question, peering into the abyss whence I came, obviously."

My jaw went slack.

"Sit." He pointed at the chair at the small table in the sunroom.

"I am not some *good dog* who does your bidding," I snarled.

"Butter—"

"Don't *buttercup* me. You took my bowl, you *broke* it, you invaded my room, you—you—" I sputtered.

"What's got you angry? That I borrowed the bowl, or that I succeeded?" He seemed smug.

Did this wolf not realize how *angry* I was? Because the baby realized it as it paddled around inside me and got fed a diet of my fury. Which only made me madder. "You think I'm upset a non-Oracle male got the Moon to let him onto Her side of things? I don't own the Tides, and if you're dumb enough to try, and she's wicked enough to accept your stupidity, fine! Haven't you figured out by now She won't save us from ourselves? She *wants* it all to go merrily to Hell."

He looked at his toast like he hadn't ever really seen toast before. "Yes, She does."

I sat down in the chair, the baby doing squirmy somersaults under my heart. "Wait. Did you see Her?"

Gabel gave me a far-away look, then he was present again. "She told me I should listen to Flint."

"Wow. *Wow.* I... I... I..." I couldn't even form words, apparently. "You had a fit about me going to the Moon to pursue a weapon and you went to Her so She could tell you *listen to Flint*?"

"There was a bit more to it than that. I wasn't satisfied by the non-answer Kiery brought back."

"Wait. Let me just make sure I understand. You were pissed about whatever answer She gave to Kiery and went full *I'd Like To See The Manager*?"

"Yes."

"And you used *my* bowls to do it. You *defiled* my workroom and my tools! After all this nice talk about how I'm still an Oracle and so on and so forth. I'm apparently not *your* Oracle, so you don't have to respect me anymore?"

He frowned. "No, of course not."

"You take your questions to Kiery, you violate my work-room, you *touch my tools*, and then you *shatter* one? Why didn't you just piss all over it too!"

He didn't reply.

"She could have *ended* you." My voice broke. "She could have destroyed you. She could have left you to rot. How could you... risk abandoning me? *Us?* You tell me not to trust Her, you howl about punching out Her Eye, and you think challenging Her is going to go *well* for you? How could you *do* this?"

Of all the things Gabel had done, this had probably been one of the most spectacularly bull-headed things.

"Butt—"

"Do *not*," I growled.

"Then sit. You're making me nervous."

"Guess you should have thought of that before you fucked off *to the Moon*."

"I knew you would be angry."

"How exceedingly forward-thinking of you. You aren't seeming to grasp *how angry* I am."

"You are not prophesying my downfall, and I was otherwise prepared for your anger."

"You *defiled my workroom and my bowls*." The tektite bowl had terrified me, and I hated the wolf who had given it to me, but losing *another* tool... and it had been... special. It'd been shattered, and it could never be put back together, and what if I needed it in the future? The Moon had slammed that door in my face at the same time She'd opened it to Gabel.

The tears started.

Stupid pregnancy blubbering.

I sniffled and bit my lower lip to hold in the sobs. Gabel got out of his chair. I snarled at him.

"I don't want you to cry, Gianna. Tell me how worthless I am again."

I just sobbed into my hands.

...Gianna...

I sobbed harder. Aaron's grip slid over my shoulders, grieving the bowl with me, whispering how much he loved me, how giving me those bowls had been more than just his duty. *He* understood.

Go away, go away, go away...

His soul crooned something and swayed me in its grip.

Gabel held out his hands like he was trying to catch my tears.

"*You* broke it," I sobbed. "Gardenia, your father, now you. Is it because *he* gave them to me?"

"No."

...Yes, it is...

I hugged myself and shook all over. "Leave me alone, leave me alone, leave me alone..."

...He destroys everything he touches...

Gabel extended his hands, then withdrew them.

I hiccuped and took a deep breath and tried to center myself. "You promised me I only had to hold on a little longer, but this isn't helping!"

"Buttercup, I had to do it. The ring, the runestone, the non-answer Kiery brought back. Things come in threes, like you said, and my question, my answer, and I went to get my answer."

"And the answer was *listen to Flint*."

"More or less, yes. And as for your bowls, I took the one that spoke to me. I couldn't see them through their wrappings and—"

"You think that is *helping*?" The pup wriggled and scratched in my belly. Needling pain started deep in my hips and spine. "You think *any* of this is helping?"

"You did throw my tourmaline spear through a window."

"So *use a fucking mirror!*"

...Gianna...

I clutched my hair in one hand, and I grabbed one of his with my other, and put it on my belly. The baby rewarded him with a kick so hard I flinched. "I can't keep doing this, Gabel. I can't. I *can't*."

He pressed his palm into my belly. The baby kicked a few more times, then settled, like they knew his touch already. With his other hand, he wiped some teardrops from my chin. "You won't have to. I took your bowl, yes. I defiled your workroom, yes. And the Moon humored me. The cost was your bowl and your anger. And I will choose a lifetime of your anger if it buys a safe den for you and our pup. I have no remorse for what I did for that reason alone."

GOOD ADVICE, BAD INTENTIONS

The koi fish seemed to avoid the pieces of the tektite bowl.

Gabel had taken my anger like an unrepentant sinner, unmoving and resolved, like Aaron had always been. I kicked him out of my bed for a few nights, but he simply did not care, and served his penance as I'd never known him to.

The anger that had held me up for the past few months, my faith that the Moon had a plan, my resolve to see the plan through... it had all been used up or chewed away, and nothing seemed to ever end, or get better.

I was fighting the Tides, and they were winning, because they carried the weight of thousands of choices that hadn't been mine.

I was so, so, so tired.

And staying angry at Gabel was too much energy.

"*Balance, courage,* and *love* were your three things that led to Hallow," Gabel had told me, "and for me, it's the ring, Kiery's non-answer, and the *comet* runestone."

The only thing that had mollified my anger was that the ring around Gabel's neck, instead of having the *dark comet* rune, had the *oracle* rune. The other three runes I had seen—*balance, faith, love*—were also not on his version. To Gabel this all seemed to make sense, but to me, it made no sense. I had always seen *balance, courage,* and *love.*

In some older runesets, *faith* and *courage* had been interchangeable, like how *balance* could mean literal balance or justice. The Moon's choice to show me a ring featuring *faith* while always presenting me with *courage* mattered, but I couldn't see how. I'd never seen *faith* anywhere else except on that ring. So why the rune-swaps?

Anytime I tried to press Gabel on his thoughts, Aaron started to pace and howl and claw at my soul, so I dropped it. Aaron hated that damn ring.

Couldn't blame him: sort of said *you were a tool all along.*

The Moon *had* humored Gabel's knocking on Her door. And She'd returned him unscathed, and only claimed my tektite bowl as the price.

Besides, there was a war to win.

And that would involve Carlos, who simply refused to wander back to IceMaw.

This *really* wasn't going to end the way he thought it would.

"Luna." Carlos half-bowed over his midsection.

"Gabel is going into the field. He's taking most of the warriors."

"An assault on SableFur?" Carlos frowned.

"Of course not. We're luring Adrianna out. We're going to throw a Hallow celebration, and I am going to issue a challenge to her. Winner takes all."

"Luna! You can't! You're *pregnant* and Adrianna has a warrior's training, even if you weren't."

Of course, instant protest. Why would I expect *anything* else from a First Beta at this point? Moon, I was so tired. "Not for conversation. I traded a human's soul for a weapon to defeat

Adrianna, and I'll use the scythe at Hallow to end her. Gabel's going to make sure she answers the challenge."

"Scythe?" Carlos asked. "The weapon is a scythe."

"Yes." At least, that was Gabel's theory, and it was as good as anything else.

"How are you going to wield a scythe?" He threw up his hands.

"I have no idea. But I need my First Beta at my hand." There, throw that little bit of meat at him and call him my First Beta in a less than sarcastic *I only do this because Aaron made it happen* way.

He straightened instantly.

"Are you the wolf for the job?" I inquired. "Lucas is going with Gabel, but if you aren't equal to what I'm about to ask of you, I know he will be. This *is* the end, Carlos, because I have *decided* it is the end."

It was also the last time I was ever going to put up with Gabel destroying everything he touched.

... He still will...

I clenched my jaw against the rictus Aaron's haunting voice sent through my bones.

Carlos needed a couple of moments to process what I'd just said, which was fine, because *I* needed a moment to regroup. I was faking this and part of me was like *this isn't happening*. But it *was* happening, just like in a few months I was going to give birth.

Gabel was reading sonnets and the newspaper to my belly while I was still trying to grasp I had to get the baby *out*.

Oh dear. Yes. That whole *give birth* thing.

"What do you need of me?" he asked.

"I'm not safe here, especially with Gabel leaving."

"I will make preparations to move you to IceMaw."

"No, this is my den, and I'm not leaving. Bring a contingent of IceMaw warriors here. Enough to keep the IronMoon tame, and Adrianna's eyes elsewhere."

His lips thinned as his jaw set. "You should consider going south, Luna."

"We're having Hallow at the old Shadowless territory. Going south would be impractical."

"Fair enough. How many wolves should I bring?"

How the hell would *I* know? That was his job. "Whatever you think is appropriate."

"Is this going to be the seat of your triumph?"

"I intend to give birth here." *That* was hard to say.

He sighed. "Fine. When is your mate leaving?"

"Four or five days?"

"Tell him to make it six."

"I also need IceMaw to send messengers. Many messengers. Use the rest of the southern alliance. A messenger, formal, from me to the Emerald Pelt Luna stating I have challenged Adrianna."

"Easily done."

"And then more messengers to everywhere that matters. Whisper in ears that all this can end if Adrianna answers my challenge. I'm going to guess Aaron didn't manage all his spies personally. He had too many of them."

Carlos grinned, his face transforming into a feral mask. "I may know something about those strings."

"So get to pulling them."

A shameless chuckle. "The packs of the southern alliance won't answer to support Gabel, but they *will* answer if your intention is to oust Adrianna. A cunning ploy to train them to your hand."

Cunning ploy, my pregnant ass. "You are welcome to bring your mate along, Carlos."

"With respect, Luna, not a fucking chance I'm bringing my family here."

"Aww, I knew I'd get you to break character eventually."

He folded his arms across his chest. "If the IronMoon rabble Gabel leaves behind get out of line, I will kill them. If they're so useless Gabel cannot even find a reason to take them into the field to die, I can't be bothered with minding them."

"You say that like *I'm* inclined to save them from themselves. And here I thought my reputation preceded me by now."

"Just trying to be clear."

"Do whatever you want to them."

"Or Gabel could simply take them with him."

"He wants the illusion of reserve forces."

Carlos sighed, and said, aggravated like the words had a bad taste. "He *has* reserve forces. He has *your* army. And if you give me leave, I can probably round up a lot of SableFur defectors as well. You *have* an army. *Your* army. Tell him to take all his beasts, you don't need them."

I thumbed my lower lip. "Get word to the SableFur that are loyal to me that they can come here, but I'm not going to ask any of the southern alliance to die for me or answer to Gabel."

He grimaced.

"Or you could just get out and take IceMaw for yourself. I'm sure Gabel or Adrianna will get around to dismantling it sooner or later."

He curled his upper lip, showing his teeth. "My choice is the Moon's Most Despised or the Obsidian Oracle."

"Sounds like an easy choice to me."

He snorted and half-bowed. "I will take my leave, Luna."

I smirked at how he said *Luna* and how tight his shoulders were as he left.

"You're playing a dangerous game," Kiery said as she stepped around the doorframe from the hallway.

"You have another suggestion?" I asked. "We've both seen the crowns. It can only end in two ways. I'm not waiting around for Adrianna to catch me."

"Don't let what happened to Ana cloud your judgement."

"*I* happened to Ana, and damn right I'm not going to let it go to waste."

"Gianna, I've warned you you're too bold."

"What would you have me do then, Kiery? I've already done all this, and I'm having a baby in a few months. Adrianna's *got* to face me."

"You don't even know what you're going to do."

"I didn't know what I was going to do with Magnes until I did it."

She pursed her lips. "Just think about why you're doing this. If it's to make it up to Ana—"

"This isn't about her," I said, frustrated. "Well, it sort of is, but it's about all of us and how it got to this point. Why am I arguing with you? You've *seen* it. You know the Moon's about to punt us into the sun and be done with it. I'm getting *one* chance at Adrianna and I have to make it count."

Kiery put a hand on my shoulder. "Gianna, I'm talking to you as your teacher and Oracle sister. Your greatest weakness as an Oracle is you are *too* powerful and *too* bold. You *still* scare me to death. But just make sure you're not doing things because it all hurts too much."

"I'm fine."

"Bullshit you're fine. It threw you for a loop when Gabel petitioned me."

I flushed with mortification. "That's his prerogative, and I can't scry for him."

"And it fucked you up, didn't it? Fucked me up the first time Lucas went to Thessa with something. Talk about mortifying."

"It's fine," I said flatly. "And I wouldn't admit to you if it wasn't. And Lucas actually consulted an Oracle about *anything*?"

"Once. One time. And I suspect it was about me. I didn't

make Elder Oracle because I'm *dumb*." She poked the tip of my nose.

I swatted her hand away.

"Right up the middle, as always, I guess," Kiery said with a sigh. "You just fuck off into the Tides with that terrifying tektite bowl. I thought you using a *mirror* was enough folly for one life."

"Technically, I fucked off to Hell."

"Are you listening to me? Talking to you is like talking to a rock sometimes. You're just going to do what you're going to do."

That's right, I was, because that was exactly what Adrianna was doing. She was already back in the heart trying to rebuild her influence. I was about to have a baby. We didn't have time to pussyfoot. The Moon had given me Her power, and the marked eye, so I was going to have to trust that I also had all the right instincts, even if it looked crazy from the outside.

Instead, I told Kiery, "Look after Ana, okay? She won't let me do it right now. Just make sure she doesn't feel alone."

Six days later, Gabel kissed me in the dim dawn light, a creature of charred metal. "Be safe."

"We'll be fine." Sixty IceMaw warriors had arrived the evening before, and now sprawled throughout the immediate heart of IronMoon, along with an assortment of other non-warrior IceMaw who had been recruited to help with getting everything ready for Hallow *and* the pup, and various SableFur I recognized from my time there had started to turn up and present themselves to me. What IronMoon Gabel was leaving behind (despite Carlos wanting him to take them all) were in the process of learning their place in the order of things.

And there was more than enough that needed to be done.

There wouldn't be enough time for anyone to get into trouble unless they were trying to piss me off.

Eroth stood on Gabel's right hand while Lucas was saying goodbye to Kiery.

"Try not to get Lucas killed," I said under my breath.

Gabel grinned. "That's going to be up to him."

He pressed his lips to mine again, then told me, intently, "We will be swift and cruel. Adrianna will not have a choice. I have sent her too many tokens of our esteem."

I gripped one of his hands while Aaron paced in my awareness. Gabel had the ring on a leather thong around his neck. It seemed to shine in the dawn shadows. I touched it, but didn't comment.

He closed his free hand over mine so that I gripped the ring in my palm. "I love you, buttercup. Both of you."

~*~ Gianna's Dream ~*~

THE ISLAND ROCK WAS WET AND WARM AND ROUGH under my bare feet.

The island. And rain, pushed sideways by the wind, soaked me within an instant. The clouds were here, but the Moon somehow remained visible on the horizon.

Aaron stood just in front of me, one of his hands entangled with mine. "My love. It's so nice to see you again."

"You—" I started to say, then stopped in horror: in the dream, I was pregnant. The pup was within me like a golden jewel. "You dragged me here!"

"I howled, your soul answered. I admit I pulled, but don't exaggerate. I didn't drag. And you even brought our pup." His other hand moved to my belly.

I smacked him away. "Don't touch me! This isn't your pup!"

"The world disagrees," he said smugly.

"Say something useful, you scavenger! Gabel goes into the field and you take your opportunity!"

"Always. You've been ignoring me." His eyes narrowed. "Do not fault a wolf for taking the prey in winter when it is there."

"Good. Take the hint, asshole. I'll go sleep in the damn basement if I have to, and you wouldn't want me sleeping down there, would you?" I asked sweetly.

Aaron looked towards the scythe-Moon on the horizon. "I will always be here, always, and I will spend eternity waiting if I have to. I will steal these moments. Even your hatred warms me, because under it, I catch the whiff of the tiny part of you that loves me. And I learned to live off crumbs long ago."

"I don't want you. But if you're going to bother me, tell me something useful. Tell me how to use the scythe when I'll be a month away from giving birth." Somehow I didn't think swinging around a scythe while I had the balance of an overfilled water balloon was going to be feasible.

"The scythe isn't what you think it is," Aaron said with a shake of his head.

"So it's not a scythe."

"No, it's a scythe, but it will be something else too. That moment is the one where you cannot falter. But it is that moment when you will hesitate."

"The Moon's told you what it is, hasn't She?" I asked, snarling at the betrayal.

He smiled, and it was a pure, handsome smile that might have melted my heart if it hadn't been filled with so much fury. "I've always known what the scythe is."

Fuck this wolf and his games.

He extended a hand towards me. "Let me closer, Gianna. Let me help you in that moment. You will need both of us, Balance-Keeper."

"No." That was a complete sentence and he could get used to it. Gabel had limits. Aaron did not.

"*I can* help *you. I can help you make sure you win, so the baby is safe.*"

He was so sweet and kind when he wanted to be. There was so much good *in him, so much aching longing in his gaze.*

Flint's lesson echoed in my head: turn away.

"*Not a chance.*" *My voice cracked.* "*I know you'll try something. You still intend to win, Aaron.*"

"*I will never stop loving you. I will never stop trying to be with you.*"

Thorns and salt choked my throat. He'd kill me, he'd kill Gabel, he'd do anything, *he'd even keep me prisoner here, because for all he was good, and noble, Aaron was deranged. And I could never forget that.*

I turned away from him. My soul tore.

I walked down the looping trail to the grotto. The rain was hot and stung slightly as it hit my skin. I glanced, and saw that the droplets each encased a small, dark glass bead.

"*Gianna!*" *Aaron called, striding after me.*

My regular sight could not see, but my marked eye saw... something. Understood something in the darkness.

"*Gianna!*

I ignored him.

"*I will never stop,*" *he said.* "*I will never stop.*"

I stepped into darkness.

GABEL - HERE,
LITTLE LUNA

G abel moved through the small hamlet. The wolves snarled and growled at his feet, clicking their jaws, smelling of hunger and barely restrained violence. The cool late-summer evening had come, with just the light of houses to illuminate anything.

Lucas, in wolf-form, padded at his heels, not betraying that he cared at all about this. In fact, the big wolf seemed to be completely comfortable.

"You aren't welcome here, monster," a male warrior told him, standing in the center of the road with several other warriors while more wolves watched from the shadows.

"I am rarely welcome anywhere, wolf, but that has never concerned me," Gabel replied. His wolves clicked and yipped. "I am in search of a volunteer."

"No one here is *volunteering* for anything except to kill you!" the wolf shouted.

So many volunteers for that particular task. So many. And yet, here he was, still very much alive. "Adrianna has not even put a price on my head. You should be insulted she values your lives so cheaply."

"*Luna* Adrianna!" one of the other wolves shouted.

At his thigh, Lucas sighed.

Indeed. Idiots. How to reveal their loyalties without a direct question. His teeth burned in his gums, and his fingernails itched in their beds. He gestured and the wolves behind him moved backwards, dissolving into the shadows and fanning outwards.

He moved towards the cluster of males. They held their ground. The most prestigious one was about his age, perhaps a bit older, and a warrior of some prestige, and while he didn't reek of fear, he had the scent he didn't want to fight—that the fights he'd expected in his life would be quick encounters with overly ambitious rogues and other cheap adversaries. That the actual *combat* would be fought by the SableFur army, that he'd have been behind rows of other, better wolves who were, for lack of a better term, *professionals.*

That he had been, what did the humans call him... a *weekend warrior*?

He had not thought of himself that way. But he was about to realize it.

Gabel walked so close he saw the cracks in their lips. They tensed and paused and reeked of anger, but under that: fear, submission. They wouldn't attack him even if he was within range. They were too afraid. They just were too stupid to admit it. And too proud to let anyone see it.

Oh, they'd see it. They were all going to see.

"I require," Gabel intoned, "a volunteer. Or a sacrifice, if you will. One of you for the many."

"You will have none of us!" the lead wolf stated.

Gabel circled them, then moved into the shadows.

"Stop!" the lead wolf snapped.

Gabel ignored him and kept walking, his nose leading him through the collected wolves. Females and pups looked at him with terrified eyes. Older wolves. An assortment of males. He moved through the herd like a dog splitting sheep until his nose led him to what he was looking for.

He grabbed the male, a few years younger than him, and a warrior, but not much of one from the shape of his shoulders. He flung the male into the light. "You will do."

"Let him go!" the lead wolf howled, and the wolves surged, and two of the other warriors twisted into war-form and snarled at him.

Exactly as expected. He held up a hand to hold his own forces, while clutching the wolf on the shoulder, his hand twisting into war-form. "And what will you do? Stop me?"

He dragged the warrior forward a step. The scent shifted to angry resolve—they'd attack over this one.

"Yes," was the snarled reply.

Gabel released the wolf and let them have their victory. He went back into the herd for the true prey: another, similar young male. Similar except for the utter lack of prestige on his shoulders.

He dragged this one forward. "Then I will take this one."

"No!" the protest came, but this time, they didn't really mean it.

Gabel dragged the wolf up the road a small way, then shoved him down onto his knees. His left hand shifted into war-form, the yellow claws digging tips into the wolf's clavicle. "Wolves of IronMoon!"

Howls in response.

Lucas sat down opposite the SableFur wolf, tail unmoving, and stared at his packmate.

"If any of these wolves try to stop me, attack that wolf! Be gentle with the females and pups, of course." Gabel grinned at the little hamlet pack.

The wolf under him held still. Every fiber trembled in anticipation.

Gabel bent over the wolf. "You know they aren't going to

bleed to save you. You know that you are one of them, but they don't value you enough to bleed for you. They just don't know it yet."

The wolf looked at him with wide, bright, fearful—and miserable—eyes. "Why?"

Interesting. None had ever begged him *why*. He lowered his tone to a silken whisper, "Your Luna has the power to end this war by answering Luna Gianna's challenge. You should ask *her* why."

He drew his claw along the wolf's cheek. A bloody line traced its path.

Time to get started.

ADRIANNA - MY
MATE'S SON

He looked so much like Magnes it was like he reached into her chest and grabbed her heart and *squeezed*.

Gabel, the Alpha of IronMoon, stood right there in the driveway, a smug, cruel smirk bending his handsome features, carved and chiseled and pure male perfection, his eyes a haunting, bright blue that seemed to glow in the fading chill of autumn evening. Some leaves drifted in the breeze around his feet, and the dark, smothering weight of his prestige and power bore down against her. The blue-gloss Mark on his arm glowed a soft, unnatural blue. A metal ring sat on a leather thong around his neck.

"Adrianna." His voice reminded her of smoldering ashes.

"Gabel." His name tasted bitter on her tongue. This beast. This *monster*. This degenerate piece of trash that gnawed on her hide, the spawn of that *fucking* acolyte who had let Magnes play his stupid games.

"You have not answered Gianna's challenge." Gabel had a cruel, wicked smile playing on his lips.

"I *am* the rightful Luna of SableFur and do not need to defend it from wolves like *her*."

"And how do you answer your pack?" He studied his filthy hands, and as he turned one hand, it extended, grew into a claw. "I will keep taking your fathers and sons. You have failed to stop me, and you will continue to fail. I will have my entertainment."

Adrianna pursed her lips as the weight of her wolves turned on her. Behind her, her sons—who had as much trouble obeying as their father had—crept around her.

Gabel looked at them, attention momentarily taken.

"Is that him?" her oldest asked, trying to push around her.

Gabel flexed his claw, the fetid tips flickering in the fading sunlight.

"That's him," Adrianna said, seething. "Gabel, the Alpha of IronMoon, and your half-brother."

Gabel turned his attention back to her, his tone lower and more cruel. "I have no desire to hurt them. I *will* kill them if you force me to, stepmother. But they are as innocent as my litter-mates, and do not deserve the life you will create for them. My father drove my mother into the darkness and winter and forests. There were six of us. Your sons have five siblings who are dead."

Stepmother. Never. "Lupine spawn. Your mother was a fool for birthing any of you."

"And my father is now a puddle on the floor of the Hall. Don't make my brothers' innocent lives more complicated with your unholy demise. Or your shameful refusal to accept a challenge. The pack will make you answer sooner or later."

"I think not, IronMoon."

"Gianna is offering you what you want: the two of us, on our knees, should you prevail."

"And if *she* prevails?"

"You will face whatever fate the Moon has planned for you. Or you *could* change course. You could admit your role in all this and avoid damnation."

She smirked as her pups clung to her. Avoid damnation?

No. There was no *avoiding* damnation. And what was eternity without Magnes? He was *gone* and a great hole had been cleaved in her soul. The only thing waiting for her was hell. "I have nothing to admit, and nothing to answer for."

Gabel moved his claw, waving the talons slowly in the light. "I will keep taking your wolves. I will keep desecrating them. They are lanterns of horror, spreading the stories of what I am capable of, what I will do, without remorse. What I force *them* to do. How I plumb the depths of their souls and show them how small and pathetic and selfish they are."

"He looks like Dad," the older gasped.

Adrianna snarled. "He is *nothing* like your father."

Gabel took one step forward. "Little brothers, what your mother has not told you is that your father committed a grave sin, and the Moon destroyed him. That your mother knew about it—"

"Be silent, lupine! Do not speak to my sons!"

"You mean *my brothers*?"

"Don't use them as a pawn in your sick games."

"I have *no* interest in using them for anything." He stopped dead, cold and serious. "I am telling them the truth, which perhaps you should do. You are not dead because your death does not interest me. In fact, I am building you a crown of bones and a throne of gore for your pack to behold. You don't appreciate my gift?"

"You deranged lupine piece of garbage!"

He glanced around, shrugged slightly, and said, "Well, to be fair, stepmother—"

"Do not call me that."

"—this isn't exactly what I had in mind when I promised Gianna I would build you a crown of bones. Answer my Luna's challenge, or my construction efforts will continue. I will dismantle this pack until nothing is left but rotted bones under your tail. The longer you wait, the less you will gain. Your pack already howls songs to summon you, soon they will demand to know why you permitted me to work my craft so long. Oh, you will sit on the throne of bones and wear my skull as a crown, but you will rule only shades and death. It is your *destruction* I seek, not your death. The only way you will ever stop me is through Gianna, and she has offered you such a nice opportunity."

Adrianna held them tighter. "I have nothing to answer for."

"The challenge has been issued. She is the Luna of IceMaw and IronMoon. Don't continue to pretend that you are somehow above her." Gabel's cruel smirk returned, and he looked at SableFur's cold, dead heart.

She'd been unable to stop Gabel taking her wolves to Iron-Moon, and the horror stories of what he'd done to his victims circulated through her pack like word of Magnes' destruction. She couldn't drive his forces out of SableFur. The territory was too large, her once-great army scattered and more than half of her best lieutenants gone or dead.

Gabel's forces were too small, too nimble, too ruthless, and he chose his targets at random. He had even sent word—via IceMaw—to her sister: *tell your sister this can end quickly.* She had urged Adrianna to take the offer.

They won't expect you to accept. The longer you hold out, the longer they'll have to prepare.

And her inquiries and messengers and calls to the southern SableFur wolves had gone—officially—unanswered. They did not answer anyone else's calls for help, either. They warned each other: *do not bring the Destroyer here.*

While in the very far south, the IceMaw's influence remained: Gianna was a good Luna. Gianna could manage Gabel. Gianna was the Moon's Chosen. Gianna was carrying a pup despite having been silvered not a year earlier. The message was clear: *do not get involved. Do not bring the Destroyer here.*

And her plan to foster a rebellion under Gabel's nose? Fail-ure. Not because the remains of IronMoon loved Gabel or

Gianna. No, they hated them—but they'd spat on her overtures as well. They humiliated themselves eating out of IronMoon's hand, but IronMoon wanted nothing in return. The wolves who had moved closer to the IronMoon heart to live in its protective shadow seemed content enough with the choice, and the reports from MidSummer were that Gabel was very civilized when he cared to be.

It was all the same: *do not get involved. Do not bring the Destroyer here.*

And here he was, on her fucking front lawn.

Her loyal wolves pressed her with questions that needed answers. She and her loyal wolves rattled around the heart like they were scavengers. Not a *single* wolf from the heart had returned.

Magnes had always thought he could manage the IceMaw Alpha and had not listened to her. Aaron had cultivated influence within SableFur, and his loyal slavering pets in the south flocked to Gianna and the child she carried, while Gianna had chosen this bastard lupine, and he marched past her guards, into her territory, and strewn this bloody carcass at her feet.

Gabel, a monster in the night that spirited wolves away to suffer unholy torture. The wolves feared the Destroyer, and none doubted that Gabel was some horrible creation of the Moon.

And that only *Gianna* could stop him... if she cared to.

At first, everyone had believed she'd been a young Oracle turned victim turned puppet Luna. Now everything was different. She was no one's puppet and no one's victim. She was Gabel's measure, both the hand on his ruff and the bitch at his side. She'd survived two Marks, and the rending of two bonds. She'd ordered one mate to kill the other. By all rights, she should be dead a dozen times over.

The wolves had started to whisper her name with fearful respect. They had started calling her the *Obsidian Oracle.*

She could just kill Gabel where he stood. But the scent of doubt was already thick: killing him when he'd come under parlay would confirm she was the Moon's Most Despised. And it wouldn't kill Gianna. "Your Luna is pregnant, wolf. She's in no condition to offer a challenge, and she won't be for some years after birth."

"And she was never a warrior. Obviously, a suitable champion will be named." Gabel's claw retreated back into a hand. "Will you be naming a champion, or will you fight with your own claws?"

Instantly, a few of her most loyal warriors jumped forward and howled.

Interesting proposition: she *did* have a warrior's training, and IronMoon did not have female warriors of any caliber. It might be an easy win.

Except... *fuck Aaron*. She bit down a snarl. The IceMaw and southern alliance had a number of serving female warriors. *Gabel* could not source a worthy female champion, but *Gianna* could.

Adrianna hissed between her teeth. "I will not take myself or my sons deep into your territory, wolf. I am not a fool."

"Hallow will be in the old Shadowless territory. Where it all began for all of us is where it will end for some of us," Gabel said with that maddening smirk.

Her fingers itched, and the cleaved part of her soul howled for a wolf that no longer existed. He did not answer her. Only the sound of emptiness.

Her warriors moved close and whispered, urging her that *they* could defeat whatever IronMoon champion was offered, and that it was a quick end to this war that would otherwise grind on for years.

Gianna was desperate if she was willing to gamble like this, and no surprise: she was pregnant, and that pup was due very soon. Her sources said around Solstice or later in the new year, based on when Aaron had taken her. The urge to have the den in order was *overwhelming*. It got worse, and worse, and worse, until even a single curtain out of place made strands of hair fall out from anxiety.

"She will not have an easy time putting herself back on the throne," one of her most senior warriors murmured. "The starlight wolves couldn't do it, and this is a mortal challenge. Even if you lose, your sons can flee to EmeraldPelt. Your sister will help them reclaim their birthright. Gabel will have to spend the rest of his life taming SableFur. There will be opportunities."

Murmurs of agreement.

"You can't keep ignoring the challenge," another wolf murmured. "He's destroying us by sparing the southern part of the pack while defiling the north. She is the undisputed Luna of two packs. You will look weak if you refuse."

A third wolf whispered, "If you win, Luna, you will have the Destroyer, the Obsidian Oracle, *and* their offspring. Three jewels for your crown."

Three jewels.

She glanced at the wolf who had said that. "True."

Years earlier, the morning after she'd taken her vows to Magnes, she'd asked Anita *what should I know?* And Anita had had a vision of Adrianna wearing a crown made of a monster's skull—the future Gabel—set with a piece of white quartz as the right eye, tourmaline as the left eye, and a new-moon sliver of obsidian across the brow. She had also been wearing a pelt of silvery-blue—an Oracle's pelt. Anita had also been clear the conquest had come on a dark, moonless night surrounded by torches.

They'd both believed the silvery pelt had either been her own abandoned training as an Oracle—acknowledgement that she herself was a Seer who had chosen to be Luna instead, or perhaps a nod to Magnes' indiscretion with the acolyte. Adrianna had made peace with the fact that both of those things had displeased the Moon, and would haunt her, so to be wary of them. The remaining details hadn't made much sense. Not until Gabel had come out of the forests and begun empire-forging.

It had *always* been leading to this. Nothing had changed.

Nothing.

She grinned.

She could erase the IronMoon. She could give her pups their future. And she would have the best trophy of all to prove her triumph: Gianna's unborn pup. The heir to IronMoon and IceMaw.

Which she would raise as her own... fairly. Kindly. It would love her. It would call *her* "Mother."

And anyone who had loyalty to Gianna would hesitate to kill her heir. Gabel's acknowledge child, and Aaron's spawn.

How delectable.

Three jewels for her crown.

And it all, *all* made sense.

Her soul was forfeit, but apparently it always had been, and her life was not *nearly* over.

She slid her hands along her sons' hair. Her pups would rule, and they would even have a new sibling: the three of them could rule the vast SableFur kingdom. Three thrones, three jewels, three pups.

She grinned at Gabel. "I accept the challenge, wolf. Tell your mate that she and I will settle this war, and who has the right to sit on that cold, dead throne at Hallow."

Gabel returned the grin. "As the old ways require, wolf. Until then, your wolves may sleep well. But only until then."

The Scythe of
Waning

The autumn night was cold and wicked and dark. Only the barest sliver of the new moon was visible in the sky. The only light was from the dozens of lanterns and torches arranged around the property. The leaves were off the trees; the branches rattled in the breeze. The air was thick with the scent of burning oil from the many, many torches I'd asked to be set along the walkways, and while I didn't have fangs, like in my visions of the temple, I asked for bones.

I did not ask where the bones had come from.

The bones on their strings rattled and clacked in the wind too, glowing a ghoulish shade in the torchlight. The platform had been built of hay bales, not stones, but the shape was right, and a stone altar had been set to one side, aligned with the position of the moon.

On the flat, open land that had once been Shadowless' heart, it was a wasteland of darkness with just the torchlights to illuminate the way, and shadowy forms of wolves milling about, shifting and rising like the dark tides in all my visions.

Adrianna's forces were on the western side, and we were on the east. She'd come with an army at her back, and the rest of her forces just across the border. Adrianna had us outnumbered. If this failed, it would not end well for IronMoon.

I watched from the same hillside that Gabel had originally watched the Shadowless house from. It was almost time. The baby wriggled in my belly, then delivered a boot to my side. I winced.

"Luna?" Lucas asked.

"I'm fine," I said. "Just the baby kicking."

"Are you sure?"

"I might be waddling but the baby's not due until Solstice." The midwife had been pretty plain on that. Baby was firmly in its den for at least another few weeks. And that despite how exhausted and waddly I felt, everything was going fine, and I was just fine to challenge Adrianna for the salvation of our kind.

Great.

Gabel placed a hand on my belly, running his hand along the curve while he watched the procession below us.

"How many wolves do you think are here?" I asked Lucas. I placed my hands over Gabel's. He kissed my hair and growled deep and low under his throat.

"Hundreds," Lucas said. "There are more in the trees. Down the road, waiting, see?"

He pointed to the many points of light dotting the trees and road and then stretching out into the tundra beyond Shadowless.

"Good," Gabel rumbled. "There will be many witnesses. Adrianna had to answer the challenge. Her power is too poisoned. Too broken. They want answers for why she can't stop me, and I continue to build her a throne of bones and gore."

"If she dies, she turns into a martyr," Lucas said.

"If this goes as planned, we won't get to the bloody part," I said.

"Buttercup, there is always a bloody part," Gabel said.

I sighed at him. "Fine, fine, but *after* I do my part."

I glanced back at Ana, who was waiting wrapped in just a fluffy cow-print robe. "You ready?"

"Me? Yeah, sure, I'm great," she said, clutching the robe at her throat, eyes wide and bright. "Yep. *Totally* great. I ever tell you how I puked all over everyone during the third grade play?"

"If the worst thing that happens is you vomit, it will be a complete success," Gabel commented.

"Gabel," I hissed.

Ana laughed. "Yeah, I guess so."

"Just do not wet yourself," Gabel warned her. "It's submissive. Only pups can wet."

"Right. Puke or shit myself, don't piss myself."

"These standards are perilously low," Lucas commented dryly.

"Then things can't get much worse," Carlos retorted.

"Do *not* dare the Moon."

"Knock it off." Kiery swatted both of them on the back of the head. "Don't stress out Gianna. The last thing we need is for her water to break and that pup to come with an audience."

"The pup isn't coming." I sighed as Gabel twitched, not previously considering the possibility.

"Technically, the pup could come *any* time," Kiery added.

"You're not helping. Focus, Gabel, we're fine. Nothing's happening." I patted his hands and grasped his chin. I turned his head towards the scene below. "Focus."

Without the moon, it was hard to judge time, and the night was *so* dark and *so* cold. Wolves milled about, then the ocean of bodies seemed to settle, calm.

Flint strode down a path created by torches. He stepped up onto the tower of hay bales. He was golden in the light, except for the eerie blue of his tattoos. A hush settled over the meadows.

"Here we go," Ana muttered under her breath.

Adrianna stepped up the hay bales and stood on the western side of the platform. "Gianna of IronMoon, howl your challenge. I am prepared to answer!"

Gabel and I walked down the path created by lines of torches. The only sound was the crackling and snapping of the flames. The cold breeze pulled my white dress, my hair whipped around my shoulders. Our Marks glowed faintly in the night, distinctly different from Flint's.

Gabel offered me his hand to help me up the hay bales to the top platform, and remained one step below, just opposite his brothers, who flanked their mother.

They looked terrified.

All around us, wolves pressed closer, a dark sea of bodies with just flickers of light reflecting off their eyes.

Adrianna's upper lip curled. In the darkness, her pale skin was revealed, her nature as a Seer. She surveyed the dark tide of wolves, then turned her attention back to me. "I am here to answer your challenge, usurper."

I raised my voice. "Then I name your sins. You knew your mate's crimes. You know the name of the Oracle of Mirrors, and contributed to her fate, and the death of five lupine children. You killed your own Seer sisters, you moved to ensure only SableFur had the Voice of the Moon at their table. You killed Anita to cover the truth. You knew all these things, you let them happen, you *caused* them to happen."

She smiled and shifted slightly. "I knew nothing. I did nothing. That SableFur had all the Oracles in the world is madness, because Shadowless had *you*, did they not? My mate's sins were his own and his alone. *You* are the Obsidian Oracle. Your duty was to put your claws through the monster, and you have *failed*! Instead, you carry a scoundrel's spawn and intend to let *that* monster raise it."

Hundreds of eyes were points of light scattered through the

dark night like a reverse sea of stars. The pans of the scales jangled in my mind. "Then you accept my challenge."

She grinned. "Gladly. Show us your champion and I will see mine seal the challenge in blood!"

The jangling was insane, the wind whipped across me, my blue-gloss Mark writhed and burst with faint blue light while the other Mark gnawed on my bones.

...now...

I raised my left arm. My marked eye went blind, searing with a brightness/darkness that overwhelmed my senses. Something scalded my palm, and the jangling stilled as quickly as it had started. I brought my arm down as my hand closed over something and a sound like metal striking stone rang across the darkness. Water rushed over my feet.

My vision returned, and I held a scythe taller than I was. The bent, blackened curve of the blade was the only brightness, a wicked sliver, and the blade was not metal, but not obsidian.

It smoldered and gave off a dark, wicked heat.

Tektite.

With the staff wrapped in a thousand strips of mottled, rotting hide like Gabel's—the hides of Hounds, and the staff itself was a thousand bone splinters, wound together under those hides, and blood, dark blood, drained over my hand as the entire thing bled and wept and raged.

Blue-green Tides bubbled from the hole made in the hay bales under my feet, poured down the sides of the structure.

I raised the scythe. Smoke rose off the arc. "I am the Obsidian Oracle, the Wielder of the Scythe of Waning, the point on which light and dark turns. The scythe moon has fallen, and the sun has set!"

The crowds shifted and muttered.

"Nice trick," Adrianna said dryly.

"This weapon did not come cheaply," I said, fury in my throat. "I traded the soul of a human for it. All here know my pet human, but catch her scent now. She is a wolf, claimed by the Moon Herself!"

I pointed at Ana.

Ana obliged by coming up onto the platform, dropping her robe and naked in the firelight. She looked terrified for a moment.

Guilt cut through me.

Then, as we'd discussed, she twisted into wolf-form.

The crowd howled.

Ana couldn't hold the shift and wrenched back into human form, and threw up on the platform while gasping in pain.

I am so sorry.

I couldn't hesitate. Not for an instant. I turned back to Adrianna as Ana howled in pain. "I call my champion!"

I flicked my wrist, and the lightweight scythe swept down, singing through the air and the crowd gasped as the blade cleaved the veil between worlds.

The smell of burning glass and stars choked everyone, and in the distance, the horrible howls of Hounds.

"Hai hai hai! Obsidian One, we bring you your champion! Hai hai hai!"

Lucas was supposed to be my champion. What the hell? I looked around. Lucas had one foot on the platform, while Gabel had a cruel grin on his face.

The song hit a terrible hungry crescendo, and the world sealed itself again.

Hix stood at my side, the light of an unseen Moon flowing over the blue-gloss tattoos burned into his body.

Holy shit.

Aaron's presence twinged in my mind, reminding me of his warning that I'd hesitate at a critical moment.

Now Adrianna jerked back, raising one hand as if to block Hix. "You're dead!"

I slammed the butt of the scythe into the platform at my feet. It made a sound like bells and stars. "Bring forth your champion, Adrianna! Mine is the First Beta you butchered, returned from beyond the Black Thorn Gate, released by the Pack That Never Surrenders a Quarry! Surrendered to *me*, to serve *my* pack! All of your wolves remember him. All saw him die! Well, *here he is*."

Nobody moved. Not even the baby.

Hix, still smoldering a luxurious blue, stepped forward. He pointed at Adrianna, the eye she had gouged out now a crystalline blue shade. "Call your champion, Adrianna. Unless none is willing to face a dead wolf?"

Adrianna was the one who moved first, looking around at her wolves, stricken, shocked, disbelieving, and her wolves, almost as one, slunk backwards or dropped to wolf form. The crowd was absolutely, completely, silent.

I turned to the crowds, the tektite crescent dark and terrible and smoldering in the cold air. "The Moon has spoken and showed Her favor. This is the end, wolves! It is the end because *I* say it is over!"

Gabel broke from his position and moved across the platform.

Adrianna hissed at him, he ignored her, and seized her by the back of the neck. His fingers extended into claws, cupping her in a crushing grip. He dragged her forward to the center of the platform and drove her to her knees.

No one moved. A thousand eyes watched in the darkness.

Gabel spoke softly to Adrianna, but his voice carried to the edges of the light. "Look at your army, *stepmother*. See how it rots and withers. I harried you into the ground, and my mate has struck swift and true. I am the Destroyer, and I have destroyed all you built."

Tears streamed down her face, but her teeth remained barred in a mask of desperate hatred. "And that is all you will ever be, *hound*. You will destroy everything you touch. Now remember your promise and get it over with."

"I remember all my promises." Gabel cradled her head against his chest, and raised his marked left arm, his forearm and hand twisting into his leathery war-form claw.

Then he lowered his claw.

He released her.

Took one step back.

"Go," he rumbled with a voice of burning and thunder, "take my brothers and leave."

Another heartbeat, then he spun and faced all of us. "Adrianna has been defeated. She is not to be harmed. She-wolf," he pointed at her, "take my brothers and leave!"

Gabel pointed into the darkness.

"I don't want your mercy," she spat at him.

Gabel laughed, acrid and thick and smoldering. "But my brothers do. I spare you for their sake. I know what it's like to be an orphan. They're old enough to remember what happened here. Old enough to know no matter how much they love you, you are damned for your sins. Enjoy what time you have with her, brothers. And you, Adrianna, will enjoy a life where your sons look at you and see who they thought you were."

Gabel passed Hix on his way back to me. He paused, shoulder to shoulder, with the returned-from-the-dead First Beta. "I assume you're staying."

"It would seem so," Hix said in his usual brittle tone.

"Excellent."

Gabel took in the smoldering scythe, slid a hand along the curve of my belly, his fingers finding a chronically itchy spot with ease. The pup delivered a sound boot to my side and his smile intensified.

Behind him, Adrianna staggered to her feet, gathered up his brothers and disappeared into the darkness, broken and ruined.

WEAR IT

G abel turned to the crowds in the silent dark. "Wolves! It is over! The anger and ill-fortune has been devoured by the Hounds of Hallow!"

A few shaky howls and a little applause that died out quickly.

I shifted my grip on the scythe. It twisted in my hand, cracking and snapping like brambles and branches and bones underfoot. It materialized into the crown of bleeding bones.

Blood trickled down my wrist, dropped onto the wet hay below. Tangled bits of small bones branched and twisted like brambles, clutching obsidian, quartz, and blue tourmaline.

A crown for a female's head.

The Bond twisted with Gabel's sudden, dark realization.

This was *my* crown.

Will you make him king?

It is over, because I ended it.

I shifted the crown to hold it with both hands, brought it eye level. Blood dripped from it.

A crown made from death, yet warm and alive.

You will hesitate at the critical moment.

Asshole, *this* was what he meant. *This* moment.

The thing about endings? They're just beginnings.

With shaking hands, I lowered the crown onto my head.

Aaron howled his glee and laughter and smugness.

Gabel suddenly shifted, like clouds moving away from the moon, and smiled, laughing under his breath. It blocked out Aaron's gleeful howls. "It suits you, buttercup. I always knew it would. Shall I be the first to kneel before you? You always do enjoy that."

I extended my right hand. The blue-gloss of my Mark slithered down my wrist, coiled in my palm, whipping and squirming like a crystalline snake. It twisted itself into a tangled crown of smoldering, blindingly-polished tektite tipped with silver barbs.

I carefully gripped the edge in both palms, wary of the silver. It was hot and misted in the cold air. I saw my reflection in the exquisitely perfect surface.

Will you make him king?

Fucking wolf, he'd seen how this ended lifetimes ago.

I raised my hands, stretched slightly, so I could place the crown on Gabel's unbent head. "I have no intention of watching our kingdom crumble into nothing. Don't make me regret this."

He cupped my chin in his hand and ran his thumb over my lower lip. The dark silver-tipped tektite crown was oddly perfect on his brow as it sent up a heat haze in the cold autumn night, the silver reflecting the torchlight as it danced and writhed. "Have you regretted your time with me?"

"Not yet." Regretted? No. Hated him for a lot of it? Sure. Not the same thing. I bit the tip of his finger.

"Frisky," he murmured. "What have I told you, buttercup? Don't taunt me."

"That's your hangup, not mine. The midwife said it was fine."

He smiled and seemed like he took up the whole sky, so I saw and perceived nothing else. He took my other hand and tugged at the collection of ornaments on his hip. One came free: the ring from the shack. He held it up, and it seemed to glow like the full moon in the torchlight.

"This wasn't my mother's ring. My mother never had a ring. This is *your* ring."

He slid it onto my finger.

"It's a bit early for a pup-ring, isn't it?" I asked, voice hoarse.

"Only by a few weeks, and the Moon clearly intends you to have it. This is our pup, mate, and I will hear no more to the contrary." He shot a look at Carlos, who bowed his head. The IceMaw present seemed to collectively hunch over in submission.

I gripped his hand tightly. "This is over because *we* ended it. Now it is the beginning."

"Or it will be." He slid his other hand over my belly, then behind my back. He tangled the fingers of his other hand with my be-ringed one. "Will you rule justly and wisely at my side?"

"I will," I answered reflexively.

"Will you bring this pup to our den, and will it be mine to raise and value?"

"I will."

"Will you temper my cruelty with wisdom, and goad my fury when required?"

"I will." Or at least I would keep trying my best.

"Your turn," he whispered.

"Will you protect our den, our pack, our pups, with every drop of blood and fiber within you?"

"I will."

"Will you accept this and all the other pups I bring to the den, that you will raise them and love them as the Moon expects an Alpha and father to?"

"I will."

"Will you cherish me and love me so that I know no other

will ever be worthy of my glance?" My voice choked, and I stumbled over the words.

...Gianna....

"I will. If you are lost on the Tides, I will find you. If he howls for you, I will speak so to be the only voice you hear. If he distracts your eye, I will shine too brightly for you to see. And if it all goes on forever, then I will be endless."

My throat was too full of thorns and Tides to speak.

He kissed me lightly, his tongue swirling briefly over my cheek to taste my tears, then slipping between my lips to offer me the taste.

The wolves howled the song of triumph.

THE GRIEF OF JOY

I t still didn't seem real.

Then again, I was about to have this pup in another week or two, and *that* didn't seem real either.

I ran my hand over Gabel's Mark, now no longer blue-gloss and just a regular Mark, beautiful and bone-white against my skin. The pup wriggled and kicked in my belly. Things were getting too snug for *both* of us.

The scythe? It remained. Gabel had added it to his collection of weaponry and armor in his office. The crowns? Those remained too. They were on pedestals in the foyer by the koi pond for anyone who wanted to look at them: the cruel bone crown that threatened to start bleeding again, and the smoldering tektite and silver nightmare.

Adrianna and Gabel's brothers had arrived in EmeraldPelt, and what had happened to her loyalists? No idea.

And somehow I'd ended up Queen, and I had, in fact, made Gabel King.

Which hopefully would have a better outcome than Gabel making *himself* King. Because that had always ended with gore and glass.

"Still can't believe it?" Ana asked, looking at the two crowns.

"No." I shifted on my aching feet. Standing felt wretched, but laying down? Couldn't breathe. Basically, this pup needed to come, and the midwife suggested sex to help that along (ironic), but Gabel was still bashful about it even when the midwife laughed at him and said it was the last chance before he had to wait a good long while.

I glanced at Ana, emotions twisting under my chest. There was something far away in her gaze. She was still *Ana,* but I'd done damage, and our friendship... it seemed like she was on her own little island and wasn't inclined to come back.

"Can't believe Hix is back," she said. "Seeing him at breakfast is... well."

I did not comment that Hix also had what Ana liked: ink. Hix's blue-gloss was glorious, but he'd declined to discuss *anything* about how he'd ended up back on this side of the Black Thorn Gate. Or why She'd sent him—hadn't Ana and the scythe been enough? Hix had been like the weird bonus prize.

But if Hix had been offered a chance at redemption like Flint had been offered redemption? Then that was Hix's business. After seeing Hell, can't say I blamed him for taking the first chance he got at a second chance.

And he was back to his old self, like he'd never left, except the Moon had left him with all the scars Adrianna's brutality had given him.

"I know," I agreed.

She frowned. "Fuck."

"Yes." I agreed again, sadness settling over me like a blanket.

Because today was the day. And as much as I'd known it was coming, and as glad as I was that it was here.

Ana wiped at a tear. "Fuck. I'm *glad* for him. It all ended pretty goddamn well, you know? War's over, you're Queen, I'm a wolf, Hix isn't dead anymore, you're about to have that baby, and the world didn't end. And here I am sad about this little thing I knew was gonna happen."

"I promised myself I wouldn't cry."

"And if *you* can do it, why the fuck can't I?"

"Well, I can't breathe, so maybe that's helping." The baby was laying square on my lungs. *And* my bladder. Somehow. At the same time.

Gabel came down the stairs. He was wearing a black kilt with the black tektite *comet* runestone on its chain, and I had never seen him look more sober. Ana melted backwards towards the corner as Gabel slid his arm around my back and kissed my cheek, then pressed his cheek to mine.

"I know." I ran my hand through his hair, my throat thorns and salt. "I know."

"I don't," he said, his voice oddly strangled as the Bond twisted and flailed with confusion and the knot of emotions.

"You don't have to. It just *is*." I closed my hand over his. He gripped my palm.

Flint came down the other hallway, wearing just his usual battered kilt and a serene expression, but his green eyes were bright. He didn't say a word to us as he headed out the front door.

Gabel watched him go, expression gaunt and confused.

Ana made a sniffling noise.

Gabel followed Flint out the front door into the cold, crisp morning. The sky was hazy with incoming snow, and some snow already clung to the trees and blanketed the front lawn. Eroth, Carlos, Lucas, Hix, and Kiery, Cook, some others, all joined us while Flint took in the world.

"She's been waiting long enough, old man," Gabel told him.

Flint actually grinned at him, a sort of handsome, cagey wolfish grin. Then he came back up the walk and took Gabel by the shoulders. His fingers squeezed into Gabel's muscled flesh. Gabel gripped Flint's wrist but didn't say a word.

Then Flint hugged him. Long. Hard.

Flint released him, then swept low in a bow to me. "Obsidian Oracle, it has been an honor."

"The honor was mine, Flint," I got out around the thorns in my throat. "The honor was always mine."

Flint smiled, then turned and walked back down onto the snow-covered grass.

"Hai hai hai! We course, we chase, we move! Hai! Hai! Hai!"

The fine hairs at the nape of my neck stood up.

The wind kicked up a swirl of snow, and when it settled, ghostly Hounds milled about Flint's legs.

One of them was snow-tipped white, almost impossible to see in the snow. With a leg of exposed, bloody bone.

"I am ready, Hounds," Flint told them. "Take me to her."

The Lead Hound separated his ghostly self from the milling pack and whispered, "As you say, as you say, your soul is not ours to taste, the Moon bids us escort you to her in glory for your triumph. Our esteem, our esteem, Moon's Servant, for serving Her so well you have earned Her mercy!"

Flint dropped into his golden form. He threw his head back and howled the song to summon a queen to battle, then bounded off through the swirling snow.

A she-wolf's joyful song answered him—a female's song to welcome her mate home.

The snow settled.

Flint was free.

"YOU ARE LOOKING AT ME *VERY* WARILY."

"That looks precarious," I said. Gabel had our infant daughter balanced against his forearm, her head cradled in his large hand. She looked so *tiny* and she was so *noodly*. Nobody had warned me that newborns were like floppy little potatoes.

He had her perfectly balanced on his arm, which was no longer marked with blue-gloss, but a bone-white Mark like the world expected, and he gazed at her with adoration.

Which was wonderful, *except could he use both hands, please!*

I grew a couple of gray hairs while watching him before I couldn't take it anymore. *"Give."*

He chuckled and returned her to my arms. I snuggled her against my chest and took inventory of my sleepy little potato.

"I can be trusted to mind her while you sleep," Gabel said.

I growled at him and cuddled her closer, teeth partially bared. *"Mine."*

He chuckled, brushing his fingertips through my hair. Outside, snow fell, and the late afternoon was fading to night very fast. "You need to sleep when you can."

"I'm starving. Dinner first." My milk had come in, and I was *hungry*. I was also *still* exhausted. I was more exhausted six days later than I'd been six hours later. My lower body felt like Flint had used it as a training dummy, while my breasts were more or less chafed bags from my daughter's nursing attempts. Nipples, apparently, did not come pre-toughened.

And the midwife assured me I'd had an *easy* birth.

Moon spare me from a *moderately challenging* birth, because that had been the longest seven hours of my life.

But our little one was here, and she had eyes like blue ice, absolutely no hair, and for now, her skin wasn't Seer pale. She'd become a Seer later, if she did at all—and I hoped the Moon looked elsewhere for Her new generation of Seers.

She was delicate and perfect and already a fierce feeder who knew how to get her meals (as my painful, mauled nipples demonstrated), and she had her father wrapped around her little palm. You want to tame a lupine? Give him a daughter.

He'd been out hunting every day since she'd been born to bring back fresh rabbits and yearling deer out of his own crazed instincts. Cook was tired of skinning things.

Gabel was enthralled with her, and any moment I was not holding her or he was not off murdering some small forest creature, he made off with her to cuddle and whisper sonnets to, which I swear he did just to make me wake up in a twitching *where is my pup* spasm.

Gabel sidled close and offered her his finger, and she grabbed it. "So fierce, and we still count how old she is in days. She is clearly your daughter."

She wouldn't get her name until the next full moon, when we'd officially present her to the pack, and Gabel and I were still arguing over what to name her.

In the chaos of the previous year, we hadn't actually thought to discuss names.

Gabel watched as she held his finger, marveling at her little hand. "I wonder if she will be as ambitious as you."

"I did not intend to become Queen." I sighed.

"Are you sure about that?"

I rolled my eyes. "What will you do with your life now, King-Alpha, that you have everything you set out to achieve?"

"I have not achieved raising our children to adulthood, *and* we need at least one more—"

"I am still bleeding and you want *more*? I did not know I could bleed this much and not die."

"I suppose, in addition to fatherhood, I will have to turn my attention to ruling our far-flung and somewhat disobedient kingdom. I'm already getting reports that SableFur is trying to splinter, and I should introduce myself to the southern alliance, and Donovan mentioned he caught the scent of, all packs, the SaltPaw."

"The SaltPaw." I raised both brows. "Why am I just hearing about it now?"

"Well, to be fair, he brought the news while you were in labor, and I didn't give it much thought at the time. He thought that when I had been sent to find you ice chips, that would be an appropriate time to mention it."

"Why am I not surprised?"

"He seemed confused that I would be inclined to be at your side."

"How medieval."

"The southern alliance is what concerns me the most. But I sent Hix to assist Carlos. I trust Hix's estimation of the matter there."

My throat twisted on thorns. Lucas had turned Eroth into living paste to become First Beta of IronMoon, while Carlos had returned to IceMaw. Ana had waited until I'd had the baby, but then she'd left for IceMaw too. She hadn't explained herself, she'd just come to say a quick goodbye and headed out the door with her things. She needed some space. She'd been holding on for my sake, not that I deserved it.

"Do you think I'll see her again?" I asked him.

Gabel tugged, but our daughter had a firm grip on his finger. "She's gone to learn how to be a wolf doctor. And a wolf. Easier down south. She'll be back, I'm sure of it."

I nodded quickly, gulping down tears.

"The southern alliance does not call me King, but does call you Queen-Luna," Gabel said. "That will be a delicate fight to pick."

"Are you upset *you* did not make yourself king?"

A chuckle, and there was something oddly warm in his eyes. "I have my crown."

"You seem oddly at peace with it," I said.

"Do I?"

"You aren't going to tell me what's really going on in your brain, are you? Or why you actually let Adrianna live?"

"I am thinking about how to affirm my position in the southern alliance without stepping on anyone's toes, and as for the second, it's done, is it not?"

Gabel and compassion? And why did that sound like a very strange lie? "Aaron always did ask me *will you make him king.*"

I tensed, waiting for the ghostly claw at my throat, but it didn't come. I sensed him, far away, but behind some walls and veils. Perhaps he was off chasing souls across the abyss. He did not seem to be Lead Hound... yet.

I'd see him again, no doubt. He was not done with me. But until then... he had gotten much easier to ignore.

Gabel smiled at the baby.

"Do you... love her less for knowing the world thinks she's his progeny?" Nobody had *said* anything, but everyone quietly believed Aaron had sired her on me.

Gabel shook his head, still focused on the baby. "She is the only thing in the world I love more dearly than you, and you know how much I love you. All the wolves heard you give her to me. They'll forget the ugly details like they always do. Flint would be pleased. And it suits me fine you made me King. It just proved that I was right all along about your ambitious nature."

"Asshole."

"And besides, you foretold *my* kingdom would rot into the ground. Your queendom will have a better chance at survival."

Tears burned my eyes. "I really hate you sometimes, Gabel."

He bent his face to mine, blue eyes as bright and wicked as the Tides, and he kissed me once, his hands sliding over mine as I held our baby. "I know, my Queen. I know. Now. Hand her to me, and I will escort you to dinner."

AND WE'RE DONE...

MERRY RAVENELL

When I started writing *Oracle* way back now, it was just supposed to be a quick 50K word, 20 chapter, one-and-done book.

And for the first dozen or so chapters, that's what was happening.

Then things (as they tend to do) just went off into the weeds and here we are. A thousand thank-you's to everyone who has hung on this long.

There's obviously the potential for a book about Ana, so if that's of interest, drop me a line. :)

About the Author

Merry is an independent author living in the Napa Valley of California with her husband and two cats. She enjoys coffee, combat sports, casual games, and low budget disaster flicks.

---

www.merryravenell.com
(freebies, festivities, oh my!)

Also By Merry Ravenell

Mates of Planet 25XA

Spared By The Monster

Spared By The Monster Vol 2 - *2023*

The Breath of Chaos Series

Breath of Chaos

Bound By Chaos

Chaos Covenant

Gate of Chaos

Grail of Chaos - TBA

The IronMoon Series

The Alpha's Oracle

Iron Oracle

Ice & Iron

Obsidian Oracle

The SnowFang Series

The SnowFang Bride

The SnowFang Storm

The SnowFang Secret

The NightPiercer Saga

NightPiercer

Separated Starlight

Between Dark Places

Aphelion - *2023*

Other_Titles

The Nocturne Bride

On The Bit

Mirsaid